THE
CHIMERA
SECRET

Dean Crawford began writing after his dream of becoming a fighter pilot in the Royal Air Force was curtailed when he failed their stringent sight tests. Fusing his interest in science with a love of fast-paced revelatory thrillers, he soon found a career that he could pursue with as much passion as flying a fighter jet. Now a full-time author, he lives with his partner and daughter in Surrey.

Also by Dean Crawford

Covenant
Immortal
Apocalypse

THE
CHIMERA
SECRET

DEAN
CRAWFORD

**SIMON &
SCHUSTER**

London · New York · Sydney · Toronto · New Delhi

A CBS COMPANY

First published in Great Britain by Simon & Schuster UK Ltd, 2013
A CBS COMPANY

Copyright © Dean Crawford, 2013

1 3 5 7 9 10 8 6 4 2

Simon & Schuster UK Ltd
1st Floor,
222 Gray's Inn Road
London WC1X 8HB

www.simonandschuster.co.uk

Simon & Schuster Australia, Sydney
Simon & Schuster India, New Delhi

A CIP catalogue record for this book is available
from the British Library

B Format ISBN 978-1-47110-255-4
Trade Paperback ISBN 978-1-47110-254-7
Ebook ISBN 978-1-47110-256-1

Typeset by M Rules
Printed and bound by CPI Group (UK) Ltd, Croydon, CR0 4YY

In memoriam,

Douglas Ian Jarvis

1916-1997

I

FOX CREEK, NEZ PERCE NATIONAL FOREST, IDAHO

'We've got him now, brother.'

Cletus MacCarthy's voice was a whisper drifting through dense ferns that sparkled with moisture. Jesse MacCarthy did not reply as he crouched low in the foliage, kept his breathing calm and tried not to look directly at their quarry on the far side of the creek. But he could hear the ragged excitement in Cletus's voice, a volatile mixture of bloodlust and adrenaline.

The alpha-male was no more than sixty yards away and some fifty feet lower than where they crouched on the forested hillside. The rushing water in the narrow creek far below was the only sound that rose up between soaring hills that vanished into wreaths of cloud enveloping their peaks. Jesse looked down to where the magnificent creature scanned the hillsides with a cautious gaze before lowering its head to drink. At least twelve hundred pounds, and with antlers more than a metre long, Jesse had never seen a Roosevelt elk as large as the specimen they had tracked for the past four hours.

A breeze drifted down the valley from the west, the clouds drifting slowly above them in the cold sky. The elk would not have picked up their scent, allowing them to creep to within a hair's breadth of a sure kill. Either one of them could hit such a large animal at this close range.

'He's a goner f'sure,' Cletus whispered. 'Question is, who's takin' the shot, lil' brother?'

Jesse breathed his reply.

'Best you make the shot, Cleet. You've done it before and we don't want to lose this beauty. Besides, you've got the Winchester.'

Jesse saw his brother nod. He was crouched six feet farther down the hillside, his rifle cradled in his grasp. Jesse held his own rifle with the barrel almost touching the ground and the safety catch off. Sighted for long range, his Browning 7mm mag was loaded with a 175-grain bullet and zeroed-in three inches high at a hundred yards, meaning that Jesse could hit targets at more than three hundred yards using the 3x9 sniper scope. But Cletus's .308 Winchester was perfect for closer shots.

Jesse relaxed his posture, knowing that he would not have to move now that Cletus was taking the shot. His brother was a big man with a thick, russet beard that almost touched his chest. Jesse watched as Cletus moved with extreme care further down the hillside, one crouched and hunched step at a time, until he reached a cluster of small boulders scattered amid the thick grass.

The elk looked up and blinked at the hillside, its magnificent antlers looking like the limbs of a gigantic tree. Big, black eyes stared as though looking directly at Jesse. The rut was over and although the Roosevelt elk did not migrate seasonally like other species, their diet changed from sprouts to bark as the fall progressed toward winter. Cletus knew where to find the big elk, the first to reach the deep valleys, creeks and ravines they favored as shelter from the winter storms. He knew that they had to head as deep into the wilderness as their supplies would allow and avoid the well-trodden game trails. He also knew that to find the best specimen they had to go in before the season opener and the influx of day-trippers and other clueless tenderfoots out to shoot bull elk for something to tell the grandkids back home.

Cletus and Jesse were poaching.

Only thing on their side was that no day-tripper would ever hike this far out into the wilderness. Hell, the ranger service probably wouldn't make it out here, so harsh was the terrain. And with the swiftly fading light, only the hardiest hunters like Cletus MacCarthy felt confident enough to rough it in the wild until dawn before making their way back with their prize. Jesse figured there probably wasn't another human being within twenty miles of them.

The bull elk scanned the hillside, not alarmed but not entirely at ease either. Jesse watched as, inch by painfully slow inch, Cletus brought the Winchester up onto his shoulder, sighting down the weapon as his finger moved by reflex and slipped the safety catch off. The soft puffs of breath condensing on the air from Cletus's nostrils suddenly ceased as he took final aim and held his breath, waiting for the pause between his heartbeats to steady the rifle for the final shot.

Cletus's finger squeezed the trigger.

'Don't move.'

The voice came from behind Jesse, spoken without force and yet in the deep silence of the moment it seemed as loud as a gunshot. All at once the magnificent elk shuddered in alarm and whirled, leaping with extraordinary force and grace across the creek in a rustle of grass and thundering hooves. Within moments it had plunged into the treeline on the opposite side of the ravine. Cletus jerked his head back over his shoulder as Jesse whirled to see a pistol held by a uniformed park ranger pointed at him. The ranger, his jacket festooned with Idaho State patches and his field hat shielding his eyes from the drizzle, directed a steely gaze at them.

'Gavin Coltz, Idaho State Park Ranger. You'll be aware that we're ten days outside of the season opener. Lay down your weapons immediately.'

Jesse heard Cletus sigh heavily and the safety catch of the Winchester click back into place. Jesse carefully laid down the Browning at his feet as he turned and stood up from his hiding place.

Gavin Coltz kept his pistol trained in their direction, the weapon held double-handed. Jesse knew that park rangers had been shot in the past by poachers, and Coltz was taking no chances. He kept his distance, ten yards further back in the treeline. Jesse raised his hands and from the corner of his eye he saw Cletus do the same.

'We don't want trouble, officer,' Cletus said, all of the excitement now drained from his voice.

'Then you'll do exactly as I say,' Coltz replied. 'Keep your hands in the air and move ten paces to your left. Leave your weapons where they are.'

Cletus reluctantly did as he was told, casting a last glance at his beloved Winchester as he backed away. Jesse followed him, stepping carefully through the rough grass. Gavin Coltz stood his ground at the treeline until they were where he wanted them, and then glanced over his shoulder into the deep forest behind.

'Where's the third guy?' he demanded.

Jesse blinked and looked at Cletus. Cletus shook his head.

'There ain't no third guy, officer. It's just me and my brother here.'

Coltz changed his stance and gripped his pistol tighter.

'I've been tracking you for three hours, boys, and I saw somebody trailing you. Don't be messin' with me and making this worse than it already is. Call him out.'

Jesse shook his head.

'We're alone, officer. I swear it. There's nobody else come out this far with us.'

Coltz frowned. 'Then who the hell was followin' you?'

Jesse was about to answer when on the faint breeze a pungent odor filled his nostrils and coated the back of his throat with something that felt slimy. He fought a choke reaction as the stench hit him and tears welled in the corners of his eyes. Beside him Cletus coughed and glanced to their right.

'Sweet Jesus,' Cletus gasped. 'What the hell is that?'

Coltz, his pistol still aimed at them, looked to his left through the forest. Jesse looked at the ranger for a brief moment and then suddenly something tugged at his stomach, a primal terror so deep it must have been buried for a thousand generations. The strength seemed to go out of his knees as the terrible odor of decay, sweat and rancid flesh

swept on the air around them and, with an almost supernatural horror, Jesse watched as the forest came alive before
his eyes.

From the treeline a huge form surged into view, half lost
in the shadows as it rushed far faster than any man could run.
Coltz whirled as heavy footfalls thundered toward him, and
Jesse saw the ranger try to swing his pistol to meet the unexpected attack.

'Bear!' Cletus yelled. 'Get your gun, Jesse!'

The huge form crashed through the treeline in a mass of
red-brown fur, a colossal creature far larger than any bear
Jesse had ever seen. He was about to turn for his rifle when
the animal suddenly reared up, and he realized that it was
running not on four legs but two. In a terrible instant Jesse
saw immense arms and muscular legs and a tall crested skull,
the entire form covered in thick hair.

Gavin Coltz fired a single, deafening gunshot at point-
blank range and then staggered backward as one immense
shaggy arm smashed into the ranger's head with a crunch like
boots on gravel. Jesse felt bile swell in his throat as the ranger's
head was ripped from his neck in a spray of dark blood and
splintered bone to spin in a gruesome arc over their heads
and bounce with a dull crunch upon the rocks behind them.

The beast turned its gaze down the hillside and fixed upon
Jesse, who felt as if he were staring into the eyes of Satan
himself.

'Jesse!' Cletus yelled as he dashed past. 'The guns!'

Jesse whirled on unsteady legs as they rushed for the two
rifles lying in the bushes barely ten feet away. All at once Jesse
heard a low growl and he turned, looking at the beast as it

spread its arms wide. Its chest shuddered as from deep within its lungs burst a cry like nothing he'd ever heard before, rising from a guttural growl to a high-pitched wail that sent bolts of pain through his ears and soared out across the valley like the howl of a thousand wolves.

Jesse staggered backward as Cletus reached his Winchester and yanked the weapon into his shoulder, snapping the safety catch off in one fluid motion as he swung the barrel around to aim at the creature.

The gunshot burst out with a blast of smoke and flame in the half-light and Jesse felt the shockwave from the blast hammer his ears. The shot hit the creature low in the belly, and the immense beast bowed over at the waist as its thunderous cry mutated into a wail of pain.

'Jesse!' Cletus shouted as he fumbled in his pocket for another round. 'Get behind me!'

Jesse stumbled backward down the hillside as Cletus shoved a second bullet into his rifle. He grabbed the Browning and then crouched down behind his brother and looked back up the hillside at the creature.

The beast's wail of pain mutated again. Jesse heard the animal suck in air and let out a roar of fury as it charged down the hillside at them.

'It's coming right at us, Cleet!'

Cletus cocked the Winchester as Jesse threw his hands over his head and crouched down lower in the bushes. He heard the beast's heavy footfalls thundering toward them as Cletus hefted the Winchester into his shoulder and squeezed the trigger.

Too late.

The beast plowed into Cletus and hurled him backward. The gunshot blasted out as Cletus's finger snapped inside the trigger guard and fired the weapon's final round uselessly into the sky above. Jesse smelled a blast of foul air and saw a huge mass of rippling fur plunge past him as Cletus let out a scream.

Cletus span through the air with his limbs outstretched, and then his body crashed down the hillside toward the rocks far below, one arm flailing at an impossible angle. Jesse gazed in horror as his brother tumbled to a halt near the bottom of the hillside and tried to pull himself away with his remaining good arm.

'Shoot it, Jesse!' he screamed up the hillside.

Jesse didn't move. Couldn't move. His legs trembled beneath him, the neurons in his brain frozen in a paralysis of horror as the beast lifted his brother's screaming body off the hillside and hurled it down into the creek. Jesse saw his brother's head smash like an eggshell against a rock and saw his neck snap like a twig. The creature crashed into the water in pursuit, snarling and wailing its terrible cries as it picked up the limp corpse and lifted it high above its head before smashing it down again across the rocks. Cletus's bones crunched and his flesh ripped until the icy waters of the creek were stained with crimson ribbons that snaked between the rocks.

Jesse vomited into the bushes, his vision blurred with tears and his throat burning as he stumbled to his feet by automatic reflex and began running up the hillside as fast as he could, the Browning falling from his grasp.

He hit the treeline and glanced back over his shoulder. Far below lay Cletus's mutilated, twisted body. Standing over the remains, the beast's head turned and two blood-red eyes locked onto Jesse's.

Nausea overwhelmed Jesse once again as he plunged into the dense forests, chased by his own keening cry of fear. The deepening night made the woods seem darker and more threatening, the mist obscuring the distant trees. Jesse ran but he could no longer feel his legs, driven now by the adrenaline seething through his veins. Raw terror, pure and undiluted. His mind was empty, devoid of anything other than the most basic of instincts. Run. Keep running.

Because it's following you.

A tingling fear like icy fingers against the nape of his neck spread rapidly down his spine as he crashed through the forest, his hands batting foliage from his path and not feeling the thorns slicing into his skin. His legs powered him over fallen logs and tree stumps, his breath sawed in his throat and his heart hammered against the cage of his chest. He plunged from the dense tangles of trees onto a winding animal trail, his hunter's eye catching a glimpse of flattened grass stems and churned earth where countless creatures had made their way through the woods. A tiny voice flickered like a phantasm through the freezing fog of terror clouding his mind: *Stay off the easy trail, keep to the forest.*

Jesse ran straight across the trail, darting left and right between trees and hurdling dense tangles of foliage. *Don't look back.* Jesse's legs began to falter, his vision blurring and twinkling with tiny pinpricks of light as his body began crashing. His labored breathing fluttered as he stumbled desperately through the darkening forest, and in a moment of hope he glanced over his shoulder.

Straight into a pair of fearsome red eyes that towered over him.

The creature was moving with incredible speed as though it were gliding through the dense woods, its huge legs adapting to the terrain with each stride.

Jesse's cry caught in his throat and he gagged. Something huge and heavy swiped across his legs and hurled him off of his feet. He span in midair and slammed down hard onto the ground amid a flurry of fallen leaves and twigs. Jesse rolled onto his back, his arms held out defensively as he looked up into the darkened sky and saw it loom into view.

The immense bulk of the creature filled the sky above him and Jesse felt his bowels loosen and spill beneath him to soak the ground. Those terrible red eyes glared down at him and blinked once. In a moment terror seared through every fiber in his body and he saw there the face of a man upon the body of a beast.

And then Jesse's consciousness slipped away from him into darkness.

2

RIGGINS, IDAHO

'We've had a *what*?'

Earl Carpenter's eyes widened as he looked across his cluttered desk to where his assistant, a primly dressed spinster named Marjorie Bird, clasped one hand over the telephone. As the Riggins Police Department Sheriff, Earl was used to hearing bad news, but this was unusual.

'A suicide,' she repeated. 'One of the MacCarthy kids.'

Earl puffed out his cheeks and blew a gale of air across his office as he glanced up at the official notices board in the lobby outside. The station was tiny, harbouring a handful of cells that hadn't held a serious convict in thirty years. In a town of barely five hundred people, there weren't many crimes a man could commit in the morning that wouldn't be common knowledge before the sun went down.

Earl dragged himself out of his seat and picked up his hat.

'Who found him, and where?'

'His mother found him in the garage,' Marjorie said, relaying what she was hearing down the line. 'Strung himself up from the rafters in the dead of the night. No witnesses.'

Earl glanced around the office. Nothing moved fast in Riggins, not even law enforcement, so he did not immediately leave. Filing cabinets that hadn't been opened in months stood beside a board to which were tacked images of local felons wanted for minor crimes. A couple of big fish wanted by the FBI stood out, supposedly seen hiding out in the woods up near Crooked Creek by a couple of rafters, but that was the extent of the excitement. An acoustic country number spilled lazily from a radio on Marjorie's desk.

'Suppose I'd better have me a look, then,' he said finally.

'Suppose you should,' Marjorie replied, her eyes fixed back on the well-worn pages of a romance novel.

Earl waddled out of the office, grabbed the keys to the Ford Ranger parked outside and opened the front door. The bright morning sunshine blazed down from a perfect blue sky, soaring hills and ragged canyons forming a dramatic backdrop to the tiny town. Nestled deep in a valley just south of Hell's Canyon, Riggins had been built along the banks of the Salmon River and its tributary, where the mountains formed the confluence of the rivers. The nearest major towns were twenty miles in either direction on the only access road to Riggins, the US-95, and with only a couple of full-time officers available for duty, the department came under the jurisdiction of Idaho County Sheriff's Department.

Earl pulled out of the station lot and drove north down Main Street past the diner and gas station. The nearby river glittered brightly in the sunlight between the trees that hugged its banks. He didn't have to drive far. The MacCarthy family lived just off the 95 where a dead-end sign gave way to a small collection of sun-bleached clapperboard single-stories.

The truck kicked up clouds of dust as Earl mounted the ramp and cruised slowly up to where Sally MacCarthy stood on the porch of her house, her face devoid of emotion, her eyes dark orbs that didn't reflect the bright sunlight. Earl killed the truck's engine and climbed out just in time for Sally to fall into his arms as the grief finally hit her.

'Jesus, Earl.'

Earl wrapped his arms around her waif-like shoulders and held her for a long time.

He'd known the MacCarthys since he'd been knee-high to an elk. Old man MacCarthy had been a former prospector who'd thrown what little he'd made from the beds of countless rivers into a small diner on the southern edge of town. Three kids, all sons. Old Tom had gone to his maker six years previously, an early visit courtesy of smoking sixty Luckies a day for the better part of forty years. All Sally had left was her three boys: Cletus, Jesse and Randy.

Earl eased himself free of Sally's embrace and looked down at her.

'Tell me what happened, right from the start.'

Sally wiped away the tears from her face, her skin aged beyond her years like rocks weathered by decades of exposure, and spoke in a voice that sounded tiny to Earl's ears.

'He went out last night with some friends,' she said. 'I went to bed early but I din' hear him come home. He wasn't in his bed this morning but that ain't unusual, so I just got ready for work. I found him when I came round to the garage for the truck.'

Earl looked across to the right of the tired-looking house to where the open car shelter stood. Little more than some timber beams surfaced with opaque corrugated plastic, stained with the dust of years. He could see an aged flat-bed parked out front.

'Is he still there?' Earl asked as gently as he could.

Sally nodded once, struggling to hold back more tears.

'I left him in case your people wanted to do all those forensic tests on him, like I've seen on the TV. There's no doubt he's gone. Besides, I couldn't have got him down even if I'd wanted to. I couldn't bear to.'

Earl stepped away from Sally and approached the car shelter. As he rounded the corner he saw the body of Randy MacCarthy hanging from the central crossbeam. Beneath him, an old wooden stool lay on its side.

His hands hung limp by his sides, his boots a good three feet above the dusty floor of the shelter. Randy was twenty-three years old, best as Earl could recall. His two older brothers were well-known local woodsmen who often supplemented their meager incomes by taking tourists out into the wilderness on hiking trips. Randy had no criminal record, just a few minors for possession of marijuana, and worked at the hardware store.

Randy's jaw was pitched steeply by the tight rope, but Earl could see that his neck was not broken. Asphyxiation then, from the noose. Inch-thick hemp cordage, double-looped over the crossbeam above. Earl looked up at the roof of the shelter, then at the parked flat-bed, and then at the dusty floor of the shelter. He unclipped his radio from his belt and keyed open a channel.

'Marjorie, you there?'

'I gotcha, Earl, what's the story?'

Earl scanned the scene before him one last time.

'You'd better get Grangeville down here with forensics,' he said. 'Randy's definitely dead. I'll photograph the scene here and get it cordoned off.'

'*Oh Jesus,*' Marjorie replied, '*that's not good news for Sally MacCarthy.*'

'A death in the family's not good news for anybody, Marjorie.'

'*I mean that Randy's not the only one of her boys in trouble. One of the others, Jesse, just turned up at Old Meister's lodge. The old man's sayin' Jesse's brother's been killed.*'

'He knew about Randy's hanging?'

'*No, he's saying that Cletus MacCarthy is dead too. You'd better get down there right away.*'

Earl muttered a profanity under his breath as he walked back to his truck. Nothing happened in Riggins for months at a time, and then every man and his dog turns up dead.

'I'll be back soonest,' he said to Sally, avoiding meeting her eye, as he climbed in and started the engine, wondering how he was going to explain this all to her. 'Forensics are on their way, just don't touch anything.' Earl sighed as he drove back down Main Street and turned off down a track toward the river. He pulled up a few minutes later outside the hunting lodge of Charlton Meister, one of the old-school trappers who'd gotten too rickety to trek the woods anymore and too damned old to get on with the locals in town. A fierce-tempered old goat who went everywhere with a scowl behind his ragged beard, Meister had built the lodge and settled on the banks of the Salmon River a couple of miles out of town. Earl knew him well enough. Every few weeks they'd get called out to the lodge after local kids harassing the old man went squealing to their folks after Meister had gotten his hands on them and cracked their heads together or taken a horse whip to their legs.

Earl strode down a narrow track that wound its way along the banks of the Salmon River and the lodge, and glanced at the frigid waters. Breakfast might have settled in Meister's nets, providing him with yet another way of avoiding going to the grocery store in town. But Meister wasn't beside the nets. Instead, the old man was kneeling on the shoal bank over a body lying on its back, covered in blankets.

Earl hurried over, his boots crunching on the shoal alerting Meister to his approach. The old man turned, and for the first time in decades Earl saw concern creasing his features.

'This boy needs a hospital, and I mean right now, Sheriff.'

Earl looked down at Jesse MacCarthy as he lay on the shoal at his feet.

His clothes were torn ragged, stained with mud and grime. One of his boots was missing, his bare foot bloodied and filthy, while the remaining boot was torn to shreds. His hunting jacket was hanging from his frame, one arm torn off at the sleeve, but it was his face that enraptured Earl.

Jesse looked like a zombie from one of those old flicks from the seventies, his eyes wide and staring, his jaw hanging slack and his lips flecked with dried saliva and mud. From somewhere came a feeble, keening cry of despair as Jesse's eyes settled onto Earl's and registered the faintest signs of recognition.

'Jesse?' Earl knelt down alongside the kid. 'Can you hear me?'

Tears began spilling from Jesse's eyes as he mumbled an incoherent stream of noise that might once have been words. Earl frowned and looked at Meister.

'Where'd you find him?'

'I din' find nobody,' Meister replied. 'I was emptying my nets when he just walked out of the woods and collapsed right here.'

Earl looked back down at Jesse. 'Where were you, Jesse? Where's Cletus?'

Jesse's trembling lips spurted a quivering reply.

'Fox Creek. Cletus is dead. It got him.'

'What got him?' Earl asked.

Jesse's sobs grew louder as he jabbered incoherently.

'It got him. The monster got Cletus.'

3

CHICAGO, ILLINOIS

Ethan Warner was not a nervous kind of guy. He had known fear, and plenty of it. Ethan had stared death in the face several times and, so far, had survived to tell the tale. But the corrosive, gnawing anxiety grinding through his guts right now was far worse for him, especially as it was entirely irrational.

The restaurant looked out over the glittering expanse of Lake Michigan, slate-gray waves flecked with white crests rolling their way south. A pair of cutters were carving their way north against the blustery wind, tacking hard to make any progress. Watching them helped to distract Ethan from the impending confrontation. He spent several minutes wishing the moment would arrive, and then when it did he wished he had more time to prepare.

'You're looking good, Ethan.'

The brunette who strode confidently toward his table was a couple of inches shorter than he was, her long hair flowing across her shoulders, but there was a familiar arrogance to the set of her frame and a recognizable icy-gray gleam in her eyes as though they were reflecting Lake Michigan's frigid waters.

Ethan stood and hugged her. Some of the anxiety thawed inside him.

'Natalie.'

He hadn't seen his sister in four years. Natalie Warner had studied politics in New York City while Ethan had been working overseas as a journalist. An internment at the White House had followed after her honors degree, and now she worked as an analyst for Congress at the Government Accountability Office in Washington DC.

She sat down opposite him. Although only twenty-five years old she was already wrapped in a cloak of authoritative confidence that belied her years. Ethan could picture himself in her from years gone by, the same determination they shared that had gotten him into the US Marines as an officer and later through the greatest tragedy of his life. Natalie's clear eyes and flawless skin were only marred by the wide jaw she shared with Ethan, making her attractive if not beautiful.

'So,' she began, her voice husky like his own, 'to what do I owe this honor?'

Ethan leaned back in his chair as the waiter poured sparkling wine into their glasses. The restaurant was out of town and half-empty, which was why Ethan had picked it. Most people were at work. Ethan worked for himself, and Natalie was on vacation for a week to visit their parents.

'Been a long time since I last saw you, and Pa said you were in town.'

'You two are talking?' Natalie's eyes sparkled. 'Did Mom pay you both?'

'I called home a while back.'

'Jesus, is it terminal?'

Ethan laughed. Natalie had a forthright way about her. The laugh faded away as he recalled why it had been so long since he'd been home.

'It's been a tricky couple of years.'

'Want to talk about it?'

'Kind of why I'm here.'

Natalie sipped some of her wine and set the glass down before replying.

'You're off the grid for four years, then you turn up when you want something? Ethan, you live in the same city as Mom and Pop yet you've barely spoken to them in all that time.'

'I wasn't myself,' Ethan said, keeping his voice even. 'Things are better now. Kind of.'

Natalie merely raised a questioning eyebrow and sipped again at her wine. Ethan sighed heavily, not touching his drink.

'Joanna might still be alive,' he said.

Natalie froze in motion, her glass touching her lips and her eyes staring into Ethan's. She set the glass back down.

'And you know this how?'

'Can't say much about it,' Ethan replied. 'Some of the people we're contracted to have access to high-level intelligence. I did some work for one of them and in return I got information. They had footage of her, Nat. Not much, but enough.'

'How old was the reel?' she asked him.

'No more than six months old at the time. Nearly a year now.'

Natalie stared at her glass for a long moment, and Ethan could tell that the sudden revelation wasn't provoking the kind of excitement in her that he had hoped to see.

Joanna Defoe had been Ethan's fiancée and business partner. Working as investigative journalists in some of the world's most dangerous places, they had exposed corruption and in the process saved dozens of victims of abduction and incarceration from lonely, unjust deaths. But their achievements had finally caught up with them in the sinister, sun-scorched alleys of Gaza City. Joanna Defoe had vanished without trace four years previously, presumed abducted by militants. Ethan's life had collapsed in the aftermath of her disappearance, all of his money expended in a futile search for her across the Middle East. Distraught, broke and driven by little more than alcohol and bitterness, Ethan had been given the chance to search for her again in Israel just a year previously by a friend who had been his commander in the US Marines during Operation Iraqi Freedom. That had led to his work with the Defense Intelligence Agency and the information that had recently identified Joanna as alive. Among other things.

'What do you want?' Natalie asked.

She wasn't looking at him. Ethan chose his words carefully.

'I need somebody to look into where she might be, do some digging in places that I can't.'

Natalie kept her eyes on her wine glass.

'Can't you just ask your friend? Surely they would know where to begin better than I would?'

'His help was a one-off,' Ethan explained. 'I can't go back to him without having to risk my neck again for the chance of more information.'

Natalie finally looked up at him. 'What the hell are you involved in, Ethan?'

'It's complicated. We're bail bondsmen by trade, but we also do investigative work for the government.'

Natalie leaned forward. 'Who?'

Ethan paused as he figured that there wasn't much harm in telling her. Christ, she worked for Congress – she could probably find out herself with a single phone call.

'Defense Intelligence Agency,' he said. 'We pick up cases that the other agencies write off as unworkable.'

'Unworkable how?'

Ethan shrugged. 'Budgets don't justify the work, or the manpower's not available because agencies are focused on counterterrorism. We get called in to investigate in their place.'

Natalie was watching him with a steady gaze as though trying to peer through the DIA's veil of secrecy and uncover the bizarre things that he had seen.

'Who's *we*?' she asked him finally.

'Nicola Lopez, my partner. Former DC detective. She's solid.'

'She'd be solid if she was still a ranked detective,' Natalie uttered. 'She fall on hard times too?'

'Partner got killed,' Ethan replied as he felt his jaw tighten as it so often did when he thought about Lopez. 'Corruption. I don't blame her for leaving the force after what happened.'

Natalie took a deep breath before speaking.

'Ethan, the last time you went looking for Jo it nearly killed you.'

Ethan managed a ghost of a smile. 'That's why I'm asking you to do it instead.'

'Charmed, I'm sure.'

'I'm not doing any field work this time until I have a solid lead,' Ethan said. 'I don't need much, Nat, just a bit of time in the books seeing if there's anything that's been overlooked. Congress might not know anything but it's a good place to start. The National Security Agency might know something too.'

Natalie laughed.

'Sure, no problem. I'll just march into the most secure agency in the world and ask to borrow some coffee or something.'

'It's more than I'll be able to do,' Ethan replied. 'I know Congress is about to start an investigation into the intelligence community. Your team will have unprecedented access to files from the CIA, DIA, NSA and God knows who else.'

'Do Mom and Pop know about this?'

'No,' Ethan replied quickly, 'and let's keep it that way, okay? I don't want them worrying.'

Natalie's eyes flickered with sheet lightning. 'Like you didn't want them worrying when you disappeared for four years? Jesus, Ethan.'

Her words sliced through his shame, but he did not try to avoid it. Like a victim of depression who cuts for the relief the pain brings, he faced it head on, sucked it in and let it settle in his guts.

'I'm back now,' he replied, 'and I'm not going to make the same mistake again, Nat, but I can't let this go until I know what the hell happened to Joanna. I need closure.'

Natalie's gaze bore into him from across the table.

'You lost her once, Ethan, and it tore you apart. You seem

like you're finally getting over it and now you want to dive straight back in like nothing's happened. You ever think that if she's out there, she might have contacted you by now? You ever think that she might not want to?'

Ethan felt tiny pricks of pain in the corners of his eyes. 'Every day.'

Natalie's eyes softened.

'I'll do what I can,' she said. 'Just make sure that it's what you really want, Ethan.'

She looked down at her menu. Ethan glanced out of the restaurant windows at the bleak surface of the lake and asked himself the same question he'd been asking himself for six months: *Is this really what I want?*

4

RIVER FOREST, CHICAGO

The sound of his labored heart pounded in Ethan's head as he jogged along the sidewalk of Lathrop, just off Thatcher Woods. He checked his watch as he swerved by reflex around the occasional dog-walking pedestrian, glancing at perfectly manicured lawns fronting two-story condos worth more than he earned in a decade. Some even had turreted corner plots like miniature castles.

Ethan frequently jogged the route, because like almost all people he liked to dream. Nobody who lived alone as he did had any need for five bedrooms, three cars and a bathroom the size of a small apartment, but all the same it was something prettier to look at than the windy city's north side. Kind of thing he'd once assumed that he and Joanna would have aspired to: kids, a dog, big house, the whole nine yards. Instead his life, along with his aspirations, had ground to a halt when she'd disappeared. He'd lost contact with friends, become consumed by grief and rage, embittered by life's uncaring twists of fate.

He shook off the maudlin thoughts and picked his chin up along with his pace.

The cables of his earphones bounced as he checked over his shoulder and ran across the street, slowing his pace as he passed a large colonial-style house. Pure white clapperboard, broad windows, high hedges blocking access to the rear. Worth a cool two million. Ethan's practiced eye picked out a robust-looking drainage chute running down the north wall from the roof, part of the hedge that was only four feet high, and a wrought-iron gate locked with a simple bolt and padlock.

Three routes of entry and egress. No, four. The southeast corner's bedroom window opened out just above the slanted roof of the double garage below. An alarm system's claxon was attached to the wall beneath the eaves, a deliberately overt statement announcing the presence of a security system within. Not that Ethan would have to worry about that. He wasn't looking to break into the house.

He was expecting somebody else to break out.

The road opened out as he reached West North Avenue, turned right at the junction and resisted the temptation of the Starbucks on the corner. His belly was still full from his lunch with Natalie, and his mind likewise filled with thoughts about Joanna and the mysterious footage he'd seen so many months before.

'*You seen him yet?*'

Nicola Lopez's voice crackled through the microphone in his ear. Ethan replied between breaths as he jogged, the microphone picking up his voice and relaying it to his partner back at their office. Nicola Lopez was several years his junior, but as an ex-police detective she was no less capable.

'He hasn't shown. It's a long shot anyway.'

Ethan had jogged past the big colonial every day for the past five, hoping for a brief glimpse of Marty Sedgewick, a 48-year-old banker out of North Cleveland, Chicago. Marty had been one of the high fliers of the nineties and beyond, forging a serious career in investments and emerging markets. Four-million-dollar mansion. Condo down on the quays Florida way, along with a mooring for his forty-two-foot cruiser. Then the economic bubble burst. As his employers faced economic ruin, Marty faced the sudden and unexpected spectre of bankruptcy when he was fired from his post in a dramatic move by the bank for which he worked. Instead of making the smart play and downsizing his life before the shit hit the fan, Marty Sedgewick got himself an idea too good to be true. He told his wife and three kids he'd left his job and was setting up for himself.

Using his credentials as a big man in the market, he played out what was left of their personal fortune, convincing everybody that he was a businessman thriving in the middle of the recession and that they, too, could have a slice of the pie. Baffling a series of investors ranging from executive jet companies to private childcare nurseries, he sucked in almost seven million dollars before the fraudulent Ponzi scheme he'd engineered collapsed around him like a deck of cards. With four million dollars of other people's money to his name, Marty Sedgewick promptly abandoned his family and high-tailed it to Mexico. He quite possibly could have stayed there had he been able to keep a low enough profile, but unfortunately Sedgewick couldn't keep his remarkable coup to himself, and fourteen months later his overworked mouth had gained him a mugging, lost him almost a million bucks and ultimately landed him back in Chicago, this time in Cook County Jail.

Ethan was more used to pursuing hardened criminals with nothing to lose than people like Sedgewick, a pasty, balding man who worshipped greenbacks over his own flesh and blood. However, it had proven far harder to track Sedgewick down after he'd jumped his hundred-thousand-dollar bond than Ethan had anticipated. Somehow, the creep still had people willing to shield him from the law, specifically in River Forest. The trail had led Ethan to the street he now jogged every day, which unfortunately for Sedgewick was just a few blocks away from the good offices of Warner & Lopez Inc.

Ethan turned left onto North 72nd Court, jogging past a parade of shops before he reached a smallholding on the corner by a parking lot. The nondescript block held a single, security code protected door that led to the four small businesses within. He reached up and punched in his number as he entered the building and strode to the door of their office, pushing it open as he walked in and pulled off his earphones.

Filing cabinets lined one wall, and a series of pictures were tacked to another, each depicting a fugitive with a price on their head. Everything from minor two-bit felons up to hardened criminals with homicides under their belts. Two desks adorned the office; Ethan's was tidy and organized with military efficiency. Nicola Lopez's looked as though a tornado had gusted through it.

Lopez leaned back in her chair, her long black hair pinned up in a ponytail and her dark almond eyes shifting with impatience.

'Just break into the goddamned house,' she snapped.
'Hundred thousand bucks bond sitting on his ass in there just
waiting for us and you're jogging-miss-daisy past his window
every day.'

Ethan smiled as he tossed his microphone onto thick piles
of paper on his desk.

'There's no point in one of us getting busted. The cops
will only take Sedgewick into their own custody before cutting us loose. We gotta play it smart and let him come out to
us.'

Lopez shook her head and gracefully twirled a pen
through her fingers.

'*We gotta play it smart*. I'll be tapping those words onto your
head in Morse Code with a baseball bat if the police bust
Sedgewick before we do. Six weeks of work down the tubes.'

'You win some . . .' Ethan replied.

Lopez huffed and puffed for a few moments more but said
nothing as she turned back to her computer.

Ethan could understand her frustration. As a kid Lopez
had walked out of Guanajuato in Mexico twenty years before
with her family and little else and somehow made it into the
police department of Washington DC as a homicide detective. Diligent, obedient and full of idealistic enthusiasm,
Lopez had seen her partner shot and killed by a corrupt
senior officer, an event which had ultimately led her to resign
her post on the force and join Ethan in the far less secure
world of bail bondsmen and private investigations. Now she
was spontaneous, impulsive and sometimes downright
aggressive, traits that fit their chosen profession surprisingly
well but also made her unpredictable. Her silence lasted for

less than thirty seconds. She couldn't let it go and looked up at him.

'You know we've spent four thousand bucks hunting that *asquerosa*, and all the while he was hunkered down less than two hundred yards from where we're sitting?'

'He's fooled the detectives on his case too,' Ethan pointed out.

'They're on payroll. We're not.'

'What do you want me to say?' Ethan asked as he flopped down into his chair. 'You think that we should have just not bothered chasing him at all? You can't win the prize if you don't buy a ticket.'

'Very poetic,' Lopez replied, rolling her eyes. 'But right now we're just sitting here while Sedgewick stays holed up in his buddy's mansion. As long as the house owner is holidaying in the Caribbean or whatever he told the police he was doing, they'll believe the house to be empty. Maybe it is.'

'It's not,' Ethan replied. 'I've seen movement inside. Sure, no lights, television or movement of vehicles, but somebody's tucked away in there.'

'You sure you're not losing your mojo?' Lopez asked, her expression serious now.

'Why?'

'Y'know,' she shrugged. 'Because of what happened, what you saw on that video, Joanna.'

Ethan sighed heavily, and even as he did so he realized that maybe she was right. Every time he was reminded of what had happened he felt a tiny piece of his soul flutter away. He swallowed thickly.

'I can still do my job.'

Lopez kept her gaze on him for what felt like an age. 'Not saying that you can't, just wondering if you can do it as well as you used to, is all.'

'I can still do the job.'

Lopez shrugged but didn't answer as she fixed her eyes back on her screen. Ethan watched as the glowing monitor reflected in her dark eyes, a strand of black hair falling down to frame one side of her face. Under different circumstances they might have become more intimately involved by now, but a series of remarkable events just months before had extinguished any spark of romance.

During a previous investigation for their biggest and most secretive client, the Defense Intelligence Agency, Lopez had gotten too close to a client who had wound up dead. Mixing business with pleasure had resulted in tragedy for her, something that Ethan was not keen to check out himself. Soon after, like a ghost long forgotten, news of Joanna's survival surfaced, news that had both elated and haunted him ever since.

Lopez was right. A year ago, he would have busted into that place and dragged Sedgewick's cretinous bulk into custody. Now he was sitting on his ass hoping that fate would play into his hands. A lifetime's experience to the contrary told him what he needed to do. Be bold. *Carpe diem.*

'Maybe we can tease him out,' he suggested.

'Sure,' Lopez replied, not taking her eyes off her monitor. 'Every cop in the city looking for him, he's being hunted by people he's swindled out of millions of bucks and who'll ice him at the first opportunity, but we'll make him forget all about that and just walk right into our hands.'

Ethan pictured the big colonial house and ran the layout of the streets through his mind for a moment, and then made his decision.

'It's worth a shot.'

Lopez looked at him. 'Great. What kind of candy you suppose he likes?'

Ethan grinned as he reached out and picked up one of a dozen cheap, untraceable cellphones stacked neatly on one side of his desk.

'Latino.'

Ethan tapped a number into the cellphone as Lopez shot upright out of her chair, her flawless skin flushing.

'What the hell are you going to do?'

Ethan leaned back in his chair as the line buzzed in his ear.

'You said it yourself, we can't just sit here doing nothing while Sedgewick stays holed up in his buddy's mansion.'

'Yeah, but—'

Ethan raised a finger to silence her as the line connected.

'*Nine-one-one, what's your emergency?*'

Ethan responded in a shaky, nervous voice.

'I'd like to report a break-in in progress. Can you send help please, right now?'

5

Lopez's face plunged in disbelief as she vaulted across her desk toward him, scattering paperwork and old Styrofoam cups. Ethan kept the cellphone pinned to his ear as she fumed.

'*What's the address, sir, and how many suspects can you see?*'

'1454 Jackson Avenue, ma'am,' Ethan replied. 'I can see four men, but there may be more.'

'*Units are on the way. Where are you calling from?*'

'I have to go and secure my front door right now!'

'*Stay on the line please, sir.*'

'The hell I will, they might try to break in here too!'

Ethan killed the line and then switched the phone off.

'What the goddamned hell was *that*?' Lopez raged. 'You're sending units to the same block? What the hell are you going to do if they see Sedgewick?'

Ethan slipped the plastic rear of the phone cover off, pulled out the SIM card, and snapped it in two as he looked up at Lopez.

'They won't.'

'How do you know that?'

'Because you're going to give him a ride out of trouble.'

'The hell I am!' Lopez shot back. 'This is your goddamned mess and if you think I'm going to dig your sorry ass out of—'

'You've got about three minutes,' Ethan said, 'to park up near his house and wait for him to come out.'

'Why don't *you* do it?' Lopez demanded.

Ethan stood up and tossed her the keys to his Suburban. 'Because he likes Latino girls, not ex-marines from Chicago. That's half the reason he holed up in Mexico. Let's go.'

Lopez caught the keys and followed Ethan out of the office. As she headed for the Suburban she cast Ethan a final indignant look.

'What am I going to be waiting for?'

'The house I called the break-in for is directly behind the one Sedgewick's hiding in. He'll see the cop cars from inside. Judging by his profile and history, my guess is that he's a narcissist, a moral coward and prone to rash decisions based on self-preservation. The first mistake he'll make when he sees those cops pouring into the house behind his is to run for the front door. He'll think the cops are there for him.'

Lopez blinked.

'You better be right about this. And why's he going to get into my car?'

'Just be ready.'

Ethan slipped his headphones on and jogged back down toward Jackson Avenue as Lopez drove out of the lot and away in front of him. Ethan made good time, running hard down Jackson and then swinging two rights to bring him back up the block on the other side just as he heard sirens screaming inbound along West North Avenue.

Ethan ran harder as he saw, in the distance, Lopez's black Suburban pull into Lathrop and ease in alongside the sidewalk. Lopez got out, opened the rear passenger door and pretended to fiddle with something in the back.

The sirens got louder, and between the big houses ahead Ethan glimpsed an occasional flash of red and blue lights as several squad cars screeched to a halt outside. Distant shouts of armed cops echoed between the trees of the expansive lawns stretching between the two houses as he jogged closer.

Moments later, Ethan got lucky.

The front door to the colonial opened and Ethan saw a portly man hurry out. He shut the door behind him, glanced up and down the street, then blundered down the front path as he pulled a baseball cap down low over his eyes. Even from fifty yards away Ethan could tell it was Sedgewick, his ill-fitting pants and hastily pulled-on jacket doing little to conceal his bulging belly and awkward, shambling gait.

Sedgewick reached the sidewalk and cast a long glance at the Suburban before turning toward Ethan. Ethan stopped running, yanked off his earphones and pointed at Sedgewick as he shouted out at the top of his voice in the direction of the cops.

'He's here! I can see him! It's him!'

Sedgewick's eyes flared beneath the rim of his baseball cap as he looked up and stared at Ethan in horror. The fat man whirled on the spot, searching desperately for someplace to hide, and in an instant he loped across the street toward the Suburban.

Ethan watched as Sedgewick hurtled around the side of the vehicle and straight into the path of Lopez. Lopez swung an open palm across Sedgewick's face with a sharp crack that made Ethan wince. The fat man yelped in shock as he came to a tumbling halt and staggered against the side of the vehicle. In an instant, Lopez had one of his wrists wrapped in a steel cuff as she twisted Sedgewick's arm up behind his back and shoved him headfirst into the rear of the Suburban.

Ethan jogged neatly alongside the Suburban as Lopez slammed the rear door shut, then he climbed into the driver's side and slipped the vehicle into gear. Moments later, they were turning right toward the office.

Ethan said nothing, but glanced in the rear-view mirror to see Lopez looking at him.

'Slick,' she admitted with a wry grin.

Sedgewick's pallid features blanched as he looked at them in turn with wide eyes.

'Who the hell are you?'

Lopez, her hands still pinning Sedgewick's behind his back, clicked the second cuff into place and smiled sweetly at him. 'Bail bondsmen,' she informed him. 'Guess where you're headed.'

Sedgewick's eyes brimmed with tears that spilled down his florid cheeks.

'Don't send me to Cook County,' he begged. 'I'll pay you anything.'

'Or sell us one of your worthless Ponzi schemes?' Ethan asked rhetorically. 'No thanks, buddy, we'll take the state's check.'

Sedgewick's bloated features imploded in grief as he banged his head against the window and sobbed quietly. Ethan ignored him as he drove into the parking lot and pulled in alongside a pair of dark-blue sedans. A knot of apprehension formed somewhere in the pit of his belly as he noted the government plates on both cars. Lopez's eyes narrowed in his rear-view mirror as she, too, spotted the vehicles.

'Jarvis?'

Ethan nodded but said nothing as he killed the engine and climbed out.

Douglas Jarvis was a former United States Marine officer who had commanded Ethan's rifle platoon during the second Gulf War through operations in both Iraq and Afghanistan. Jarvis had long since retired from the corps, serving his country instead from within the shadowy halls of the Defense Intelligence Agency and hiring Ethan and Lopez to conduct investigations into cases that the Pentagon rejected as unworthy of attention. So far, their work had uncovered conspiracies that were beyond anything that Ethan could ever have previously imagined.

Lopez manhandled Sedgewick out of the Suburban as Ethan saw that the security door to their office was already open, a pair of DIA agents standing guard inside. Lopez shook her head.

'Jesus, what's that guy's problem with doors?'

Ethan couldn't remember a time when Jarvis had simply knocked on a door and waited for somebody to open it. He just walked in, picked the lock or had his people bust their way in.

Ethan led the way into the office, the two agents allowing him through. Jarvis was waiting inside, sat behind Lopez's desk and leafing through a series of documents detailing their recent busts.

'Good morning,' he greeted them with a smile, and then caught sight of Sedgewick's face. 'Looks like you've had a busy one, street cleaning.'

'He's worth a fortune,' Lopez snapped, holding Sedgewick like a leashed dog in the office doorway. 'No way you're pulling this one off us.'

Jarvis held up his hands.

'I'm not here to snatch your prize, Nicola, believe me. I've got more work for you, if you can fit it in.'

Lopez slammed Sedgewick down into a plastic chair that creaked under the strain. She glanced at Jarvis as she pinned the fugitive to the chair.

'What makes you think we want any more work from you?'

'Because you're hungry for it and because you enjoy it.'

'Son of a bitch . . .'

Lopez reached out for Jarvis's throat. Ethan blocked her and put himself between them, looking down at Lopez as he gripped her shoulders.

'Easy. Don't go there.'

'He killed Scott,' Lopez shot back, pointing at Jarvis. 'We got a pay check and a pat on the back. All he cares about is the goddamned DIA, not us.'

Scott Bryson had been a retired Navy SEAL who had helped them on their last investigation. A colorful character with far more personality than sobriety, he had nonetheless sacrificed himself to protect Lopez. The covert nature of their work meant that nobody would ever know of what he had done, and along with his death the injustice had poisoned Lopez with a deep-rooted hatred of government work.

'Doug didn't kill anybody,' Ethan replied. 'The government did. The Pentagon did. National Security did. Why don't you take Sedgewick here down to Cook County Jail and get him processed, okay?'

Lopez stopped straining. Ethan released her and watched as she stepped past him and reached out for Sedgewick's paperwork. Her dark eyes glowered at Jarvis as she snatched the papers out of his hand.

'Whatever you're here for,' she growled, 'you better make damned sure it doesn't get anybody else killed on our watch.'

With that, Lopez turned and stormed out of the office, reaching out with one hand to yank Sedgewick to his feet and haul him out of the room like a giant recalcitrant teddy bear. The office fell silent in her wake as Ethan turned to Jarvis.

'You really should keep your pet under control, Ethan,' the old man murmured.

Ethan hooked one boot behind the office door and kicked it shut.

'You think? You got any idea what she went through?'

'Of course I do,' Jarvis shot back. 'I don't go out of my way to get civilians killed, Ethan. It's what we're here to prevent. But Nicola has a serious attitude problem and you need to make sure she keeps a lid on it. The DIA won't hesitate to take their work somewhere else if they find out what she can be like. Discretion is what we're about, Ethan. Perhaps you should go it alone, it's how you worked best in the marines.'

Ethan ground his teeth in his jaw. 'I had a platoon behind me in the marines, Doug. I'd much rather be with Lopez than without her, no matter what you think. You here on business?'

'Not entirely. How are things? Any news on Joanna's whereabouts?'

A shadow descended upon Ethan even as the name fell from Jarvis's lips. The things that should have remained buried.

'No,' he uttered. 'I don't know where to start looking for her, or even if I should.'

Jarvis stood up.

'We can talk about that on the way,' he said.

'On the way to where?'

'The University of Chicago's zoology department,' Jarvis replied. 'We'll pick Lopez up en route. I'm sending you both up north, but you'll need to hear from an expert what's happened first, otherwise you won't believe it.'

6

CENTRAL INTELLIGENCE
AGENCY, LANGLEY, VIRGINIA

To say that the Director of the Central Intelligence Agency, General William Steel, was in deep shit was something of an understatement and nobody knew it more than he. Sitting in his office in the brand new headquarters in Fairfax County, he was the commander of perhaps the most famous of all America's many clandestine intelligence agencies.

And it was that fame that was ruining both his day and his career.

He had just received a call from the President of the United States, who that morning had received, as he always did, a daily briefing from the CIA. Within that report, compiled by analysts to give the President a broad-strokes picture of the current state of affairs around the world, was a single paragraph detailing a covert program that had been running for six years. William Steel had not authorized the program; it had been initiated during the tenure of his predecessor. The President also had not authorized the program, it had been created by *his* predecessor. Both men had inherited it, and it had blown up spectacularly in their faces to become a problem that could end both their careers.

Thus, the phone call had not been especially cordial.

The President rarely swore. He shouted profanities even less. The message had been clear: make the problem go away. Right now.

The problem with making the other problem go away was that it was a covert operation conducted not on the dusty plains of Iraq, the bitter mountains of Afghanistan or in the dangerous alleys of Pakistan, but in the picturesque hills of Idaho. Worse, the problem was compounded by a further issue: the program was one department within a larger CIA-funded and controlled program that had been running covertly for no less than forty-eight years.

William Steel sat in his leather chair, his thick hands folded on the desk in front of him and his eyes vacant as he mulled over the complex dilemma he faced, his craggy and graying features creased with the burden of responsibility.

A sharp knock at his office door snapped him out of his reverie, and he sat up straight as a tall, sepulchral-looking man strode in and closed the door behind him. The man walked across to a seat opposite Steel and sat down before regarding the director with frosty blue eyes set into an emotionless face.

'How bad?'

The man's voice was disarmingly soft, more like a doctor than an experienced field agent. Truth was, Steel did not like Mr. Wilson at all. A product of the agency's darker years after the political and military fallout of the Vietnam War, Wilson was a lethally capable trained assassin.

'You're here, aren't you?' Steel replied.

'What would you have me do?'

No hesitation. No emotions. No concern, hubris or doubt that Steel could detect. Wilson was all business. Christ, the man didn't even seem to blink. It was like sitting in front of a goddamned waxwork.

'Congress has started another investigation into CIA-sponsored paramilitary programs,' Steel said. 'After what happened in 2009, when one of our counterterrorism programs was busted open and terminated by Congressional meddling, we want to shut down some of our more sensitive operations until the dust settles.'

'I'm not an administrator,' Wilson replied without rancour.

'One of the programs is almost a half-century old,' Steel explained. 'You of course know about it.'

Wilson's eyes narrowed. 'Project MK-ULTRA.'

'The same,' Steel confirmed. 'The other is a subsidiary of the same program being run out in Idaho. That's where the big problem is. We've lost all contact with the team on site.'

Wilson leaned forward in his seat. 'You know what they've got up there,' he said, revealing for the first time a hint of concern. 'What they've been doing.'

'I do,' Steel confirmed, 'and if word gets out about it, it won't just be the end of my career or the President's. It'll probably see the end of this agency. We'll lose our independent status and with it protection from Congressional control. With the bleeding-heart liberals running operations our ability to protect the United States from our enemies, to do the things required to maintain security, will be totally compromised.'

Wilson nodded, his icy gaze never leaving Steel's.

'You didn't bring me here to send me to Idaho,' he said. 'You can use a paramilitary team to clear up the mess there and—'

'We already sent two teams,' Steel cut him off. 'We lost contact with the first of them last night. A second team is in the field at the moment and have tied up some loose ends, but they're under strict orders not to let anybody approach the site.'

Wilson stared at Steel for a long beat. His frosty eyes finally flickered as though a ray of sunlight had penetrated their glacial depths.

'It's escaped,' he said. Steel nodded but said nothing. 'Has the second team you sent maintained security?'

Steel bit his lip before replying.

'They removed one player who had obtained information regarding the site, a civilian. But the Defense Intelligence Agency got to the paperwork before we could intervene,' he said. 'It appears they've got some kind of outsourced team that investigates events passed over by the FBI.'

Mr. Wilson glanced out of the office windows.

'So they killed a civilian, and now we've got independent investigators crawling around out there?'

'Nobody's on site as far as we can tell,' Steel said, 'at least, not yet. They're probably trying to put the pieces together as we speak. If the DIA sends anybody, they can be dealt with. I'm more concerned about the possibility that Congress picks up the trail too. If the committee assigned to investigate projects that have been withheld from Congress lays its hands on hard evidence of what's been going on, we're screwed. It'll all be over.'

Wilson nodded.

'What would you have me do?' he asked again.

'Derail the investigation in any way that you can,' Steel replied. 'Hinder, obstruct and otherwise block all avenues of investigation in Washington DC that lead to either MK-ULTRA or Idaho either via the Defense Intelligence Agency or Congress.'

'That could prove difficult,' Wilson pointed out. 'I won't have deniable access to either the DIA building or Congress. If I'm seen, I'm useless to you.'

'I'll put pressure on the DIA director and the Congressional committee myself,' Steel said. 'You will apply your own *pressure* more discreetly.'

Steel let the word hang between them.

'I want assured immunity,' Wilson said, 'in writing from both yourself and the President.'

Steel raised an eyebrow.

'I can give you assured immunity from prosecution if this all goes belly up, but the President will—'

'Will want his own ass covered,' Wilson cut the director off. 'So get the Defense Secretary, or the Joint Chiefs or the goddamned Director of National Intelligence to sign the paperwork. Either way, you want me to take down American citizens on your watch, you sign the paperwork and you get it to me. Otherwise, I don't budge.'

General Steel had of course expected Wilson to demand some kind of immunity from prosecution. But it wasn't the first time that the CIA had been forced to consider the killing of American citizens. A previous intelligence chief had once testified before the House Intelligence Committee in 2010 that the US intelligence community was prepared to kill US citizens if they threatened other Americans or the United States. Assassinations, both on American soil and abroad, occurred regularly. That was the nature of counter-terrorism: sometimes, people had to die so that the majority might live. The CIA's charter was a pure white canvas of idealistic patriotism, but that canvas was regularly stained by the harsh reality of blood spilled in the name of national security.

But targeting members of Congress or their colleagues was another matter entirely.

'I'll get it done,' Steel said finally.

There was no other option. The danger of seeing the CIA shut down was simply too great. Steel knew that threats to disband the agency dated back to the Kennedy administration. As recently as 2004, senators had repeated a need to end the agency and see it broken up into smaller departments overseen more closely by Congress and other intelligence agencies. With public concern about the lack of information regarding CIA policies and activities, a $44 billion per year budget and the potential for the abuse of unchecked executive power, a scandal now could bring the agency down around General Steel, an outcome he intended to prevent with all of that unchecked power.

Wilson stood and looked down at the director.

'Focus on the outsourced investigators at the DIA,' he advised. 'That's the weak link in their investigation and the easiest way to trip them up. We need controllable government agents up there in Idaho, not freelancers.'

Steel nodded. Both the CIA and the DIA employed contractors that accounted for almost 50 per cent of the total workforce. The travesty of the situation meant that civilians were exposed to classified information which could then be leaked to the media, and the only retaliation the agency could mount would be expensive and complex court battles instead of more discreet internal investigations and punishments.

'I'll arrange a meeting with the Director DIA, Director NSA and the Joint Chiefs of Staff,' Steel confirmed. 'With luck I might be able to get this back under our control.'

'It's already too late for that,' Wilson replied coolly. 'This is damage limitation. The Idaho site needs to be removed from play entirely and anybody up there eradicated along with it.'

Steel sighed heavily but he knew that Wilson was right. Cutting the head off the Hydra was no longer an option: only total destruction would suffice.

'What about that *thing* they have up there?' he asked.

'That's your problem,' Wilson replied. 'I'll take care of this end. I know for a fact that we've had at least one Congressional official under surveillance for some time. They'll come in handy right now.'

Steel stared at Wilson in amazement.

'Who?'

7

UNIVERSITY OF
CHICAGO, ILLINOIS

The zoology department was a gothic-looking building located on East 57th Street. Ethan looked out of the window as the sedan pulled in alongside an ornate archway called Hull Gate. Jarvis climbed out and led Ethan and Lopez into the complex. Tree-lined residential halls were filled with students hurrying from one lecture to another or catching the last warmth of the fall on the neat gardens.

'What are we doing back at school?' Lopez asked.

'There's been an incident, way up in Idaho. You need some background training before you head up there.'

They turned left along a path that led to the entrance of the compound's zoology building. Ethan followed Jarvis inside, the old man apparently knowing exactly where he was going, and reached an office within. Ethan glimpsed a name-plate on the door as he walked in: Professor Giles Middleton.

The office was in part a laboratory, but one that looked as though it had been built sometime during the previous century. To Ethan it looked like a cross between Hogwarts and Frankenstein's dining room. Tall glass cabinets lined an entire wall, filled with glass jars containing the remains of bizarre creatures the likes of which Ethan had never seen.

'Jesus,' Lopez muttered. 'It's like *Pan's Labyrinth* in here.'

Ethan leaned close to one of the glass jars, peering in at what looked like a cross between a baby hippo and an alligator, suspended in some kind of embalming fluid. Small, black eyes squinted vacantly back at him from within the jar, which had a yellowing label affixed to one side.

Ivory Coast, 1874

Lopez peered in at the strange foetus. 'Whatever the hell that is, I'm glad it didn't get the chance to grow up.'

Ethan glanced around the laboratory, dust motes glinting in the sunlight beaming through the windows. The beams hit a painting on one wall that depicted what looked like a Spanish galleon being crushed in the grip of an immense octopus, terrified sailors hurling themselves from the ship's rigging into a tumultuous sea.

To his left were row upon row of specimen jars that held a thousand different species, all of them looking as though they had come from another planet. The darkest recesses at the back of the laboratory harboured shadowy forms like demons sheltering from the light, deformed skeletons and grotesque skulls peering as though from the gates of Hades.

Then Ethan looked up.

'Holy crap,' he uttered out loud.

Suspended from the ceiling beams was a skeleton of

bleached bones that Ethan reckoned must be at least fifty feet long, its remains looping back and forth across the ceiling in order to fit it all in. There was no mistaking what it looked like. Yet the only problem for him was that what it looked like was a creature from the fantasies of science-fiction authors, the long and undulating body of a fish tipped with the head of some kind of shark.

'It looks like a sea serpent,' Lopez said as she gazed up at the remains.

The reply came from the doorway behind them. 'That's because it *is* a sea serpent.'

Ethan turned to see a small man with a wizened face and short gray hair smiling at him from behind half-moon spectacles. Professor Middleton stepped into the laboratory, taking off his spectacles and polishing the lenses on his shirt as he examined the monstrosity looming above them.

'It's a *Regalecus glesne,* otherwise known as the giant oarfish,' he explained. 'This one was caught in the nets of a trawler off the coast of California in 1996 and acquired by me for the university. They can grow twice as large, although none that size have been captured. Yet.'

Jarvis introduced Middleton to Ethan and Lopez. The professor was a world-recognized expert in the subject of cryptozoology.

'I thought that cryptozoology wasn't considered a valid scientific discipline,' Ethan said. 'Pseudo-science, I think biologists call it.'

Middleton smiled ruefully as he replaced his spectacles and pointed up at the enormous oarfish above them.

'Do you think that's pseudo-science?' he challenged, but his blue eyes were bright with delight. 'Mr. Warner, throughout history people have recorded sightings of creatures so bizarre that the witnesses were dismissed as hoaxers or drunks. It has become common discipline to dismiss anything considered too out of the ordinary by science. Solid, incontrovertible evidence is required before any self-respecting researcher will even begin to consider the existence of a new species that defies conventional description.'

Jarvis took up Middleton's line.

'Over the past couple of decades there have been some studies conducted into the existence of creatures that used to be the stuff of myth. The reason that the scientific community has begun to embrace the possibility of these animals being real is the ubiquity of video cameras on cellphones. For the first time in history, people can actually prove that what they said they saw was real.'

'Or not,' Middleton cautioned. 'Many honest people have been genuinely fooled by natural phenomena or misidentification of ordinary creatures under unusual lighting conditions or at great distance. That said, sometimes what they see is truly terrifying even when it's not a new species.'

'Such as?' Lopez asked, intrigued.

'Well,' Middleton shrugged, 'a few years back somebody claimed to have footage of a giant black beast running across the wilderness in Dartmoor, England. The footage was analyzed by experts and was confirmed to be a rare black lion, an adult male and a big one at that. Obviously it's not a species native to that island, but you're still talking about a four-hundred-pound killing machine running wild out there. You can understand where the legends of a beast roaming the moors came from. It's not hard to imagine people being hunted down and killed by a giant African cat.'

'But how could it have gotten there?' Ethan asked.

'The Kings of England often kept big cats in the Tower of London as spectator attractions and symbols of wealth and power,' Jarvis said. 'Many of them escaped over the years. There was also a craze in the seventies for keeping exotic big cats as pets. When the government there changed the laws to prevent people owning dangerous animals, the owners turned their animals loose into the wild. Of course there weren't enough of them to maintain a true breeding population else they'd have been documented by now. But individual animals within huge tracts of wilderness and with an ample food supply could survive for years.'

Ethan glanced uncertainly at Jarvis. 'Why are you telling us about this?'

'You're being sent to Idaho to interview a man named Jesse MacCarthy, who is currently being held by the Sheriff's Department on suspicion of homicide.'

'Who did he kill?' Lopez asked.

'Well, that's the question: did he actually kill anyone?' Jarvis said. 'Jesse MacCarthy's case was picked up by the FBI because Jesse claimed his brother Cletus had been killed in the forests outside of Riggins, Idaho, along with a Ranger by the name of Coltz. Because Riggins sits near the border of Oregon, Montana and Washington State, and Jesse was so incoherent when he was found, the sheriff couldn't figure out for sure where Cletus was when he died. They had to assume the case might have crossed borders so they called the Bureau in.'

'Which is where you come in, right?' Lopez suggested.

'The DIA picked up the case after the FBI rejected it. Turns out that not only did Cletus MacCarthy die in the woods, but a third brother, Randy, was found hanged in his garage the following morning. The Bureau's agents on site decided that Jesse must have killed both of his brothers in some catastrophic mental breakdown. Apparently he was suffering panic attacks for about twenty-four hours after he was found, so the mental instability figures.'

'Why would the FBI drop it so quickly?' Ethan puzzled. 'Two deaths in twenty-four hours in the same family is suspicious, but I take it there's no smoking gun tying Jesse to the killings otherwise you wouldn't be here.'

'Not exactly a smoking gun,' Jarvis replied. 'Jesse has claimed repeatedly to local law enforcement and the Bureau that he knew nothing of Randy's death. But he also insisted that his other brother, Cletus, whose body has not yet been found, was killed by a monster in the forests.'

The room remained silent for a moment.

'A monster,' Lopez echoed flatly.

'His exact words,' Jarvis confirmed.

Ethan thought for a moment. 'There's got to be more to it than that.'

'Not for the Bureau,' Jarvis said. 'But when I got the case I took a better look at it. There are several things that don't add up. Randy's estimated time of death is stated as being the same time that Jesse was supposedly out in the forests. Of course he could have lied about where he was, killing both brothers in the same time frame, except that when he was found his clothes were torn to shreds and he was on the

verge of cardiac arrest. The doctors who treated him diag-
nosed extreme dehydration and exhaustion, which backed up
his story.'

'Which was?'

'That Cletus was killed somewhere near a place called Fox
Creek in the mountains to the east of Riggins. It's almost
twenty miles away from the town through severe terrain, and
Jesse swears his brother was killed the previous evening.'

Ethan got it immediately.

'He ran twenty miles, at night, through the mountains?'

'Non-stop,' Jarvis confirmed. 'Whatever he saw, it scared
him enough to flee so far and so fast that it almost killed him.'

8

In his time with the United States Marines, Ethan had been put through some severe physical challenges that had tested the limits of his endurance. That was just part of a soldier's life, accepted by all who served. But for a civilian with no prior history of extreme physical endurance to run for twelve hours across wild ground was an almost superhuman feat.

'So Jesse gets back to civilization,' Ethan said, 'finds somebody and tells them a monster killed his brother.'

Jarvis nodded.

'He's taken to hospital, but after a few hours the Sheriff's Office arrests him in connection with his brother's death. No motive had been found but Jesse won't shift from his story, which has been digging him further into trouble.'

'You want us to go in and figure it out,' Lopez guessed. 'You really sure this guy's worth all the trouble? What's that scientific rule – Occam's Razor? You don't introduce one mystery to explain another. It's more likely that Jesse killed his brothers and concocted a crazy story to throw the police off the scent.'

Ethan's gaze drifted up to the writhing skeletal coils above his head.

'True,' he agreed, 'but Idaho is big bear country. Why invent a story about a monster when he could just have said a bear got his brother? And if Jesse did murder them both then why come back at all? Why not stay out in the woods a while, then come back as if nothing's happened?'

'That's what I thought,' Professor Middleton said. 'There is no good reason for Jesse MacCarthy to falsely claim a monster killed his brother. Nor could he possibly have faked the damage done to his body in his flight from those mountains. The simplest explanation, Miss Lopez, is that he saw something that terrified him almost to death.'

'Couldn't he have seen a bear though?' Lopez suggested. 'Been mistaken?'

Jarvis shook his head.

'Two of the three MacCarthy brothers were experienced woodsmen and hunters, taught by their father. Jesse was the youngest but he knew the region like the back of his hand: well enough, if we assume he's told the truth, to find his way home in the dead of night while in a state of blind panic. These guys knew what bears looked like. But that's not what intrigues us the most.'

Middleton pushed his spectacles further up onto his nose as he took his cue. 'This has happened before.'

'To whom?' Lopez asked.

'A celebrity, believe it or not,' Middleton explained. 'Spirit Lake, near Mount St. Helens in Washington State, May 1950. Championship skier Jim Carter vanished without trace from a twenty-strong climbing party after diverting from the group in order to take photographs. He left the other climbers near a landmark called Dog's Head, in good weather at the eight-thousand-foot level, to take a picture of the group as they skied down. That was the last time anyone saw him. The next morning searchers found a discarded film box at the point where he had taken a picture.'

'So?' Ethan asked.

'Carter had left ski tracks in the snow going down the mountain,' Middleton said, 'that recorded a wild and death-defying flight. He took chances no professional skier would take, going like the devil and leaping crevasses. His companions claimed that he would only ever have done that if he was in genuine fear of his life. He eventually reached Ape Canyon and skied straight down the canyon wall, such was his evident terror. Yet his body was not found at the bottom.'

'Seattle Mountain Search and Rescue combed the canyon for five days,' Jarvis continued, 'but no sign of Carter or his equipment was ever found.'

'During the search,' Middleton went on, 'the rescuers reported feelings of being watched on the mountain, and agreed that there was something strange up on the high slopes of the Cascades. There have been about twenty-five different reports of people attacked by apelike men in the St. Helens and Cascade areas over a twenty-year period. One was a group of Boy Scouts from Centralia. Several were taken off the mountain in a hysterical state after claiming they had been attacked by what they called mountain devils.'

Ethan turned to Professor Middleton.

'I take it that you think that whatever attacked Jim Carter also attacked Cletus and Jesse MacCarthy. Do you have any idea what it was?'

Middleton walked further down into the laboratory and

picked up what looked to Ethan like a large slab of cement. The professor heaved it into the light and set it down on a nearby wooden table with a thump that sent little clouds of dust curling up into the sunbeams.

Ethan stepped forward and looked down at the huge plaster cast.

The depressions set into the cast marked the surface of what must have been a shallow pool or perhaps the bed of a stream, ripples of sand clearly formed by flowing water speckled with small pebbles and a grainy texture. But in the center of the cast was the unmistakeable shape of an enormous footprint. A plastic measuring gauge was glued along the edge of the cast, and he could see that it measured just less than seventeen inches.

'This cast,' Middleton said, 'was made from a trail of fresh prints that ran along a watercourse in Umatilla National Forest, Washington State. The inferred weight of the creature that left this print, measured by the density of the riverbed at the time, was in excess of seven hundred pounds.'

Lopez squinted down at the print. 'It looks human.'

'Yes it does,' Middleton nodded, 'and yet at the same time, it isn't. The step length of the creature that created this track was almost two metres, far greater than that of a human being. Moreover, details in the print reveal a compliant gait on a flat foot, compared to the human method of walking which uses a stiff-legged stride with distinct heel and toe phases. Essentially, this creature walks with a bent knee, using its legs like shock-absorbers and rolling the foot to keep the torso level. Humans bounce a little when we walk – this creature does not.'

'Couldn't it be a fake?' Ethan suggested. 'Some jerk with boards strapped to his feet?'

'No,' Middleton said as he gestured to details in the cast, 'because it would be physically impossible to model all of the tiny variables we see in prints like this. The roll of the foot through the sand that created these mid-tarsal pressure ridges; the slight slip of the ball that has pushed the sand backward behind the heel; and here,' Middleton pointed to fine lines in the base of the print, 'evidence of dermatoglyphics, like fingerprints, the faint ridges in the surface of the skin of all primates.'

'You're saying that an ape created this?' Lopez said. 'Like a gorilla?'

'A bipedal ape,' Middleton corrected her, 'sometimes known as *sasquatch*, or Bigfoot.'

Ethan stared at the print for a long moment before speaking.

'You think that Jesse MacCarthy's brother was killed by a Bigfoot? It's no wonder the FBI walked away from the case.'

'And even if it were true,' Lopez said, 'what the hell do you expect us to do about it? Head into the mountains and bring our homicidal Bigfoot back to trial? This is crazy. What possible interest can the DIA have in this?'

Jarvis gestured to the cast.

'The department's interest at this point is purely coincidental. The murder of Randy MacCarthy is an open and recent case, and having become involved we've been given tacit approval to head up there. Solve the murder and the case gets closed as far as the DIA is concerned. I'd like you to push a little further and find out what you can about what really happened to Cletus and Jesse.'

Ethan sighed and shook his head.

'Okay, but don't hold your breath for any spectacular discoveries this time. There have been people scouring the forests for sasquatch for centuries and nobody's found a thing. For me, the idea of a giant hairy human wandering about in the forests is about as close to myth as we're likely to get.'

Professor Middleton's eyes hardened behind his spectacles as he looked at Ethan.

'Perhaps your scepticism, although healthy, is both misplaced and out of date, Mr. Warner,' he warned. 'We humans are apes ourselves, primates, closely related to our cousins, the chimpanzees and gorillas. Our own lineage, that of the order *Homo*, until a hundred thousand years ago consisted of several different species of human wandering the earth.'

'Seriously?' Lopez asked. 'I thought it was only us?'

'The Neanderthals were a different species,' Ethan said. 'As were *Homo heidelbergensis* and *Homo erectus*, but they all walked the earth at the same time as us, *Homo sapiens*. Our species overlapped in their ranges and likely came face to face often.'

'Impressive,' Professor Middleton said, raising an eyebrow. 'Your knowledge of human evolution is remarkably astute.'

'I learned a few things about the origin of life in Israel a while back,' Ethan said without elaborating, unwilling right now to think too hard about the Gaza Strip and the things that had occurred there years before. 'But all of our competing species died out, became extinct. We, *Homo sapiens*, are the only ones left.'

'Are you sure?' Middleton asked rhetorically.

Jarvis gestured to an image pinned to the wall of the laboratory, that of a clearly human face with a thick beard and long, lank black hair. The eyes seemed too large for the face and the brow ridge was pronounced, almost like that of an ape, while the nasal bridge was wide and flat with large nostrils.

'The island of Flores, 2003,' he said. 'A team working in the deep jungles researching the migration of ancient *Homo sapiens* around the world unexpectedly discovered an entirely new species of human, *Homo floresiensis*, the remains of which were found in a place called Liang Bua Cave. Evidence of extensive tool production, use of fire, cooking and eating confirmed the species as effectively a modern human, but there was one major difference.'

'What? Lopez asked.

'They were tiny,' Professor Middleton said. 'A fully grown adult male might only reach three feet tall. It's the result of a process called dwarfism, when a species finds itself on a small island or in an environment with limited resources. Evolution through natural selection favors smaller species with smaller demands on the limited environment. Sophisticated stone implements of a size considered appropriate to the three-foot-tall humans were widely present in the cave. The implements were at horizons from ninety-five to thirteen thousand years ago and were found in the same stratigraphic layer as an elephant of the extinct genus *Stegodon,* also a dwarf species, which was widespread throughout Asia during the period and presumably the prey. They also shared the island with giant rats and Komodo dragons.'

'So?' Ethan asked.

'They didn't die out until just thirteen thousand years ago,' Jarvis explained. 'Local geology suggests that a volcanic eruption on Flores approximately twelve thousand years ago was responsible for the demise of *Homo floresiensis*, along with other local fauna, including the elephant *Stegodon*. But the Nage people of Flores still speak of the *Ebu Gogo* people: small, hairy, language-poor cave dwellers on the scale of this species.'

'They're still alive?' Lopez asked in amazement.

'It's entirely possible,' Middleton said, 'that pockets of this species could have survived until this day. Imagine, an entirely different species of human walking our planet. The dwarfism that has caused their diminutive size seems to have had little impact on their technological achievements when compared to our own ancestors of equivalent vintage.'

'What have they got to do with a sasquatch though?' Lopez asked. 'They're supposed to be huge.'

Middleton simply gestured again to the footprint.

'The opposite of dwarfism is giganticism,' he explained. 'Put simply, if a species is placed into either a resource-rich environment, or one where there are predators big enough to force an evolutionary advantage in being large, then almost any species can grow to enormous proportions.'

'Kind of like the dinosaurs,' Ethan suggested.

'Exactly like the dinosaurs,' Middleton agreed. 'Even before they ruled the earth, the atmosphere of our planet was far richer in oxygen than today, resulting in species that still exist but were far larger in the past. There were centipedes a hundred times larger than today and dragonflies with wingspans two yards across.'

Ethan had a mental image of a dragonfly with the wingspan of an eagle, then quickly exterminated it from his thoughts with a shiver.

Jarvis's cellphone trilled in his pocket. He answered it, asked a couple of brief questions and then shut the line off and looked at Ethan. 'There's been a development.'

'What?'

'They've found the remains of park ranger Gavin Coltz,' Jarvis said sternly. 'Whatever killed him, it sure as hell wasn't a man.'

9

DEFENSE INTELLIGENCE AGENCY HEADQUARTERS, JOINT BASE ANACOSTIA–BOLLING, WASHINGTON DC

Lieutenant General Abraham Mitchell was a tall and powerfully built African-American who had served the United States of America his entire adult life. An aura surrounded him like a force field, staff veering out of his way as he strode down the seventh-floor corridor to his office.

The Chair of the Military Intelligence Board and a deeply respected figure at the Pentagon, Abraham Mitchell had the ear of the President and could, provided with sufficient evidence, order an air-strike on any location on earth whether on enemy or allied soil. Yet today, for all of his ribbons and all of the respect, Mitchell knew that trouble was brewing within the intelligence community and that he was close to the epicenter.

He walked into his office and closed the door as the two

men awaiting him rose from their seats. One was a former Green Beret by the name of Foster, who in his career as a field man had served in more theaters of war than even Mitchell. As a soldier, he was a man with whom Mitchell could identify. The other man was General William Steel, Director of the CIA. A visit from DCIA only happened when there was something wrong. Very wrong.

'Gentlemen,' Mitchell greeted them without preamble. 'What can I do for you?'

Foster and Steel sat down opposite Mitchell as he eased his 220-pound frame into his chair. Foster spoke with a gravelly voice, the result of two decades of screaming at recruits down Fort Benning way.

'We've been sent up here regarding a possible breach of security protocol by one of your team.'

Mitchell raised an eyebrow. 'Whom?'

'A Douglas Jarvis,' Foster replied. 'Former United States Marine officer, works under your watch on a new program of some kind. Homeland sent us here in person because they have no access to files pertaining to this program he's running. We were wondering whether you could fill us in?'

Mitchell remained motionless for a moment. Foster was maintaining a formal bearing but he was clearly trying to project a reasonable persona at the same time. Mitchell could see it in his expression and body language that was saying: *hey, we're both on the same side here.* General Steel, on the other hand, simply watched Mitchell with an unblinking gaze. Reptilian, Mitchell thought.

'Jarvis is responsible for the overseeing of a classified

research program for the agency,' Mitchell replied. 'It's an autonomous outfit, so neither Homeland nor the Pentagon would have direct access to it.'

'Why is that?' Steel asked, speaking for the first time. His voice was both soft and threatening, a forged-in-granite confidence born of thirty years in the CIA.

'Intelligence security,' Mitchell replied, unfazed. 'The program has assets on the ground, and exposure of their activities could render them at risk from potential hostiles.'

Foster's controlled expression slipped slightly. Steel remained silent. Mitchell became aware of people walking past his office door as the silence stretched out for several seconds until Foster finally spoke.

'Sir, we have managed to identify two individuals who have been connected to this program within the DIA.' He slid a pair of glossy images across the desk to Mitchell. 'Do you recognize them?'

Mitchell looked down and saw a black-and-white mug shot of Ethan Warner staring up at him. It was typical of the CIA that they would source a shot of Warner taken in Cook County Jail, and not one from the much easier to acquire service record at the US Marine's primary training base at Quantico, Virginia. Beside Warner's haggard features was a shot of Nicola Lopez, again taken via a surveillance team and not a more formal shot of her proudly wearing the blues of the Washington Police Department.

He looked up at Steel and Foster. These boys had an agenda all right.

'They work for Jarvis,' he replied. 'They're his primary agents.'

William Steel nodded and leaned back in his seat, folding his hands in his lap as he spoke.

'You are aware of the joint Pentagon and NASA operation down at Cape Canaveral, Project Watchman?'

Mitchell nodded. Watchman was a major defense initiative launched by the National Reconnaissance Office that used orbiting KH-11 Keyhole Satellites and immense super-computers to record events on earth in real time and compress the data into a virtual world through which operatives could move. The project had been running for over ten years now, and represented for the intelligence community the ability to do what no other government agency on earth could do – effectively look back in time, anywhere on earth.

'Watchman is something that the DIA has a close relationship with,' he confirmed.

'Too close,' Steel replied. 'Your man Jarvis recently allowed both Ethan Warner and his partner, Nicola Lopez, into the facility. Not only that, but he allowed them to actually *use* the program themselves.'

'They were involved in an investigation that ultimately saved thousands, if not millions of lives,' Mitchell said. 'Their exposure to sensitive programs is more than justified by their success in utilising the information obtained.'

'That would be true,' Steel said, 'were Warner and Lopez not civilian contractors. It's not in the interest of our intelligence services to bring unqualified risks to our work.'

Mitchell leveled Steel with a stony gaze.

'More than half the workforce of the CIA's most important directorate, the National Clandestine Service, is outsourced, so don't come in here telling me that my outfit is jeopardizing

national security. Warner and Lopez are only given cases that
the rest of the intelligence community has already rejected as
unworkable, and their resulting investigations have been
unqualified success stories. Perhaps you should ask yourself
why it was that the Pentagon have turned away from at
least three major investigations that presented clear and present dangers to both American security and the lives of our
citizens?'

'This isn't about blame,' Foster intervened. 'We're being
asked to ensure that the security of our most sensitive operations cannot be blown by two people over whom we have
no control. This program that you're running represents a
very weak link in a long chain of carefully orchestrated security measures. I can't just go back to the Secretary of Defense
and tell him that, hey, everything's just fine, chill out. If
Watchman or a comparable program were exposed to the
public, all of our careers would be on the line.'

Mitchell remained impassive.

'Who sent you, exactly?' Neither Foster nor Steel replied,
which pretty much was an answer in itself. Mitchell let a
bitter little smile curl from one corner of his mouth. 'So,
nobody sent you. The spooks at the CIA have finally taken
an interest in what Doug's achieved down here.' He glanced
at Steel. 'Let me guess: Warner and Lopez have done what
you guys couldn't, you've gotten all upset about it, so now
you're looking to take over the operation.'

'This is about security,' Steel replied in a crisp tone.
'Nothing more.'

'Of course it is,' Mitchell replied without losing the smile.
'So much so that you want me to breach my *own* agency's

security protocols and tell you everything about one of our programs.' He let the smile slip. 'Not going to happen.'

'We're on the same side here, Abe,' Foster said, trying to keep the mood cordial. 'We just need to keep everybody's borders tight is all. If this program is such a big deal then maybe you could run it through the NRO and cut Warner and Lopez loose. That way it's all internal and we're not farming work out to people like that.'

Foster gestured loosely to the images of Lopez and Warner.

'People like *what*?' Mitchell rumbled.

'A convicted felon and an amateur gumshoe,' Foster almost chuckled in response. 'Come on, we've got much better people available for this kind of work who won't set off alarm bells in DC.'

Mitchell's fists balled of their own accord.

'If you'd bothered to look into the history of these two investigators, instead of just sucking up the crap that the CIA is obviously feeding you, you'd know that Ethan Warner is a decorated former United States Marine, as is Doug Jarvis, and that Nicola Lopez is a former DC police detective. Neither of them is amateur at anything.'

'They're both liabilities,' Steel snapped. 'Ethan Warner has a reputation for opposing and directly disobeying authority and Lopez is known to be a short fuse at the best of times. Yet they're both wandering around the country with access to all manner of classified materials. Jarvis has twice used assets of our Navy and Air Force to achieve his aims in support of these investigations, which have often led to extreme expo-sure events such as exploding civilian apartment buildings, violent incidents in allied countries such as Israel and repeated firearms violations in public areas throughout the country. Our business, sir, is both covert and classified. These two . . .' Steel gestured at the photographs. 'They're a danger to national security, not an asset to it.'

Mitchell leaned across the desk, his dark eyes glowering into Steel's.

'Left to you, none of those cases would ever have been investigated, let alone solved. The Pentagon has acquired extraordinary technology as a direct result of these investigations and I'll be damned if I'll let the CIA kick the door down now.'

Foster sighed heavily as Steel bolted upright from his seat and stalked out of the office. Mitchell waited until the door had closed behind him before he looked at Foster. The soldier's expression said it all.

'Are you really in bed with the CIA?' Mitchell asked.

'Transferred out of the army for medical reasons,' Foster explained. 'My knees gave in. I'm too damned old to learn the intelligence game and all that computerized crap, so they attach me to field agents instead for mutual training.'

'Watch your back,' Mitchell warned. 'The CIA has a long history of self-preservation at the expense of its agents.'

'Don't worry, I've got myself covered,' Foster said as he stood. 'But they'll get what they want in the end.'

He was right, Mitchell knew. That was just the way of things. He knew that Jarvis had hoped to have cracked a few more cases before the Pentagon really started taking notice, which would have given him more information and evidence to defend Warner and Lopez. Jarvis had a lot of time

for Ethan Warner, and to his surprise Mitchell had also been
quietly impressed with the man's tenacity and success.

'I know. Just going to try to hold them off for a while
longer, is all.'

'Don't try too hard. There's too much at stake, for all three
of us now that we're involved, and for your man Jarvis,' Foster
warned him. 'It's better for you all if you handle their investigations directly through this office and keep us in the loop.'

'Why's that?' Mitchell asked.

'Because I'm only here due to Warner's military history,'
Foster replied. 'Truth is, Abe, I've got very little control over
what CIA might try to do. I'm consulting, not controlling.'

'Steel's in charge of this?' Mitchell asked in surprise. Foster
nodded. 'Under whose mandate?' Mitchell pressed.

'It went past the Director of National Intelligence,' Foster
replied.

'Which means an executive order,' Mitchell rumbled
unhappily. 'Jesus, what are they trying to keep under the
carpet now?'

'I don't know,' Foster admitted, 'and I don't want to know.
Last I heard there's another Congressional investigation run-
ning, looking into CIA projects that haven't been seen by
Congress. If Steel's gotten himself knee-deep in something,
he'll want to clear the decks and tie up loose ends before
Congress gets hold of anything solid.'

Mitchell nodded. William Steel was a good man and an
undoubted patriot, but he was also ruthless in maintaining
secrecy at the CIA and hated the interventions made by
Congress in the past. Mitchell wasn't sure just how far Steel
would go to ensure his agency remained free from interference,

but he was damned sure the general would not be made a patsy for a previous director's indiscretions.

'Who's the enforcer for all of this?' Mitchell asked as Foster turned to leave. 'Steel must have somebody on the ground picking up the pieces if everything goes south.'

Foster's hand rested on the door handle as he replied.

'I don't know, but keep your people in sight. The administration is maintaining complete deniability for this little clean-up operation of Steel's. If his back is forced to the wall, Ethan Warner and Nicola Lopez are likely to end up as targets themselves.'

10

NEW MEADOWS
AIRPORT, IDAHO

The chartered Beech Twin Bonanza thumped down onto the grass runway and rumbled along beside the tiny town of New Meadows. Ethan peered out of rain-streaked windows at the soaring mountains nearby, their peaks lost in dense wreaths of gray cloud and the fields below sodden and damp.

A light drizzle had enveloped the airplane all the way up from Friedman Memorial Airport, the thick clouds obscuring Ethan's view of the mountainous and forested terrain as the pilot guided them over tumultuous bumps in the air. The mountains caused violent updrafts and downdrafts that tossed the little aircraft about as though it were a leaf in a gale.

Ethan knew that Idaho was not a densely populated state, but even so the vast tracts of wilderness that had stretched into the gloomy distance beneath them had seemed so immense that he could not imagine how one might begin systematically searching it for any creature unknown to science, much less one that had made these lonely forests its home for untold millennia.

'We're digging ourselves a hole with this one,' Lopez said, peering out of her window as the aircraft taxied off the runway and bumped along a track. 'A big, damp, cold hole.'

'Sheriff's picking us up from here,' Ethan replied as he unbuckled from his seat. 'Maybe there have been more developments since we left Chicago.'

The pilot shut down the aircraft's engines, and as Ethan clambered out of the airplane he saw a portly sheriff ambling his way across the rutted, rain-sodden soil toward them.

'Earl Carpenter,' he introduced himself, 'Riggins Sheriff's Department. Welcome to Idaho.'

He said it with a cheery smile and a twinkling eye, and Ethan wondered whether the drizzle and cold was something folk just got used to up here. The sheriff proved himself a helpful soul, carrying their bags to his patrol car before they climbed in and set off north on the U-95.

'Riggins is about thirty-five miles out,' Earl informed them as he drove away from the airport. 'Say, where did you guys come from? All I got told was that you were working for the government or something?'

'Private contractors,' Ethan replied by way of an explanation, 'the FBI don't have the manpower to dedicate a team to this investigation, so we help fill in for them.'

Earl Carpenter frowned as he glanced in his mirror at Lopez.

'You qualified for this kind of work, ma'am?'

'Worked homicide as a detective in DC for six years,'

Lopez replied without bridling. 'Ethan here is ex-marines, recon.'

Earl raised an eyebrow and smiled apologetically at them. 'I guess that's good enough for me.'

'What's the story so far?' Ethan asked. 'You've got two dead bodies, another supposed dead but still missing and a kid who swears that his brother was killed by an animal, right?'

'To cut it short,' Earl agreed, 'but there's a whole lot about this that doesn't fit right.'

'Tell us,' Lopez said.

Earl puffed his cheeks and blew the air out as he drove.

'Hard to know where to start. I get me a call about a local lady whose son's been found hanging in the garage.'

'Randy MacCarthy,' Ethan said.

'So I goes down there,' Earl went on, 'and I check out the scene before the county coroner gets called in. Sure enough, Randy's swinging in the wind. There's a stool underneath him and he'd been dead for a few hours.'

'How did you know?' Lopez asked.

'Body was cold,' Earl replied. 'His neck weren't broken, so he died on the rope.'

'Any history of prior convictions?' Ethan asked. 'Anything that might motivate this kid to take his own life?'

'He'd been busted a couple of times for possession but nothing serious, got held by the local police department for forty-eight hours but no charges were filed as he wasn't dealing,' Earl replied. 'Made a lot of claims about conspiracies and said that he had evidence of government agents working in and around Riggins. Watched too many TV shows, you ask me. But there's no evidence of foul play. I took some photographs before forensics moved in, and Randy's post-mortem confirmed death by asphyxiation.'

'You got copies of the photographs on you?' Lopez asked from the rear seat.

Earl reached down into the side pocket of his door and pulled out a manila envelope before passing it to the back seat. Ethan watched as Lopez pulled out a wad of six-by-eight images and began sifting through them. If there was anything unusual about the crime scene, she would notice it soon enough.

'What about the other brothers?' Ethan asked. 'And the ranger who was killed?'

Earl Carpenter rested one arm on the sill of his door as he drove. Ethan noticed that the hills around them were getting steeper as they traveled, thickly forested with pines or coarse grass, and the roadside flanked by occasional shacks and game crossings.

'Well, that there's a mystery. Cletus and Jesse go off huntin'' out in Nez Perce Forest, and it turns out that the ranger, a local man called Gavin Coltz, spotted them tracking a game elk. Season's out right now so he decided to follow them and catch them in the act. He was a tenacious soul, Gavin, and he stuck with them for almost four hours before they tried to take their shot out near Fox Creek.'

'Then they get attacked?' Lopez guessed.

'By a bear,' Earl confirmed. 'Gavin is killed, so is Cletus, and Jesse runs for his life. Turns up next morning in Riggins lookin' for all the world like he was dead already.'

'You don't believe his story about a monster killing his brother?' Ethan asked.

Earl Carpenter looked Ethan in the eye.

'I've been working out here since I was a boy,' he said, 'and I've seen a lot of people come close to dying after attacks by bears and cougars. This kid, he din' have no reason to claim what he did, that some kind of other creature had at them. In all my years I've never seen fear like that in the face of a man, but then if he'd just killed two members of his family then I'd guess he'd be all shook up. Truth is, I don't know what to believe.'

Ethan glanced up at the foggy mountains looming either side of the car as it drove between the steep hillsides. 'It's a mystery all right.'

'It's not the only mystery,' Lopez said from the rear seat.

'What you got?' Ethan asked.

'You say you found Randy MacCarthy hanging just like this?' Lopez asked Earl Carpenter. 'And you hadn't touched him at all?'

'Exactly like that,' Earl confirmed. 'I only touched him once to search for a pulse. Needless to say I din' find one, and his body was cold.'

Lopez nodded.

'Then this isn't a suicide, Sheriff, it's a homicide.'

Earl's old eyes flicked up to meet hers in the rear-view mirror. 'You shittin' me, lady? The boy's a suicide for sure. There's nothing that suggests foul play in my book.'

Lopez handed the photographs to Ethan. 'Tell me what's wrong with the picture,' she said.

Ethan looked at the six-by-eights one after the other. Randy dangling from the noose, his tongue swollen and poking from his mouth, his eyes half-closed and lifeless.

The toppled stool three feet below him. Ethan shook his head.

'I'm not seeing it,' he admitted.

'The body was cold,' Lopez said. 'Been there a few hours. What's missing?'

It took only a moment for Ethan to realize what she meant. Images from his service with the marines in Iraq and Afghanistan flashed through his mind, of the shameful sight of the dead lying in the streets or in bitter, lonely caves in the mountains.

'The body hasn't voided,' he said finally. 'Randy didn't die where he was found.'

'That's my boy,' Lopez smiled.

'Crap,' Earl Carpenter uttered, and slapped a hand across the steering wheel, angry with himself. 'Should've realized that.'

'When a person dies their sphincter muscles give way and they void their bowels,' Lopez said. 'This kid had been hanging for some time but there was no residue beneath him from the moment of death.'

'So he died elsewhere and was moved,' Ethan said. 'Any further clues here?'

'None,' Earl shook his head. 'Whoever hanged him there was careful enough to sweep the floor, which covered their tracks but I guess also proves they were there.'

'Exactly,' Lopez said. 'That was my next point: they cleaned up after themselves, which means premeditated homicide.'

'I'd better call ahead to Grangeville,' Earl said, and reached for the patrol car's radio. 'Inform them of what you guys have figured out.'

'Can you think of any likely suspects?' Ethan asked Earl.

'Only Randy's ma, Sally, who found him,' Earl said. 'But I don't think she's on the cards for this. She had three sons and loved them all. Besides, there's no clear motive. Randy had no life insurance and no savings. The mother's penniless and all three of her sons contributed to the upkeep of their household from their own pay checks, all of which were from menial jobs in town.'

Ethan mentally scratched a financial motive to the killing from his list.

'So it's a homicide disguised as a suicide, and done badly,' Lopez said. 'That suggests somebody inexperienced, maybe a local person who doesn't know much about crime.'

Earl Carpenter chuckled bitterly.

'Sure does, which means most all folk in Riggins. Our population work in local business or make the run over to McCall and Grangeville for work. Anybody wantin' bigger cahoots in life gets out of the county altogether.'

'Anything from forensics or the coroner's office?' Ethan asked.

'Nothing much,' Earl replied. 'Randy died of asphyxiation by the same rope that was found around his neck, that much is for sure. So whoever did this, they had a vehicle to transport him and there was probably more than one of them. Hard to carry and hoist a body on your own.'

Ethan struggled to get his head around it.

'So they're dumb enough to botch the apparent suicide, yet smart enough to leave no trace of their presence at the scene or on the body? Were there any tire marks or tracks?'

'None but my own vehicle when I arrived,' Earl replied. 'Which means they cleared their own trail out of there.'

'We were told that the ranger's body had been recovered,' Lopez informed him. 'Anything you guys have learned there?'

'Oh yeah,' Earl replied. 'We'll head up past Riggins to Grangeville first. I'll let the doctors fill you in about that, because I don't even like talking about it.'

II

IDAHO COUNTY CORONER, GRANGEVILLE, IDAHO

Ethan stood in the clinical surroundings of the autopsy room and looked down at the corpse before him. The body was that of a young, athletic male, probably no more than thirty years old. Broad chest. Narrow waist. Long, strong legs and muscular arms. Only one thing was missing.

'Where's his head?' Lopez asked, her normally olive skin pale and her eyes wide with horror.

The body of Gavin Coltz ended abruptly at his neck. A bloodied stump of bone protruded from the flesh, the remains of where his spinal column and vertebrae had been snapped off with unimaginable violence.

The consulting pathologist, Dr. Jenny Shriver, gestured to a nearby box concealed beneath a sheet of blue plastic.

'It was found fifty feet below where he died, in the bed of a shallow creek. It's not in good shape.'

Jenny Shriver was a middle-aged woman whose features might once have been considered attractive but had been creased by years of seeing human bodies tragically mutilated or decayed to the point of being unrecognizable. Ethan guessed that no matter how detached a person might become to death, it still left its somber imprint on their faces.

'Did the water accelerate the rate of decay?' Lopez asked.

'No,' Shriver replied. 'The impact shattered the skull like a bag of chips under a car tire. The jaw was broken in fifteen places and both of the eyeballs had been blasted from their sockets. We weren't able to recover them.'

Ethan looked at Gavin Coltz's corpse. The skin was a pallid white but the upper chest was stained with huge purple bruises, each the size of Ethan's hand and surrounded by a halo of sickly yellow skin.

'What are those?' he asked, gesturing to the marks.

'Compression fractures,' Shriver identified them. 'Caused by blunt trauma.'

'So he was attacked by another human and not an animal?' Lopez suggested. 'Somebody must have hit this guy with a truck to cause that much hemorrhage.'

Shriver did not reply, simply casting a serious gaze in Lopez's direction before she rested one gloved hand on the body.

'He was not attacked by a human being, Miss Lopez.'

'What happened to him?' Ethan asked, eager to cut to the chase. 'We have a man locked up in a cell in Riggins under suspicion of murder who swears that he didn't do it, and there's still one other person missing. We need to know what we're up against here.'

Shriver lifted her hand from the corpse, took a deep breath and gestured to the various lesions lacing the body as she spoke.

'The victim was killed by a single blow to the head that resulted in decapitation, the neck severed between the fourth and fifth cervical vertebrae. That blow was sufficient to send the severed skull flying more than thirty feet through the air to land in the creek bed.'

Ethan ran what she had said through his head for a moment.

'But you said that the skull landed in the creek, causing the massive damage.'

'The impact that blew this man's eyeballs out of their sockets was caused by the blow that killed him,' Shriver corrected. 'The skull hit the water below but not with enough force to cause this kind of damage. All of the major fractures were caused by that first, single, lethal impact.'

'That's impossible,' Lopez said. 'Nobody could hit a man that hard, certainly not Jesse MacCarthy.'

'Correct,' Shriver replied as though congratulating a schoolgirl. 'The amount of force required to physically tear a man's head from his shoulders via a single impact is the equivalent of being hit by a thirty-pound sledgehammer traveling at sixty miles per hour. No human being can produce that kind of physical power.'

Ethan looked down at the bruised, battered corpse.

'So something hits him so hard that it kills him instantly, and then it continues striking him?'

'The sign of a frenzied attack,' Shriver acknowledged. 'A crime of rage.'

'So maybe it's a bear attack, a mother protecting its young or something?' Lopez suggested.

Shriver walked across to the box beneath the blue plastic.

She lifted the sheet off and picked the clear acrylic box up. The head within the box was a macabre visage, the empty eye sockets black and lifeless, the tongue poking fat and bloated from a slack mouth. The once-clean line of the man's jaw was crumpled and bulky, shards of shattered jaw-bone trying to push through white skin. But it was the impression on one side of the skull that instantly caught Ethan's attention as Shriver set the box down on top of the corpse's chest.

Gavin Coltz's head had been stoved in on one side, the skull crushed almost flat but the skin unbroken. Shallow depressions ran from the rear of his skull across the side of the face, like channels beneath the skin.

'We made a scan of the face and skull,' Shriver informed them, 'to digitally preserve the details of the impact. One of my lab assistants reversed the image to try and deduce the shape of whatever hit this man.'

'What did they find?' Lopez asked.

Shriver turned and picked up a glossy black photograph, then pinned it to the wall nearby. Ethan felt something squirm through his guts as he looked at the image, like a primal fear seldom felt but never forgotten.

'Jesus,' Lopez whispered.

The image was that of the base of an enormous clenched fist, the channel-like depressions crunched into Coltz's skull formed by broad, fat fingers with an opposable thumb folded beneath them.

'The hand was clenched into a fist but struck the victim flat on the side of his head,' Shriver explained. 'It's a way of strik-ing somebody without risking the damage to the hand that can be the result of punching in a more classic, knuckles-first way.'

Earl Carpenter looked away from the gruesome imagery and caught Ethan's eye.

'Now you see why we didn't want to deal with this alone,' he explained. 'The Bureau walked before we found Coltz's body, and frankly I don't see the need to bring them back in. Sure, we might possibly have the world's largest fugitive on our hands, but my guts are telling me that this isn't a human being.'

Ethan stared at Coltz's remains for a moment before replying.

'You say that you didn't find any other remains at the scene.'

'Nothin',' Carpenter confirmed.

Ethan looked at Shriver. 'So this mystery animal kills Coltz with a single blow, beats the hell out of his corpse, then carries off another body without leaving a trace? Why attack one so savagely and then carry another away while letting the third, still-living witness, flee the scene unharmed?'

Dr. Shriver shrugged.

'It's not my place to solve the crime, Mr. Warner. All that I can tell you for sure is that whatever killed Gavin Coltz was more powerful than any human being could ever be, and it most likely will kill again if it encounters people out there in the woods.'

Ethan briefly recalled an image that had haunted his thoughts for months, when Jarvis had used Project Watchman to show him a glimpse of the future. Time had blurred his memory, but he remembered enough to know that whatever was hunting people in the forests of Idaho truly was something inhuman and that Lopez would inevitably find herself in danger.

Ethan forced the images from his mind as Lopez gave the corpse one last glance and then turned to Ethan.

'We need to talk to Jesse MacCarthy. He's the one that witnessed Coltz's death.'

12

GOVERNMENT ACCOUNTABILITY OFFICE, UNITED STATES CAPITOL, WASHINGTON DC

Natalie Warner swept into the GAO building. A barrage of security checks followed and she was scrutinised with hand-held scanners before being cleared to enter the building.

Natalie was an analyst and researcher at the GAO, a job she had obtained after her internship in the White House. Perhaps due to her family connection with the military through the Marine Corps, Natalie had found herself fascinated by the world of intelligence gathering since her childhood when her father had told her stories about presidents and foreign countries and the battles they had fought since the Revolution. Although she had possessed very little security clearance at the White House during her two years there, it had been readily apparent that all of the interesting stuff happened behind closed doors in meetings attended by the Joint Chiefs of Staff and the heads of the various intelligence agencies. Natalie had decided within the first six months of her tenure that she wanted to know what went on in those kinds of meetings. A job working for Congress had been her way of getting in on the act.

Aside from legislative activities, Congress devoted a great deal of time to investigations that had uncovered wrong-doing within the executive branch, from obscure agencies up to the president's office. The GAO was the body through which investigative work was done on behalf of members of Congress. By uncovering this information and informing the public, investigations had often led to important reform legislation. Natalie knew that critics in the media often dismissed Congressional investigations as an opportunity for politicians to make headlines, and pointed out that many investigations produce no solid evidence and failed to lead to any legislation at all, but she figured that some investigative ability was better than none. Since 1792, Congress had kept an eye on the executive branch: it had the power to investigate anything related to legislation or oversight and the monitoring of the activities of executive agencies.

Now, under Democratic Congressman Howard J. Faulkes, New York, Natalie was part of a Congressional investigation into the intelligence community's alleged withholding of defense program budgets and details from Congress.

The first shock upon arriving at her new post in the Capitol and visiting a CIA monitoring station had been the antiquated equipment. Far from being a hive of ultra-hi-tech computers and real-time satellite links, the intelligence agencies all preferred to use slightly older, tried and tested equipment that had proven its value and reliability in the field. That, and the painfully ordinary-looking ranks of offices and desks, was the reality of modern intelligence gathering. Her visions of valiantly dealing with Homeland agents while protecting Jack Bauer's back in the field quickly degenerated into dealing with acres of paperwork, hours of mind-numbing computer files and long hours. But slowly, as her experience grew, she began to identify her small but essential role in the bigger picture of United States security, and with that recognition returned the enthusiasm and excitement of having a pivotal role in ensuring that those agencies remained within the laws they had sworn to protect.

Natalie was one of a team of twelve analysts assigned to assess documents being provided by the CIA's Clandestine Service. She cast a quick glance across at her colleagues as she strode through the office. Most were adopting 'The Nod', a semi-affectionate name for the head-down attitude of analysts in the department.

'Morning, Natalie.'

Larry Levinson, a 28-year-old analyst attached to the investigation from Fort Benning, waved at her with a thick wad of computer print-outs in his hand. Thin, diminutive and with big brown eyes, he was the epitome of the high-school chess champion and the butt of continuous bullying from the administration manager, Guy Rikard. Natalie smiled back at him as she weaved her way across the office toward the desk of another colleague.

Ben Consiglio was an analyst one grade below Natalie who had come to the department from the military two years previously after he had been wounded during an intense fire-fight in Cykla, Iraq. The heroic work of surgeons at the Landstuhl Regional Medical Center in Germany had seen the bullet that had shattered Ben's skull removed and his life saved by a titanium plate across his skull. Young, energetic and quietly competent, he got on well with Natalie and they had developed a personable sense of trust. Both had a reputation for getting the job done, and occasionally relied upon each other for assistance handling particularly complex data streams.

Ben looked up as she approached and kicked away from his desk on his roller chair.

'Morning,' he smiled. 'You look like a woman on a mission.'

Frustration was as much a part of being an analyst as any other job, regardless of how interesting the data or essential the work. But Natalie needed somebody else to perform the search she had in mind. Although the keystrokes of every employee within the Capitol could, in theory, be traced, it was almost standard procedure that new recruits would search for their own names within the system just to see if they had ever been watched by a government agency. Few, of course, ever had. But Natalie was indeed on a mission: to achieve higher office, and she wasn't about to let some tech-head identify what they would no doubt class as a frivolous use of resources and hold it against her. She hadn't entered a personal search since her first days in the office.

Natalie had known Joanna Defoe personally, and needed to keep her distance.

'I've got something for you,' she said to Ben as she reached his desk. 'Tedious, boring and most likely non-productive.'

'Another day at the office,' Ben shrugged. 'What is it?'

'Data stream for a name, Joanna Defoe. Can you fit it in for me?'

'For you?' Ben smiled, and scribbled the name on a pad beside his computer terminal. Natalie passed on the date and place of birth, nationality, and blood group.

'What's the purpose?' Ben asked her.

It was a question that would be asked by any analyst worth their role.

'Missing persons,' Natalie replied.

Secrecy was an immense part of security within the Defense Department, naturally enough, but a surprising amount of that security came down to nothing more elaborate than trust. Fact was, many employees of the NRO or the NSA had inadvertently walked out of their shadowy halls carrying extremely sensitive defense files that would be worth millions on the black market to rogue states and foreign dictators. True, some had taken those papers for just that purpose, but the number who did so was minuscule. Despite employing literally tens of thousands of people, the department rarely had to contend with anything other than an equally apologetic administrator who had forgotten to return the offending articles before leaving for home late at night. Such was the pride of thousands of unnamed citizens serving their country.

'Any next of kin?' Ben asked.

'Orphaned,' Natalie replied. 'No dependants or siblings. If we've got anything useful it'll be under her name alone.'

Ben span around in his chair and accessed the department's search engine before tapping in the name.

JOANNA DEFOE

Natalie watched over his shoulder as the search engine began a systematic trawl through the Defense Department's database for any information. Since the contentious debacle of the Patriot Act it had been possible, although not easy, for the US intelligence community to intercept the communications of any single person on earth, including American citizens. Few people realized, for instance, that when they sent an email, that mail did not go direct to the recipient but went first through servers based in the United States, allowing electronic eavesdropping by US intelligence. The idea that the military actually listened to *everything* was a myth, technically. Huge super-computers at the ultra-classified National Security Agency in Maryland ran complex programs that watched for keywords in communications. What keywords were sought depended on what Human Intelligence, referred to as HUMINT, had been gathered by agents on the ground. For all the wizardry available to analysts like Natalie, ultimately the keystone of intelligence gathering still lay largely with the brave but vulnerable spy concealed in a foreign, most likely hostile country.

The search engine finally spat out a single response.

JOANNA DEFOE, b.1978 – Mt. Vernon, Ohio
Missing (presumed deceased)
No Active File.

Ben shrugged and leaned back in his chair. 'The file's been closed.'

A voice called over Natalie's shoulder.

'What you got there?'

Natalie turned and looked straight into the squinting eyes of Guy Rikard. A twenty-year veteran of the department, Rikard had never achieved higher office mainly due to a long history of complaints by female colleagues of physical harassment. Rikard fancied himself as a sort of eighties cop-show rogue whose rough-edged charm and habit of talking over people could let him get away with anything. In reality he was considered by one and all as a feeble-minded chauvinistic jerk, tolerated only because of his near-photographic memory, a valuable asset in the world of intelligence gathering.

'A bad attitude,' Natalie snapped back at him. 'Want some of it?'

Rikard held his hands up, his bald head glistening in the heat from the overhead lights.

'Easy, tiger, just making conversation.' He squinted at the screen. 'Defoe. Why you looking for her again?'

'Again?' Natalie asked, and instantly regretted it. She had, of course, been tempted to search for people during her first days on the job out of nothing more than curiosity and had gone so far as to type their names into the database. The difference was that she had never actually hit the 'Search' button for most – just one. It hadn't crossed her mind at the time that Rikard might have seen what she was doing.

Rikard eased himself closer until she could smell his cheap cologne, and let his gaze drift thoughtfully up to the ceiling.

'Let's see,' he droned nasally. 'Two years ago, not long after you started here, you were searching for that name in the database. It was a Wednesday, and you were wearing a gray two-piece with a white blouse and one of those little gold necklaces that dangle right between your—'

'Get out of my face, Guy,' Natalie rumbled, 'while yours is still intact.'

Rikard smiled, his chubby cheeks glowing red with the effort.

'No need to get all shy on me, honey,' he murmured in delight. 'Not that I would mind you getting on *my* face.'

Natalie jabbed her biro up between Rikard's legs like a spear. Rikard let out a brief high-pitched yelp and wobbled off-balance as she held the point of the pen in place.

'Trust me, Guy, this is as close as you'll ever get.' With her free hand, she tapped Ben's monitor screen. 'What did the search results say when I last did this?'

Rikard's eyes swiveled to look at the screen.

'Search results listed her disappearance from Gaza City a few years back, can't remember the date.'

Natalie jabbed the pen higher. 'Remember harder,' she encouraged.

Rikard gasped and shook his head.

'There wasn't a date, but it did say that she was last seen in a place called Jabaliya, some sort of refugee camp in Gaza.' He sucked in a strained breath. 'Something about militant abductions.'

Natalie held the biro in place for a few more moments as she remembered the details of what she'd seen, and then she dropped the pen. Rikard let out a sigh of relief as he staggered sideways and leaned on her desk for support.

'That's what I thought,' Natalie said, looking at the screen.

'But that extra information has since been removed. Why would somebody do that?'

Rikard shook his head as he regained control of his breathing and discreetly massaged his wounded crotch.

'Don't know,' he wheezed. 'Probably cleaning out old data.'

Natalie shook her head.

'No need, there was hardly anything here anyway, maybe just a few kilobytes of text.'

Rikard stood up slowly as he tried to reassemble his dignity.

'You sure got a quick hand, honey, I like a firm touch.'

'So do I,' she replied, without looking at him, 'which is why you repulse me.'

Rikard's hastily erected smile collapsed as he sneered at her.

'Some people got no sense of humour,' he muttered, and walked away.

Ben Consiglio grinned up at her. 'You sure got a way with folk. He's your boss, remember?'

'He's an ass,' she replied as she stared at the monitor screen for a moment longer. Fact was, Ben now knew that this wasn't the first time that she'd tried to help Ethan in his search for Joanna Defoe. Ben's smile melted into understanding.

'You got a stake in this, Nat?'

She nodded. No sense in messing around now. Besides, she trusted Ben.

'She's my brother's fiancée. I was trying to keep this under the radar.'

'Until that dick showed up,' Ben nodded, jabbing a thumb in Rikard's direction.

She glanced across the office to see Rikard now back at his desk, his pallid cheeks flushed red with embarrassment and impotent fury.

Last she'd heard, Rikard was separated from his wife. No children. The fat idiot had somehow managed to snare himself a spouse and then insulted her by playing out of school, or at least trying to, with a succession of co-workers. Lived alone now and never got invited to after-works drinks. She'd feel sorry for him if he wasn't such a jerk, and not for the first time she wondered why people found it necessary to devote such energy to pissing others off. Despite her anger with her brother for all that he had done, she could only admire him as a man.

She looked back down at Ben.

'Can you do some digging, find out why the file on Joanna was closed or by whom?'

'Sure,' Ben replied. 'What's your brother's name? I'll start there.'

13

IDAHO COUNTY JAIL, GRANGEVILLE

There was only one chief jailer and seven detention officers staffing the jail, which given Idaho's low population density Ethan did not find surprising. Whereas back home in Chicago the jails were a teeming mass of drunks, hobos and gang hoods filled far beyond their design capacity, out here in north-central Idaho there were an average of just eighteen inmates each day passing through the system.

Earl Carpenter took them to an interview room with a one-way mirror, where Ethan and Lopez waited with obligatory Styrofoam cups of coffee until Earl returned with an inmate shackled to his wrist and led him into the next room.

Jesse MacCarthy was a thin, pale-looking kid with messy black hair and eyes sunken beneath the weight of too many sleepless nights. He looked up briefly from behind the veil of hair at the mirror behind which Ethan and Lopez watched and then dropped his gaze away again. Earl directed him to a chair and the kid sank into it without resistance. Earl's voice reached them through a speaker set into the wall.

'You want to talk again about what happened?'

Jesse sat silent and still, his dark eyes staring into nothingness.

'Shock,' Lopez murmured as she watched the kid.

'Traumatic stress,' Ethan confirmed with a nod. 'I saw something similar once, after engagements with the Taliban. Some of the guys had that thousand-yard stare of terror.'

'Jesse,' Earl said to the unresponsive kid. 'I can't help you if you won't speak to me.'

'He's closed up,' Lopez went on. 'He might go into denial if we don't break him.'

Ethan nodded, and grabbed his coffee. 'Let's go.'

They walked out of the observation room, and Ethan knocked on the interview room door before walking in with Lopez.

'Jesse, this is Ethan Warner and Nicola Lopez,' Earl introduced them. 'They're trying to figure out what happened and how to help you.'

Jesse peered up at Ethan but said nothing. Lopez smiled down at him.

'We're not cops,' she said.

'You don't look like cops,' he observed in a voice that might once have been bold but was now scoured of confidence. 'Why would you want to help me?'

'Because you didn't kill your brothers,' Ethan said.

A glimmer of hope appeared in Jesse's eyes.

'They don' believe me,' he said, glancing briefly at the sheriff.

'It's not an easy story to believe, son,' Earl said.

Ethan slid into a seat at the table and looked at Jesse. 'You ever heard of a giant oarfish?' he asked. When Jesse shook his head, Ethan went on. 'It's about sixty feet long and looks like a sea serpent, like one of those things that sailors used to swear attacked ships hundreds of years ago. People didn't believe them, until they caught one. Now there's a skeleton of one hanging in a university in Chicago.'

Lopez sat down next to Ethan and leaned forward on the table. She took Jesse's hand, her rough-edged persona melting as she smiled at the kid.

'We need to know what happened, Jesse, what you saw up in those mountains. Whatever it is, we need to prove it exists before the state of Idaho decides that you're insane and puts you behind bars for the next fifty years.'

Jesse bit his lip, his attention fixed on Lopez's disarming gaze.

'I din' kill my brothers, or that ranger. That . . .' He struggled for words. 'That *thing* got them.'

Ethan watched the kid closely. His hands clenched as he spoke of the animal that had killed his brother. A fingernail paled as it was crushed against the Formica surface of the table.

Ethan could see it wasn't an act, the kid wasn't lying. Most teenagers tended to be full of vigour and arrogance: they didn't cry in front of others. Jesse MacCarthy had not just been frightened beyond belief but had been psychologically transformed from a cocky, fearless youth who had spent an entire childhood out in the woods into a cowering child, afraid of his own shadow.

Lopez squeezed Jesse's hand gently.

'Can you describe it? How did you find it?'

Jesse sucked in a trembling lungful of air.

'Headed east out of Riggins and followed the animal trails into the mountains. We went up that way because the elk move to the valleys in the fall, and most all the hikers stay close to the towns with the tour parties. We figured there was nobody out there to watch us. Cleet, he was the shooter, I was the back-up in case our mark bolted.'

'Season was out though, right?' Ethan said. 'Why not wait?'

Jesse managed a brief, bitter chuckle, staring at the table top as he spoke.

'Cleet hated the tourists. He was like our old man, reckoned that the forests were better without the people in them. Exceptin' himself, of course.'

'We found the ranger's body out by Fox Creek,' Earl Carpenter said. 'Did he follow you all the way?'

Jesse shrugged.

'Guess so. We tracked a big male elk out that way. Cleet wanted to take his shot at dusk, when we could get real close in the half-light and make sure of the kill.' Jesse shivered. 'I guess the creature that killed the ranger was thinking the same thing.'

Lopez's dark eyes narrowed. 'You think that it hunted you on purpose?'

Jesse nodded, his voice haunted as he spoke.

'The ranger collared us before we could take our shot,' he explained. 'He asked us who was with us. When we told him it was just the two of us, he din' believe it and said that somebody was following us. Before we could figure out who the hell it was, we all smelled something.'

Ethan frowned. 'You smelled something?'

'Worst thing ever,' Jesse confirmed. 'Was like a soccer team's used kit rubbed in crap then left in a steam room for a month. I nearly puked, it made my eyes water up, it was so bad. Then . . .' He trailed off. 'Then it broke cover and went for the ranger.'

'Describe it,' Lopez encouraged him. 'As if it was a person.'

Jesse swallowed thickly, his hand gripping Lopez's tightly enough that his knuckles showed white beneath the harsh glare of the lights.

'Big, way bigger than a man or even a bear. Russet-brown fur, and it walked on two legs the whole time except when it charged down the hillside after Cleet. God, it moved so fast, and it screamed.' Jesse stumbled over his words as fear poisoned his veins anew. 'I've never heard a noise like it. It echoed down the valley and was so loud it hurt my ears.'

'This thing was standing when it hit the ranger,' Ethan said. 'Can you tell us how tall it was?'

'Nine feet,' Jesse replied through his repressed sobs as he ran a wiry hand through his thick black hair, 'maybe ten. Fucking hell, man, it was huge, made the ranger look like a little kid. Then it hit him. His head came clean off and went into the creek and I freaked. I just froze and couldn't move. Cleet tried to protect me and fired at it. Hit it straight in the guts with a .308 slug from no more than fifteen yards – might as well have been at point-blank range.' Jesse slowly shook his head. 'If he'd have shot the elk that close it would have been dead before it hit th'ground. Man, it just made the thing madder. It went after him, hurled him into the river and broke his neck.'

Jesse went abruptly silent as he realized perhaps for the first time that his brother was truly dead.

'Then what did it do?' Lopez asked softly.

'Beat 'im up real bad,' Jesse uttered. 'Was shaking him about and breaking all his bones. Didn't care that he was dead already. Then it came at me.'

Ethan leaned forward. 'But you got away.'

Jesse shook his head, but his entire body was shaking just the same as he replied in staccato tones, his words broken by fear.

'No, I ran but it caught me just as easy as if I'd stayed right where I was.' He looked at Ethan in confusion. 'Then it let me go. It had me, was standing right over me. I must've passed out or something, and when I came around it was just walking away like I wasn't worth the bother.'

Ethan leaned back and looked over at Earl Carpenter.

'That sounds like a conscious decision,' he said. 'Not the kind of thing a bear would do.'

'Bear probably wouldn't kill more than once out of rage either,' Earl admitted. 'Sure, they take hikers from time to time and chew on them a bit, but this doesn't sound like a bear attack.'

'It was no bear,' Jesse snapped. 'Cleet was a fine shot, one of the best. If it had been a bear he'd have killed it long before it reached us. All I can think is that he was as scared straight as I was and didn't make a clean shot.'

Ethan glanced across at Earl.

'If there's some dangerous animal out there in the moun-

tains, wouldn't the ranger's office have posted warnings by
now or sent teams out to track this thing down? Technically,
it's a man-eater, right?'

'So are bears,' Earl replied. 'This is big bear country, Mr.
Warner, and those critters don't have much issue with hunting humans, especially unwary tourists who dump trash
around their camp sites. It's virtually a welcome sign for a
hungry bear.'

'They've been known to smash their way into cars,' Lopez
agreed, 'because somebody's left a window open and food on
display inside.'

'No way any ranger's office could track all the bears at
once, much less prevent them from crossing paths with
people in the woods,' Earl said.

Jesse MacCarthy looked at Ethan, his fists clenched and
tears staining his cheeks.

'Like I said, this weren't no bear. It's smarter, bigger and
more dangerous, and it sure don't like people.' Jesse leaned
in toward Lopez. 'Whatever it is, don't be goin' after it. Get
the goddamned marines out there, they might stand a
chance.'

'Would you be willing to lead us out there, Jesse,' Lopez
asked, 'maybe help us track this thing and—'

Jesse recoiled from her, the cuffs on his wrist snapping
taut. 'No way,' he choked, 'no fucking way. I'm not goin' out
there ever again.' He looked up at Earl, panic in his eyes.
'Don't make me.'

Earl unlocked Jesse's cuffs and led him back toward the
holding cells as Ethan and Lopez made their way out to the
station's lobby.

'What do you think?' Lopez asked him as they stepped outside.

The sun was out again, the soaring hills around the Salmon River looking like an idyllic haven for nature lovers, not the shadowy domain of some murderous beast.

'Tough to know. We've still got one missing body, that of Cletus MacCarthy, but from what Jesse just said that could have been smashed to pieces and eaten by now.'

Earl Carpenter stepped out of the station office and joined them, pulling a Lucky from a packet in his shirt pocket and offering one to Ethan and Lopez. They both declined. Earl lit the cigarette and puffed a billowing cloud of blue smoke into the air.

'So, what you want to do now?'

'I want to talk to Jesse's mother,' Ethan said. 'There's got to be something we can follow up on here. Two brothers die on the same night, one out in the woods and one in his own garage. I don't care if there's a monster prowling the hills, it's too much of a coincidence.'

'You think you can connect the two killings?' Earl asked in surprise. 'With what?'

'We'll find out when we get there,' Lopez said.

Her dark eyes brooked no argument, and Earl shrugged as he flicked the butt of his cigarette away into the parking lot and headed toward his truck.

'You suit yourselves,' he said. 'Sally MacCarthy lives up off the main road. I'll drop you there on my way through.'

14

RIGGINS, IDAHO

Ethan stood in front of the lean-to garage and looked up at the heavy crossbeam from which Randy MacCarthy's body had been hanged as Earl Carpenter drove away down the dusty track toward the main road.

Lopez stood next to him and gestured up at the beam.

'One person couldn't sling a dead body over that beam unless they fashioned some kind of rig. If they'd hauled the body up and over, the rope would have scored the beam.'

Ethan nodded.

'We're looking for more than one person but right now the mother's going to be the prime suspect in the eyes of the law.'

'Earl didn't think so,' Lopez pointed out, 'and he knows the family better than us.'

'That's not evidence,' Ethan said, 'it's bias. In the absence of any other known players I can't see where else to take this.'

The voice that came from behind them was quiet.

'I didn't kill my boy.'

Ethan turned to his left, where a frail-looking woman

watched them from behind the porch door, half in shadow as though she was afraid of the light.

Lopez took a pace toward her.

'Mrs. MacCarthy? We're here from the Sheriff's Office on behalf of—'

'I know who you are,' Sally MacCarthy replied as she turned from the door and vanished into the house. 'In a small town, word travels. Won't you come in?'

Ethan followed Lopez into the house and pulled the porch door shut behind him.

Homes always had a feeling to them, that first impression: a mixture of sights, smells and instincts that flood the senses, and in an instant Ethan felt an odd mixture of warmth and tragedy. Pictures of a family across a mantelpiece. The lounge, clean and uncluttered, well looked after. Warm colors on the walls. Soft carpet underfoot. A small, floppy-eared dog napped in a basket beneath a stairway. Sunlight beamed through from the kitchen.

But the faces in the pictures were of Sally MacCarthy's sons and deceased husband. The dog's eyes were open and it was slumped listlessly. The house was silent, perhaps for the first time in decades. Sally moved with weary steps that dragged her feet across the carpet, as though every step was now a labor that she would rather not undertake.

'You from the government?'

Her voice called from the kitchen above the sound of a kettle, her tones a little brighter now. Ethan caught a knowing glance from Lopez. Denial was a difficult emotion that they had both witnessed in the relatives of murder victims and those of tragedy. Sally's movements suggested resignation to the fate that life had dealt her, while her voice was laden with the stubborn defiance of a woman who has suffered and yet refuses to quit.

'Contracted,' Lopez replied as Sally returned from the kitchen with a pot of coffee and three ornate cups. 'We're trying to figure out what happened here.'

Sally set the cups down on a small table and sat down, Ethan and Lopez taking a seat opposite her on the couch.

'So is everybody,' Sally replied, and picked up her cup. 'But they're all one step forward and two steps back. Two of my boys are dead, one's in a cell likely to be charged with their murder and I'm here on my own wonderin' how the hell this could have happened.'

Ethan saw the cup trembling in her hand, beads of coffee spilling from the rim.

'You said that you found Randy in the garage and that he had already passed away,' Ethan said as gently as he could. 'Did you notice anything else out of place?'

Sally looked at him over the rim of her cup.

'I was kinda focused on my boy, mister.'

'We know,' Lopez replied. 'But we believe this may have been a homicide. Forensics haven't turned anything up and there aren't any other leads. We just want to know if something has been missed, anything at all.'

Sally stared into the middle distance for a long beat before speaking.

'I don't know, it was just a—'

'A what?' Lopez pressed. 'Anything could be helpful.'

'It was just a feeling,' Sally replied. 'Right before I found Randy I came through here and it just felt like somebody had been here. I can't explain it, nothing was out of place and yet nothing seemed quite the way I'd left it. I felt sure that somebody had searched our home – that's why I went straight out to the truck. I thought that maybe somebody had stolen the keys.'

'And there was nothing about Randy's behavior that struck you as unusual in the days leading up to now?'

She sighed.

'I've told the sheriff and the rangers everything. Randy was a complicated boy, always into everything. He din' get out much, unlike his brothers. Last time he made wild claims about government agents at work in Riggins he was locked up for forty-eight hours by the sheriff. But mostly he preferred to stay in on his computer.'

'Could we see his room, please?' asked Ethan.

Sally's eyes closed for a moment and then she nodded and stood up. Ethan knew that the chances of her having set foot in that room since Randy had died would be minimal. The door would have been kept closed, everything left as it had been. Perfect for an investigator – perfectly miserable for Sally MacCarthy, the room forever a shrine to her lost son.

Sally led them down a hall to the rear of the home and a series of doors, all shut. Only the last one, to the bathroom, was open.

'That one,' she said, pointing to one of the doors. 'I'll wait for you out here.'

Ethan nodded and took the lead. He opened the door and stepped inside with Lopez behind him.

The room was dark, thin curtains glowing with the sunlight from outside. The room smelled stale, devoid of fresh air. The walls were black, painted roughly by hand with a broad brush that had left visible strokes. Randy had clearly decided to redecorate, the gloomy walls and worn carpet giving the room a neglected air.

'Jeez,' Lopez whispered, 'what does this remind you of?'

The black walls were covered with images of UFOs, sea serpents, posters of movies like *Independence Day* and *Star Trek*. Plastic models of weird alien creatures adorned hastily erected shelves.

'It's Fox Mulder's holiday home,' Ethan replied softly, not wanting Sally MacCarthy to hear him. 'Randy got himself a slice of science-fiction city.'

Lopez moved across the room to the wall opposite the bed, where a computer sat atop a table cluttered with headphones, discarded mugs and potato chip packets. She reached out and turned the machine on, the hard drive whirring into life. Within moments a password request appeared.

Lopez walked to the door and peeked out at Sally.

'Do you know the password to your son's computer, ma'am?'

Sally nodded as a glimmer of a smile touched her lips.

'Randy liked to think that he was very careful covering his tracks, but he always forgot that he was my boy and that I knew him too well. His password was *RandyLucPicard*.'

Lopez smiled. 'A wise choice.'

Ethan tapped the name into the password bar, and the screen changed to an image of Scott Bakula and Jolene Blalock in their full Starfleet regalia. Surrounding the screen's wallpaper were dozens of files and programs.

'This could take a while,' Lopez said as she scanned the files over Ethan's shoulder.

'We're not exactly in any hurry,' Ethan pointed out. Fact was, this was pretty much the end of the road as far as any investigation they could make. The only remaining avenue after Randy MacCarthy was an attempt to locate the remains of Cletus, and Ethan had serious doubts that they would find anything larger than the scattered bones of the unfortunate hunter.

'What's that?'

Lopez pointed at a file folder entitled, 'Research'.

Ethan double-clicked on the folder, and a window opened with dozens of documents all labeled by date and time. The earliest went back at least four years. Ethan scanned the scrupulously named documents, and then glanced around at the room. Under the bed were shoved old clothes and discarded games consoles, while little pieces of junk littered every available surface. Randy had not been an organized sort of person, yet here on his computer was evidence of a long and systematic project of some kind.

Ethan clicked on one of the documents, dated two years previously.

An image flicked up in a new window, a high-resolution shot of a muddy riverbed or creek, and in the center of the shot a huge footprint. A ruler placed alongside the print showed a length of some fifteen inches.

'That's like the cast we saw in Chicago,' Lopez said.

'A little smaller, but otherwise identical,' Ethan agreed.

The possibility that Randy MacCarthy was some kind of fantasist had not escaped Ethan's awareness. The kid had clearly been a nerdy recluse, dreaming of science-fiction worlds while in reality he spent his days in self-imposed incarceration in a darkened room, locked away from the world outside. It would not have taken much for his imagination to overcome his need for reality, and that would naturally have left a need for the impossible to be made possible. Fakery was almost exclusively the reserve of con men and attention seekers, and Randy fit the second category like a glove.

Ethan zoomed in on the image and scanned the very edge of the prints.

'Dermatoglyphs.' Lopez spotted the faint lines in the soft mud. 'Hard to fake.'

'Randy had time on his hands,' Ethan shrugged. 'An attention seeker will go to great lengths to achieve perfection in something like this.'

Ethan began opening more of the files, and each held another image of a huge footprint compressed into soft mud, sand or even gravel. Any of them could have been faked, if not by Randy then by somebody else: maybe even local kids who knew of Randy's obsessions and who silently taunted him from afar with their pranks.

Ethan clicked on another image, this one showing a trail of prints crossing a creek and heading off into deep forests beyond. He was about to close it when his finger froze on the mouse and he stared at the photograph.

Beside him, Lopez peered at the image.

'That one's got scenery in it,' she observed.

The photograph had been taken to show the trail of prints, and in doing so had caught the horizon line and soaring mountains beyond that dominated the sky in a row of jagged peaks. Ethan frowned, and turned to Lopez.

'Where'd you think this was taken?'

The answer came from behind them.

'That's the Pioneer mountain range,' Sally said. 'I'd know that skyline anywhere.'

She walked over to join them, her arms folded protectively around her and her gaze fixed rigidly to the computer monitor's screen, as though she didn't want to look at the rest of the room around her.

'How'd you know?' Lopez asked.

'Cletus loved it down that way,' she replied. 'I recognize that mountain: Pyramid Peak. It's near Fox Creek.'

Fox Creek was where Jesse alleged that he and his brother had been attacked, and Gavin Coltz killed. Ethan scanned the image one last time as a new train of thought formed in his mind.

'Randy was a recluse,' he said, turning to Sally. 'You said he didn't get out much.'

'He wasn't a woodsman like his father and brothers,' Sally replied.

'Then who took this photograph?'

Sally looked at the image for a moment and seemed momentarily surprised.

'I hadn't seen these pictures before on Randy's computer.'

'But you knew his passcode,' Lopez said.

Sally sighed and nodded.

'I worried about Randy, not gettin' out and all. It wasn't healthy, him stayin' in his room all hours of the day and night. I worried about what he might be getting up to, so I . . .'

Sally broke off, and Ethan offered her a reassuring grin.

'Parental concern isn't something to be ashamed of,' he said. 'You were looking out for him is all.'

'I was spyin' on him,' Sally protested, but her regret faded in the wake of a smile that briefly lit her features. 'But I never found anything more incriminating than friends he'd chat to from other countries and science-fiction fans forums that he subscribed to. And those files, his research.'

'You ever ask him why he had these images on his computer?' Lopez asked.

'Couldn't,' Sally confessed. 'I'd have had to tell him I was watchin' on him. I couldn't do that.'

Ethan looked at Lopez.

'Randy didn't take those photographs. His brother Cletus must have shot them while he was out in the forests.'

Lopez raised an eyebrow. 'Really? Maybe Randy went wanderin' now and again.'

'Never,' Sally said. 'He'd have gotten lost before he'd set foot out of Riggins. The Pioneer range is at least twenty miles drive from here, most of it off-road, and Randy didn't get his license yet.' She looked at Ethan. 'You think that they were working on something together?'

'I'm hoping so,' Ethan replied. 'We'll need to download these files so that we have a copy. We might find something else on them that could help us. Is there anybody else we could talk to who might be able to help?'

'You could try Olivia, Cletus's wife.' Sally's face fell again. 'Widow.'

15

CAPITOL HILL, WASHINGTON DC

Nobody knew much about agents working for the Central Intelligence Agency. They thought that they did, their supposed knowledge provided by a wealth of television dramas depicting elaborate underground facilities with satellite links and hotlines to the White House and beyond.

Mr. Wilson knew better.

The nondescript dark-blue Cadillac Catera in which he drove ensured that he drew absolutely no attention to himself whatsoever. The windows were lightly tinted, just enough to shield his face from traffic cameras and casual observers. Virginia plates, a child-seat in the back and a Virginia Cavaliers sticker in the rear window completed the illusion that it was a family car. He pulled into the sidewalk near the corner of 4th and Independence, opposite a Presbyterian church. His close proximity to the building allowed him to exit and be inside in the shortest amount of time. Mr. Wilson liked to observe the world around him without himself being observed. Where possible he traveled at night, a shadow flitting like a dangerous thought from one pool of darkness to the next. Today, however, was a special day.

Mr. Wilson climbed out of the car and strode across to the church. A handful of anonymous pedestrians on the sidewalk parted either side of him like chaffs of wheat gusted by a passing tornado. Whether by instinct or knowledge, people had avoided Mr. Wilson for as long as he could remember, as though somehow they sensed the undiluted violence veiled behind his unassuming exterior.

He reached the church, where on the north side a narrow iron gate led to a concealed path hidden between the church walls and rows of trees and bushes lining the sidewalk. Wilson vaulted lithely over the gate, into the shade of the trees and out of sight from the road.

Wilson walked only a few paces along the path before a man emerged ahead from where he had been leaning unobtrusively behind the church's ornate brickwork. Wilson stood in front of him and, unlike the pedestrians before, he saw no signs of intimidation in the man's eyes as he removed a pair of expensive Ray-Bans.

'You were able to get out without alerting suspicion?' Wilson asked.

'It's not a problem,' came the reply. 'They work flexible hours in there. It's like a holiday.'

Wilson did not smile. The agent before him was extremely capable and used to operating in far harsher and more dangerous climes than the center of the district.

'Our program has been stepped up,' he announced.

'Collateral is no longer an obstacle.' Wilson hesitated, and then added: 'Within reason.'

'None of the staff is a problem,' the agent replied. 'Only one is doing any real digging, Natalie Warner. I'm not sure what she's after but it's beyond her remit.'

'Keep a sharp eye on her,' Wilson ordered him. 'If she becomes an issue, ensure that she is removed from play.'

'Time-scale?'

'The problem at hand will be resolved entirely within twenty-four hours, probably less. All you are required to do is ensure that the GAO does not collate enough evidence to warrant Congressional intervention in CIA programs. If they should do so, then you are to prevent that information from reaching either the committee or the inspector general.'

The man nodded. 'Where will you be?'

'Here in the district. I'll maintain a watch on the key figures personally. If any should show signs of making a case against the agency, then we will make every effort to prevent them from doing so.'

The man raised an eyebrow.

'That might be easy out here on the street, but taking down a Congressional aide in the accountability office is another matter entirely. It will be difficult to maintain cover.'

'Use your imagination,' Wilson replied. 'As soon as our task is complete you will be extracted and placed far from any inconvenient inquiries or investigations.'

'Fine,' the agent replied. 'I'll keep the office covered. If anyone leaves, I'll inform you immediately.'

16

RIGGINS, IDAHO

Olivia MacCarthy was a bulky, businesslike woman with a florid, round face and brown hair that hung in thick tresses across her shoulders. Her dark eyes squinted at Ethan and Lopez as though they had landed outside her creaking homestead from another planet.

'Have the both of you lost your minds?'

Lopez took the photograph that Olivia shoved back in her direction.

'This is where the evidence has led us,' Ethan said. 'Crazy as it sounds, we think that Cletus and his brother Jesse were attacked by something in the woods.'

Olivia's face screwed up on itself.

'I ain't heard such rubbish since years gone by. That boy Randy lived in a world all of his own. You look hard enough you could probably find evidence that Cleet and Jesse were abducted by aliens.'

'That's probably true, ma'am,' Ethan replied, 'but right now your brother-in-law is facing a triple-murder charge on his brothers and a park ranger and we can't ignore that.' Olivia's haughty demeanour faltered slightly and Ethan pressed his advantage. 'It was Jesse who said they were attacked by something, ma'am. We're just trying to find out what.'

Olivia relented, and stepped back as she opened the porch door for them to enter.

It appeared that Olivia and Cletus MacCarthy had lived a Spartan lifestyle. The house was more like a cabin, set amid deep forest near the Salmon River. The smell of wood smoke and dried meat tainted the air, but somehow it seemed cleaner than the clinical whiff of air conditioning.

Coals smoldered in a fireplace in the main room, still hot enough to warm the cabin to a comfortable temperature despite the chill air outside. Ethan realized that there was no mains electricity, just a diesel generator he'd glimpsed outside in the yard.

'You're off the grid?' Lopez asked Olivia, noticing the same thing.

'Don't got no need for the grid,' Olivia replied. 'The land provides most of what we need, if you know where to look.' She smiled faintly. 'Cleet taught me that.'

'How often did Cletus go hunting?' Lopez asked her.

'Quicker to ask when he *wasn't* hunting,' Olivia replied. 'He was either acting as a tour guide in the summer months or hunting for game in the winter. I'd reckon him to be out five or six days a week come rain or shine.'

'Was Randy ever with him?' Ethan asked.

Olivia looked at him as though he'd turned blue.

'That boy didn't know how to get out of bed, let alone go hikin' out into the mountains.'

Lopez opened a slim folder she had brought with her,

containing a series of photographs taken from Randy's computer. She showed them to Olivia.

'These were taken out in the wilderness, but we found them on Randy's computer. We think that Cletus took them for him and passed them along.'

Olivia looked at the images and Ethan saw her eyes flicker with recognition, as though she had seen the pictures before. She balked and turned away from them.

'Kids, most likely, playing pranks in the woods.'

'Did Cletus ever hunt out toward the Pioneer range?' Ethan asked her.

Olivia nodded.

'Sure he did, but I never saw him with pictures like that ... God knows who Randy might have got talkin' to on the Internet, swapping fools' pictures and talking their fantasies out.'

Lopez shook her head.

'These were downloaded from a digital camera direct to Randy's computer, Olivia,' she said gently. 'Had to have been taken by somebody local. Did Cletus take a camera with him on his hunts and tours?'

Olivia's lip quivered, and Ethan realized he was witnessing the collapse of a once robust and content woman. Fat tears welled across her eyelids as she turned abruptly to hide her face from them, her hand flying to her mouth. She did not reply, but nodded instead.

'Can we see it?' Ethan asked as gently as he could. 'It might prove that Cletus took the photographs.'

Olivia pointed one heavy arm at a window shelf nearby. Ethan instantly saw a camouflaged camera case lying open there, the silver camera within clearly visible. He walked over and slipped the camera from the case, turned it on and flipped through the menu's picture history.

Within thirty seconds he found what he was looking for and showed it to Lopez.

'One of the shots from the computer,' she said, seeing the image of a gigantic footprint in soft sand.

Ethan shut the camera down as he looked at Olivia MacCarthy. She stood beside the fireplace, one arm outstretched to balance against the wall as she angrily wiped tears from her face.

'Ma'am, we know that Cletus was working with his brother, searching for what I think is called sasquatch here.'

'I don't want to talk about it,' Olivia muttered.

'Cletus might have been killed by something out in the woods,' Lopez pressed, 'and his brother might go to prison for a crime he did not commit if we can't find evidence to back up his claims. Is that what you want, Olivia? Is that what Cletus would have wanted?'

Olivia stared at her feet for a long moment.

'We need to find him,' Ethan said. 'I think we all need to find Cletus.'

Olivia looked up at him, and for the first time he thought he caught a glimpse of understanding in her eyes. She sniffed mightily, then gestured to the door.

'There's something I need to show you,' she said.

Olivia led them out of the cabin and round the back to the yard. Ethan saw a tidy-looking vegetable garden housed in a chicken-wire mesh wall, a pair of small sheds and two kennels that backed onto the dense forest stretching beyond.

'It happened two or three years back,' she said as they walked. 'Don't never seen anything like it before or since.'

As they walked, two heads appeared from the kennels. Ethan felt his pace falter as two huge Rottweilers loped from within, drool spilling from between thick white fangs. Olivia waved the two dogs over without apparent concern.

'Don't worry, they look like pure evil but they're totally docile, which is the problem.'

'Problem?' Lopez asked as Olivia ruffled the menacing dogs' heads.

Olivia stood up straight and looked into the forest as she spoke.

'Two years ago these dogs were only let loose after dark, because if you'd visited here then they'd have eaten you both alive. They were trained to attack intruders because some of the farms about here had been broken into by thieves and vandals, so we trained 'em that way.'

'What changed?' Ethan asked.

Olivia was still focusing on the forest ahead as she replied.

'We used to get all kinds of animals passing through here,' she said, 'deer and the like, even elk sometimes. The animal trails ran right through here and up into the hills to th'north. I used to watch them from the kitchen window. Then, couple of years ago, they all vanished just as quick as that.'

She clicked her fingers and the sound seemed to echo away into the forest. Ethan realized belatedly that he could hear little birdsong and see nothing moving in the dense woods. Beneath the low, brooding clouds and with the air cold and still, it felt as lifeless as the surface of the moon.

'Anyways, I came out here one night at dusk to feed the

dogs like I always did. Everything was half-light like it is at that time, and about this time of year too. As I was walking out here, I felt something . . . strange. It was the weirdest sensation. You ever have a dream where you see a ghost in the dream, or something impossible happens and it raises your heckles like you've been tapped on the shoulder by Death himself?'

Ethan nodded but did not elaborate. Olivia went on.

'The dogs were both out of their kennels and they was growling out at the woods. I couldn't see much but the dogs started howling like I've never heard 'em do before or since. I don't mind tellin' you that I panicked and set them loose on whatever was agitatin' them.'

Lopez, her own eyes cast out into the lonely woods, spoke softly. 'What happened?'

Olivia gestured to the forest.

'They ran no more'n twenty paces toward the treeline and then both of 'em came up short like they'd hit a brick wall. They came runnin' right back past me, into the house and neither of 'em came back out for more than a month.'

Ethan looked at her. 'You think they saw something?'

Olivia nodded slowly. 'It wasn't just that, it was the smell.'

'The smell?' Lopez echoed.

'Like nothing you've ever smelled before,' Olivia said, her nose crinkling up at the memory of it. 'Imagine fifty people hiking through a rainforest together for six months, not taking a shower or washing their clothes or cleanin' up after themselves, and then being packed into a small room with you for a week.' She shook her head. 'I nearly threw my guts up. We're standing here a hundred yards from the treeline, and whatever it was that smelled so bad was somewhere beyond that and it still nearly made me hurl, y'know what I'm sayin'?'

Ethan scanned the treeline and reassessed the property. Clapperboard walls, single-glazed windows, no land line. Vulnerable and exposed.

'Did you see it?' he asked her finally.

Olivia nodded.

'Only briefly,' she replied, her voice now a whisper. 'I couldn't move, the smell was so bad and the feeling of being watched just had me rooted to the spot. I must have been here for twenty minutes or more, and then it moved just across there in the trees.'

Olivia pointed to a dense clump of pines jutting out toward the homestead, and an animal trail that ran alongside it and into the forest.

'What did it look like?' Lopez asked, unable to contain her curiosity.

Olivia looked like she was going to throw up all over again, her face pale now.

'Big,' she uttered. 'Biggest damned thing I ever saw, and hunched over a bit like a gorilla or something. But it was lookin' at me. Jesus, makes my skin crawl just thinking about it. It must have been watching me for a long time because the rest of the wildlife had taken off a few days before I saw it.'

'Is that when Cletus started taking pictures for Randy?'

Olivia recovered herself, and nodded.

'I told him about it, and he said he'd seen things when

he'd been out and about in the woods but never told me on account of me thinking he'd lost his mind. We neither of us spoke of it to anybody else but Randy.'

Ethan took a breath, and took a chance.

'Did Cletus keep a record of what he and Randy learned about this creature?'

Olivia MacCarthy stared out into the forest for a moment more and then turned to Ethan. She reached up the collar of her shirt and undid two buttons before delving in and retrieving a slim black flash drive that was tied to a thread. She snapped the thread before handing the drive to Ethan.

'Randy used to say that Cleet should save a copy of everythin' they found, because someday people might threaten them. I told them both they were fools to think anything they might find out here would make them that important.'

'And did they?' Lopez asked. 'Find anything important?'

Olivia nodded.

'Whatever's on that drive is what Randy and Cleet were doing, and whatever they found is there. Cleet kept it buried in a plastic box out in the yard, but since what happened ... I've kept it on my person, just in case.'

Ethan looked at the drive in his hand, and glanced at Lopez.

'Didn't Sally MacCarthy say that she was sure her house had been searched by someone, after she found Randy's body?'

Lopez nodded.

'Maybe this is why. Maybe there really is something on that drive that incriminates somebody enough to lead them to kill, and maybe Randy's claims of government agents working out here weren't so wild after all.'

'Whoever they are,' Olivia MacCarthy rumbled, 'find them and make them pay. Don't let my Cletus have had his life ended for nothing.'

17

GOVERNMENT ACCOUNTABILITY OFFICE, WASHINGTON DC

'I've got something.'

Natalie saw Ben hurrying toward her, a sheaf of papers in his hand. Guy Rikard looked up at him and smirked as he passed.

'Is it catching?'

Ben ignored him; he grabbed a chair, hauled it across to Natalie's desk and sat down beside her.

'What is it?' she asked.

She saw Ben's features creased with concern. He was too cool to let Rikard notice it, but now as they huddled at her desk he let some of his tension spill out.

'I did a bit of extra digging on Joanna Defoe, okay? Disappeared Gaza City four years ago.' Ben laid down the papers he held on her desk and spread them out before her. 'I found her in the database right away, no problems. Seems like there was a bit of a diplomatic spat between the administration of the time and the Israeli government, who claimed they had no responsibility for foreign journalists working in Gaza.'

Natalie nodded, recalling all too well those dark days. Ethan should, to all intents and purposes, be something of a non-event in the immense databases of the intelligence community. A former Marine Corps officer, he had served with some distinction in both Iraq and Afghanistan before resigning his commission to pursue a civilian career. Her brother had rarely come home, racing into war zones with the marines and then afterward living and working with Joanna in a succession of volatile countries where violence, abduction and corruption seemed less of a problem and more of a way of life. Columbia, Peru, Gaza, Israel, Somalia and others, each more dangerous and obscure than the last.

Their mother had repeatedly warned Ethan that, sooner or later, his luck would run out.

But it wasn't his luck that had failed him. It was Joanna's.

'Israel kept out of it,' Natalie said. 'Ethan started a campaign to try to force Israel to commit resources to locate her and negotiate her release, but nothing came of it. Joanna was just another journalist who had disappeared and after a brief flurry of media interest she was forgotten.'

'Figures,' Ben said, 'the information on her file stops just a few weeks after her disappearance. But that's what bothered me the most.'

'How come?'

Ben shifted one of the pieces of paper toward her. 'Because not only did the department shut down the file on Joanna, which is odd as she was not yet presumed dead, but they opened an entirely new one.'

Natalie looked down at the sheet of paper and her heart skipped a beat.

ETHAN WARNER
US Marines, 15th Expeditionary (Ret.)
Surveillance active and deployed.

'Ethan,' she whispered.

Ben's voice reached her ears as though from the opposite side of the world.

'Your brother has been under surveillance by at least one intelligence agency ever since he was thrown out of Israel several years ago. Ethan spent a year in Israel trying to find Joanna Defoe and harassing the Knesset to assist him in finding out what happened to her. Israel finally had him expelled from the country when he ran out of cash and threatened legal action against the government.'

Natalie leaned back in her chair and stared out of the office window as she considered the implications of what she had just heard. The intelligence community was keeping at the least a watching brief and quite possibly 24/7 surveillance on Ethan. Such endeavours required a significant amount of manpower, equipment and money. In a day and age when there were so many threats to United States security, to devote time and money to watching a former officer and patriot in such a way was highly unusual. Natalie had no doubt that her brother did not harbour any secret desire to blow up Congress or sink a Navy frigate, and was in fact absolutely certain that he was immensely proud to be an American.

'Maybe it's a result of what happened in Israel,' she said,

looking at the page. 'Maybe he got involved in something sensitive enough for them to want to keep an eye on him?'

'It gets weirder,' Ben said, tapping a finger on another piece of paper. 'Your brother is repatriated to the United States, heads home to Chicago and then promptly goes off the radar for almost three years. Doesn't move much, doesn't do much. No job, no pay checks, no nothing. Looks like he was renting a small apartment on the Lower East Side and paying for it with menial jobs, cash in hand. He didn't even have a bank account.'

'We didn't hear from him the entire time,' Natalie replied. 'I was at college for most of it and would have visited but he refused to reveal his address. He could have been dead for all we knew.'

Ben nodded and slapped down a black-and-white photograph of Ethan stepping out of what looked suspiciously like Cook County Jail, Illinois. His face was bruised as though he'd been in a fight, a cut on his left cheek half-concealed by thick stubble, his clothes tattered and dirty.

'You didn't know where he lived but somebody did. Took this shot of him a couple of years ago: I found it on his file. Up until this time there's not much in the files, just general movements. It seems that the watch got careless, didn't stick close enough to him. Then, Ethan vanishes into thin air.'

Ben slid another piece of paper in front of her and his features became animated.

'The CIA goes ape-shit! I've never seen so much traffic in such a short space of time around a single individual since Osama Bin Laden started getting big ideas back in the 1990s. They put agents all across Illinois trying to track him down.'

'Jesus,' Natalie whispered. 'What the hell's so important about Ethan that they'd commit so much to finding him?'

For intelligence agencies to pursue an interest in an individual and commit funds and resources to doing so would have to be justified to the chain of command, probably to field office level if the Bureau was involved. That would leave a record, a series of authorizations that could be traced back to an agent on the ground. And yet here there was nothing, no leads to follow.

'The orders must have come from the top down,' Natalie realized out loud. 'Christ, this isn't about Ethan, it can't be. He's just not important enough to warrant a surveillance operation this large.'

Ben leaned closer to her, his blue eyes wide.

'It's not Ethan they're interested in,' he said.

'What do you mean?'

Ben didn't take his eyes off of hers, but he slid the final piece of paper across to her. Natalie looked down at it. What she saw there chilled her to the bone.

NATALIE WARNER
Surveillance active and deployed.

Natalie backed away from the page on her desk as though it were a poisonous insect. Her heart fluttered briefly in her chest as her eyes cast further down the page.

HENRY WARNER / KATHERINE WARNER
Surveillance active and deployed.

'That's my entire family,' she uttered, feeling almost sick.

18

'When Ethan disappeared the government placed watch-cells on all of you,' Ben informed her. 'This is high-level covert surveillance, with all that it entails. I've never seen so many resources directed in this way at a single family before. The surveillance itself is not uncommon, but this level and persistence is. I'm guessing it's because they hoped that Ethan would turn up either at home or at your university.'

'But he didn't,' she said, struggling to understand why on earth anybody at the CIA would be keeping her entire family under surveillance. She worked at Congress, for Christ's sake, so wasn't hard to find. Her parents were retired and rarely left Illinois, their mother now too frail for long-distance travel. The level of surveillance simply wasn't justified.

'No,' Ben said, 'he turned up in Israel. That's where everything closes.'

Natalie looked at him. 'Just like that?'

'Totally,' Ben replied, looking up at Guy Rikard's desk to ensure he wasn't listening in. 'It's like suddenly the entire department just shuts down the files as though it had never had the slightest interest in Ethan Warner.'

Natalie frowned. 'But it says the surveillance is currently active?'

'That's what I don't get either,' Ben agreed. 'They're still watching you all, Natalie. Weirder still, whatever Ethan got up to in Israel has been completely rinsed from the system.' He turned to her. 'What happened to him out there?'

Natalie sighed and shook her head.

'Nobody knows and he certainly doesn't talk about it. All I know is that he went out there at short notice then came back a few days later. Suddenly he had an apartment, money and was hooking up with a Latino woman called Nicola. She's some kind of ex-cop or detective out of DC.'

'Ah,' Ben said, shuffling through his handful of printed pages. 'Yeah, here you go. Nicola Lopez, formerly one of DC's finest. She founded Warner & Lopez Inc with Ethan the year before last. Bail bondsmen and investigators. Quite a turnaround for your brother. You think this Nicola had something to do with it?'

'Maybe,' Natalie said absent-mindedly as she thought about her brother. Members of staff walked to and fro between the ranks of desks, and she waited for a pair to pass out of earshot before speaking. 'But he only starts working with her upon returning from Israel. So whatever happened to him probably occurred beforehand.'

Ben cast a glance across the pages. 'Joanna then?'

Natalie nodded, thinking hard about the video footage of Joanna that Ethan had mentioned back in Chicago. Not having seen it herself, she did not feel as though it could be used as evidence to further her cause. Besides, Ethan had said he had seen the footage only recently.

'Maybe he found something else out there in Israel, some new information that gave him hope. Not long after he founded this company with Lopez, he showed up at home and started talking to our pa again. Believe me, *that's* a big deal.'

Ben leaned back in his chair.

'Doesn't explain why the government is still watching Ethan, unless it's not Ethan they're interested in.'

'Joanna,' Natalie agreed. 'There must be something about her that they're keen on. It's maybe why they put us all under surveillance, in case she showed up.'

'Which means they also think that she's alive.'

She forced herself to calm down, taking slow deep breaths and clearing her mind of obstructive thought. *Focus.*

'File gets opened when Joanna disappears,' she murmured to herself, 'gets closed a while afterward, then gets opened again when Ethan heads back to the Middle East for reasons unknown . . .'

Natalie saw in her mind's eye Ethan sitting opposite her in the restaurant. The name popped into her head of its own accord.

'Defense Intelligence Agency,' she said.

'DIA?' Ben echoed. 'What connects them to Ethan?'

'He mentioned them,' she said. 'Ethan told me that he and Lopez do work occasionally for the DIA, something to do with cases that are rejected by other agencies.'

'Cold cases?'

'No,' Natalie said. 'He was kind of cagey about it, wouldn't say what they were about.'

Ben thought for a moment.

'It would explain how Ethan got back into Israel so fast, and also why the CIA were taken out of the loop. The DIA runs its business with a certain amount of autonomy from the other agencies. CIA might have gotten pissed about that and kept Ethan under watch.'

Natalie felt a sense of dread creep across her shoulders. 'They could be watching me right now,' she said. 'They could have bugged my phone, my apartment, anything.'

Ben nodded. 'Especially now you're part of an investigation into the CIA,' he said. 'You can't trust anybody, Natalie. Not right now, anyway.'

They sat in silence for a long moment before a voice cut in between them.

'Does that say what I think it says?'

Natalie turned and saw Guy Rikard's beady little eyes scan the pages spread across her desk. She hastily swept them aside but Guy smiled at her.

'Too late,' he said, and tapped his head with one stubby finger. 'All in here now.'

Ben stood up and confronted Guy. 'How about you take off?'

Natalie stood up and put herself between them. She placed a hand against Ben's chest to hold him back and shot Rikard a dirty look.

'Good advice, don't you think, Guy?' she said.

Rikard's face flushed red but his eyes flickered with panic as he looked at Ben.

'Go ahead,' he uttered. 'You'll be in jail by this afternoon.'

Natalie felt Ben press toward Rikard, but the older man backed away with a sneer and strode off back toward his desk.

Natalie turned away from him and thought for a moment before making a decision. The first thing she needed to do was confirm whether or not she was actually under surveillance, and there was really only one way to do that.

'I'm heading out,' she said, and picked up her bag and keys.

'You want help?' Ben offered.

'I'll be fine,' she replied. 'Try not to kill Guy while I'm gone, okay?'

Rikard saw her leaving and called across to her.

'I can't make lunch today, honey, maybe tomorrow if that's okay?'

Several faces looked up in surprise. Natalie smiled back at Rikard as she swept from the office.

'Sure, Guy, let me know when hell freezes over.'

A flutter of chuckles followed her out of the door.

19

WHITE BIRD, IDAHO

Ethan found the settlement of White Bird just off the US-95, nestled between the highway and soaring hills of sandy rock peppered with hardy cedars clinging to life on their barren slopes.

'You sure we're going to find our man here?' Lopez asked, looking out of the window of their hired Taurus.

'This is where Earl Carpenter told me he lives,' Ethan replied. 'Best tracker in the business, so he said.'

White Bird boasted a population of less than one hundred souls, and most of the homes were single-story clapperboard affairs with neatly kept yards. A colorful swing-sign welcomed visitors to the town, emblazoned with 'Est. 1891'. The Sacred Heart Church was painted a pure white and the town boasted both a post office and a library. They passed a bar called the Silver Dollar, a bunch of well-polished trucks parked outside. The trees around the residential areas gave the little town a splash of greenery that contrasted with the rugged hills looming around it.

Ethan pulled in alongside the address he'd been given

when he'd asked the sheriff for an experienced woodsman to act as a guide. The small, immaculate homestead looked like many of the others in the town except for one small detail. The truck outside was caked with mud and dirt, the mark of a four-by-four used for what it was actually designed for. Off-roading.

Ethan got out and let the Labrador that wandered over lick his hand and snuffle the cuff of his jacket as they walked toward the porch. The door opened before they even got there and a young girl of maybe eighteen or nineteen peeked out at them.

'Can I help you?'

Ethan offered her an easy smile.

'We're looking for Duran Wilkes. We were hoping to hire the best tracker in Idaho.'

The silhouette of a man appeared in the hall behind the girl, who stepped back as the door opened fully and a bearded, wizened face peered suspiciously at them.

'Who sent you?' the old man demanded.

'Sheriff Earl Carpenter,' Lopez replied. 'Said you were the go-to guy for tracking.'

'Did he now?' the old man asked, one hand reaching up to tug at his straggly beard. 'Well, that all depends on what it is you'll be wantin' to track.'

There was a chance that the old guy might have gotten wind of the arrest of Jesse MacCarthy, and maybe even heard of the story that the missing Cletus had been taken by a *monster*. But Ethan doubted it. This man looked like he wasn't in the slightest bit interested in the affairs taking place outside his own picket fence, much less in a town down the road. Ethan took a chance.

'A man,' he replied. 'By the name of Cletus MacCarthy. He disappeared out in the forests of Nez Perce and we were hoping you could help us try to find him.'

The old man chuckled as though relieved.

'A man? That'll be easy. Cretins leave a trail like a herd of bison through a wheat field.'

Duran Wilkes stood back and held the porch door open for Ethan and Lopez to step through. He closed it behind them and followed them into the lounge. Ethan's gaze was drawn immediately to what looked like half of a tree affixed to one wall. It was only when he saw the elk's head in the middle that he realized what it was.

'Jesus,' Lopez said, flashing the old man a bright smile. 'You bring that down with your bare hands back in the day?'

He cackled a laugh as his frosty demeanour melted.

'Just last week, honey.' Duran gestured to the teenage girl who watched them from the kitchen doorway. 'This is Mary, my granddaughter. She travels with me and knows the land just like I do.'

Ethan nodded at Mary, who perched herself unobtrusively on the edge of an armchair. Duran gestured for Ethan and Lopez to sit down and looked at them both for a moment before speaking.

'I like you, both of you,' he said. 'You don't have the air of the city-boy jerk-offs I get coming down here offering a thousand bucks for day trips to shoot shit for the hell of it.'

'For a thousand bucks I'd get some other asshole to shoot for me,' Lopez replied.

Ethan leaned forward as he spoke.

'We need you for a couple of days, is all. We have a good

idea of where Cletus MacCarthy was when he vanished. The plan is to pick up his trail from there and see where it leads us.'

Duran nodded and waved airily as though he'd heard it all before.

'What's the last known location?'

'Fox Creek, Nez Perce Forest.'

Duran Wilkes's features froze in motion for an instant, as though he'd briefly forgotten where he was. He reached for his beard again as he spoke.

'Okay,' he said, his voice softer now. 'What happened out there, anyone know?'

Ethan sensed an obstacle and let Lopez do the talking.

'Cletus and his brother were out poaching elk when they were caught in the act by a park ranger named Gavin Coltz. As he was about to arrest them the ranger was attacked and killed.'

'An accomplice,' Duran said, 'and a violent one. If it's criminals we're tracking my price doubles, you understand?'

Lopez, cornered already, glanced at Ethan before she replied. 'We're not tracking a criminal.'

Duran watched her for a long moment. 'What happened to this Cletus fella?'

'Cletus was also killed by the attacker,' Ethan replied. 'His body is missing. The only survivor was the younger brother, Jesse, who is now under suspicion of homicide.'

'What's his story?' Duran asked.

Ethan again let Lopez lead, hoping it would soften the blow somewhat.

'Jesse swears that his brother and the ranger were attacked and killed by some kind of animal.'

Duran Wilkes's gaze remained fixed on Lopez as he nodded slowly.

'I'm takin' it that he was smart enough to know a bear when he saw one?'

'He knew bears,' Lopez agreed, 'and he was adamant that it wasn't a bear, despite the fact that had he said it was he wouldn't be under so much suspicion.'

Duran Wilkes's head dropped for a moment as he examined his own hands, folded before him as he sat on the couch. He sighed softly before speaking.

'You found the ranger's body at the scene, but not Cletus's?'

'That's what was strange,' Ethan said. 'This animal, whatever it was, killed both of the victims but only took one body with it. More than that, Jesse said that the creature let him go. You ever hear of a bear doing that?'

Duran glanced at his granddaughter, Mary, and Ethan detected a look of apprehension pass between them.

'You know something about this?' Lopez asked them.

Duran Wilkes became even more subdued. It was Mary who spoke, her voice small yet confident, the blood of her hardy frontier-women ancestors still running strong within her.

'My grandmother disappeared near Fox Creek eight summers ago. Grandpa spent the next three seasons looking for her out in the forests, searched everywhere for her and—'

'That's enough, Mary,' Duran interrupted.

'No, it's not,' she insisted. 'She disappeared, and the National Guard went up there, found nothing and claimed a bear must have got her.'

'You don't think it was a bear,' Lopez guessed.

'Harriet, my grandmother,' Mary replied, 'carried a Marlin lever-action with .450 caliber rounds with her whenever she went out into the woods. Never even went to the out-house without it.'

Duran finally spoke.

'We were all out camping near Fox Creek,' he said. 'Harriet went to the river to check on our fishing nets. Couple of minutes later we heard two shots from her carbine. You can tell the noise from a Marlin that big, foot-and-a-half barrels that kick like all hell. Drop a grizzly flat on its back so fast it'd be dead before it hit the ground.'

'What happened?' Lopez asked.

Duran rubbed his forehead with one hand, then ground the points of his fingers into his eyes as he spoke.

'We found the nets and the Marlin, lying on the shoals. There was blood on the stones, real fresh. Of Harriet, we never saw anything again.' Duran looked up at Lopez. 'Whatever it was that took her, she hit it with both barrels at point-blank range and all it did was leak a bit.'

Ethan waited for a moment before speaking.

'We're heading out there,' he said. 'We've got one suspect facing charges for a murder that we feel certain he did not commit, and we've got strong evidence of something stalking the forests out here that attacks and kills humans regularly enough to be a hazard. We need to take this opportunity to stop it and we need your help, Duran. Anything you can tell us, anything that you can do, will help.'

Duran Wilkes sighed heavily and then stood from his couch.

'I'm sorry, but we're done here.'

'You sure that's the right decision?' Lopez asked. 'You might even be able to find out what happened to—'

'We're done here,' Duran interrupted. He gestured to the front porch with one stiff movement of his hand.

Ethan felt his shoulders drop, but he could hardly blame the old man. Lopez stood and joined him as Duran followed them to the front door. She turned to look at the old man before they left.

'Is there anything that you can tell us that might help?' she asked. 'You searched for your wife all that time, maybe you figured something out?'

Duran's rheumy old eyes looked into hers for a long beat before he replied.

'Don't climb above the six-thousand-foot line in the mountains,' he said. 'There's something up there, and I wouldn't wish meeting it face to face upon my worst enemy.'

20

RIGGINS, IDAHO

The guest house that Ethan and Lopez had checked into was not the most luxurious they had even seen, but it was sufficiently well equipped to afford online access in all of the rooms. Ethan had wired their spare laptop up to the Internet using a cable, which was more secure than the wireless system, and now Doug Jarvis stared at him from out of the monitor screen.

'What's the story so far?'

High-level encryption slowed the laptop's processor down, meaning that the conversation lagged slightly.

Ethan held up the flash drive in his hand.

'I'm sending you the contents of this drive right now,' he said. 'The files inside allegedly contain evidence of sasquatch living out here in the mountains. According to the deceased's mother, whatever is on this caused her son to become extremely paranoid and worried, to the extent that he hid this evidence with his brother-in-law in the hope that it would come to light should anything happen to him.'

Jarvis appeared unimpressed.

'Didn't hide it very well then, did he?' he replied. 'And I take it that you're referring to Randy MacCarthy, a renowned local drop-out and social recluse?'

'He was a fantasist and loner,' Lopez cut in from one side, 'but he was harmless and not enough of an outcast to have turned weird on anyone. Plus he found enough stuff that his brother got involved, and everything we have on Cletus says that he was a straight-up guy.'

'No convictions,' Ethan agreed, 'worked hard, married and lived out near the forests. We spoke to his widow. She's the one who gave us this evidence.'

'Have you looked at it yet?' Jarvis asked.

'It's encrypted,' Ethan replied. 'No way we can get into it here so you'll have to get your tech-heads onto it.'

Jarvis nodded.

'There's not much commercially available encryption that our guys can't crack within an hour or two. We should have results back by the end of today. What's your plan from here?'

Ethan leaned back in his chair as he spoke.

'Mostly we're up against dead ends but something's going on all right. This is the last real avenue of investigation that we can follow up in Riggins.'

'What about Jesse MacCarthy?' Jarvis pressed. 'What did he have to say?'

'He was pretty shook up by everything,' Lopez said. 'The kid's not much out of his teens and has just seen both of his brothers turn up dead. Whatever he saw out there in the woods it scared the bejesus out of him and he's sticking to his story. He's telling the truth, Doug.'

Jarvis nodded.

'And it's that truth that's going to see him serving twenty to life if we can't prove that he didn't kill his brothers.'

'No way he's lying,' Ethan said. 'He knows he could go down for this but he's not changing his statement. He'll be psych' evaluated and found fit to stand trial. Prosecution will tear him apart, defense will try for a guilty plea or some other crap, he'll refuse and he'll do time.'

'He doesn't deserve that,' Lopez added. 'He goes down, he won't last a year inside.'

Jarvis nodded.

'Then we'd best get you out into the woods.'

'I was afraid you'd say that,' Lopez uttered. 'You didn't see what was left of Gavin Coltz's head.'

'Only way you can keep working on this now is to find Cletus MacCarthy's remains and hope the coroner can pin the cause of death to the same perpetrator who we think killed Gavin Coltz,' Jarvis explained. 'One anomaly in the cause of Coltz's death isn't enough to convince an attorney of Jesse's innocence, but two will ring enough alarm bells to halt any prosecution pending further investigation.'

Ethan frowned thoughtfully.

'I don't know,' he replied. 'Seems that the law here considers Jesse guilty as hell and isn't doing anything with the evidence already at hand. Sure, Randy's suicide was clearly staged, but Gavin Coltz was killed by something far stronger than a human being. Jesse's just a kid and not a big one at that. He just couldn't have decapitated a man with his bare hands. I know I sure as hell couldn't and I'm twice his size.'

Jarvis understood immediately.

'You won't be going out there alone,' he assured them. 'I'll request an escort to be sent out from Gowen Field. I've already got a couple of mission specialists on stand-by – they'll join you in Riggins. The troops will meet you at a pre-assigned location outside of the town so we don't attract any local media attention.'

'What kind of specialists?' Lopez asked.

'Cryptozoologists,' Jarvis replied. 'They've both spent years studying sasquatch, including time in the field in Oregon and Washington State. They're qualified anthropologists, so they should have experience and knowledge enough to assist you.'

'And the troops?' Ethan asked.

'National Guard,' Jarvis said. 'I'll have to go up top with my cap in my hand to get them deployed.'

'They'll need to be tooled up,' Ethan warned. 'This thing supposedly shrugged off a direct hit from a .308 slug like it was swatting a fly, and we've seen what it can do when it gets hold of people.'

'Fine,' Jarvis agreed. 'Leave it with me.'

'What about Jesse?' Lopez asked. 'As long as he's in that cell in town he's vulnerable to just about anybody who wants a piece of him. Word spreads fast and people can react without thinking.'

'Not much I can do for him,' Jarvis said. 'But there's nothing that the sheriff can do either until a trial date is set. They won't transfer him into a prison population unless formal charges have been made, which I take it hasn't happened yet?'

Ethan shook his head. Despite the sheriff's dismissal of their questions over Jesse's presumed guilt, he had so far made no formal charges.

'Good. Let's get you out there doing what you do best, and in the meantime I'll see what legal stalling I can create to protect Jesse. I should be able to get him a decent lawyer. Right now I've got to go – been summoned by the high and mighty at the NSA.'

Ethan reached over and switched off the laptop before looking at Lopez over his shoulder.

'Fancy a hike?'

Lopez's dark eyes watched his for a moment but they were devoid of humour.

'You got any idea what you're doing?' she asked. 'I'm all for getting Jesse off the hook but this isn't a fool's game, Ethan. If there's something out there, we're headed right into its back yard and all the evidence suggests that really pisses it off.'

Ethan raised an eyebrow.

'You're buying into this monster stuff?'

'You're not?'

'Jesse saw something,' Ethan agreed, 'but a bear might have hit Gavin Coltz hard enough to take his head off. Heat of the moment, being charged by a wild animal having seen it smash your brother to death on rocks? I'm just saying chances are it's a wild animal, although no less dangerous, and that Jesse mistook a bear for something more sinister.'

'A bear that made a conscious decision to overkill his brother, but then let Jesse go?' Lopez challenged. 'Hell, that's one smart bear you got there, skipper. He developed a con-science? Regret?'

Ethan stood up, smiling as he fished his cell out of his jacket pocket.

'I gotta make a call.'

Ethan made his way to the lobby and then outside into the lot. The surrounding mountains were still wreathed in cloud, the horizon between them lit like a sliver of molten metal as the sun sank into oblivion beyond. Ethan checked behind him to ensure that Lopez had not followed, and then hit a quick-dial and waited. The voice answered on the third ring, sounding like it was outside.

'*Ethan?*'

'Hi, Natalie, how's things?'

Her reply made something instinctive inside of him tense up.

'*Interesting.*'

21

NATIONAL SECURITY AGENCY, FORT GEORGE G. MEADE, MARYLAND

The National Security Agency's facility at Fort Meade could possibly be described as the most classified intelligence building in the entire world. A parking lot for 18,000 vehicles gave some sense of scale to the operations conducted by this most clandestine of agencies. A huge oblong building in the center was coated with mirrored black windows that reflected the surrounding Maryland hills and likewise shielded its interior from prying eyes, a Pandora's Box of classified information-gathering so sensitive that it was said that any form of communication, whether verbal or electronic, could be intercepted and eavesdropped by specialists laboring within.

Doug Jarvis strode into a briefing room on the top floor four minutes late for a meeting, the importance of which had been flagged on his internal mail system as 'Stellar' by Director Mitchell. When he got into the room, he realized why.

Before him sat the Joint Chiefs of Staff, the United States military's highest-ranking officers and the men responsible for the overall command of the Army, Navy, Air Force and intelligence community. It wasn't quite like being summoned by the twelve apostles, but it wasn't far off either.

Jarvis hesitated before closing the door behind him.

A single spare chair awaited him, which meant that he was the only department head invited to this spectacular display of rank and medals. It was a wonder that the sheer volume of brass wasn't showing up on the agency's spy satellites. Heading the table was DIA Director Abraham Mitchell, flanked by the Director of the National Security Agency, Morris Tyler, and CIA Director William Steel. The Chiefs of Staff sat alongside each other on each side of the table, and at the far end was the empty chair.

A dense pall of foreboding fell upon Jarvis's shoulders as Abraham Mitchell's voice rumbled like an avalanche of boulders toward him.

'Jarvis, good of you to join us. Please, take a seat.'

Jarvis kept his back straight and his chin held high as he strode with more confidence than he felt and took his place at the end of the table. Mitchell wasted no time in getting down to business.

'Your operation has been flagged by the CIA as having flouted a number of pivotal security protocols, during which civilian contracted workers have been exposed to classified projects and data which, if exposed, could lead to serious repercussions.' Mitchell glared down the table at him. 'Why?'

'In order to protect the same interests you have just described,' Jarvis replied instantly, knowing that to hesitate would seal whatever fate awaited him in this room. The Director was clearly unable to offer Jarvis much room for manoeuvre. 'Without the intelligence provided, the cases upon which we were working could not have been solved as efficiently as they were. It was a necessary step for which I take full responsibility.'

Mitchell's features creased into a tight smile. Although Jarvis knew that his boss harboured no ill feeling toward him, the presence of so much high-level muscle left him in no doubt that Mitchell was under pressure. He decided to fight fire with fire.

'A necessary step,' Mitchell echoed, 'which you had no authority to make.'

'This isn't about authority,' Jarvis snapped, provoking a look of surprise on Mitchell's craggy features. 'This is about getting the job done with the resources we had available at the time. And I cleared every usage of classified projects with the relevant chief of staff.'

William Steel glanced down the table at him.

'Those chiefs of staff are no longer on the service record, Mr. Jarvis,' he said softly but with enough restrained energy to convey force. 'The list of people you can call in favors from is rapidly shrinking.'

'I don't call in favors,' Jarvis growled back. 'I do what is required to protect national security. That is what all of us should be doing, not coming here from the CIA and shoving our little noses into piles of bureaucratic crap in order to get brownie points back at the Pentagon.'

William Steel's eyes flew wide in surprise. Jarvis didn't wait for the director's response.

'Can we stop beating about the bush and get down to the problem here?' Jarvis asked the Joint Chiefs. 'I take it that this is about my department's hiring of Warner & Lopez Inc. to carry out investigations on our behalf?'

'It is,' Morris Tyler acknowledged before any of the chiefs could reply. 'The Department of Defense believes that it is a tactical folly to employ civilians in what should be an internally sourced investigative outfit.'

'Then the department should look more goddamned carefully at its own charter,' Jarvis snapped back. 'All of the intelligence agencies outsource work, even clandestine operations. Every single one of Warner and Lopez's investigations at the DIA was previously rejected or denied resources by other agencies, including the CIA and FBI, before we picked it up at the DIA. We got results precisely because we were willing to look into things when other agencies were not.'

'Which is admirable,' Tyler agreed, 'but which could still have been internally sourced. Why put these things into the hands of civilians at all?'

'Budgets,' Jarvis replied, 'resources, equipment, time. The logistics of life mean that quite often a case will come up that requires intervention immediately. I put in a call to Director Mitchell for men on the ground and I might be waiting hours before a team can even be confirmed, let alone assembled. With Warner and Lopez, they're on the spot on demand, and they're just as reliable as any government agent.' Jarvis shot a look at William Steel. 'Sometimes even more so.'

Admiral John Griffiths, Chief of the Navy, leaned forward on the table.

'We were briefed this morning on the scope of your

operations. I know that everybody in this room is aware of the full details of each of these investigations, so I'll make this simple. Since starting this department of yours, for which I understand you turned down the role of Director-DIA, you've overseen investigations into alien remains found in a seven-thousand-year-old tomb in Israel; into immortalized veterans of the Civil War living in seclusion in New Mexico; and the arrest and death of the philanthropist Joaquin Abell, who had used his fortune to build a device capable of seeing into the future. And you put all of this into the hands of a washed-up former marine and a DC detective turned bounty-hunter?'

Jarvis maintained a stern expression.

'Yes, sir, that's *exactly* what I did. And respectively that washed-up former marine and DC detective saved the life of a prominent senator, prevented a serious biological attack on the United Nations and put an end to a takeover of the democratic process of this nation within those investigations. If it weren't for their efforts, half the population of our planet would have died of a lethal virus by now. What's wrong with you all? Have they not done enough to prove their worth? Shall I call them and demand that they double their efforts because the CIA's little puppy dogs think that they can do better?'

William Steel's tone betrayed no rancour as he replied.

'No, Mr. Jarvis. Only that they can be more closely monitored and their allegiance assured.'

Jarvis's eyes narrowed.

'That's utter crap and every man around this table knows it. What's the CIA's stake here?'

Tyler Morris raised a hand, silencing Steel's response.

'Gentlemen, the fact remains that we have a situation here that is best resolved by ensuring a return to more traditional methods. Outsourcing is all well and good for administration purposes, but for sensitive investigations I propose that we require trained, qualified agents to take over within this department of the DIA.'

Jarvis raised an eyebrow at Tyler.

'The same trained, qualified agents that tossed those same cases aside before we picked them up and solved them?'

'We'll review our analysis procedures,' Tyler Morris rumbled back.

'Sure you will.'

General Hank Butcher, Chief of the Army, shook his head.

'What's your problem with this?' he asked Jarvis. 'Why are you so opposed to military influence in your investigations?'

'Because it's not influence the CIA wants,' Jarvis replied. 'This is about control. They dropped the ball time after time when these investigations came up, passing them off as the stuff of myth and mystery. Now, they see that we're getting results at the DIA and they're throwing a hissy fit because they want to play.'

'That's not the case,' William Steel snapped, finally showing his anger. 'We're interested only in what you haven't done, not what you've achieved.'

'Fine,' Jarvis said. 'I'll send Warner and Lopez down to Quantico for some training and get them badged officially to the agency. Satisfied?'

Steel squirmed. Jarvis could see him grinding his teeth in his jaw.

'No,' he replied. 'This operation is over, period.'

'Is that an order now?' Jarvis mocked. 'I thought that in terms of rank you were the smallest fish in the room.'

Abraham Mitchell intervened, his voice quiet but forceful enough to cut through the tension.

'Doug, for now I think it's best if we draw this operation to a close until something can be worked out.'

Jarvis looked at Mitchell and slowly shook his head.

'Y'know, I had you down as pretty solid, Abe. Didn't realize you'd fold so easily just because the JCs are flashing their pretty medals and ribbons at you.'

'It's practicality, not pressure!' Mitchell growled back. 'Every man at this table is in basic agreement except you. We can put it to a vote if you like, Doug, make it real fair.'

'Fair?' Jarvis uttered. 'Nothing's fair when it comes to inter-agency squabbling. I don't suppose this has gone up as far as the Director of Intelligence, has it?'

'This is a manpower issue,' Steel replied. 'It's not something we need to off-load on him.'

'Perish the thought,' Jarvis said as he looked at the Director of the CIA and got up from his seat. 'He might disagree and wonder whether the CIA has an ulterior motive for shutting us down, and then what would you do?'

'Shut you down anyway,' Steel uttered.

Jarvis shot Mitchell a look of pure contempt. 'Are we done here?'

Mitchell nodded once, curtly. Jarvis turned, and had almost made it to the door when Steel's voice reached him.

'Jarvis. Where are Warner and Lopez right now?'

'Busy,' Jarvis said as he opened the office door.

'Busy *where?*'

Mitchell looked at Jarvis. 'Doug, their whereabouts is not a big deal.'

'Busy in Idaho,' Jarvis replied finally. 'Why?'

'Pull them out, immediately,' Steel snapped.

'They're dark, out of reach,' Jarvis lied. 'I'll pull them out when they make contact, or are we intending to put their lives at risk by going in there and searching for them in plain view of potential enemies of the state?'

Jarvis saw a tremor of unease flicker like a shadow behind the director's eyes.

'What are they doing in Idaho?' Steel demanded.

Jarvis smiled at him, then stepped out of the room and closed the door behind him.

'He's up to something,' General Butcher said. 'Had it written all over his face.'

'He's supposed to be up to things,' Mitchell replied defensively. 'That's what we pay him for.'

Steel leaned on the table.

'It's not his job to risk the exposure of classified projects to—'

'Oh, cut the crap,' Mitchell interrupted him. 'We all know that the CIA just wants to take control of Jarvis's operation and the credit that goes with it. If you had sharpened up in Israel when Warner first appeared on the scene we wouldn't be having this conversation.'

'He's a liability, a wild card,' Steel snapped back. 'He's got his own mission and he'll prioritize that before any concerns for national security. Look what happened in Israel – he damned near caused an international incident because he doesn't know when to stop.'

'By his own mission, I presume you're referring to his fiancée, Joanna Defoe?' Mitchell asked.

'Warner's still hung up on her,' William Steel acknowledged, and then backtracked. 'But she is irrelevant to this. It's his attitude and methods that are our problem.'

'Strange,' Mitchell said, 'that you should know so much about a bail bondsman. If I didn't know better I'd say you've been watching him.'

'Beyond the scope of this discussion,' Steel muttered.

There was silence for a moment before John Griffiths spoke.

'Warner's fitness report from the marines says it all: he'll either do nothing or he'll go at something full-on like a bull at a red flag, regardless of orders. From what we've seen of his history working with the DIA he's illegally crossed international borders, blown up apartment blocks, damned near got a senator killed and is now doing God knows what in Idaho. As for his partner, Lopez, I wouldn't trust her as far as I could throw her.'

'I'm aware of their volatile nature,' Mitchell replied to the Joint Chiefs as one. 'I'm also aware of their extraordinary devotion to their work. They get results where, frankly, other agencies do not.'

'What are they working on in Idaho?' Steel asked. 'Can they be pulled out without Jarvis's help?'

Steel stared expectantly at Mitchell, who decided to give Jarvis the benefit of the doubt once again, just to see the spook's irritation.

'Not if they're dark,' Mitchell said. 'Jarvis requested an armed unit to support them, which I forwarded to the 116th Brigade at Gowen Field. Whatever they're up to, it needs firepower.'

'National Guard units are easily tracked,' Morris Tyler noted. 'Shouldn't be too hard to keep them under surveillance, even in the field.'

General Butcher opened his hands palm up on the table. 'So, what do we do with them?'

Mitchell sighed.

'I'll ensure that when they return from this latest expedition Jarvis retires them from operations and revokes any clearances they might have. Beyond that, there's very little more that I can do.'

'You can surrender all of the paperwork pertaining to their operations to me,' Steel said. 'That way, we can assess what happened and ensure there is no repeat performance when the CIA takes over.'

Every man in the room looked at the CIA director for a long beat before Butcher spoke.

'What's the big deal?' he asked. 'You've already got what you want. Where's the fire?'

Steel hesitated, as though unsure of whether to address the question or not.

'Covert ops,' he replied finally. 'There's a danger that Warner's work in one area might uncover CIA investigations in another. It'll be a lot easier for us all if Warner's out of sight and out of mind.'

Mitchell leaned forward on the table. 'What investigations?' he demanded.

'There are no secrets at this level,' John Griffiths said to Steel, 'unless the CIA are up to something that Congress doesn't know about, which I'm sure they would be most displeased to hear.'

Steel stood from the table and made his way to the door without replying. He opened it just as Abraham Mitchell spoke again.

'Interesting, that you have gone to such great lengths to protect a covert CIA op when you didn't actually know where Ethan Warner and Nicola Lopez were. Or did you?'

Steel made no reply as he closed the door behind him.

22

DIXIE–US FOREST SERVICE AIRPORT, NEZ PERCE NATIONAL FOREST, IDAHO

'Remember the last time we tried to pull a stunt like this? It didn't end so well.'

Lopez's voice crackled into Ethan's antiquated headphones above the clatter of the Cessna's engine as it descended toward what was little more than a dirt-strip buried between soaring mountains deep in the forest. As the aircraft bobbed and weaved on the wind currents and the pilot struggled to keep the wings level, Ethan shrugged.

'We're no good to anybody sitting in a motel in Riggins. This is our only option right now.'

The Cessna thumped down onto the dusty airstrip as the pilot pulled the throttles back to idle. The engine settled down to a soft chugging as he taxied off the strip into a parking area flanked by a scattering of low sheds. What struck Ethan most of all was how completely devoid the area was of evidence of humanity's presence. Just thirty miles east of

Riggins, it may as well have been another planet. There were no roads and no vehicles. Dense forest surrounded the entire strip, with only Forest Service trails disappearing into the trees in various directions. Low clouds obscured a pale flare of light where the sun was struggling to break through.

'Here we go again,' Lopez said as the aircraft's engine spluttered to a stop.

The pilot helped them unpack their gear from the rear of the aircraft then bade them farewell and good hunting. He climbed back aboard and within a couple of minutes the Cessna soared back into the air, giving them a quick wiggle of the wings before turning and departing to the west.

Within sixty seconds it was out of sight and the forest was deathly silent around them.

'Supposed to be very scenic out here,' Ethan said to Lopez as they stood alone beside the airstrip.

'Jeez, forgot my camera,' she uttered in reply. 'What the hell are we doing out here, Ethan? Look at this place. It's bigger than God's garden and we don't have a damned clue where to start looking for Cletus MacCarthy's body. Plus there's nobody here to meet us.'

'Fox Creek,' he replied, unpacking a map from the back of his heavy bergen and unfolding it. 'That was where Jesse said the attack happened. And our scientist friends will be here soon.'

'Yeah,' Lopez agreed, 'and I'm sure our big-footed killer left us a signposted trail to follow. This is the outdoors, Ethan. Horrible creatures live and die here, decompose and then get eaten by other horrible creatures. We'll be lucky to find bones.'

'You don't like the outdoors much, do you?' he smiled as he studied the map.

'Not when it's full of bad-mannered, head-smashing giants, no.'

'Could just be a wounded animal of some kind.'

'Thank God for that. Five hundred pounds of enraged grizzly makes me feel a lot better.'

'It's out that way,' Ethan said, pointing to the northeast, 'about five miles along this trail.'

'What is?' Lopez grumbled as she hauled her bergen onto her back.

'Dixie,' Ethan said. 'The scientists are probably already there, so we'll meet them on the way and then head into the forest to rendezvous with the escort team.'

Lopez made a disapproving sound but said nothing as they set out along the track.

Ethan could see that there were tire marks in the dusty sand of the track. Dixie was a small settlement nestled deep into the hills, mostly farmsteads and smallholdings. It had taken him a moment to find it on the map, so small was it amid the immense wilderness, but the people who lived there needed access to the highway in their trucks. That meant that if the scientists used their no doubt prodigious intellect, they would drive out to meet Ethan and Lopez and save them the trek.

'You ever think about the places that your friend Jarvis keeps sending us?' Lopez asked as they walked, her voice sounding strangely loud in the silence.

Ethan shrugged. 'Not so much. He's our employer, we just do what he asks.'

'I guess,' she replied. 'Just it seems that with time we're getting put up against ever more dangerous odds and in ever more remote locations. It's like he's *trying* to get us killed.'

'You don't trust him.'

'Nope,' she replied without hesitation. 'He's got his own agenda, Ethan, and we're not high up on his list of priorities.'

Ethan stared at his boots as they walked, Natalie's recent revelation ringing in his ears. They, and their family, had been kept under observation by at least one government agency in an operation running for years. The implications were too great for him to even begin considering, the questions far too many. That Doug Jarvis was behind it seemed remote, but then how could he be sure?

'My sister and family have been under surveillance,' he said finally. 'Natalie found out during her work at the Capitol.'

Lopez looked at him as her jaw dropped open. 'When did you find that out?'

'Yesterday,' Ethan admitted.

'And you didn't figure on telling me about it then?'

'I'm telling you about it now.'

'Honored, I'm sure,' Lopez muttered.

'It's not Jarvis doing the surveillance,' Ethan said.

'And you know that how?'

Ethan found himself stumped. Between serving as his lieutenant in the Marine Corps to working for him at the DIA was a six-year gap where they'd had no contact. Who knew what the old man might have gotten involved with during the intervening years?

Then he remembered all that Jarvis had done for him,

what he had now compared to when the old man had first approached him years before when he had been barely scraping through life, living in a battered apartment in downtown Chicago.

'He gave me my life back,' Ethan said finally. 'Doesn't mean much to you, I know, but when we need him to he goes the distance for us. He damned near got himself killed in New York last year trying to help us.'

Lopez said nothing for a while, but Ethan could see that she was mulling it all over, and he could hardly blame her for questioning the risks they were taking. Six months ago they'd almost died 2,000 feet beneath the surface of the Florida Straits. The year before that they'd almost been buried alive in New Mexico, and prior to that Ethan had almost lost his life in Israel. Now, they were strolling out into immense wilderness to search for a wild creature that had already killed at least two people.

Bail jumpers, by comparison, seemed tame foes.

'I just wonder when the money we earn from doing this is outweighed by the likelihood of, y'know, dying,' Lopez said. 'I've got my family to think about.'

'We've been here before,' Ethan said. 'We agreed it was worth it. Besides, it was your idea to work for the DIA.'

'That was then,' Lopez pointed out. 'This is now, a lot further down the line. I thought we'd be apprehending high-profile criminals, not running around in the woods looking for man-eating monsters.'

'We're well paid,' Ethan answered her.

Lopez smiled, her neat white teeth contrasting with her olive-brown skin.

'And you get access to all kinds of technical wizardry so you can keep searching for Joanna,' she said demurely.

Ethan stopped on the trail and looked at her. 'You think that's all this is about?'

'Is it?' Lopez challenged. 'You're a risk-taker, Ethan, just like me. But is what we're doing for the DIA *too* much of a risk? What good are you to Joanna if you get your head ripped off by the homicidal long-lost relative of the gorilla?'

'Finding her means a lot to me,' Ethan replied, and was surprised by how easily it came out. Once upon a time, he would not have found the words.

Lopez sighed and nodded, took a pace closer to him.

'I know it is,' she said. 'And I also know that Doug Jarvis keeps dangling a damned carrot in your face to keep you hoping that you can find her.'

'He doesn't do it like that.'

'No?' Lopez asked. 'Like the fact that he let you see the footage that proves she's still alive, then refuses to let you use the same intelligence information to track her movements?'

'He said that national security would not allow me to—'

'Bullshit!' Lopez almost shouted, loud enough to scare a nearby bird into flight. The flapping wings chased the echo of her voice into the distance. 'He had us inside what was probably the most secret installation in the entire United States' secret arsenal of secret places, lets you have a quick glimpse of her, then suddenly you're not allowed to see any more? Jesus, Ethan, wake up and smell the beans.'

Ethan felt momentarily deflated as he looked into her angry eyes and realized that she was right. He hadn't even noticed, so focused was he on the chance that Joanna might still be found.

'If it's all so bad,' he said finally, 'then why do you stick with me?'

Her eyes flickered and she blinked.

'Because . . . we're partners; that's what we do.'

Lopez had lost her previous partner, a DC homicide detective, years before during an investigation in the city that eventually led her to Ethan. Lucas Tyrell had died a hero, and Ethan knew that Lopez still blamed herself for leaving his side.

Ethan swallowed thickly. Words tumbled out of him as though he were listening to a recording of his own voice.

'I'm not leaving you,' he said. 'If you're done with this, I'll follow you.'

Lopez stared at him and he saw a smile blossom across her features that she tried, and failed miserably, to hide.

'Asshole,' she muttered. 'Got a goddamned answer for everything.'

Her smile was infectious and he found himself grinning back at her. He took a deep breath.

'I mean it,' he said. 'I've got your back, Nicola, whatever happens.'

Lopez stared at him for a moment longer, then took a pace closer.

'Okay,' she said, almost a whisper. 'We got that settled. What happens if you find Joanna?'

'What happens?' Ethan echoed.

'To us?'

Ethan had never really seen Lopez as closely as he was

looking at her now. Her dark eyes were staring up into his as though she had opened a window to her soul.

'I haven't figured that out, yet.'

'You wanna start thinking about it?' she asked.

He was about to reply when a shout hollered across the canyon toward them.

'There you are!'

Ethan turned his head to see a small man in khaki shorts, sneakers and a blue T-shirt emblazoned with a *Superman* logo walking toward them, a map in his hand as he waved. Ethan bit his lip and looked down at Lopez, who was also staring at the newcomer. She shot Ethan a wry glance.

'Saved by Superman, huh?' she murmured.

Ethan grinned, relieved. 'The caped crusader's got my back too, it would seem.'

'Dr. William Proctor,' the man said breathlessly as he hurried up to them, flashing a smile of big white teeth that clashed with a frizzy mass of wiry black hair. 'Great to meet you both, really great.'

Proctor was a carnival of enthusiasm, his eyes ablaze with excitement.

'You're assigned to our expedition?' Lopez asked quizzically as she looked him up and down. 'You know we're going to be out in the forest for several days, right?'

'Oh, don't worry,' Proctor replied with another big smile and a short burst of chortling laughter. 'I once spent three weeks in the Amazon jungle searching for specimens of beetle larvae. I'm used to being outdoors.'

Lopez nodded slowly. 'But you still don't get out enough, right?'

Proctor hesitated, and then honked another laugh and nodded. 'Got it, right, yeah. Good one.'

'Where's your colleague?'

'Back at Dixie,' Proctor said. 'We'll meet up with her and then head out. C'mon, there's a lot we need to talk about. We've already found some interesting tracks.'

23

'How old is it?'

Ethan crouched alongside Dana Ford as she indicated a row of 17-inch-long depressions in loose soil climbing a hillside less than a mile out of Dixie. The trail crossed a canyon wash where runoff from the hills swept down toward a creek a quarter-mile behind them. The long, slender prints were capped with toe marks and what might have been three or four nail-prints where the toes had dug into the soft earth.

'Three days, maybe four,' Dana replied. 'There hasn't been any heavy rain for the last week or so, so the prints have held up. But they're too faint now to cast.'

Lopez and Proctor looked on as Dana traced the outline of the print with the tip of a pen in her right hand. Her long mousy hair was pinned back in a ponytail tucked beneath the hood of her waterproof jacket. Tall and slender, she wore fashionable square-lensed glasses that made her look a bit like Sarah Palin. The big difference was her Ph.D. and the excitement sparkling in her eyes as she pointed with the pen.

'Look at this,' she said in wonderment. 'Seems like a huge human print, right?'

Ethan nodded. Dana smiled at him.

'Well, it isn't,' she explained. 'This was made by a three-hundred-pound bear.'

'How do you know?' Lopez asked, glancing furtively around them at the soaring hills wreathed in thick banks of swirling cloud.

'Because we see this all the time,' Dana replied. 'People take photographs like this and pin them up on Internet sites claiming them to be evidence of bipedal creatures wandering the woods, but it's nothing of the sort.' She gestured to the depressions. 'There's only four toes, for a start, which kind of gives it away. The toe scratches are caused by claws, and the length of the print is caused by the bear's paw sliding backward in the soil as it climbed out of the creek, probably foraging for fish.'

Ethan pictured the scene for a moment and figured it out.

'The creek was flowing at the time, enough that the bear was sliding slightly on the surface soil under the water.'

'Bingo,' Dana grinned. 'Mystery solved.'

Proctor gestured to the hills as they stood up from examining the prints.

'History is full of these kinds of genuine mistaken identities,' he explained. 'You ever see all those photographs taken by climbers in the Himalayan Mountains, with the trails of huge footprints crossing snowy valleys?'

'Sure,' Lopez agreed. 'The climbers always lay their pick-axes alongside the prints for scale.'

'The same,' Proctor confirmed. 'Thing is, those shots are always made at dawn, when the climbers wake up and come outside. It took investigators years to realize that the prints were made by wonderful but normal animals like snow leopards when they had walked past at night. As the sun rises it strikes the tops of the prints in the deep snow, melting the edges and expanding them to gigantic proportions. When somebody tracked the trail into the shadow of another mountain, the prints returned to their normal size, betraying the illusion. Of course, that inconvenient fact never makes it into the reports.'

Ethan hefted his bergen onto his back as they set off again, heading north into the wilderness.

'So you guys are sceptics?' Lopez asked Dana, confused.

'*All* scientists are sceptics,' Dana replied. 'That's our job, to not take things at face value but to test them to ensure that they are real. A lot of people talk about having faith, about believing. Scientists don't want to believe, they want to *know*, so the criteria for evidence that has to be met is much more demanding.'

'You came out here, though,' Ethan pointed out.

A drizzle hung like a fine mist of rain so light that it could not fall, only float on the cold air. It enshrouded the forests as they tracked alongside the edge of an icy stream winding between the soaring hillsides.

'Because being a sceptic doesn't mean you have to be an ass,' Dana replied. 'Wanting to test evidence is one thing. Writing it off before you've even looked at it is another entirely. Most scientists wouldn't dare put their name to a study like this because it would be virtual career suicide. I don't think that's the most productive way to advance human knowledge.'

'Is this an official visit then?' Lopez asked.

'Not exactly,' Proctor admitted. 'We were made to sign non-disclosure agreements.'

Ethan chuckled and shook his head.

'So if you come out here and you find what you were looking for, you can't tell anybody about it.'

'No,' Dana agreed as they hiked up between boulders littering the side of the creek. 'But what we learn here can go into our next study. I figured that if the government wanted advisors out here who had some knowledge of cryptozoology and were insisting that we sign non-disclosure agreements, then there had to be something juicy waiting to be found.'

Lopez nodded as she glanced across at Dana.

'Oh, there's something out here all right.'

Ethan was about to put his foot down as he walked when he heard a faint metallic snicker from within dense trees to his right. He froze with his boot inches from the ground and turned his head fractionally to the right.

The dark maw of the treeline stared back at him, the misty dew-laden air drifting past in silence above the soft gurgling of the creek. Lopez's voice reached him.

'You smell somethin'?'

Ethan squinted into the woods for a moment longer.

'We're being watched,' he replied.

'By what?' Lopez asked.

'By whom, you mean,' Ethan replied, then called out into the woods. 'You guys want to come out or are you just going to sit there watching us all day?'

The voice that replied came from behind them.

'We're here.'

Ethan turned in surprise and saw seven soldiers now

standing in plain view behind them, all wearing full battle-kit and cradling M-16 assault rifles. He turned back to the treeline and saw a single soldier stand up and make his way toward them. *Caught in crossfire*, he realized, an easy and deliberate way to distract the attention of enemy troops to a supposed error while the real danger emerged from behind them.

Ethan turned back to the seven soldiers, one of whom stepped forward. Tall and square-jawed, his face smeared with camouflage paint, he looked every inch the infantryman. There was no rank insignia on his fatigues, but his steady gaze and age marked him out as an officer. He offered Ethan a leather-gloved hand.

'Ethan Warner? Lieutenant Jim Watson, Idaho National Guard,' he introduced himself with a shake of Ethan's hand. 'We're here to baby-sit you on your little camping trip.'

The line was delivered with a genuine smile and Ethan found himself warming to the officer immediately. Watson introduced his men to them as they stepped forward. His sergeant was a man named Kurt Agry, a couple of inches shorter than Ethan and maybe twenty pounds lighter, but he was stout and compact and his features had been hewn into hard lines by the axe of military training. His hair was shaved down to a gray stubble that stained his almost square head. The corporal was a younger guy called Jenkins, tall and rangy.

The rest of the soldiers were amiable but reserved toward their civilian charges. He caught their names; Milner, Simmons, Archer, Klein, Willis. Most wore black basketball-style caps over their heads and generally kept their faces vaguely concealed as though concerned about their identities. Ethan smiled inwardly.

National Guard soldiers were occasionally prone to inflating their appearance to mimic battle-hardened front-line troops. Ethan didn't care much: what mattered to him was that they had firepower, and plenty of it.

'You guys got a game plan here?' Lieutenant Watson asked Ethan. 'Our brief was exactly that: brief.'

'Fox Creek,' Ethan replied, and showed Watson the position on the map. 'This is the closest we have to a location for the disappearance of a man named Cletus MacCarthy. Finding him is the key to proving the innocence of his brother Jesse, who is currently facing trial for his murder.'

The lieutenant frowned at the map. His sergeant, Kurt Agry, shot Ethan a confused look.

'Civil case?' he guessed. 'Why are we down here and involved in it?'

Ethan decided not to beat about the bush.

'Because whatever killed Cletus was strong enough, or mad enough, to decapitate a park ranger with a single blow.'

The soldiers glanced at each other, their interest piqued. Ethan folded the map away as Watson shrugged and smiled.

'Well, no sense in standing here debating. We'd best move out.'

Kurt Agry raised an eyebrow at his lieutenant.

'You got any idea what could do that to a man? There was nothing in the brief about bear-hunting.'

'We're not sure,' Ethan replied. 'The suspicion is that it might have been a sasquatch.'

Watson and Kurt stared at Ethan for a long, silent moment. 'Seriously?' Watson murmured.

'Apparently so,' Lopez replied. 'Hence you guys and the heavy weapons.'

Ethan scanned the soldiers. All carried M-16s, probably service pistols too, but he saw no grenades other than 'flash-bangs', designed to stun and blind unprepared opponents. Each man carried a bergen, filled with equipment and extra ammunition. Two of the troops carried Mossberg 500 pump-action, 12-gauge shotguns.

The sergeant did not look impressed.

'We've been deployed to hunt down a sasquatch?' Kurt Agry asked. 'What's after that, werewolves?'

The soldiers behind him chuckled. The voice that replied didn't.

'That might be safer.'

The group turned as from the forest walked an old man and a young woman. Ethan recognized Duran Wilkes and his granddaughter Mary as they walked toward the group.

'We can track animals,' Kurt Agry murmured to Ethan, suddenly changing his tune. 'There was no need to bring in the rednecks.'

'Local knowledge,' Ethan countered him. 'No amount of training can equal that.'

The old man and his granddaughter stopped in front of the group. The man spoke in a voice imbued with the confidence of a man entirely at home in the wilderness.

'Duran Wilkes,' he announced. 'This is my granddaughter, Mary.'

'Welcome aboard,' Lieutenant Watson said. 'More the merrier, I suppose.'

Kurt Agry thrust himself into the conversation.

'Thanks for coming, but from what Warner here says it's probably best if we take point right now.'

Duran Wilkes raised an eyebrow at the soldier. 'How's that, son?'

'Experience and training,' Kurt replied. 'We're kitted out for this whereas you're not. This is a big group to move through the hills without being detected, and we've already had a chance to get a lay of the land since we arrived so we've got a bit of a head start on you guys.'

Duran Wilkes stared at the soldier for a long moment and then chuckled.

'Sure thing, mister,' he replied. 'You boys go ahead and take the lead.'

Kurt Agry nodded, and with a brief flick of his head gestured to the other soldiers.

'Let's move out!'

Ethan watched as the soldiers fanned out into a loose phalanx and turned north to follow the stream up into the mountains. He turned to Duran.

'Thought you weren't coming out?'

'Change of heart,' Duran said. 'Doesn't mean I like bein' here.'

'You've got local knowledge,' Lieutenant Watson said. 'That counts for a lot. Don't mind my sergeant, he's old school. Personally I'm glad you showed up here today.'

Duran looked up at him and a twinkle of light gleamed in his ancient eyes.

'We didn't get here today, we turned up yesterday evening. Been watching your troops all night.'

Lieutenant Watson grinned beneath his heavy camouflage paint, looking at the old man with new respect.

'I'll be damned,' he replied. 'Sergeant Agry didn't spot either of you.'

Ethan hefted his bergen onto his shoulders and gestured for Duran to lead the way.

'Looks like we'll be following you after all.'

24

GOVERNMENT ACCOUNTABILITY OFFICE, WASHINGTON DC

Natalie Warner pressed the button on her key fob and the lights of her Ford Taurus flashed briefly as she walked toward it. The bright sunshine was warm on her hair as she opened the door and climbed inside.

She pulled out of the lot slowly and eased the car out onto 3rd Street.

Fact was, she had no idea what she was doing. Natalie did not have the first clue about how a surveillance operation was run. It had been an instinctive decision to leave the Capitol and drive out of the district toward Maryland. Her reasoning was simple enough: if she was the subject of a surveillance operation then somebody would be following her.

Natalie felt an almost childlike sense of anticipation as she briefly scanned the handful of cars visible in her rear-view mirror as she cruised west on Madison, the nearby Washington Monument towering into the powder-blue sky. A dark-blue sedan, a silver GMC, two cyclists hugging the sidewalk and a glossy red Pontiac. She remembered watching cop shows shot on these very streets as secret agents sought to foil the impenetrable plans of unspeakably evil organizations bent on world domination.

The excitement waned as she reminded herself that this was the real world and that this surveillance, whatever the reason for it, was also just as real.

She drove up onto the Arlington Memorial Bridge, the Potomac glittering beneath the bright sunshine, and looked again in her mirror. The Pontiac was gone, as were the cyclists, left far behind. The silver GMC was still with her, and the blue sedan, two people inside it.

Interesting, but hardly a cause for concern. There was plenty of traffic flowing from the district across the Potomac. Ahead, the bridge descended down to a circular near the National Cemetery. Two lanes on the right headed north for the Memorial Parkway. The left lane was for traffic heading south on the Parkway or toward Fort Myer. Natalie stayed in the central lane and scanned her mirror.

The GMC loitered about four cars back in her lane. The sedan had taken the Fort Myer lane and was two cars back.

Natalie waited until the last moment, and then just before the lanes split from each other she switched lanes abruptly.

Behind her the GMC swerved to match her, tucking in behind a deli van with bright fruits emblazoned across its side.

Natalie's previous excitement vanished, to be replaced with concern. The GMC was a slightly modified version with flared wheel arches and tinted windows, the kind of thing a college student might possess if he had too much money to blow.

She followed the circular round and headed down the Esplanade. The GMC stayed with her, three cars back. She took the first exit onto the switchback and joined the Jefferson Davis Highway headed south. The sedan had vanished. The GMC stayed with her, now the same distance behind but with only one car separating them until they hit the highway.

Natalie settled down into a steady cruise and watched carefully as the GMC matched her speed in the outside lane. It had closed on her slightly and moved into a position off her right that was hard to monitor without checking over her shoulder.

Paranoia prevented her from looking. If they guessed that she was onto them they might break off. She glanced ahead. Highway One crossed overhead less than a mile away and signs for Washington and Pentagon City showed for the next exit.

Natalie waited until the last possible moment before hitting her turn signal and switching lanes as she took the exit for Washington. Having come from the district, she was now heading straight back there. The chances of the GMC needing to do the same were unlikely in the extreme.

She checked her mirror as she rounded the switchback and joined the US-1 headed straight back toward the Potomac. The GMC didn't show. Natalie joined the flow of traffic and wondered briefly if the whole thing had been just a waste of time and gasoline. By the time she made it back to the district again and got parked she would barely have time to grab something for lunch before she would be due back at her desk.

'Dammit.'

She thumped the wheel and turned on her signal to change lane as she glanced in her mirror.

Her heart skipped a beat.

The dark-blue sedan was two cars back. She blinked, checked again. Same vehicle, same plate. Only the driver was alone now, his passenger gone. Natalie's mind went into overdrive. The sedan had pulled off somewhere between the Esplanade and the switchback south for the Jefferson Davis Highway. It could have been someone dropping a work colleague home, or a friend to the metro, or just a family member who got out for a walk in the sunshine over the bridge. Anything. And now they were headed back to the district.

Natalie saw a truck cruising slowly in the inside lane ahead. On an impulse, she switched lanes and dropped in behind it as she grabbed her cellphone from the inside pocket of her jacket. Driving one-handed, she selected the cell's camera and activated it as the now faster-moving sedan was forced by the flow of traffic to pass her. A Cadillac Catera, Virginia plates, child-seat in back, Virginia Cavaliers patch in the window.

As it cruised by, Natalie looked straight across at the driver.

Male, maybe in his forties. A long and angular face, short gray hair. Looking studiously ahead to avoid looking directly into the camera, the windows of the vehicle tinted enough to obscure detail. Natalie clicked the camera button as the sedan moved past, and then shot another picture of the tailgate. As she lowered the cell she saw the driver glance in his wing mirror as he cruised away in the faster flow.

She wasn't imagining it, she knew. The guy was tailing her. Quite possibly two vehicles watching her, switching places to try and avoid being noticed. A new sense of anxiety swelled within her as she considered this. Two vehicles, multiple individuals, all dedicated to watching the every move of a lowly analyst at the Capitol.

She picked up her cell again and tapped a quick-dial number.

'*Ben Consiglio.*'

'It's Natalie. I'm being followed, Ben.'

There was a long pause.

'*You sure about it, I mean, really sure?*'

He didn't sound convinced. She gripped the cell tighter.

'Dammit, Ben, I've got pictures on my cell, I'm bringing them in.'

'*You took pictures? Jesus Christ, Natalie, you sure that's a good idea?*'

'I just drove across the Potomac and back, came right round the switchback and they followed me the whole way. It's too much of a coincidence, Ben.'

'*Holy crap,*' Ben whispered down the line. '*What do you want me to do?*'

'Keep this to yourself, okay? I don't want anybody to know about this until I've figured out what the hell's going on.'

'*Okay.*'

Natalie racked her brains for a moment, trying to think of a way forward.

'Do you think that there's some way we can figure out who's behind this?'

'*What do you mean?*'

'Y'know, track them down. Run the plates or something?'

'*I don't know. I'm not a cop. I'd have to check if we can even legally do something like that.*'

Natalie focused on the road ahead as she replied.

'I'm pretty damned sure that it's illegal and an invasion of privacy to monitor the movements of any American citizen without some kind of probable cause, regardless of what the Patriot Act says.'

There was a long silence down the line before Ben spoke again.

'*Let me see what I can do. Just get back here right now, okay? And don't do anything else that might let them know you're onto them. Just act normal.*'

Natalie shut the cell off and drove across the Potomac, but instead of heading back to the office she took Ben's advice and drove to her apartment. People didn't just pop out for a drive in Washington's busy traffic, so she pulled into her parking space and got out. A quick trip home to collect something, anything, and she could head back to the Capitol.

She opened her apartment door and hurried inside.

Then she stopped.

It wasn't that she could tell instantly that something was wrong. It was more like a sixth sense, like the sensation of being watched. From where she stood she could see that there was nobody in the apartment with her, but her keen eye picked up on the dislodged rug in the center of the living room; the kitchen door not quite as open as she had left it; the pictures on the mantelpiece above the faux fireplace at slightly off angles.

Somebody had been here while she was at work.

25

DEFENSE INTELLIGENCE AGENCY ANALYSIS CENTER, JOINT BOLLING–ANACOSTIA AIRBASE, WASHINGTON DC

'It's not much to go on.'

Doug Jarvis stood behind Marty Hellerman and looked at his monitor, where a window displayed the apparently empty files contained on the flash drive Ethan had sent from Idaho. Another smaller window displayed the DOS boot screen and a flashing cursor beside an 'ACCESS DENIED' message.

'Do you recognize the encryption?' he asked.

Hellerman stroked his top lip with one finger. Barely out of his teens, he was a graduate of MIT and Jarvis was lucky to have him. Most of the promising information technology big guns were hoovered up through recruitment drives by the National Security Agency. Hellerman shook his head.

'No. We could send it to NSA.'

Jarvis shook his head. His recent meeting had reminded

him that whatever was going on in Idaho had repercussions that affected a great deal more of the American intelligence community than just the DIA. Somebody, somewhere, was hiding something, and while it was easy to assume that the CIA were behind it, it was just possible that they were as much in the dark as anybody. The thought of that sent a tremor of apprehension down his spine. If not the CIA, then who – and why?

'Where the hell does some kid from the backwoods get encryption good enough to stop a professional code-breaker?' Jarvis mused. 'Even for a moment?'

Hellerman waved a hand airily about as he replied.

'You'd be surprised. Sure, we've got top-notch decryption software and access to super-computers, but all of it's for nothing if an entirely new code is generated, something unique. Think about it. All a code or encryption really represents is the means to conceal a message within randomness. As true randomness is very hard to generate in any system, so clues and hints to decoding the encryption can be found.' Hellerman swiveled around in his chair. 'But if somebody encodes their data based on some piece of encryption derived from, say, private events in their personal life, then there's no baseline from which we can begin decryption because we know nothing about their personal lives. There's no pattern to follow, and so the code becomes, in essence, unbreakable.'

Jarvis peered at the monitor.

'So if I created a code based upon the number of times I've been to the dentist, it would be unbreakable?'

'If you broke those visits down into individual times, plus

say the length of the visit and then formulated a way to con-vert that data into strings of characters, then yes, it could be unbreakable,' Hellerman agreed. 'There would probably be a pattern that would emerge somewhere within the data, perhaps because most visits would last roughly the same amount of time or occur at regular intervals, but if you then added another layer of encryption like a simple character cipher even that pattern might cease to exist.'

'The individual who owned this data was a computer geek,' Jarvis said, and saw Hellerman raise an eyebrow. 'No offence. He might have been able to encode stuff but he doesn't have the profile of somebody who would go to quite such lengths to hide this information or even have the knowledge to do so.'

Hellerman smiled up at him.

'And yet he did, so whatever's on here he considered important enough to hide well enough that even we're not getting in here. There must be a key, Doug – something that can get our encryption software started. Once we find it, my guess is that your code will be cracked in seconds. But we can't do that from here. It'll be down to your guys on the ground to figure out what the key is.'

Jarvis searched his memory for the details of the file that had been handed to him by the FBI agents assigned the case. Having written it off as a cut-and-dried multiple homicide, he had made it his business to read the file from front to back before contacting Ethan Warner.

'The geek's name was Randy MacCarthy,' he said to Hellerman. 'This guy was right out there, if you know what I mean. He'd been busted by the local PD a couple of times for possession of cannabis but nothing serious. What made him stand out to local law enforcement was his conviction that there was a sinister government conspiracy at work in his area.'

'Another one?' Hellerman said. 'Let me guess: CIA covert ops? Corrupt FBI agents? Buried alien remains?'

Jarvis decided it best not to mention Ethan Warner's recent investigations in Israel's Negev Desert.

'Randy MacCarthy claimed that he had photographic evidence of government agents at work in and around Riggins, Idaho. Thing is, when he said this the local Sheriff's Department hauled him in and held him at their station for nearly forty-eight hours without charge.'

Hellerman blinked in surprise.

'Maybe an overzealous sheriff?'

'Sheriff's as clean as can be,' Jarvis replied. 'No complaints from people on his watch in the last twenty years.'

Hellerman thought for a moment.

'Outside influence? Maybe this Randy really was onto something and the local sheriff is under some kind of leverage?'

Jarvis inclined his head thoughtfully.

Fact was, when the security and intelligence agencies went to work on or with local law enforcement, they normally got the cooperation they required without complaint or condition, not because of jurisdiction but because the police were happy to have the help. Although inter-departmental rivalry was a real factor, it did not manifest itself in the manner of a TV cop show, with rival department heads or conflicting agents thrashing it out on the street. It was more of a behind-closed-doors kind of deal: withheld information, confiscated data and suchlike. Everybody wanted to catch the bad guys, but nobody wanted somebody else to get there first.

'It's not impossible,' he conceded. 'Problem is, why? Randy would have had to uncover the mother of all national secrets to get himself killed by a military or government agency. I mean, this is Idaho. There's nothing of ours there that would generate any real interest, just a few airbases and training grounds, none of which is hard to find.'

Hellerman thought for a moment.

'Maybe whatever's there isn't on the official list,' he suggested. 'Maybe this guy Randy stumbles upon it, takes a few photographs or whatever, and then hightails it out of there. He hides the evidence but then blabs about it to anybody who will listen to his conspiracy theories.'

Jarvis frowned.

'Randy rarely left the house as far as we can make out,' he said slowly, and then it hit him. 'But his brothers were hunters and woodsmen, *always* out and about. If one of them had seen something or taken photographs . . .'

'Then Randy would have been able to encrypt them, but maybe not been able to keep his mouth shut about what they contained.'

'Because he didn't have direct access to whatever was seen,' Jarvis enthused. 'He wouldn't have feared whatever it was as much as the other witness, the one who took the pictures.'

Hellerman nodded.

'Then all three brothers get taken out, but one survives and his story is too incredible to believe so he gets put inside for it.'

Jarvis let the pieces fall together inside his head. It was a wild story, but if any one piece of evidence stood up then they could pursue it and maybe uncover the key they needed to access Randy MacCarthy's images.

Jarvis gestured to the screen.

'Keep working that through our filters, maybe we'll get lucky.'

As Hellerman got back down to work, Jarvis pulled out his cellphone and dialed a number. He checked his watch: a quarter of five. Ethan and Lopez would probably have met up with the military team that Director Mitchell had assigned to the case, but they still might be within range enough to ...

The line cut dead in Jarvis's ear and he lowered the cellphone.

They were already out in the forests, which would make communication difficult even with the advantage of satellite phones and the escort team's advanced radios. Jarvis decided to change tack and try to figure out what the CIA might have an interest in all the way up in Idaho.

26

NEZ PERCE NATIONAL FOREST, IDAHO

Ethan Warner pushed up with his right leg around the edge of a massive gray boulder that was lodged deep into the hillside, the damp, dark surface sheened with rainwater. The incessant drizzle dripped in a symphony of tiny splashes through the gloomy forest of Ponderosa pines around them as they climbed into the mountains.

To his right, far below, a churning river gouged its silent way through a canyon, much of its course lost beneath wreaths and ribbons of cloud drifting through the cold air.

'Does it ever stop raining here?' Lopez asked, her voice sounding tiny.

Duran Wilkes, his graying features semi-concealed behind the hood of his waterproof jacket, shook his head.

'Not so much at this time of year. You get used to it after a while.'

'That so?' Lopez mumbled, picking her way around a

fallen tree trunk thickly laced with damp creepers and vines. 'Hard to believe.'

The team of soldiers were fanned out in a loose wedge formation ahead of them, the troops apparently oblivious to the cold and the wet as they advanced with their weapons held at port-arms before them, safe but ready. Behind the soldiers labored Dana and Proctor, hindered by their lack of physical fitness but equally driven forward by their enthusiasm. Ethan and Lopez trailed them by a dozen yards, alongside Duran and Mary Wilkes.

'Who called those guys in?' Mary asked, gesturing ahead to the troops.

'They were sent as protection by our boss,' Ethan explained. 'At least two people have died out here at the hands of something extremely strong and aggressive. We didn't want to take any chances and risk lives, ours or yours.'

Duran Wilkes snorted beneath his hood.

'Mighty thoughtful of you, son,' he muttered, 'but I've been walking these hills for the best part of sixty years and whatever's hiding out here, a few pop-guns aren't going to stop it.'

'Bears, you mean?' Lopez asked.

'Black bears,' Duran nodded, 'elk, raccoons, cougars. There's plenty of critters out here that'll attack humans if they feel threatened, but they're fine if they're left alone.' He gestured up ahead to the soldiers. 'Those trigger-happy goons, waving their weapons about, will be the first to get hit if they stumble across a sleeping bear.'

Ethan decided not to say anything. Kurt and his men were from the National Guard, which to some people was held in the same regard as the Boy Scouts. But in reality the guard was highly trained, highly motivated and often manned by former regular soldiers. They were far from amateur.

'They're here to protect us,' Lopez said. 'I don't suppose they'll lead us into danger.'

'They already are,' Duran said.

Ethan looked at the old man. 'What do you mean?'

Duran didn't reply, instead giving a low whistle that sounded like a bird but immediately caught the attention of the soldiers. Lieutenant Watson looked over his shoulder and raised his hand to halt his men as Duran beckoned him back.

'What is it?' Kurt Agry demanded as he joined them alongside Watson.

'Light's getting low,' Duran pointed out. 'We need to find shelter before dark.'

'We've got that covered,' Kurt snapped in reply. 'We know what we're doing.'

'Then you'll know that we're close to the six-thousand-foot line,' Duran said.

Lieutenant Watson looked at the old man. 'So?'

Duran leaned on his cane and gestured around them at the dense forest.

'All of the attacks that have gotten your friends here so excited have occurred above the six-thousand-foot line in these mountains. Nobody has been killed in the lowlands. Whatever it is you people think you're hunting for, this is where it lives.'

The scientists and soldiers had fallen back to listen, and Dana wasted no time.

'Great, we should set up the motion sensors and cameras

around any camp we make, and start working out a watch–rota.'

'We're not camping here,' Kurt said. 'We can make another five hundred feet before dark, enough to get us into some open country.'

Duran Wilkes shook his head.

'You'll lose the cover of the woods from the rain if you do that,' he replied. 'And it's colder out in the open.'

Lieutenant Watson offered Duran a reassuring smile.

'Clear fields of fire are more important to us than staying warm.'

'Fields of fire against what?' Duran asked. 'You haven't been attacked, so why would you need them?'

'We're done here,' Kurt uttered before Watson could reply, and turned to the men. 'Move out! Half an hour more, then we start looking for good ground for our LUP.'

The soldiers responded instantly, melting back into their wedge formation and advancing through the forest.

'What's an LUP?' Mary Wilkes asked as they began following the troops.

'Laying-Up-Point,' Ethan replied. 'A camp, basically.'

'Easier just to say that, isn't it?' she suggested.

They marched for another twenty minutes, climbing ever higher. Ethan could see that as they climbed so the forest began to thin out. The Gospel Hump Wilderness held the highest mountains north of the Salmon River and east of the Bitterroots on the Montana border. The dramatically varying elevations produced different climes depending on altitude, from deep fir, spruce and pine forest in the depths of the creeks and valleys to permafrost on the lonely, high peaks.

There was an altitude, usually referred to as the treeline, above which permafrost, snow and lack of soil prevented trees from growing. Anything above the treeline was essentially a dead zone, used by most animals only to traverse from one hunting or feeding ground to another, or in desperate times to hide or forage.

The last of the feeble light was fading as the soldiers gathered on a narrow strip of clear ground between ranks of spruce that stretched into the night on either side of them. In the distance to his right, Ethan could just about distinguish clouds between the trees where the edge of the hillside fell away toward the valleys below. To his left, the forest was as dense and dark as anything he'd envisioned as a child reading *Grimm's Fairy Tales*.

'We'll set up here,' Lieutenant Watson announced. 'Jenkins, Klein and Simmons, you're on watch for the first stretch, three-point placing from north. Kurt, Milner, on me. The rest of you get some shut-eye before the next watch.'

Three of the soldiers peeled away without a sound and vanished into the blackness of the night as the remaining infantrymen began unpacking equipment from their heavy bergens.

'Looks like we're camping here then,' Ethan said, and dumped his bergen onto the damp, springy moss of the forest floor.

Lopez dropped her own burden miserably down alongside his and scanned the forest around them. The haunting darkness was reflected in her eyes as she looked at Ethan.

'Jesus, this place scares the crap out of me.'

27

Duran and Mary Wilkes wasted no time in gathering fire-wood from the surrounding forest and piling it up in the center of the camp. Ethan noticed Duran building a simple pyramid fire stack, but then laying a lattice of thicker sticks and branches alongside it: the pyramid structure would burn quickly to get the fire going, with the lattice placed into the flames afterward to provide a longer burn.

Nearby, the warm orange glow of chemical camp lights that Dana Ford and Proctor had brought with them began illuminating their tiny patch of land as though they were the last humans alive on earth.

Ethan and Lopez unpacked their tents alongside Duran and Mary Wilkes, joining up with Proctor and Dana's tents to form a large semicircle facing the fire that Duran was now lighting in the center of the camp.

'I'm not happy about having a fire here,' Sergeant Agry muttered as he walked past. 'We'll be visible for miles. You might as well let off fireworks.'

Duran gently nursed a cigarette lighter from his backpack, but did not look up from his work as he replied.

'Didn't realize we was hidin' from anyone.'

'Maybe your big monster,' Kurt shot back, and glanced at Ethan with a sly grin. 'Besides, the woods here are sodden with moisture. It'll take a while to get that fire going properly.'

Duran did not respond, so Kurt moved on by with a pack of motion-sensors tucked under his arm, heading out into the woods to set them up. Duran reached into his pocket and pulled out a dense wad of fibers that Ethan recognized as having been peeled from the bark of a tree. Duran must have pocketed them to help them dry for kindling while they climbed up into the hills.

Duran used a cigarette lighter on the fibers, which caught quickly despite the damp conditions. He gently blew on the kindling until it glowed and flamed in his hands, holding it with all the care one would hold a newborn baby, before he set it down deep inside the dense tower of thin, tall twigs he had constructed.

The flames caught vigorously, and Ethan watched as Duran slowly added the thicker, heavier sticks to the fire until it was crackling and snapping and casting a wide, flick-ering glow out into the forests around them. Finally, Duran set the lattice in place and stood up to look out into the woods as Kurt returned and glanced at the roaring flames.

'You think you'll find your monster by firelight, old man?'

'You don't find sasquatch,' Duran replied. 'It finds you.'

Kurt chuckled as he made his way across the camp. 'Yeah, and he sure as hell won't find it hard now.'

Proctor and Dana, their small tents secured and ready for use, gathered around the old man with anxious, tense expres-sions.

'That's the first time you've used that name,' Dana said. '*Sasquatch*. So you do believe in it then?'

Duran looked at her, his wizened old face creasing in bemusement.

'Believe? Why would I believe in something like that?' He looked down as he emptied a sachet of what looked like beef stew into a tin cooking pan. 'No need to believe in something that's plain to see. You don't believe that the sun will come up tomorrow, do you?'

'No,' Proctor replied, 'because we know that it will.'

Duran inclined his head as he set his pan on top of a steel rack to cook.

'When people talk about faith, what they really mean is: *I don't know*. But they can't admit that to themselves or to others, so they hide behind words like belief and faith.' He looked up at Dana. 'But I know damned well what I've seen with my own eyes.'

Ethan watched Dana lean forward, her gaze fixed upon Duran's face.

'When? Where?'

Duran stirred his stew, Mary placing her own meal alongside her grandfather's on the rack. She answered for him.

'Three years ago, about ten miles east of here out near Bitterroot, close to the border with Montana.'

Proctor almost fell over himself. 'You both saw it?'

'Same time,' Duran confirmed. 'We were making our way down to a creek for water. I suppose it was doing the same.'

Dana shuffled closer to the old man, enthralled.

'Height? Weight? Could you tell the sex? How would you classify it?'

Duran shot her a bemused look.

'We didn't sit down for coffee with it, ma'am.'

'Your best guess is fine,' Dana replied.

Duran stirred his stew and tested it.

'Eight feet, maybe nine feet tall,' he said finally. Dana produced a slim recording device that she held out as Duran spoke. 'Way too large for a bear or any other large animal. I'd guess it was about six hundred pounds. Very muscular. I could see its abdominals even through the thick fur.'

'Did you see its face?' Proctor gasped. 'Did it look human?'

Duran sat back with his bowl in his lap and stared at the fire for a moment.

'Very much so, but at the same time it was different. It had a high crested skull, deep-set eyes and a flat, flared nose, much like a gorilla. But it had more expression than a gorilla, like with a person, when you can see what they're thinking sometimes even when they don't say it.'

'What did it do?' Ethan asked.

Duran shrugged as he shoveled in a mouthful of stew. 'He just sat there and drank water by scooping it out of the creek into his mouth. We were downwind of him, so he didn't realize we were there.'

A voice spoke to them from the edge of the firelight. 'You didn't try to shoot it?'

Kurt Agry stood over them, spooning food out of a silvery ration pack. Duran looked up at him.

'Why would I?' he asked. 'It wasn't causing me no harm.'

'Only because it hadn't seen you,' Kurt pointed out. 'Probably a mangy bear or something.'

'Bears drink straight from the stream,' Dana Ford pointed out. 'They don't scoop water into their mouths. Only primates do that.'

Kurt shrugged and foraged deeper into his ration pack.

'Did you smell it?' Proctor asked. 'We get a lot of reports that these things have an unpleasant odor.'

'Yeah,' Mary nodded, 'we could smell it. It's a wonder the damned thing can creep up on anyone stinking that bad.'

Lopez looked at Proctor. 'Why would anything smell bad like that on purpose? Surely it would make it difficult to hunt. Is it some kind of defense mechanism, like a skunk?'

It was Dana Ford who answered.

'The sasquatch is a primate, so therefore is also an omnivore. But, like most great apes, in a natural environment it's mainly herbivorous so it would have no need to sneak up on prey.'

Kurt Agry scoffed over his ration pack.

'We're carnivores,' he chuckled. 'We've got canines.'

Dana Ford shook her head.

'It's not the kind of teeth we have that define our diet,' she replied. 'It's the shape of our gut. We've evolved to be good at digesting both meat and plants, but we're far better at digesting plant matter. Carnivores have totally different stomachs to ours. Besides, there are plenty of herbivores with canines, they just don't use them any longer for what they originally evolved for. Evolution is always in motion, always a work-in-progress.'

'So this thing stinks,' Ethan conceded her point. 'Why?'

'It may not be a facet that evolved for a particular reason,' Proctor replied. 'If we assume that the sasquatch is indeed a primate, which all of the evidence suggests that it is, then it must have come here from elsewhere, as all bipedal primates evolved in Africa and spread from there over millions of years. So for instance at some point one of our ancestral species crosses from Asia into North America, perhaps across the Bering land bridge during an Ice Age, and settles here in America's northwestern territories.'

Dana nodded as she continued.

'The process thereafter is straightforward. Even if the progenitor species of what we're calling sasquatch did not possess excessive body fur, it would soon become an evolutionary advantage because those that possessed the genes for extra fur to combat the cold winters here would begin to dominate. Over time, you would have a series of evolutionary responses occurring that predominate survival in cold climates: greater physical size, thicker fur, flared nostrils and suchlike. The Neanderthals evolved much in this way to deal with severe cold in Europe during the last Ice Age.'

Duran Wilkes, silent now for some time, looked up at Dana.

'You think that what I saw was a man?' he asked.

Dana inclined her head.

'Perhaps not a man, but much closer to a man than we might think. You see, we sweat from our skin to keep cool, an evolutionary trait stretching back to our earliest ancestors in Africa. There's no reason to suppose that the ancient cousins of sasquatch would have been any different. But now it's been living in a frozen environment for tens of thousands of years. It evolves the heavy fur and facial features to endure severe cold, just in time for the Ice Age to come to an end.

Suddenly, it's sweating to keep a five-hundred-pound-plus body cool beneath a thick fur coat. Imagine having thick hair all over your body and not taking a shower for ten years. You'd stink real bad too.'

Ethan nodded in the firelight.

'Doesn't explain the aggression we've heard about recently,' he said. 'Whatever these things are, they may have been taking people for decades and we never knew a thing about it.'

'Cannibalism is a survival strategy,' Proctor said. 'When times are hard many primate species resort to killing their own species, even members of their own families in order to survive. Sasquatch may be a long-lost cousin of ours but it's unlikely they'd see a human as anything more than prey.'

'Then why let a human victim go?' Lopez challenged. 'Why kill two men with unbelievable savagery, then let the last one go?'

'Efficiency,' Dana Ford replied. 'You've gotten one meal, the second one shoots you so you kill him in self-defense. The last meal runs away but is no threat and you can only carry so much meat anyway. You let him go.'

Ethan smiled ruefully in the dark.

'That would work, except that the creature took one of the bodies, left another there for us to find, and let the third victim go. Three different targets, three differing responses. You know what that says to me? That whatever this thing is, it *thinks*.'

Kurt Agry's voice called across the camp to them from where the soldiers were sitting.

'Only thing it's going to be thinking about is the end of its goddamned life, as seen down the barrel of my M-16!'

Two of the soldiers laughed and clashed palms. Agry grinned as he slowly polished the barrel of his rifle.

Dana Ford watched the soldiers for a long moment and then shook her head.

'Even if we do find one there'll be nothing left of it by the time those assholes have finished blowing it to hell.'

Duran Wilkes's voice replied to her from out of the darkness.

'I wouldn't be too sure of that, ma'am.'

Ethan was about to speak when he heard the hoot of a bird calling out in the forest. He had barely turned his head when he realized that it was not a bird, but something much further away.

'You hear that?' Lopez asked.

Ethan was about to answer when a low, alien cry swept across the camp from somewhere deep in the forest.

The laughter of the soldiers died away as across the valley the cry became a keening, strained howl that soared up into the night sky. The sound seemed to shudder through Ethan's body and creep beneath his skin.

The mournful howl died away softly to be replaced by the crackling of the flames.

Ethan glanced across at Duran Wilkes, but the old man simply sat and sipped his coffee as though nothing had happened.

28

GOVERNMENT ACCOUNTABILITY OFFICE, WASHINGTON DC

'You're absolutely sure?'

Ben looked at the images on Natalie's cellphone of the blue sedan.

'No question about it,' Natalie replied. 'Look, I even got a close-up of the guy driving the sedan. It's not a perfect shot but it might be enough to identify him. And that's not all. Somebody broke into my apartment.'

'Are you sure?' Ben asked, stunned.

'Definitely,' Natalie insisted. 'They barely left a trace but I could tell that things had been altered, moved.'

Ben looked at the photograph, thinking hard.

'Without hard evidence the break-in, if one happened, means nothing. This photograph is probably enough to identify the agent in question, if he is an agent, but this isn't enough for you to take it to the House Intelligence Committee. Even if they did turn out to be CIA, they could just say that the agent was out for a drive or something. Christ, all of the major agencies have field offices in the district.'

Natalie's shoulders sagged as she realized that Ben was right. Her suspicions about her apartment could be dismissed as paranoia and the photographs couldn't be used as evidence of a conspiracy. Even when combined with the evidence that she was under surveillance, it wasn't enough to place Natalie as a witness to misappropriation of resources by any agency. It might even raise questions about her own loyalty and patriotism, something that Guy Rikard would no doubt exploit.

'So we're back to square one,' she said finally. 'And we need to stay quiet about what we've discovered here, so it can't be part of the committee's evidence. Not yet, anyway.'

'Pretty much,' Ben agreed. 'Keep the images, they may come in handy later, but right now all we've got is the search for Joanna Defoe and the fact that your brother showed up as a result of it.'

Natalie rolled it around in her head as though she were chasing food around a plate with a fork.

'Ethan's been working with the DIA, that much we know,' she said.

'Which means it's unlikely that they're the ones doing the surveillance,' Ben said. 'They already know where Ethan's going to be when he's working for them, so there wouldn't be much point. We could possibly take this to them and see what happens?'

'No,' Natalie replied. 'They may be a government agency but we don't really know anything about them and I'm not sure I want to go cap in hand to a bunch of strangers asking about surveillance operations on my brother.'

'You need to get to the bottom of this, Nat,' Ben tried again. 'Whoever is behind this could be doing it for their own ends and not for national security.'

'Ethan just got back on his feet after what happened in Israel,' Natalie insisted. 'I'm not going to wreck that. I don't like that he's working for the DIA but as long as he's got something to focus on I'm not willing to risk derailing his life. Plus, he's got that partner of his, Nicola Lopez. She seems to keep him on the straight and narrow.'

Ben glanced at the paperwork strewn across his desk.

'What about her?' he wondered out loud. 'You ever meet her?'

Natalie shook her head.

'She's never been with Ethan on the rare occasions when he's come home,' she admitted, 'but I can tell by the way he talks about her that they're close.'

Larry Levinson's voice infiltrated their conversation. 'Why not run a search for her too?'

Natalie glanced at the diminutive man in surprise, and he blushed. 'Sorry, Natalie, but you guys have been working on this all day. Sooner or later Rikard's going to corner you about it, so why not check out this Lopez, and see if she ties in with it all? If she does, you might be able to take the search out of the office and get away from Rikard.'

Ben shrugged, turned to his monitor and tapped Lopez's name into the search engine.

'Let's see if she shows up,' he said, sitting back and waiting for the engine to complete its search.

'Why would she be on there?' Natalie asked. 'Surely she's got nothing to do with our family.'

'Maybe not,' Ben said, 'but like you said, what if this isn't about your family?'

Ben gestured to the monitor screen as it flashed up the results of the search.

NICOLA LOPEZ
b. 1981, Guanajuato, Mexico.
Surveillance active and deployed.

'I'll be damned,' she whispered.

'Holy crap,' Larry whispered. 'Is this for real?'

Ben nodded as he prodded his chin with the tip of his pen and looked up at Natalie.

'You, your brother, your brother's work partner and your folks are all being watched simultaneously, presumably by the same agency. Lopez is the odd one out here as she is not family and yet is connected to you via Ethan, so best guess would be that this operation isn't about direct family at all. Lopez is being watched simply because your brother's always with her. This is about somebody who connects you all.'

'Joanna Defoe,' Natalie said softly.

'Who, according to our database here, is not under any kind of surveillance whatsoever,' Ben said. 'Which kind of makes sense, seeing as she disappeared years ago.'

Natalie frowned in confusion.

'Then why the surveillance on us?'

Ben tossed his pen down on his desk as he replied.

'It's a fair bet that nobody actually knows where Joanna Defoe is or even if she's still alive for sure, so this surveillance operation is a kind of sleeper-cell gig. The agency in question has exhausted all leads and has set this up as a last resort in the hopes of catching her if she hightails it home to Ethan in Chicago.'

Natalie ran one hand through the thick tresses of hair hanging down across her shoulders.

'That's a long shot, especially seeing as she disappeared so long ago and in Gaza City of all places. The likelihood of her waltzing straight back into Illinois is just about zero.'

'Like I said,' Ben replied, 'a last-resort action. There's nothing else that they can do but sit tight and hope that Fate throws them a lead.'

Larry Levinson spoke softly beside Natalie. 'You know what would bother me the most about all this, if it were me?'

'What?' Natalie asked.

'Why?' Larry replied. 'What could be so important about a journalist that a government agency would spend so much time and effort on even the smallest possibility that she might turn up alive?'

Natalie stared at the monitor screen and wondered for the first time whether she actually knew Joanna Defoe at all.

They had first met when Ethan had brought her round one Sunday to meet the family. The pair had already been dating a while but Ethan had always been naturally cautious when it came to relationships. Joanna was one of just a handful of girls he had brought home. Natalie had taken to her instantly, which wasn't hard to do. Joanna had one of those smiles that was infectious and bright, a genuine enthusiasm for other people's lives and a willingness not to speak but to listen. Natalie had, in retrospect, embarrassed herself by confiding to

Joanna her entire past semester at college, including several fumbling encounters with a fellow student.

But Joanna had listened without complaining, all the while fielding questions from Natalie's parents and also carefully observing the growing animosity between Ethan and their father over his resignation from the Marine Corps. Joanna had effortlessly mediated, endearing herself to their parents as a result, and had proven herself the perfect catch for her troubled but decent brother.

Natalie had not been surprised at how hard Ethan had taken her disappearance years later in the dark and dangerous alleys of Gaza. For such a personality to simply vanish from the face of the earth must have been like witnessing the sun blinking out and plunging a warm summer's day into a frozen darkness.

'We could try some of the other databases,' Ben suggested, 'see if she turns up there.'

Natalie blinked herself awake from her reverie and forced herself to think. Fact was, nobody was looking for Joanna because she had disappeared too long ago for there to be any real hope of picking up any trail she might have left behind.

The answer popped into Natalie's head almost immediately and she kicked herself for not thinking of it earlier.

'The agency responsible for this must *know* that she is alive, somehow. That's the reason they're willing to commit to surveillance operations. The odds must not be so long after all.'

'But I thought you said that Ethan told you he was starting the search for Joanna again?' Ben said. 'Did he find evidence of some kind that confirmed she was alive?'

'Yes,' Natalie replied. 'He had proof of life, video footage.'

Beside them, Larry frowned uncertainly.

'Proof of life usually concerns abduction victims,' he said, 'and is used in order to provide leverage for ransom negotiations or whatever the kidnappers want. If they've got proof of life of Joanna but are watching your family then surely she must have escaped from somewhere.'

Natalie nodded, a sudden urgency to her thinking.

'It makes sense,' she said. 'Ethan told me that he wanted closure on all of this, that he just wanted to know what happened to her so that he could finally shut the door on all that happened to him. He'd been shown footage of her alive in Gaza, and said the reel was a year old. So if she's still alive . . .'

'He'll go after her,' Ben finished her sentence for her. 'If he's as tenacious as I've heard, he won't let it go.'

Natalie clenched her fist and thumped the desk.

'The DIA must know what happened to her,' she said. 'They're the ones employing Ethan and Nicola, they're the ones who showed Ethan that reel and they're the ones who sent Ethan to Israel.'

'Where he had his mysterious experience and came out a changed man,' Ben agreed. 'But there's no way we're going to get near any documentation of what might have happened out there.'

Natalie shook her head.

'Maybe, maybe not,' she said, and looked at her watch. The sun was just descending toward the horizon outside the office windows.

'What are you thinking?' Ben asked.

'This surveillance and all that it entails,' Natalie replied. 'What if Joanna knows something of immense importance, or perhaps has evidence of some kind? She was abducted by militants in Gaza, and then apparently escaped. So why didn't she run to the cops or to Israel? Why disappear? Only reason I can think of is that she wasn't abducted by militants but by somebody else, and then escaped with evidence of her abductors. If it was a government agency, that would be reason enough to hunt her down before she could blow the whistle.'

'Extreme rendition,' Ben conceded, 'civilians apprehended and taken to foreign countries outside of the Geneva Convention for interrogation as enemy combatants. But how can we figure out if it's true and why? We don't know any more than whoever's searching for her does.'

'It depends on whether Ethan still works for the same guy he served with in the corps,' she replied. 'Can you find out if a Douglas Jarvis still works at the DIA? Maybe I'll pay them a visit after all.'

29

NEZ PERCE NATIONAL
FOREST, IDAHO

'You want to tell me what the hell that was?' Lopez asked.

Ethan sat down alongside her in front of the fire, the haunting howl that had echoed through the forests bothering him far more than he dared admit.

'Coyote or something,' he said.

It sounded lame and he knew it.

'Coyote,' Lopez repeated. 'Well, that sounded like the biggest, meanest and most unfriendly coyote I've ever goddamned heard.' She glanced across at Dana Ford. 'You ever heard anything like that before?'

Proctor and Dana sat side by side as Dana replied.

'We've been sent a thousand recordings that sound just like that,' she said. 'Sometimes the howls are long, low and mournful like that one was. Other times, they're high-pitched and warbling. The worst ones aren't the howls at all though.'

'No?' Lopez murmured. 'You figure that, how?'

It was Proctor who replied, awkwardly playing with his mug as he spoke.

'It's the ones that sound like dialect,' he said. 'It's horrible to listen to, the strangest combination of growls, whoops and gabbling you've ever heard. It sets the hairs of your neck on end because it's something so familiar and yet so odd.'

Proctor seemed to shiver where he sat and clasped the warmth of his mug with both hands.

'How many of these things have you gone after?' Ethan asked them.

'We've uncovered evidence for bipedal apes in almost every state but how many of the encounters are genuine we just don't know, and we have to do it in our own time and pay for it out of our own pockets because we'd never get grants for this type of work,' said Dana.

'Yeah,' Proctor snapped. 'You even utter the word crypto-zoology in the halls of residence and you're out on your ass by the end of the week. Nobody wants to fund research into sea monsters or North American bipedal apes, but if you find anything suddenly everybody says they suspected it was there.'

'People have found monsters?' Lopez asked, prodding the fire with a stick.

'Sure they have,' Dana replied. 'It happens surprisingly often, believe it or not. Scientists working in remote areas on unrelated projects hear about local legends of creatures out in the wild, so in their spare time they go wandering about looking for them.'

'Such as?' Ethan challenged.

'Well,' Proctor said, 'there are two main types: living fossils, animals believed to have been extinct that are later found:

and then there are species believed to be the product of myth that then turn out to be either real or based on real observations of undiscovered species.'

'Probably the most famous living fossil in history is the coelacanth,' Dana Ford explained. 'It's a large fish, fossils of which had been found fairly regularly dating back some three hundred and sixty million years. Other, more recent fossils revealed later species some eighty million years old. But nothing had been found dating after the extinction of the dinosaurs during the Cretaceous-Tertiary extinction event, so quite understandably science believed the species to have died out.'

'Until 1938,' Proctor said, 'when one was found swimming happily along off the coast of South Africa. It wasn't until 1998 that a live specimen was actually caught, off Indonesia. Point is, these things are quite large and have been present off the East African coast for the past sixty-five million years, yet we've only just caught a live specimen. Think what else could be out there. Seventy-five per cent of our planet is ocean, and the same percentage of that ocean is utterly unknown to us. We have absolutely no idea what's down there.'

Ethan shrugged.

'Finding a fish isn't exactly going to rock the world, Proctor,' he said.

Dana Ford smiled faintly and set her mug down at her feet as she wrapped her arms around her knees and leaned forward, her face flickering in the snapping light of the fire.

'There is a place, out in the Pacific Ocean, west of the southern tip of South America, where in the sixties the

United States Navy laid an array of hydrophones to monitor the passing of Soviet submarines. The network was called SOSUS, an acronym for Sound Surveillance System. The phones lie far below the ocean surface in what's known as the "deep sound channel", where temperature and pressure allow sound waves to keep traveling and not become scattered.' Dana leaned forward even further, her eyes fixed on Ethan's. 'In 1997 the sensors detected a sound that freaked out just about everybody who ever heard it. The varying frequency of the call bore the hallmark of a marine animal and was confirmed as a biological species by marine biologists who examined the recording. The call rose rapidly in frequency over a period of one minute and was of sufficient amplitude to be detected on multiple sensors.'

Lopez raised an eyebrow. 'So?'

'The sensors were more than five thousand kilometres apart,' Dana replied. 'The frequency of the sound means that the living creature that made the call would possess a mass five times greater than that of the blue whale.'

A silence descended around the camp as everybody pictured in their mind's eye a creature that would dwarf even the largest of the dinosaurs.

'It's not the only time it's happened,' Proctor confirmed. 'The US National Oceanic and Atmospheric Administration have even given names to the occasional but disturbing sounds they have detected, calling them things like Train, Whistle, Upsweep and Slow Down. Upsweep turned out to be an undersea volcano. But the 1997 sound was confirmed as biological, and they named it the Bloop. Likewise, Slow Down was recorded in the same area as the Bloop, lasted for seven minutes and was powerful enough to be detected on sensors two thousand kilometres apart.'

'Every other possible cause of the noises has been eliminated,' Dana continued. 'Ice floes calving in Antarctica, submarine earthquakes, volcanoes and man-made events. Whatever made those noises is alive and five times larger than a blue whale, and it's living in the deep ocean right now.'

Proctor stared into the flames as he spoke.

'Sailors from around the world have reported tales of huge monsters of the deep for thousands of years. For the most part it was always dismissed as the effects of embellishment and alcohol, but those same sailors would also speak of rogue waves a hundred feet high that would rear up and swallow vessels whole. Science dismissed those tales too, until an orbiting satellite detected rogue waves all across the world's oceans and large vessels started filming their encounters with them.'

Ethan, mesmerised by the tales, looked at Dana.

'So you're saying that the Kraken might actually exist?'

'No,' Dana smiled. 'We're saying that sailors' tales of a gigantic sea creature able to take down large vessels were born of encounters with something very real. Dead giant squid have been washed ashore that were sixty feet long, but there is no theoretical limit to the maximum size for a cephalopod.'

Kurt Agry snorted as he leaned back against his bergen and swilled a mouthful of coffee around his mouth.

'Big fish in the vastness of the ocean is a bit different to a ten-foot-tall ape in the mountains of Idaho,' he said. 'People have been looking for sasquatch for decades, yet nobody has

ever found a single bone, let alone solid evidence of its existence.'

Dana Ford rocked her head from side to side as the soldier
spoke and then casually wafted his comments aside with a
swipe from one hand.

'Same old story,' she said. 'No evidence, so therefore it can't
be true. But have you ever thought about it for a moment,
about what people are trying to find out here? For a start, it's
likely that we're looking at a fairly small population living in
the largest wilderness anywhere on earth.'

'The USA?' Lopez asked in surprise. 'I thought the largest
wilderness would be Africa or something.'

'So do most people,' Proctor said, 'but in fact in this country we have the greatest proportion of land classed as
wilderness in the world, with most of it entirely unoccupied.
And where we're sitting, the Gospel Hump Wilderness, is
the largest continuous tract of forest in all of North America.
That's more than enough room for a population to live virtually unobserved for millennia.'

'A small population would not have enough genetic diversity to survive,' Lopez pointed out as she warmed her hands
near the fire. 'I've read about it. Without enough variability,
breeding becomes impossible and the species goes extinct.'

'Absolutely true,' Dana replied. 'And how many do you
need to maintain a healthy population?'

Lopez blinked. 'I don't know. A few hundred?'

'Thirty or so,' Proctor replied with a smile that was surprisingly bright in the firelight, 'provided those thirty
individuals come from a varied enough pool themselves.
There are probably thirty to forty Amur leopards living out

in the snowfields of Siberia. They rarely meet, and breed even less, but they're considered surprisingly genetically healthy. Large numbers are not required, just the genetic diversity itself.'

'No bones or remains have been found,' Ethan challenged. 'Odd, if this species of animal has been living here for tens of thousands of years.'

'How often do people find bear remains?' Dana replied. 'Not that often, given the large numbers of bears living out here. In the wild a large carcass can be completely consumed within five to seven days, even less in warm weather. Carnivorous scavengers break up the larger bones and chunks of flesh, birds and small mammals strip the smaller remains and bacterial action breaks down the rest. That's without the tendency of many species to find a hiding place in which to curl up and die, if the moment of their passing is not due to an accident or predation. They literally find somewhere they won't be disturbed and die there completely concealed.'

Proctor shrugged in agreement, but gestured to the fire.

'See this fire,' he said, the flames glinting off his mug. 'It was the ability to make and control fire that set us apart from all other species, maybe as long as four million years ago. The scorch marks of human fires hundreds of thousands of years old can be found all across Africa and Europe, the scars of our ancestors' struggle for survival in a wilderness where almost every other creature was a beast, something that could kill you. But in 2003 researchers working in the deep jungles of Indonesia came across probably the closest thing we'll ever see to a real *Lost World*.'

Lopez chuckled.

'You mean they found Doug McClure and some cavemen being chased by giant lizards?'

Dana grinned and raised an eyebrow.

'Almost. A species known as the Komodo dragon lives there, a two-metre-long lizard with a lethally poisonous bite, that will happily hunt humans and eat them. But that was not what fascinated them the most.'

'In a cave,' Proctor picked up the tale, 'deep in what has been described as some of the toughest and most remote jungle terrain the team had ever encountered, they found the remains of a fire that was started by humans a thousand times. Littering the floor of the cave were the bones of creatures consumed thousands of years ago, but there was something special about them and the humans that consumed their prey: all of them were dwarf species, the humans barely a metre tall when fully grown.'

Kurt Agry burst out laughing. 'Jesus Christ, was Aragon there too?'

'*Homo floresiensis*,' Ethan said, and was rewarded with looks of surprise from the gathered team.

'Another species of man,' Lopez added, clearly not wanting to miss out. 'That was definitely alive just twelve thousand years ago and may survive to the present day in the deep jungles of Indonesia.'

Dana Ford nodded and smiled at her.

'It's good to know that we're not the only ones who are taking this all seriously, because *Homo floresiensis* wasn't all they found out there. Just to the north, and across China, India and Vietnam, they found a species of ape that was the opposite of *floresiensis*: a giant.'

'A giant?' Ethan echoed.

'Gigantopithecus,' Proctor said, 'an extinct genus of ape that existed until around one hundred thousand years ago, a species that ancient humans would have encountered. The fossil record suggests that they were the largest apes that ever lived, standing up to ten feet tall and weighing over a thousand pounds, three times heavier than a gorilla. Big males may have had an arm span of over twelve feet.'

Lopez stared at Proctor for a moment. 'Meat-eater?' she asked cautiously.

'The species probably inhabited bamboo forests, since its fossils are often found alongside extinct ancestors of the panda,' Dana replied. 'It would appear that Gigantopithecus was mostly a plant-eater, but there's nothing to suggest it wouldn't have been omnivorous and capable of consuming meat.'

'You think that's what attacked Cletus McCarthy and Gavin Coltz?' Lopez asked.

'It's one of the possible explanations for the suspected existence of sasquatch,' Proctor explained. 'The Bering Strait was a land bridge throughout the Ice Ages, which means that members of the species could easily have crossed into North America. As it was so huge, Gigantopithecus probably had few enemies when fully grown and could have survived the cold conditions in North America at the time.' Proctor looked into the flames of the fire. 'People expect sasquatch to be some kind of human, but a far more logical explanation is a primate species more closely related to the apes: Gigantopithecus is most closely related to modern orang-utans and closely fits the description of Bigfoot in its appearance and habitat.'

Lieutenant Watson chuckled as he squatted down nearby alongside the fire.

'Don't get too comfortable, doc, you're still outnumbered here. I don't know what's swimming about in the ocean or walking about in the mountains, but Kurt's right – I doubt there'll be any weird and wonderful monsters stalking us out here.'

Ethan was about to respond when from somewhere in the inky blackness surrounding the camp a deep, sharp crunch shattered the silence. Then he heard a low, rattling growl so deep it sounded as though it were underwater. Ethan felt the hairs on the back of his neck prickle up as the soldiers leapt to their feet, their rifles in their hands.

30

'Cover all points!'

Lieutenant Watson's command snapped out harsh in the night as he and his men rushed outward from the fire in different directions, scattering to the impenetrable blackness at the edge of the treeline. Their M–16s glinted wickedly in the darkness as they hurried past.

Kurt Agry keyed his microphone and called urgently down it.

'Klein, Jenkins, radio check and status.'

The radio clicked once, but nothing verbal came back in response. Kurt cursed and ran low and fast out of the camp toward the perimeter.

'What was that?' Lopez asked, shooting a nervous glance at Ethan.

'Probably a bear,' Lieutenant Watson replied. 'Nothing to get too excited about, but stay close to the fire.'

Dana and Proctor were on their feet, their features taut with a volatile fusion of excitement and fear. Ethan glanced at Duran Wilkes and saw that he had not moved and still sat with his mug in his hands, looking into the fire. Mary was curled up beneath a blanket alongside him.

'That sounded too damned big for a bear,' Dana Ford uttered, searching the darkness uselessly with her eyes.

Ethan moved to the edge of the firelight and squatted, deliberately looking into the deepest, darkest bit of forest that he could find in an effort to let his eyes adjust to the night. He had some sympathy with Kurt Agry's desire to not have a camp fire – the bright light and heat destroyed the human eye's ability to see in the dark.

He heard Kurt's anxious voice float to him from the blackness.

'You see anything?'

Ethan started to distinguish the soldiers as they fanned out toward the perimeter of the camp, their M-16s aimed in front of them as they edged toward the treeline. Somewhere out there were the two sentries, concealed in the undergrowth.

'No, sir,' came a series of hushed calls.

'Hold the line,' Kurt Agry whispered back, and then Ethan heard him try the two sentries again on the radio. Again, Ethan heard a faint click in response and then silence. He guessed that one man was responding by keying his microphone only, and that meant that, for whatever reason, he could not speak.

Lopez crouched down alongside him.

'What's going on out there?' she asked.

Ethan shook his head, not sure what to make of it. They had all heard something, but there was no point in them chasing every noise in the woods. The wilderness was filled with animals following trails.

The soldiers held their positions, all of them down on one knee with their weapons trained on the forest. Ethan was about to move forward when a hand pressed down on his shoulder. He turned and saw Duran Wilkes squat silently down alongside him. In his hand he held a rifle's sniper-scope, and he could see a faint glow coming from the optics. It was an infra-red device, designed to detect heat signatures against the cold backdrop of the damp woods.

Duran leaned down close to Ethan's ear and spoke so softly that he could barely hear him.

'Hundred yards,' he said, and pointed out into utter black-ness to Ethan's right.

Ethan pivoted on his heel and lifted the scope to his right eye.

A thick wall of trees loomed into his vision, dark blue against the deeper black of the forest beyond. The perspec-tive shifted slightly as he moved, but he could see nothing but the empty forest.

'Be patient,' Duran said as though reading Ethan's mind. 'Just watch.'

Ethan calmed his breathing like he used to do before taking a shot when he was with the marines. The image steadied. For several long seconds he saw nothing. Then, quite suddenly, from between two large and distant trees a tall, bright sliver of heat appeared, as though something had peeked out. The object remained stationary for several sec-onds before vanishing once again into cover.

Ethan dropped the scope from his eye and looked at Duran. 'A hundred yards?'

Duran nodded and then gestured to the soldiers nearby.

'Like I said, you don't find a sasquatch,' he repeated. 'It finds you.'

'Is it out there?' Lopez asked.

'Something sure is,' Ethan replied, and handed her the scope. He turned to Duran as Lopez began scanning the woods with the IR scope.

'How did you know it would be there?' he asked the old man.

Duran stroked his beard as he replied.

'I've been out in these hills for most of my life,' he said. 'Time to time you see one of these things walking about. Most all the time they mind their own business, but I've learned that they're like us in one real important way: they're curious. They're interested in what we're doing and they'll come have a look-see if they get the chance.'

Ethan surveyed the immense forest around them.

'That was a pretty fast catch,' he said admiringly. 'It could have been hiding behind any tree in the woods within a hundred yards.'

Duran nodded.

'Yup, but they'll always track in from downwind so they don't drop their scent. Then what they do is approach from a direction that allows them an easy and quick escape, while also providing a lot of cover for their approach. They watch from behind and between trees, and must have pretty decent eyesight because I've never seen one come as close as this. Most times they're a couple of hundred yards away.'

'I can see it,' Lopez murmured. 'Sneaky little bastard, isn't he?'

Ethan smiled wryly.

'He's not little,' he pointed out. 'If he's a hundred yards out he must be over eight feet tall.'

'Nine,' Mary Wilkes corrected him as she joined them, a scope to her own eye. 'A big one even by their standards, and very close to the camp.'

Lopez looked at the old man.

'You're not going to tell Lieutenant Watson where it is?'

Duran scowled in the darkness and shook his head.

'Why, so his sergeant can take a pot-shot at it and carry home a trophy? Like hell. It hasn't done anything to us.'

Ethan frowned uncertainly.

'Then what the hell was that noise, and the growl?' Ethan asked. 'And if it can watch us from a hundred yards out, what was it doing right beside the camp?'

Ethan did not hear Duran's reply. From the forest nearby a shout of alarm was followed by Kurt Agry's voice bellowing in the darkness.

'Man down! Light 'em up!'

In an instant the soldiers turned on the Maglites on their weapons, the bright white flashlight beams cutting like lasers into the forest. Banks of mist glowed like ethereal clouds and tree trunks gleaming with moisture as they swept the woods with the beams.

Ethan jogged with Lopez to a dense clump of foliage where Lieutenant Watson was kneeling, his rifle slung over his shoulder. As he reached the officer's side Ethan saw the prostrate form of Simmons slumped on his back on the ground, thick blood snaking across his face from a deep wound in his head.

'What happened?' Lopez stared down at the fallen soldier in disbelief. 'He didn't make a sound.'

Kurt Agry was unpacking a reel of medical dressing as he replied.

'I don't know, but we need to get him into the camp right now.'

The soldiers were pulling back toward them, circling protectively around their fallen comrade, when the remaining point-man suddenly appeared from the forest and ran toward them with his breath condensing in billowing clouds in the flashlight beams that whipped around to aim at him.

'Where the hell have you been?!' Kurt Agry snarled at him.

Corporal Jenkins looked down at his fallen colleague, his face stricken.

'It came right past me,' he said. 'I couldn't move or speak.'

'Who moved past you, Jenkins?' Lieutenant Watson asked as he stood up.

The soldier rubbed his face.

'I couldn't see it that well,' he admitted, 'but I could hear it breathing. Sounded big, heavy, but it moved in total silence.'

Ethan looked at Duran, who was standing with Mary nearby.

'We saw one of them,' Ethan said.

'You saw them?' Kurt Agry snapped as he rounded on Ethan. 'And you didn't say anything?'

'It was a hundred yards out,' Ethan shot back. 'It wasn't a threat.'

Jenkins stared at Ethan in disbelief. 'But I was only fifty yards away. What could move that fast in total darkness?'

In a split second, Ethan came to the conclusion that the deep crunch they had heard had in fact been caused by something hitting the fallen soldier on the head and crippling him. An image of the distant, watching figure in the woods snapped into his attention.

Ethan turned toward the camp nearby.

'It's a distraction,' he uttered.

On the cold night air a stale odor drifted to stain Ethan's nose. The smell intensified until he felt his throat contract and his eyes stream. He turned away and gagged instinctively from the smell as he heard Lopez cough beside him.

Behind his disgust he heard Lieutenant Watson shout out a command.

'Protect the camp!'

The soldiers had barely started to move when a heavy rock slammed down into the center of their group with a heavy thud that stripped a chunk of bark from a nearby tree. Another smashed into the foliage at their feet as a third hit Kurt Agry square in the back. He stumbled forward and crashed down into the undergrowth.

'Cover! Return fire!'

Agry's cry was followed by a sweep of flashlight beams and a deafening clatter of automatic fire as every soldier let off a pair of three-round bursts into the forest around them. The bullets shattered tree bark and zipped through leaves and branches as Duran Wilkes shouted out above the noise.

'Cease fire! You're wasting your time!'

Ethan and Lopez ducked down as the soldiers ignored the old man and fired controlled bursts into the inky black woods. Ethan, squinting against the noise and the fluttering flames of the muzzle blasts, crouched down alongside Lopez and looked across at the flames of the camp fire.

In the midst of the firelight, he felt his breath catch in his throat as he saw a gigantic form plunge through the camp. The battering noise of the rifles and the sweeping flashlight beams confused his eyes, but he saw a glimpse of thick fur and a huge arm that smashed through piles of equipment. The fire flared in a blossoming cloud of sparks that spiralled up into the night sky as whatever was thundering through the camp crashed through it and sent the embers sprawling across the forest floor.

31

DEFENSE INTELLIGENCE
AGENCY ANALYSIS CENTER,
JOINT BOLLING–ANACOSTIA
AIRBASE, WASHINGTON DC

Natalie walked into the agency's foyer with her visitor's pass attached to the lapel of her jacket. She felt like an imposter as she strode through a series of security checks and into the building proper. Truth was, she wouldn't have gotten into the building at all were it not for Ethan's friendship with Douglas Jarvis, even on the back of the Congressional investigation's mandate. People didn't just walk into the DIA for a chat. You asked, you waited, and you generally got denied.

Jarvis had, for whatever reason, agreed to meet her.

Natalie had taken the time to pull what files the committee could access on Douglas Jarvis. Born in 1950, Brooklyn, New York, Jarvis had been educated in New Jersey and had joined the corps right after graduating.

Jarvis had shipped out to Vietnam in 1968 and served with

the 1st Battalion, 3rd Marines near Da Nang during the Tet Offensive, surviving two tours before the division was pulled out of the country in 1971. Battle-hardened and no doubt scarred as so many were after the horrors witnessed during the conflict, Jarvis had served the corps with distinction but had not sought the higher ranks. He had been just a captain when he had commanded Ethan's rifle platoon with the 15th Expeditionary Force in 2003, and by then his age precluded his participation in front-line combat duty. Frustrated by his limited operational options, Jarvis had finally left the corps at the age of fifty-four and joined the intelligence community at the Pentagon before transferring into the DIA to head up some kind of paramilitary unit within the agency.

That, apparently, was where the story ended.

Natalie suspected that it was almost certainly where the story began.

An elevator carried her up to the fourth floor and, moments later, she was outside an unassuming office door with Jarvis's name upon a polished aluminum plate attached at eye level. Natalie reached up and knocked before entering the office.

That Doug Jarvis had been waiting for her was obvious. He was leaning against his desk with his hands in the pockets of his dark-blue pants, his jacket undone and his tie loose. He looked more like somebody hanging out in a bar after work than a senior officer in one of the most secretive agencies in the world.

'Mr. Jarvis? Natalie asked as she closed the door behind her.

Jarvis pushed off the edge of the desk and smiled at her.

The window of his office looked out over the airbase behind them, the runway lights twinkling in the night.

'You look a lot like him,' he said by way of a greeting. 'Although you're attractive.'

Natalie grinned, thrown off guard by the old man's affable nature and firm but gentle handshake.

'He says the same,' Natalie replied. 'He's always full of bluff wit and charm.'

Jarvis gestured for her to take a chair at his desk, and as she sat down she saw two cups filled with steaming coffee, surrounded by a bowl of sugar and a jug of milk. Two possibilities infiltrated her thoughts: one, that Jarvis was just a decent guy who wanted her to feel at home; and two, Jarvis had plenty to hide and was hoping to fob her off with idle chatter and a sweet old smile.

'Sugar?' Jarvis asked, reaching for the sachets.

'I've got it,' Natalie said, and picked them up herself.

Better safe than sorry, she decided. Whatever this guy was up to he had plenty of power and probably access to things so secret that neither Natalie nor the most far-reaching Congressional committee in the history of the United States of America would ever get close to.

Jarvis pulled his own cup closer as he sat down and looked across at her.

'Your brother's a paradox, you know,' he said conversationally. 'One of the best officers and soldiers I ever served with, but a stubborn son of a bitch. Sometimes I think he used to disobey orders just to see what chaos he might cause.'

'I thought that Marine Corps officers would be beyond that kind of thing,' Natalie said. 'All by the book and ship-shape.'

Jarvis chuckled.

'If only. Officers are the worst law-breakers sometimes.'

'You were a captain in the corps yourself, weren't you?' she asked sweetly.

Jarvis inclined his head as he stirred his coffee. 'Touché,' he said, 'although I was going to add that those same officers only break the rules to protect and to serve.'

'Of course,' Natalie agreed. 'Ethan loved the corps. I think he only left to be closer to Joanna.'

Jarvis slowed in his stirring, pulled the spoon out and set it down.

'You're here for something, Natalie,' he said finally. 'You could be here on behalf of the Congressional committee but they're investigating the CIA, not us, so I have to ask why you are here.'

Natalie silently inhaled and ordered her thoughts. Jarvis was a straight talker, which helped, but it also meant that he was a sharper tool than most and wouldn't be easy to trip up.

'What kind of work does Ethan do for the agency?' she asked.

'I'm not at liberty to answer that question,' Jarvis replied, and took a sip of his coffee.

'How does the agency feel about having a private contractor working on some of its most classified projects?'

'I'm not in a position to ponder the preferences of this agency, only to achieve results from our investigations as best as I can with the resources at hand.'

Natalie bit her lip and went for the kill.

'Congress cannot access much of the material that we know is handled here on a daily basis, but we can organize a complete and thorough access to the files of Warner & Lopez Inc, and by way of that obtain warrants for relevant and connecting files within the DIA.'

Jarvis's eyes narrowed.

'That's not a legally valid course of action for a Congressional investigation.'

'It will be,' Natalie replied. 'One way or the other we'll find a way to break into whatever's been going on here. You can make it easier for us by telling me a few simple facts about my brother.'

'I'll tell you what I can,' Jarvis said, and smiled over his mug.

'Is Ethan your friend?'

Jarvis's smile vanished and his blue eyes fixed on hers for a long beat. For a moment Natalie thought she saw there the man himself, with all the years of soldiering and secrecy stripped away to reveal just another human being struggling to do what he felt was right.

Jarvis set his mug down.

'In this business, you try not to make connections because they're all too often severed by circumstances beyond your control.'

'That's not what I asked,' Natalie replied.

Jarvis hesitated only for a moment longer before he spoke again. 'Yes.'

Natalie reached down to her bag and pulled out a file. From within she produced a series of printed pages that Ben had prepared at her request. She tossed them onto Jarvis's desk and fanned them out with one hand.

'Documents uncovered earlier this afternoon. These search

strings revealed the names of subjects currently under observation by unknown government agencies in direct contra-
vention of statute laws protecting citizens of this country
against invasive acts of observation.'

Jarvis looked down at the images, and as he read the names
on the files Natalie saw the old man's eyebrow raise, saw him
take a slight breath. The subtle body language told her that
whatever else Jarvis might know, he did not know about this.

'How long have these been running?' Jarvis asked.

'Four years,' Natalie said. 'Ever since the disappearance of
a journalist from Jabaliya, Gaza Strip.'

Doug Jarvis looked up at her from the files.

'Joanna Defoe,' he said.

The old man was showing all the signs of somebody expe-
riencing revelation after revelation and struggling to link
them all together. He furrowed his brow as his eyes danced
from one sheet of paper to the next. Natalie leaned forward
and swept them away from his gaze and back into the file.
You've got him on the run now. Keep control of him.

'You'll have noticed that not only was Ethan's name on the
files and that of his partner Nicola Lopez,' Natalie said, 'but
my name is on these files as being under surveillance, as are
those of my parents, and I'll be damned if I'm going to let
some secretive agency snoop around our personal and private
lives without telling me *exactly* why they're doing so.'

Jarvis looked at her. 'This isn't a DIA operation.'

'How would you know?' Natalie asked. 'You're not the
director. They could have something going on above your
pay-grade. Hell, they could be watching you too.'

'I have no doubt that they are,' Jarvis replied smoothly,

catching her off guard. 'Difference is that we would have a tangible reason for doing so. I don't see anything here that suggests to me that this surveillance is anything other than some kind of training exercise. You're on the committee's list of investigators, Ethan and Lopez work for the DIA – maybe everyone's keeping tabs right now.'

'And my parents?' Natalie pushed. 'Are they being watched due to your supposed cautionary measures? My father's a former United States Marine and my mother's both elderly and suffering from arthritis. Are you expecting them to be behind the next major terrorist attack in this country? Does the DIA suspect that right now she's working out how to build a rocket launcher from her goddamned walking stick?'

'I think you're overreacting,' Jarvis replied. 'And all of this is just paperwork without evidence to support it, which I don't suppose you . . .'

Natalie slid her cellphone smoothly across the desk, the device spinning round as it came to a stop in front of Jarvis. He looked down at the image of a blue sedan, taken on what looked like the freeway over the Potomac.

'What's the chances of that turning out to be an agency pool vehicle if I run the plates through the committee's investigation?' Natalie asked. 'It followed me for almost an hour this morning, along with another acting in support.'

'It could be,' Jarvis replied, his gaze still fixed on the image of the sedan. 'But it won't be DIA.'

'I don't care who the goddamned hell it belongs to,' Natalie snapped as she grabbed her cellphone back. 'I'm being followed. So are my family. I want to know why. I want your official assistance in this investigation, Mr. Jarvis.

I want you to find out why my family are of such interest to the government, and I think that you already know more than you're letting on.'

Again, the raised eyebrow and look of bemusement. 'Really?'

Natalie felt a surge of anger at the old man and his casual disregard for her plight.

'Y'know, for a friend of Ethan's you sure know how to short-change him,' Natalie shot back. 'Who the hell do you people think you are?'

Jarvis sighed softly.

'We're the ones who have to make difficult decisions every single day of the year,' he replied, 'often decisions that conflict with what we would morally consider to be the right thing to do. There is no easy way to say this, Natalie, but Ethan, Nicola, yourself, your family, even me and mine, are nothing more than pawns in the epic sweep of mankind's tale. Our priority is to protect and to serve this country for the benefit and security not of ourselves but of people who are not even born yet. It is they who will reap the rewards of our efforts, as we now reap the rewards of countless men and women who died in war zones to protect our way of life.'

Natalie sat in silence for a long moment. 'Even if it costs innocent lives?'

Jarvis, his face impassive, nodded once.

'Even then. It's horrible, unfair and tragic, but sometimes our people are lost to enemy action through more than just a knife or a bullet. Sometimes it's simply unavoidable that col-lateral damage will occur from operations and individuals can become exposed, their identities revealed to the enemy before we can protect them.'

Natalie realized that she was grinding her teeth in her skull. She forced herself to stop.

'This surveillance,' she said finally. 'It's not about my family, is it? It's about Joanna Defoe.'

'I don't know,' Jarvis replied.

'You say that Ethan is your friend. I know that he respects you, Mr. Jarvis, although right now I'm struggling to figure out why. Surely you must consider it worthwhile to find out what happened to her, even if not in an official capacity?'

Jarvis remained impassive.

'It is not within my remit to use the resources of this agency to satisfy personal grievances, no matter how tragic.'

Natalie pushed away from the desk and stood. Jarvis stood with her and extended his hand. Natalie was momentarily surprised. She looked into his eyes and saw swimming there a regret that she had not noticed before, like a long-forgotten dream breaking the surface of his thoughts.

'I'm sorry that I can't help you, Miss Warner,' he said.

Natalie shook his hand and for a moment wasn't sure what to say.

'I know,' she replied finally. 'But rest assured, I will not stop until I find out what happened to her, regardless of your collateral damage.'

Mr. Wilson sat in silence in his car and watched from a distance as Natalie Warner drove out of the DIAC building's lot and joined the freeway headed north for the district. He made no attempt to follow her, for to do so now could jeopardize the entire operation. Clearly, the analyst shared her brother's soldiering instinct: Wilson knew he'd been spotted by Natalie on the freeway near Washington DC. Her keen eye had surprised him, but he would not be caught out so easily again.

He lifted his cell to his ear.

William Steel's voice echoed down the line, distorted by the intense electronic shielding.

'*What news?*'

'Natalie Warner just visited somebody at the DIA, presumably Doug Jarvis. They're onto something here, something beyond what we're trying to protect. Without access I can't tell what they're up to.'

'*Then there is no longer any other option,*' Steel replied. '*We cannot afford to take any chances. Bold action is all we have left. Ensure that the analyst is prevented from furthering her investigation.*'

'Understood,' Wilson replied, and shut the line off.

He tossed the cellphone onto the passenger seat next to him and set off for Washington.

He would not be able to fire his gun easily in the city. He would have to use his imagination. A smile curled from the corner of his mouth.

32

NEZ PERCE NATIONAL
FOREST, IDAHO

Kurt Agry's voice screamed out above the gunfire.

'Fall back! Protect the camp!'

The soldiers turned and fired into the camp, rounds plowing through tents, boxes and bergens as they swept the camp with a lethal hail of bullets. Ethan flinched as more rocks arced down on them from above and thumped down onto the forest floor. One slammed into Klein's arm and smashed the rifle from his grasp as he cried out and dropped to his knees.

Ethan sprinted forward and grabbed Klein's M-16, then turned his back to the camp and squinted out into the darkness behind them instead. A massive form plunged through the trees away from him, barely visible. He lifted the rifle and fired two three-second bursts out into the woods, but the shadowy form was gone before he could determine if he'd hit it or not.

The gunfire ceased and the falling rocks vanished as quickly as they had come.

'The camp's on fire!'

Ethan turned to see flames curling and writhing up the walls of the tents, the burning embers from the fire scorching anything upon which they landed. Kurt Agry dashed into the center and hurled handfuls of dirt on the flames.

Ethan ran in alongside him and tossed the soldiers' bergens clear of the flames, kicking out fires as Lopez joined him with Dana, Proctor, Duran and Mary. Ethan grabbed for another bergen and hauled it away from the fire. The top of the bergen spilled open as he yanked it away, and the flap of a canvas satchel toppled from within. As Ethan hauled the bergen clear of the flames, he almost leapt into the air as he saw the insignia on the satchel.

CHARGE ASSEMBLY, DEMOLITION

Ethan dropped the rucksack as though it were itself aflame and stared down at the satchel charge now laying half out of the bergen. He recognized the product instantly from his service in Iraq and Afghanistan with the US Marines. An M-183 Demolition Charge was essentially sixteen blocks of Composition C-4 explosive packed in a case, each block wrapped in a Mylar-film container. Two priming assemblies would also be packed in the case. Each of the blocks, designation M-112, were easily cut and molded to fit specific targets and could be initiated with any number of high-energy devices. The entire kit had been extremely effective in the field of battle, able to be adapted to all requirements for general demolition.

Just beneath the charges lay a box detonator, which

contained the electronics to set off the explosives either by direct connection or wireless signal. Ethan realized that this was Simmons's bergen, and that he must have been the demolition man on Lieutenant Watson's squad.

Ethan looked up and saw Sergeant Agry frantically hauling one of the other bergens away from nearby flames. Ethan dragged the bergen away and resealed the top before he returned to the center of the camp and began hurling clumps of dirt on burning tents.

After several minutes of furious activity, the fires were out. Ethan stood in the center of the camp as Duran began rebuilding the original fire, while the soldiers carried their fallen comrade into the camp on a collapsible stretcher. One look was all Ethan needed to know that the young soldier would not be continuing on their journey. As Duran got the fire organized and the light flickered again, he could see that the man's skull was badly fractured.

'He needs a hospital,' Lopez said. 'Fast.'

Kurt Agry looked down at the injured man and nodded.

'Get on the radios,' he ordered Klein. 'We'll need an extraction.'

'Radios are all smashed,' Klein responded. 'That *thing* that came through here pretty much wrecked most of our communications gear.'

'What about the satellite phone?' Agry snapped.

'Fire damage,' Jenkins reported. 'It was in my bergen. Most of the other stuff wasn't damaged but the phone was in a side pouch and got burned. It's useless.'

Sergeant Agry dragged a hand across his stubbled jaw. 'You're saying we've got no comms.'

'None,' Klein confirmed.

For a moment Ethan glanced across at the bergens now piled up away from the camp fire. Lieutenant Watson's men were trained National Guard soldiers, tasked with escorting them through the forests in a search for a body. There was no requirement at all for demolition, and it wasn't standard practice for infantry to carry charges: the M-183 weighed around twenty pounds, a significant burden for troops operating in mountainous terrain.

For the first time, Ethan looked at the soldiers in a different light. They had just come under attack from unknown creatures, were stranded in the middle of the mountains without communications and with one man wounded. National Guard would likely be pissing in their pants right now, but Ethan saw no panic in the men around him. More than that, they were each hauling an extra twenty pounds of explosives in their bergens and had shown little sign of exhaustion. That required levels of fitness beyond that of a standard infantry soldier.

'What's your EVAC plan?' Ethan asked.

'We return to our infiltration point after twenty-four hours and are pulled out,' the sergeant replied. 'Standard procedure. A chopper will be there if we need it.'

Lopez glanced at her watch and shook her head.

'No way we can get him back down the mountains to Dixie in the few hours we've got left.'

'We should try,' Mary Wilkes insisted. 'He'll die if we don't.'

'He'll probably die if we try it!' Kurt Agry snapped. 'We need to reassess the situation. No radios, we've lost two tents and several days' supplies and we're one man down.'

Duran Wilkes looked up at the sergeant.

'Not one man down,' he replied. 'Two.'

Ethan looked at the old man and saw him pointing out into the woods near the edge of the treeline, right where the glow from the freshly burning camp fire ended.

'Oh no,' Lopez uttered.

Ethan followed Sergeant Agry and his men across to where the body lay sprawled across a thick bed of damp ferns and moss.

Lieutenant Watson was lying on his front but his face stared lifelessly up at them. In the flickering firelight Ethan could see that his head had been twisted back upon itself until his spine snapped like a twig, killing him instantly.

'You definitely need to reassess your situation,' Lopez said to the sergeant. 'You're in command.'

In a moment of terrible realization, Ethan understood what had happened.

'It planned this,' he said finally. 'It took Simmons down as a distraction, to get us out of the camp so it could be destroyed.'

'It must have attacked Simmons because he was a sentry,' Milner said. 'Only way through without being spotted by the other two was right through the middle.'

Jenkins nodded, and wiped droplets of fine drizzle from his face as he spoke.

'Came from downwind of us, so if it's some kind of wild animal it could probably home in on our scent. Hell of a thing, something that big to creep up on Simmons without him seeing it.'

Sergeant Agry looked down at his commander's remains, and then lifted his chin.

'There's nothing we can do for him or for Simmons tonight. We get our heads down and reassess our situation in the morning.'

'Reassess our situation?' Lopez uttered in amazement. 'Our situation is that we're in deep shit!'

Ethan stepped forward. 'He's right, Nicola. Moving in this terrain at night is suicide. We've got to wait for first light.'

Lopez fumed but took a breath and nodded once. Sergeant Agry said nothing as he stared down at his commander's remains. Duran Wilkes looked across at the sergeant without sympathy.

'Like I said, son, we shouldn't have crossed the six-thousand-foot line. It's onto us now and, believe me, it's not going to let up.'

33

The dawn broke cold and damp and was enveloped in an eternity of silence, as though the thick veils of mist draped across the hills had trapped all sound somewhere above. Ethan rolled out of the warmth of his sleeping bag and let the cold air caress his skin. He rubbed his face with one hand and then clambered out of his tent.

The chill air was sharp in his nose, tainted by the smell of wood smoke as Duran Wilkes tended to the flames of a meager fire in the center of the camp. Mary was gathering firewood nearby on the edge of the treeline, Klein watching her protectively with his rifle in his grasp.

'Any word?'

Duran looked up at Ethan and shook his head. Ethan made his way across the camp to where a tent slightly larger than the rest had been erected close to the fire, its entrance facing the warmth of the flames. Inside, he could see Kurt Agry tending to the injured soldier, who lay comatose and silent. Ethan crouched down at the tent entrance.

'How's Simmons doing?'

Kurt glanced briefly at Ethan as he checked a saline

drip jury-rigged to the roof spar of the tent. He shook his head.

'Not good,' he admitted. 'Hard to do a proper analysis in the field, but I'm thinking multiple skull fractures, probable hemorrhaging and it's quite likely his neck's broken.'

Ethan felt his guts plunge inside him as he looked at the stricken, unconscious man and knew that without a hospital and professional care he was doomed.

'We've got to get him off the mountain,' he replied. 'There's nothing we can do while he's here and I'm not willing to risk his life for this expedition. One of us could head back down and call in a helicopter.'

Kurt Agry turned to face Ethan.

'We came here to get a job done and we're not leaving until we're finished.'

Kurt made his way past Ethan and out of the tent.

'We can't carry on with this guy on a stretcher,' Ethan protested. 'One false move and you're talking about the difference between him walking again or spending the rest of his life in a wheelchair.'

'Simmons knew the risks.'

Ethan stared at Kurt Agry in disbelief and was joined by a sudden chorus of voices. Dana Ford and Proctor were alongside him in moments, along with Lopez.

'He's dying,' Dana said. 'He's our priority now.'

'Abandon the search for somebody who's already dead,' Lopez agreed. 'This is about keeping your man alive.'

Kurt whirled to face them all.

'Yes it is, and that man is my responsibility, not yours! I'll decide how and when we get him back to civilization.'

'The longer you wait, the greater the chance it is that we'll have two dead bodies coming back with us,' Lopez pointed out.

Kurt Agry barged past her as he replied. 'Maybe. Maybe not.'

'The hell's that supposed to mean?'

Duran Wilkes stood up from the fire when Kurt did not reply, and spoke quietly.

'We can't move him safely at all, whether up or down the mountain. The risk is too great to his injuries, especially his neck. Only way that boy's going off this mountain is by helicopter and that's no option at all right now.'

Ethan realized the truth of Duran's words and turned to look at the camp around them. The military radio carried by the soldiers was smashed beyond repair, as though somebody had taken a sledgehammer to it. Many of the cellphones, the satellite phone and other radios and emergency beacons had been burned and melted in the fire that had taken down the supply tent the night before.

The bergens were carefully cached beneath the watchful eye of Corporal Jenkins.

Ethan looked at Kurt Agry. 'What's your real mission here, Kurt?'

'This is a milk-run,' Kurt shot back. 'It's not a real mission at all. Riggins is only twenty miles away. We could march out of here in six fucking hours if we wanted to.'

'Not now you can't,' Ethan said, 'and in my experience there's no such thing as a milk-run.'

'Your experience?' Kurt uttered in disgust. 'And what would that be?'

'Lieutenant, 15th Marine Expeditionary Unit, 1st Battalion,

4th Marines,' Ethan shot back. 'Operations Enduring Freedom and Iraqi Freedom.'

The other soldiers looked up at Ethan with renewed interest in their eyes, but they said nothing as Kurt screwed his face up at Ethan.

'Congratulations, you got your colors and I've got mine. Right now it's not worth rat shit.' He gestured to the tent. 'Best option is to leave him here and pick him up on our way out once the job's done.'

Duran Wilkes took a pace toward Kurt and pointed at him.

'That's as good as a death sentence, son, and you know it. If he's hemorrhaging then he may only have a few hours left to live.'

Kurt nodded, his features hardened by years of learning to bury emotion.

'That's right, so we'd better get movin', hadn't we?'

'Lieutenant Watson wouldn't have left him here,' Lopez pointed out.

'Lieutenant Watson is dead,' Agry snarled. 'I'm in command now and this is the way it's going to be. Any of you don't like it, you're free to leave.'

Duran Wilkes watched as Kurt turned his back on them and walked toward his tent. The old man shook his head as he called after the sergeant.

'Am I the only one here who thinks that leaving this poor man to die is the wrong thing to do?'

'No,' Lopez cut in. 'You're not.'

'Me either,' Ethan said, facing Kurt. 'You ever hear of the saying "No man left behind", Kurt? Or would that be something that gets in the way of the mission?'

'The mission objective is my priority,' Kurt replied as he hauled his bergen onto his back. 'Everything else is secondary.'

'You ever get left behind, Kurt?' Ethan pressed, already sure of the answer.

'You wanna stay here and baby-sit his ass, you go ahead!' Kurt snapped, pointing directly at Ethan. 'But we've got a job to do and I'm not going to let you and a bunch of crack-pot scientists stand in our way.'

'That's funny,' Lopez murmured, 'I could have sworn you were sent out here to *escort* us.'

Ethan saw Kurt hesitate and glance across at the other sol-diers. They were watching their sergeant with interest, as though they had never seen him challenged in this way before. Fact was, he probably never had been. Military troops most often dealt with their tasks using the black and white logic of mission goals. They did not often have to deal with the annoy-ing gray area of civilian morality and compassion.

Kurt stared out at the trees for a long moment and then back at the lonely tent stranded in the middle of a cold, des-olate forest. Ethan saw the man, not the military machine, make the decision.

'Prepare him for movement,' he snapped finally at the sol-diers. 'We'll get him below the six-thousand-foot line and secure him there on one of the ranger trails.'

Duran Wilkes nodded at Kurt as the soldiers dashed into action. 'Relief to see you're still a human being.'

Kurt didn't respond. Ethan was about to say something when Mary's voice screamed out across the camp.

'Grandpa!'

34

Duran moved with surprising speed for a man his age, breaking into a low run and sweeping his rifle up into his hands as he went. Ethan followed, cleared the camp perimeter at a sprint and leapt foliage and rotten tree trunks. Lopez appeared alongside him with a pistol in her hand, her long black ponytail flying as she hurdled through the forest.

Ethan reached Duran's side as they smashed through thick branches that sprayed clouds of sparkling water droplets into the air.

'Mary?!'

Duran's voice was hoarse with the effort of running and the anxiety searing through his veins. They heard the girl's voice shout back and moments later reached a clearing maybe a hundred yards back in the forest.

Mary Wilkes stood near a huge fallen cedar trunk, a thick bundle of firewood under her arm as she looked at a strangely shaped branch protruding from the trunk.

Ethan and Lopez slowed at the edge of the clearing as Mary raised a hand to forestall them.

'Watch where you step,' she said. 'Grandpa, you need to see this.'

The soldiers jogged up behind them from the forest as Duran carefully walked across the clearing, Ethan and Lopez following behind him.

'Down there,' Mary pointed ahead of them.

Ethan looked down as Duran deftly skirted the edge of a deep depression in the soft forest soil, half-concealed by rotting leaves. Ethan felt a tingle of what he could only describe as fear as he saw the immense footprint, and two more ahead of it. The tracks led to where Mary was standing.

Lopez crouched down beside the footprint as the soldiers looked on, and pressed her hand into the soil alongside it. She whistled softly.

'The ground's not soft, Ethan, it's hard, cold from the fall. Whatever made this—'

'Must have weighed maybe six hundred pounds or more,' Ethan finished her sentence for her. 'I'm nearly two hundred pounds and I'm not leaving much of a mark on the leaves, let alone the soil.'

Ethan looked up ahead to the next track and tried to walk alongside them and stretch his legs to match. After two attempts it was clear that his legs simply were not long enough to match the stride.

'Jesus,' one of the soldiers muttered, 'that thing must be ten feet tall.'

Dana and Proctor dashed breathlessly into the clearing, coming up short as they spotted the huge prints. Proctor almost laughed in disbelief as he literally dropped to his knees alongside one of them.

'Oh my God,' he whispered reverentially. 'Oh my God. Oh my God.'

Dana Ford knelt next to him and draped one arm across his shoulder.

'This is it,' she uttered. 'This is the one. A new species. We've discovered a new species of hominid.'

'I've never seen a print so clear, so fresh,' Proctor gasped. 'We must make casts, right now.'

'There's no time,' Kurt Agry said as he marched into the clearing and cast an uninterested eye across the prints. 'You wanted my man off this mountain, we gotta move now.'

Ethan looked around at the clearing and then back in the direction of the camp.

'This was where it was watching us from, last night,' he said, and looked at Duran. 'The one we saw.'

Duran nodded in agreement, but he was busy examining the branch of the fallen cedar with Mary. Ethan stepped up to join them, closely followed by Dana and Proctor.

'Oh my God,' Proctor whispered again, seemingly in some kind of trance of excitement.

Ethan looked at the branch, which protruded vertically from the main trunk about six feet. As thick as Ethan's thigh, the branch was contorted in a strange pirouette about halfway up, yanked around on itself until the upper half of the branch was parallel with the ground. Dense fibers of bark and wood had splintered outward and twisted the elbow of the branch, but it had not broken or snapped.

'What the hell is it?' Kurt snapped as he stormed over and looked at the branch.

Duran Wilkes ran his hand gently up across the bark and then stood back from it.

'It's rage,' he said.

It took a moment for Ethan to realize what he was actually looking at. The immensely strong branch had been twisted as easily as Ethan might twist a straw in his bare hands, bent sideways with such grip that it had not snapped off or otherwise shattered.

Dana Ford stepped reverentially closer to the branch and touched it gently with one hand.

'Stress relief,' she said finally. 'Like Duran said. It's taking out its frustration about something on the tree. Do you have any idea how much force it must take to do something like this?'

'Why would it do it, though?' Lopez asked, gesturing back toward the camp. 'You think that's why it attacked us and trashed our equipment last night?'

'Different species of animals show signs of stress in different ways,' Proctor replied. 'Cats lick their fur or excessively mark their territory, for instance. These creatures, whatever they are, seem to twist and bend branches. There's no other explanation for it, as they would not expend energy like this without good reason.'

Ethan looked around them at the forest.

'It knew what it was doing enough to plan an attack.'

'We're in its territory,' Lopez guessed. 'You don't get a lot of humans this far off the trails, so maybe it got upset?'

Dana Ford shook her head slowly.

'The stress relief here I can understand, but the attack last night doesn't make any sense. If it wanted us to move on, surely it would have remained silent and just let us go on our merry way. That seems to have been what these creatures have done in the past. Either that or they've left the area, because human encounters out here are so rare.'

'Rare for us,' Duran Wilkes said quietly. 'Just because we don't see them, doesn't mean they don't see us. Humans aren't that good at living in the wild anymore because so few of us do it for any length of time. We've lost the ability to sense what's around us. These sasquatch live out here permanently and probably have done for tens of thousands of years. They're about as in tune with their environment as it's possible to get and probably are stumbling over noisy, stupid humans almost every day. That might be stressful for such a quiet, solitary creature.'

Kurt Agry shoved his way to the front of the group.

'Getting your skull crushed is stressful, in case you hadn't noticed. I don't give a damn what these things are out here, what they want or what you all think we should give them. Right now I've got to get one of my men off this mountain and then finish what we came here to do. Now you can all either stand here and sing your happy fucking songs about how at one with the world these creatures are, or we can all get on with our jobs. What's it going to be?'

Dana Ford stepped forward. 'If we want to survive this, we need to understand what we're up against. Isn't that what you soldiers are taught? Know your enemy?'

'If my enemy,' Agry snarled, 'is a nine-foot-tall bear then that's all I need to know. Thing that big, it's a wonder hunters haven't shot dozens of them by now, so excuse me if I don't believe your ape-man stories.'

Duran's aged features creased into a crooked smile.

'Oldest excuse in the book,' he said. 'How come hunters haven't shot one of these before now. You want answers to that? People think that the forests here are crawling with hunters and poachers, but that's dead wrong. The wilderness is far too big, and unless you're walking the forests in-season you won't see one. Hunters are also under all kinds of restrictions: where they can hunt, when they can hunt, what weapons they can use and so on. Even those that do spot a Bigfoot say their first reaction is not to shoot because the damned things look so human, despite their size.'

'Ninety eight per cent of hunters don't poach,' Proctor added. 'Most observe all local laws, which means that most of the time they're out in the forests they're poorly equipped to take down something as large as sasquatch. The hunting dogs that often accompany them are trained to track certain scents like elk or whatever and ignore all others, not track *any* scent they encounter. Besides, a creature like sasquatch would likely see them coming long before they got a decent shot off: they seem to avoid humans wherever possible and move off silently at high speed, too quick to track down.'

'Sure,' Agry muttered, 'like I'd not take a shot at something as big and famous. Take one of these things down and it's fortune city.'

'Maybe,' Dana Ford said. 'Except if you killed a nine-hundred-pound primate miles from anywhere, how would you get it home? A body will decay rapidly, and photographs are always open to interpretation. Only thing that would guarantee you fame and fortune is a live specimen or excellent footage of one.' Dana smiled at the sergeant. 'Virtually every person who has set out to shoot and kill a sasquatch has ended up bringing only a camera with them, because a dead sasquatch would be close to useless in every respect, financially or otherwise, not to mention the social and moral disgust you'd eventually receive. Would you shoot a chimpanzee in cold blood?'

Agry turned away from them with a sneer. 'If it had just killed two of my men, you're damned right I would.'

Dana Ford and Proctor looked at each other before they turned and headed back toward the camp. Kurt Agry ignored the apprehensive looks on the faces of his men.

'Let's move out!'

Ethan watched as the soldiers marched away back toward the camp until he, Lopez, Duran and Mary stood alone by the prints and the fallen cedar trunk.

'What's his rush?' Lopez asked. 'Only time limit we've got is between now and the Sheriff's Department charging Jesse with homicide. Sure, we need to get Simmons off the mountain, but Kurt and his little army are only supposed to be here to watch our backs.'

'They're here for more than that,' Ethan said.

'How do you know?' Duran Wilkes asked.

Ethan watched the elite troops disappear through the woods.

'Kurt Agry said it himself, this was a milk-run for them. That's the whole problem for me. Doug called in back-up for us out here, and the DIA sent in elite troops when an ordinary squad of infantry would have been just fine.'

'Elite troops?' Duran asked. 'I thought they were local guard units from down at Gowen Field?'

'Too fit, too composed,' Ethan replied. 'The troopers are

young but they're too well trained to be reservists. They wouldn't have had enough time to become so professional.'

'That's thin, Ethan,' Lopez said. 'Not nearly enough to get me worried about them.'

'I know,' Ethan replied. 'How about a hundred-twenty pounds of C-4 explosive then?'

Lopez's dark eyes flared with alarm. 'You're kidding?'

'They're tooled for demolitions work,' Ethan said. 'I spotted the charges in Simmons's kit last night when the camp got raided.'

'You think they're up to something else?' Lopez asked. 'Earl Carpenter said that whenever people have gone missing up here, the search and rescue element has come from the National Guard and not locally. Maybe there's something up here in the mountains that they don't want hikers to stumble across.'

'Makes sense,' Ethan admitted. 'But if the military had an outpost up here surely they'd just secure it? They've got Mountain Home Air Force Base not so far from here, plenty of space there for installations.'

'Maybe they're not military?' Lopez suggested. 'But paramilitary?'

Ethan knew that paramilitary units were often attached to government agencies like the DIA to act as instructors to foreign armies or as security to heads of state. Putting them out in the middle of Idaho on what was effectively a state police case was not standard procedure by any means. Jarvis would not have bothered using such units as back-up to their mission. He would have known that firepower was their main requirement, not explosives.

'We need to watch our backs,' he said to Lopez and Duran. 'Until we figure out for sure what's going on here.'

'You think that we're a target?' Lopez asked. 'The surveillance on your family? You think it's Doug Jarvis after all?'

'I don't know,' he admitted.

Duran Wilkes stepped forward.

'Whatever this is about, your man Kurt has his own agenda and I'm not sure I want to be a part of it. This was supposed to be a search for a missing woodsman. Now we're without communication, one man dead and another who's severely injured and we're being attacked by a wild animal that clearly doesn't want us here.'

Ethan pulled his jacket tighter about him to fend off the cold.

'You saying you want more money to be here?'

'No,' Duran said, and glanced at his granddaughter. 'I'm saying that I want to get off this mountain alive.'

35

NATIONAL ARCHIVES AND RECORDS ADMINISTRATION, CONSTITUTION AVENUE, WASHINGTON DC

'This is a long shot, even for you.'

Ben Consiglio walked alongside Natalie up the steps toward the administration building's entrance.

'If this thing is as big as I think it is,' Natalie replied, 'then long shots are all that we'll have. Everything else will have been classified way out of our reach.'

The Rotunda entrance to the NARA on Constitution Avenue held the Declaration of Independence, the Constitution and the Bill of Rights, along with other major historical documents like the Louisiana Purchase Treaty and the Emancipation Proclamation. However, Natalie and Ben were climbing the steps to the research entrance on Pennsylvania Avenue, well away from the tourist crowds.

An agency independent of the United States Government,

NARA existed to preserve and document historical records as well as publish acts of Congress, executive orders and various federal regulations. The archives included vast records of once sensitive documents declassified after periods of time determined by the administration that created them. Natalie knew that within were documents over fifty years old yet only recently released into the public domain.

'You're not going to find everything you need in here,' Ben warned her as they walked inside toward the public desk. 'The administration reclassified many documents back in 2006.'

Natalie knew that certain government agencies had withdrawn from public access many documents considered a threat to national security. In what was described as an 'understanding' between the agencies and the Archivist of the United States, those withdrawals would also be conducted in such a way as to prevent researchers from realizing that the documents ever existed. The public enquiry that revealed the collaboration had provoked an outcry in the media, one that the government of the time had simply ignored.

However, Natalie had a simple way around that.

'It won't affect what we're looking at,' she replied. 'Not yet, anyway.'

'How'd you figure that?' Ben asked as they collected their identity badges and affixed them to their jacket lapels.

'Joanna Defoe disappeared after that protocol was enacted,' she replied as they entered the archives. 'I'm guessing that the surveillance has been in place sometime since then.'

Ben frowned as he followed her.

'Sure, but wouldn't that mean that any further documents

or files wouldn't have made it into the system here? They'd have been pulled beforehand and never made public.'

Natalie nodded as she walked.

'That's right, but my thinking is that whatever it is about Joanna Defoe that attracted the attention of government agencies occurred long before 2006. I'm here to find out what I can about her past, see if there's anything here that might have been overlooked.'

Ben didn't sound convinced.

'If the government has a reason for silencing this woman's history they're not going to have just missed a couple of things. They'll have cleared out everything, every incriminating reference.'

Again, Natalie nodded.

'Yes, but Joanna Defoe was an investigative journalist. Her work was made public before any agency would have known about it.'

Ben stopped walking and thought about it for a moment. 'You figure that she did an article on something, maybe dug too deep, and that was where it all started.'

'Something like that,' Natalie said. 'There has to be a catalyst and that something must be in the public domain because Joanna never served in the military or on an administration. She completed a college degree in photojournalism just like Ethan did, but she then went straight to work as a freelance journalist. There's nothing to suggest that she did anything else in her life.'

Natalie worked her way through the halls of the archive and began tracking down the documents she felt would most likely lead to new information on Joanna Defoe. Ben remained by her side as the hours passed, carefully documenting and filing the papers that she found until they had a stack of documents and printed images of magazine covers and articles that both Joanna and Ethan had written that had reached the public domain.

Ben leaned back in his chair and examined the pile.

'Okay,' he said, 'so the picture is simple. Joanna starts work as a journalist and right from the get-go she's focusing on corruption in political circles, but not in North America. She travels to Palestine, South Africa, the Malay Peninsula and South America.'

Natalie nodded. 'It's like she wanted to get abducted. Most of those places harbor the most dangerous cities on the planet.'

'Either that or it was a Pulitzer she was after,' Ben said, a little more cynically than Natalie would have liked. 'These journos have a habit of putting themselves in the middle of a shit-storm in the hope of breaking the next big news scoop.'

'True,' Natalie conceded, 'but look at the stories she wrote. Government-sponsored abductions in Colombia; same thing in Palestine and South Africa. Corruption in the aftermath of the Boxing Day tsunami in Aceh. It's like she was more interested in hitting government fraud than anything else, and governments have a way of preventing the media from championing their journalists when it's not to their advantage.'

'Maybe she's got an anarchistic streak?' Ben mused out loud. 'That would justify our government keeping one eye on what she was doing.'

Natalie laughed. 'Even if she was, waving anti-nuclear flags and joining Greenpeace don't warrant twenty-four-seven surveillance on your family. It's not enough.'

'What about after she got together with Ethan?' Ben asked.

Natalie looked through the papers, flipping forward, and then flipped back again as she realized something.

'That's odd.'

'What is?' Ben asked.

'She goes back around and does the whole thing again, same countries, same order,' Natalie replied. 'After their work in Iraq and Afghanistan, they pull out and head back to Colombia.' Natalie sat back thoughtfully. 'I remember Ethan saying once that because everybody else was reporting on the War on Terror, they decided to change tack and start covering smaller, more personal stories.'

Ben inclined his head. 'Sounds like a smart move. Did it get them anywhere?'

Natalie leafed through the reports.

'They were able to expose repeated acts of injustice within the police force in Colombia, which resulted in several high-level figures being forced to resign or even sent to prison. Death threats followed, so Jo and Ethan pulled out.'

'To where?'

'Gaza City.'

'Not such a smart move.'

'No, wait,' Natalie said, checking back. 'They were right here in Washington DC for six months before flying out to Gaza. Joanna only wrote two or three articles during that period, mostly concerning the presidential election and allegations of fraud in southern states.'

'Maybe she was working on something else?' Ben hazarded. 'A bigger, longer-term project?'

Natalie traced a line of article titles that Ben had compiled, and stopped on one of them.

'Here,' she said, turning the page to face Ben as they sat together. 'The presidential primary of two administrations ago: Joanna gets a piece published about alleged ties between the front-running candidate and an arms company called Munitions for Advanced Combat Environments – MACE.'

Ben nodded.

'I remember them from my army service,' he said. 'Big contractor, strong ties to several governments around the world. They used to provide a lot of high-tech equipment to combat troops, aerial drones, that kind of stuff. Went down spectacularly a couple of years ago.'

Natalie nodded, grabbing relevant articles off the computer beside her as quickly as she could.

'Byron Stone, CEO of MACE, was killed by a car bomb in Jerusalem,' she read aloud from the first news archive she found, before turning back to the files and quickly flipping through them. 'I've seen that name before here,' she said, and then found what she was looking for. 'Here, got it.'

The document was a small piece in a newspaper that would not have been easily traced by archivists who were looking for Joanna Defoe's work.

'It's in Spanish,' Ben said, surprised.

'Joanna must have not been able to get it into the big broadsheets here in the States, so she settled for the next big thing, a national in Colombia. I can't read Spanish, but I know what that says.'

She pointed to a couple of lines in the text, and Ben nodded.

'Byron Stone, and MACE,' he read the English words in the line. 'Any idea what the article is about?'

Natalie shook her head but sifted quickly through the text looking for words that were recognizable.

'Corruption,' she said, 'fraud, weapons.' Then she paused. 'Abductions.'

Ben's eyes narrowed.

'Wasn't MACE shut down by the FBI because of links to abduction cases around the world?'

Natalie nodded. 'They acted as both abductors and hostage negotiators,' she said as she read from the computer screen. 'They earned millions from high-level figures in ransom money. Turns out that in Gaza they were supplying militants with high-quality improvised explosive devices, bypassing Israel's blockades on weapons-grade material and allowing the conflict there to continue. Which then justified the sale of MACE weaponry to Israel, to defend itself against the attacks.'

'Nasty,' Ben uttered. 'Kit like that probably made its way into Iraq and Afghanistan, taking out our own troops.' He looked at her. 'So you think that maybe Joanna dug into this MACE company long before they were exposed and got herself noticed?'

Natalie nodded.

'That's not all. The period that Byron Stone got himself blown up in Israel is the same period that Ethan was out there.'

Ben looked at the dates. 'But that was long after Joanna had disappeared, right?'

'Two or three years,' Natalie confirmed. 'So, Joanna and Ethan are in Gaza, possibly searching for links between MACE and abductions or weapons supplies there, which would be a big story if it broke during a presidential race. Joanna gets abducted, possibly by MACE, and vanishes. No ransom, no nothing. Ethan eventually returns home, alone.'

'Ethan crashes out of life for a couple of years,' Ben said, 'then this Doug Jarvis from the DIA appears and offers him . . . something?'

'The chance to find Joanna,' Natalie said with near-clairvoyant certainty. 'Probably he dangled that carrot in the hope that Ethan would do something else for the DIA while he was there, but what?'

Ben shrugged, not sure where to go next.

'There's nothing much in the media from the time, just another failed peace process in the region. If anything major happened, politically or in terms of intelligence, it would have been wiped clean by now.'

Natalie nodded. It was pointless searching for evidence of covert operations in what was already one of the most sensitive places on the planet. With presumably both American and Israeli forces on task, no stone would have been left unturned.

'Ethan comes home from whatever he was doing there,' Natalie murmured, 'and suddenly he's going into business with Nicola Lopez. How did he meet her?'

Ben sifted through a handful of papers and pulled out a news report from the *Washington Post*.

'Nicola Lopez left the force after the death of her partner, a detective called Lucas Tyrell, who was investigating a case involving . . .' Ben smiled, '. . . Byron Stone, CEO of MACE.'

Natalie snatched the paperwork from Ben, scanned it quickly and then tossed it down.

'I'll be damned,' she said. 'So this was all to do with MACE being involved in various types of fraud and treason. Only reason for covering that up would be if the company was linked to a high-level government figure, maybe one of the presidential candidates.'

Ben nodded.

'Ethan gets asked to investigate MACE, with the payoff being some kind of information on Joanna. He does the job and gets paid for his work, which helps put his life back on track. He goes into business with Lopez and everyone moves on with their lives. It's a sealed deal, everything's here.'

Natalie shook her head.

'Everything's *wrong*,' she insisted. 'Why send Ethan? He was a wreck at the time, the last person you'd send into a war zone on a high-risk mission.'

'Deniability,' Ben said. 'He would have been out on his own.'

'Deniability *why*?' Natalie demanded. 'There's something missing here, something big enough for it to have been wiped from the public record.' She thought for a moment. 'We're getting off track, looking too hard at the recent stories. Joanna's our target, let's stay with her.'

Ben shrugged as he picked up a sheaf of papers. 'Okay, but I think you're chasing rainbows. Joanna Defoe studied photojournalism and then went to work as a freelance, that's all there is to it.'

'How?' Natalie asked. 'Who financed her college degree? How did she survive working freelance with no previous experience? Who supported her? Her parents?'

Ben frowned as he scanned through the papers in his hand.

'No evidence of any financial concerns,' he said. 'Joanna was an orphan, her father died when she was eight years old. Raised in an orphanage – ah, here you go. Her father's estate passed to Joanna. Not a huge amount but enough to see her through to adulthood and cover her education.'

'How did her parents die?' Natalie asked. 'She never mentioned them.'

'Mother died in childbirth,' Ben said, the timbre of his voice softening. Natalie liked that about Ben – he had a heart. 'Father raised her, then he died of a heart attack.'

Natalie thought for a few moments. 'What was his name?'

'Harrison Defoe,' Ben replied, 'born Kansas, 1948.'

Natalie typed the name into the search engine and a list of hits flashed up almost instantaneously. She scanned down them, searching for relevant articles about his life. And then something else appeared.

'Project MK–ULTRA'. Natalie frowned at it. 'What's that?'

Ben Consiglio glanced at the acronym and his features darkened.

'I know what it is,' he replied. 'And it's not good. Not good at all.'

36

NEZ PERCE NATIONAL FOREST, IDAHO

The forest was as thick with fog as it had been at first light as Ethan checked his watch. A quarter of two, and the sun was a feeble orb of pale light hovering in the murky gray sky.

'Easy there, watch those roots,' said Duran Wilkes.

Ethan hefted Simmons's stretcher onto his shoulder and carefully stepped over the thick, damp and gnarled roots of a fallen tree blocking their path. The hillside was steep, the terrain treacherous and slick with water from the incessant drizzle drifting down around then. Ethan guessed that the temperature was no more than forty degrees, probably a lot less, although the effort of shouldering his corner of the injured soldier's stretcher was generating a lot of heat beneath his waterproof jacket.

Duran had the other corner, with two of Kurt's soldiers manning the rear. Mary, Dana and Proctor walked ahead, picking the easiest path they could find, while Lopez and the remaining soldiers formed a loose guard around the group.

'How much farther?' Proctor called as he looked back at Duran Wilkes.

The old man glanced up at their surroundings for a moment before he replied.

'Another four hundred feet.'

Proctor's face creased with misery beneath his hooded jacket as he turned and followed Dana down a steep animal trail that descended into deep forest below the ridge line.

Ethan could see that the valley below them was deep, almost like a ravine, with thickly forested slopes either side that led to a narrow exit to the south. There was no river in the valley, although it was possible that there might be a creek deep inside the forest that he couldn't see from up on the slopes.

'We're not going to get him down before the sun sets,' Lopez said as she edged in alongside Ethan. 'Captain America over there is getting agitated about it already.'

Ethan glanced across to where Kurt Agry was leading his men, stopping impatiently every few minutes to observe the progress of the cumbersome stretcher.

'There's no rush,' Ethan said. 'We know Cletus MacCarthy is dead and we know that his remains may well be scattered by now. I don't give a damn about his agenda. He's here to escort us and we're here to find a body. Period. He's probably just bored.'

'After last night there's nothing boring about this expedition. There's something out here, Ethan, and it's not friendly,' Lopez said. 'Why don't we just hike down with our injured friend here then come back in helicopters? Preferably the gunship kind.'

Ethan smiled with gritted teeth as he and Duran slipped and slid down a muddy track and onto firmer ground, the stretcher rocking and shuddering as the soldiers followed them down.

'The weather's too heavy here for flying,' he replied. 'We'd never see a thing.'

'Oh no,' Lopez murmured, 'what a great shame that would be. Then we'd have to go back to Illinois or maybe take a vacation down Bermuda way.'

'*Now* you're tempting me,' Ethan grinned at her.

Duran Wilkes looked across at them as they walked through trees that were once again densely packed but on mercifully level ground. 'You can't run away from destiny.'

'You're damned right there,' Lopez replied, 'and it's my destiny to live out my years on a beach with a small army of servants tending to my every need.'

'Your *every* need?' Ethan enquired.

'Keep it clean, Warner,' she said, watching him from the corner of her eye. 'This is my fantasy world we're talkin' about, not yours.'

'You might want to put that fantasy on hold,' Duran said quietly.

'You okay?' Ethan asked, looking at the old man.

Duran nodded once.

'So far,' he replied, 'but we're being watched.'

Ethan turned and looked out across the forest. He saw nothing but the endless, densely packed ranks of cedars and pines, the carpet of damp foliage shivering as drops of water fell from the canopy above in a constant torrent.

'I don't see anything,' Ethan replied.

'Nor do I,' Duran replied. 'And I don't hear anything either. That's my point.'

Ethan attuned his ear to the forest around them and suddenly became aware of the absolute silence, so quiet that it almost seemed tangible. No birds sang. There was no rustle of animals in the bushes. Just the endless pattering of raindrops stretching away to infinity around them.

Lopez whispered across to Ethan.

'You remember what Cletus's wife said, about the woods outside her home?'

Ethan nodded. 'The wildlife left when the sasquatch appeared.'

Ahead, Kurt Agry slowed down and raised a clenched fist into the air. Ethan stopped walking and watched with interest as the soldier stood motionless, looking around him at the forest as though uncertain. He glanced back at Ethan and the stretcher, then continued to survey their surroundings.

'You think he's noticed?' Lopez whispered.

'Definitely,' Ethan said. 'He may be an asshole, but you don't lead a paramilitary platoon if you're not a great soldier.'

'How did he figure it out?' Lopez asked.

'Sixth sense,' Ethan whispered back. 'You'd be surprised how common it is with soldiers.'

Ethan knew that although there was little time for the supernatural among the military, there was a sincere appreciation for the strange but undeniable ability of people to detect the watching gaze of an observer, often from great distances. Ethan himself had been trained never to look too long into the eyes of a target, especially an animal if hunting for food. Sooner or later, they would sense the presence of the hunter and flee.

Likewise, human targets occasionally detected snipers with supernatural accuracy and avoided the bullet that would otherwise have opened their skull like an axe through a melon. There was no predicting when such a bizarre event would occur, but the fact that it did meant that the military took the ability seriously.

Lopez looked around her at the woods and shivered.

'It's out there, isn't it,' she said.

It was Duran who replied.

'It's been out there the whole time. There are birds ahead of us that take off too soon to have been spooked by us.'

Ethan watched for a moment as he considered what Duran was saying.

'It's in front of us.'

'No more than two hundred yards.'

Kurt Agry waved a signal to his men and they began drawing back toward the stretcher, their rifles raised and aimed out into the woods around them. Ethan watched as they pulled back, and Kurt turned to them.

'There's something moving ahead of us,' he said. 'We'll check it out. Warner, Lopez, you cover the stretcher.'

'Great,' Lopez uttered as the soldiers moved out, and pulled her pistol from its holster.

Ethan lowered the stretcher down onto the ground, glancing at Simmons's pale face and guessing that he had hours to live. The build-up of pressure on his brain due to the hemorrhage would kill him before nightfall.

Ethan checked his own weapon and squatted down alongside Duran as Kurt and the troops moved out.

'This isn't going to work,' Duran said. 'We need to get out of here.'

'You were the one voting to get this guy off the mountain,' Ethan said.

Duran turned slowly to look at him. 'That was before we were being hunted.'

Lopez grabbed the old man's jacket. 'What's that now?'

'High ground on all sides,' Duran said, and gestured to the valley around them. 'A natural choke point ahead. Perfect for an ambush.'

Ethan scanned the woods ahead. 'You're saying this is deliberate? The terrain is perfect for an attack, but would they even be capable of something like that?'

Duran opened his mouth to reply but he never got the word out.

A crackle of machine-gun fire smashed the silence of the forest as one of the soldiers blazed automatic rounds into the woods. Ethan barely spotted him before a dull, wet, gray rock smashed down barely three feet from where he crouched.

'Shit, not again,' Lopez shouted as she whirled and aimed out into the woods to their left.

'We need to move, now!' Duran shouted. 'Grab the stretcher!'

Dana and Proctor lifted the rear of the stretcher as Duran and Ethan grabbed the front.

Another heavy chunk of rock sailed down from above as if tossed on a high arc out of the woods toward them. This one hit the ground just behind Proctor and made the biologist leap into the air with fright.

'Keep moving,' Ethan shouted as they plunged forward through the dense foliage.

Another burst of gunfire cracked the air, followed by the splatter of bullets hitting tree trunks, the impacts echoing through the forest around them as Ethan stumbled and struggled beneath the weight of the stretcher, his boots slipping on mud and dead leaves.

A pair of rocks smacked the ground nearby, one of them bouncing off the trunk of a cedar and narrowly missing Lopez's head.

'I can't see it!' she shouted, aiming wildly into the woods but not firing.

'You'll never hit it at this range even if you could see it,' Duran said. 'Keep moving.'

Ethan led the way into the ravine, hitting a slope near the bottom. He saw through the trees a narrow creek that ran through the forest toward the valley exit. The soaring slopes of the ravine rose up around them as Ethan deliberately descended toward the creek.

'You're giving up the high ground,' Lopez said as they slipped and slid down the hillside.

'It's useless to us now,' Ethan shouted. 'We'll make faster progress in the creek.'

Lopez hit the bottom first and landed in thick mud beside water that was only a few inches deep but was flecked with a thin flotsam of ice. Moments later two heavy rocks crashed into the water either side of her, fountains of frigid water splashing her jacket.

'It's still with us!' she shouted, squinting up into the woods for a target.

Ethan got down the slope with Duran, Dana and Proctor struggling along behind them as they splashed into the creek. The icy water flooded into their boots, so cold it felt as though it were leaking directly into Ethan's bones as they jogged unsteadily along the creek toward the end of the valley.

'What the hell do we do when we get out of here?' Lopez asked.

Ethan did not have a good answer for her.

A terrific scream shrieked across the valley from somewhere ahead, like something between a bird of prey and a cougar, and loud enough to ring in Ethan's ears. His legs shuddered to a halt beneath him, frozen still by the terrifying pitch of the cry.

Duran, Proctor and Dana all froze at almost the same instant, the stretcher quivering and swaying as they stood motionless in the water.

'That's not good,' Duran spat. 'It's between us and Kurt's men.'

Ethan scanned the creek ahead and made his decision. He turned toward the bank and walked out of the water, forcing Duran and the others to follow his every move as he set the stretcher down on the mud.

Then he drew his pistol and set off on foot down the creek.

'Where are you going?' Lopez whispered urgently.

'We can't run away from it,' Ethan said. 'We've got to show it that we won't be intimidated. It's more wild animal than human, right? That means it can be fooled.'

Lopez stared at him for one disbelieving second, and then she drew her pistol.

'What did I tell you about us getting in way over our heads?' she muttered.

Ethan nodded as they started off down the creek.

'This is the last time, trust me.'

37

Ethan edged forward in the bitterly cold water, keeping himself in plain sight to get a better look at the two hillsides flanking his position. Hugging the banks would get him out of the water and provide cover, but then he would not be able to see any attack coming.

The creek bubbled softly around rocks and fallen branches that were rotting in the damp, moisture-laden air. The bed of the creek was a cobbled morass of polished stones as big as his fist and as smooth as eggshells. He stared thoughtfully down at them for a moment, the water rippling around his boots. Ethan could no longer feel his feet and his hands were numb from the cold.

'You see anything yet?' Lopez asked.

'Nothing,' he replied, 'but it's not throwing rocks now.'

Lopez seemed surprised to realize that the bombardment had indeed stopped. The screech that had echoed through the forest moments before had clearly spooked her and he could hear her breathing coming in short, sharp bursts as she stayed close to him.

Ethan squatted down, and picked up a handful of the big

round stones from the bed of the creek. He shoved them into his pockets and zipped them up.

'What the hell are you doing?' Lopez asked in confusion.

'Tell you later,' he promised as they moved forward.

The creek ahead rounded a gentle corner to the right, a cedar tree growing right out of the bank at a 45-degree angle making a huge arch that loomed over the creek. Ethan glanced up at the immense tree as he eased forward.

'Our pistols are going to be useless against it,' Lopez said.

Lopez was right, but he figured they were better with any weapon than without. He realized that the ghoulish scream had affected him more than he thought. He blinked rain out of his eyes and focused on rounding the corner, one finger ready on the trigger and the other tucked behind it in the guard, just in case the cold made him fire by accident.

'I can't hear the soldiers,' Lopez said softly.

Kurt Agry and his team were somewhere up ahead, and the sudden silence after the blasts of automatic fire unnerved Ethan further. More than that, the firing had sounded more sporadic, more panicked. He wondered if Kurt's men were beginning to crack under the strain of being hunted by an unknown enemy.

'Kurt's hold over them is failing,' Ethan said. 'It's unlikely they were briefed in detail about what they would be facing out here.'

Lopez didn't reply as they slowly rounded the corner and ducked down to pass beneath the thick trunk of the cedar, a web of gnarled and twisted branches forming a dense net in front of them. Fat drops of icy rainwater plopped down around Ethan into the creek as he ducked beneath the trunk, trickling down the collar of his jacket and smelling of rot and stale, musty air.

They emerged from beneath the fallen cedar and edged their way down the creek. Dense coils of dead creepers spilled down from the banks to Ethan's right, surrounding the rotten core of a tree that had probably fallen years ago, the bark black and sodden.

Ethan led Lopez up to the tangle of creepers and vines and peered over the top down the creek ahead.

A blast of noise crackled toward him and a spray of sodden woodchips spat across his face as he flinched away and ducked back out of sight.

'Hold your fire!' Lopez shouted.

Ethan swiped shards and splinters of wood and bark from his face as Lopez, her hands in the air, stepped out into plain view in the creek.

'Agry?' she called out. 'It's us.'

'I told you to stay put!' came the bellowed response.

Ethan cursed as he stepped out in time to see Kurt and three of his men emerge from the cover of pine trees flanking the creek fifty yards further downstream. They jogged through the water toward them, Kurt's face stained with camouflage paint that had smeared in the damp conditions.

'We were following it,' he said to Ethan. 'Saw you moving and assumed it was waiting for us.'

'It didn't come through here,' Ethan said. 'We left Duran and the others with the stretcher and headed down this way after it shrieked.'

Kurt nodded, wiping rainwater from his brow. 'Yeah, we

heard it too and figured it had somehow gotten around behind us.'

Lopez frowned, scanning the hills either side. 'Where the hell did it go then?'

Ethan shrugged, but then a chill pierced him deep as he remembered the raindrops falling from the huge cedar behind them. He turned slowly as the chill crept up his neck, and looked back up the creek at the dense morass of coiled branches and dripping vegetation of the fallen giant cedar.

Now, he could see pinpricks of daylight through the branches and pines that hadn't been there before.

'It was in the tree,' he said in disbelief. 'I smelled it.'

'You serious?' Lopez asked, suddenly nervous.

'The rain,' Ethan said, 'it's hiding the creature's odor, but I ducked under the tree and it smelled like rotting wood and stale air.'

Kurt Agry and his men responded instantly, weapons flicking up to aim at the tree as they fanned out across the creek and advanced toward it. Ethan and Lopez followed, circling out wide and staying behind the soldiers.

'Freakin' thing must have run from us and headed back toward the group,' Jenkins uttered. 'Why the hell did it do that? And why didn't it drop down on Ethan and Lopez?'

Kurt Agry replied as he edged closer to the tree, his cheek pressed against his rifle.

'It lured us toward each other, trying to force us to shoot our own.'

Ethan nodded. 'That's what I figured.'

'This thing tried to outwit us?' Lopez asked in amazement.

'Damned near worked too,' Kurt Agry said.

The soldiers watched as Kurt Agry moved underneath the tree, aiming up into the branches, and then lowered his rifle. 'There ain't nothing here,' he said.

Ethan and Lopez lowered their pistols as the soldiers regrouped around their leader.

'Okay, let's re-form and get the hell out of this valley while there's still enough light to see,' Kurt said.

The soldiers did not move, and Corporal Jenkins raised a black-gloved hand apologetically.

'Sergeant, we want to know what this thing is that's following us.'

Kurt Agry turned and looked at the corporal for a long moment.

'It's a bear, sergeant. A very clever, very agile, very strong bear.'

Beside Jenkins, one of the troopers swallowed thickly and took a pace toward the sergeant.

'All due respect, sir, that's a fine line of bullshit you're smoking.'

Kurt Agry paced across to the soldier, who stood a good three inches taller than he did, and squared up to him.

'You got a problem with that, Willis?'

The trooper shook his head. 'No, sergeant!'

'Then secure that shit, take point and lead us out of this godforsaken place or I swear I'll gut you from bow to stern and leave you here to rot, is that clear?'

'Yes, sergeant!'

Kurt Agry glared at his corporal for a moment longer, and then dismissed him with a flick of his head.

Willis turned and dashed back underneath the tree before

jogging away toward the valley exit. Kurt Agry turned to the rest of his men. 'We'll form a phalanx, staggered file. This thing hurls any more goddamned rocks at us, I want somebody to have a clear shot at it.'

The troops turned and were about to duck under the tree when a dull thump, like a baseball hitting the glove, echoed through the forest to be followed by a horrendous, blood-chilling scream of agony as though a grown man was having his innards torn out from within him. Ethan winced and Lopez cringed at the terrible noise as Kurt Agry and his men hurled themselves back under the tree and up the other side, sprinting away down the creek after Willis.

Ethan and Lopez crashed through the water behind the soldiers until they came to an abrupt halt in the center of the creek.

'Oh Jesus,' one of them uttered.

Ethan staggered to a halt and looked down into the water.

A cloud of dark-red blood was dispersing into the flow of the creek, some of it staining the smooth round rocks protruding from the water. There, lodged between two of them, was a black combat boot, a torn tangle of flesh spilling from the top and a wedge of splintered bone poking out into the air from within.

Lopez covered her mouth as Kurt Agry stepped forward. Lying in the water a few feet in front of him was Willis's M-16 rifle, unfired and abandoned where it had been dropped.

Kurt grabbed the weapon and lifted it from the water with one hand as the other kept his own rifle aiming at the valley exit. Slowly he slung the abandoned weapon over his shoulder and then began backing up toward Ethan.

'We're out of here,' he uttered.

'What about Willis?' Lopez whispered.

Kurt Agry shook his head.

'This thing's running fuckin' rings around us,' he growled back. 'We gotta make some tough calls or we'll all be dead by tonight. Let's move out.'

Lopez began backing up. 'You think it's trying to lure us in there?'

'Or keep us out,' Kurt nodded. 'Right now I don't give a shit. We back out of this mess and make a new plan.'

Ethan looked at the valley exit and shook his head.

'Only way off this mountain is through that valley,' he said. 'We could go around if we were all on foot, but with your man on a stretcher we'll never climb out of here.'

Kurt nodded in agreement.

'I ain't arguing with you, but until we figure out a weakness in whatever this thing is we can't risk going through that choke point.'

Ethan followed Kurt back to where Duran, Mary, Dana and Proctor were sitting with the soldiers around the stretcher.

'We're cut off,' Kurt informed them. 'Can't risk heading back out of the valley to the south.'

'What are our options?' Dana Ford asked.

'Few,' Kurt replied. 'We head north for Highway 14, but the easiest way to do that is to cross into the next valley to our west. To do that we'd have had to exit this valley, which we can't do.'

'No chance of going over?' Proctor hazarded.

'Not with that stretcher,' Lopez replied for Kurt.

'Can we send two men out?' Mary suggested. 'Get them to come back with help?'

Kurt shook his head.

'We're vulnerable as it is with six armed troops. Two men on their own are going to get taken down. This thing is too well adapted to this environment to be outpaced and I'm not willing to lose another man.'

Duran Wilkes raised an eyebrow.

'Perhaps if you listened as well as you dictate, you wouldn't have lost people in the first place.'

Kurt turned to face the old man.

'We underestimated it,' he replied. 'That good enough for you? We figured there was no threat out here. There is and now it's got us on the back foot. I'm not interested in playing a blame game here, Wilkes. All I'm here to do is get all of you and my team out of these hills and back to safety.'

'You sure about that?' Lopez uttered. 'Seems to me that you've had bigger things on your mind than just our expedition.'

Kurt Agry glanced at Lopez but he ignored her accusation.

'Our best bet is to head back through the valley and make camp as best we can.'

'He won't make it through the night,' Duran said, gesturing to the stretcher. 'If we don't get him into a hospital today, he'll die.'

Kurt's features twisted with barely concealed frustration as he weighed the life of one man against the lives of ten more. Ethan watched as he made his decision and stuck with it.

'We camp again,' he insisted. 'There's nothing else we can do right now.'

'You're just going to sit on your ass and hope for the best?' Lopez snapped.

'Nobody's going to be sitting on their ass!' Kurt yelled at her. 'This isn't a fucking democracy. You either do as I say or you're on your own. Your call!'

Ethan stepped in.

'Okay, enough. We camp for the night and we formulate a new plan of action. Kurt, I think that you need to face up to something, as uncomfortable as it might sound.'

'What's that, Warner?' Kurt uttered.

'That for whatever reason, this creature out here has deliberately blocked our only way home.'

Kurt winced and turned away, but Duran Wilkes stood up.

'He's right, Kurt,' he said. 'There's no doubt about it, this thing's picking us off one by one. We're being hunted.'

38

DEFENSE INTELLIGENCE ANALYSIS CENTER, JOINT BOLLING–ANACOSTIA AIRBASE, WASHINGTON DC

'What do you mean, we've lost contact?'

Doug Jarvis stood in the center of a communications hub, one of several within the DIAC, where signals intelligence and other sources of information were gathered and consolidated into a constantly moving picture of global intelligence.

'Last night, twenty-one hundred hours Pacific Seaboard Time,' Marty Hellerman said as he sat behind a console that controlled over forty plasma screens in the hub. 'Total loss of communications and they haven't fulfilled the emergency evacuation protocol.'

Jarvis dragged his hands down the sides of his face and looked around him. The particular hub in which he stood collated information from all of the intelligence community concerning North America. Others in the DIAC covered

South America, Europe, the Middle East and so on, coordinated with the military's regional command centers. In principle, any major operation by US forces could be monitored from this room, while at the same time data from the NSA, CIA, FBI and local law enforcement would also be assessed, providing a uniquely real-time picture of global political, military and diplomatic operations.

But in this case, all the technical wizardry in the world was useless if there was no way to communicate data from the field to the DIAC.

'They had multiple radios,' Jarvis said, 'satellite phones, emergency beacons. Christ, they get high enough even their cellphones might work. It's not like they're in the Sahara, they're in Idaho.'

'The terrain is severe,' Hellerman explained, 'and the weather out there right now precludes any kind of aerial search or communication attempt. We could assign another team to attempt to track and locate the first, but I doubt that the Director will go for that.'

'He won't,' Jarvis agreed. 'You don't send a fresh mission in pursuit of a doomed one unless you know where they are and why they're in trouble in the first place. We have no information at all. When was the last check-in?'

'Twenty hundred hours,' came the reply.

Jarvis thought for a moment.

'They'd have made camp,' he said. 'Probably did so before last light as it would be extremely dark out there so far from civilization and with heavy weather.'

'Pitch black,' Hellerman agreed. 'You can't see your hand in front of your face. I camped with my brother in the backwoods of Wyoming for two nights when he was working forestry out there. Scariest damned thing I ever did.'

Jarvis nodded. Ethan, Lopez and the National Guard escort team were probably all smart enough to rough it in the woods for a few days without support, but ultimately the region was extremely challenging in terms of survival. The late season meant that much of the available game was either hibernating or migrating away from the winter. The cold was an enemy not to be underestimated, as was the rain. Shelter would be thin on the ground, with the dense forests offering only brief respite.

What Jarvis could not mention was the fact that those very forests were home to something that was killing anybody it came across.

'Let me know the moment any contact is made with the team.'

Hellerman nodded, and Jarvis cast a last glance across the banks of plasma screens before he strode out of the hub and down a corridor toward the decryption lab. He felt pursued by a foreboding, as though something was building like storm clouds on the horizon but remained tantalizingly beyond his grasp.

The team at work on Randy MacCarthy's files were confident that they would crack his decryption, but all of them had their heads down as Jarvis walked in and surveyed them.

'Anything?'

Several heads bobbed up from behind monitors, and shook from side to side.

'We know that most of the files are images,' said one. 'We

can tell by the digital imprint they leave on the overall size of the system folders. Simple maths, really. The rest, about ten per cent of what's on here, are just text documents.'

Jarvis thought for a moment. Ethan had said that Cletus MacCarthy was the one who had shot most of the images on Randy's computer, because Randy himself never left the house. Chances were that whatever he had found and photographed was sensitive enough that he'd kept two banks of images, maybe to help throw off whoever the kid thought was following him.

If somebody was indeed watching Randy, or any of the brothers for that matter, then if they believed that classified information had somehow been obtained then they may have taken matters into their own hands in order to plug the leak. Then there was the matter of disappeared hikers and locals in the region, all of which had been reported to the Sheriff's Office and yet no official search and rescues launched. The National Guard had instead been employed, a force which could in effect be controlled in its work and thus anything sensitive out in the Idaho wilderness protected from observation or discovery.

Jarvis turned to one of the men sitting nearby.

'Can you access the Idaho Army National Guard database? I need the dates and locations of all call-outs regarding missing persons in the Nez Perce National Forest area.'

The technician's fingers rattled across his keyboard as he accessed a search engine and tapped in the search strings. Jarvis moved around to his workstation as his computer flashed up a response.

'Okay,' the technician said, 'fifty-six call-outs over the past thirty-eight years, mostly involving the 116th Cavalry and associated aviation units out of Gowen Field, Boise.'

Jarvis nodded.

'Right, now can you cross reference those searches with matching missing-persons reports from either Grangeville Sheriff's Office or Riggins.'

The keys rattled and the computer screen blinked as a new, refined search appeared.

'Thirty-nine of the call-outs match,' the technician said.

Jarvis looked at the list on the screen.

'Okay, can you locate the approximate locations where the missing persons vanished, if the information was available at the time?'

Jarvis watched as the technician transposed the various latitudinal and longitudinal coordinates of the disappearances. The process took several minutes as the handwritten reports naming the locations were found and then placed on the map.

When he had finished, Jarvis looked at the final image.

'They're all within about five miles of each other,' he said.

The disappearances were clustered around a deep valley and mountain complex near the very heart of the Nez Perce National Forest, north of a place called Moore's Lake.

'Wild country,' the technician said, 'I'm seeing gorges here that are some of the deepest in the country. Anybody suffers an injury or gets stranded in any way out there, they're in for a rough ride.'

Jarvis glanced at a second monitor, where the names and personal details of the missing people that had vanished over the past three or four decades were listed. He saw immediately that the technician was right: apart from one or two hardy survivalists, almost all of the missing persons were local guides and hunters, people who knew the area.

He looked back at the image of the forest where the people had disappeared.

'Can you blow this up to high resolution, get it up on a bigger screen?'

'Sure,' the technician said, and gestured across the laboratory to a pair of plasma screens. 'I'll send it to the workstation there.'

Jarvis made his way across the lab, the image beating him to the screen as it flashed up ten times as large as the original and with the tags marking the last known locations of the vanished people still visible. Jarvis leaned in close.

In the very heart of the forest was a deep, winding gorge that twisted its way west and then north to a spot where several valleys converged on a single point buried deep in the forest. All of the disappearances seemed to be centered close to the middle of the gorge, within about a kilometre of each other and with a slight bias to the west, where high mountains soared up from the valleys around Fox Creek.

'There,' Jarvis tapped the screen. 'Those mountains. They were all close to something up there when they vanished.'

The technician joined him, squinted at the screen and shrugged.

'Looks like virgin forest to me,' he said. 'At this resolution, anything there much bigger than a camp fire would be visible.'

Jarvis could almost make out individual trees amid the vast swathes of dense forest, and in fact on part of the hillside he could actually identify where large patches of forest gave way to gray rock and what looked like shale.

'What are those?' he asked the technician, pointing to the rocky outcrops.

The technician called across the lab to one of his colleagues, who jogged over and peered at the screen.

'Joe here has a degree in geology,' the technician said by way of an explanation.

Joe looked at the image for no more than a few seconds before he spoke.

'It's caused by runoff from mining operations,' he said. 'The hills in Idaho were hugely popular for hard-rock mining, but the work often poisoned the soil around the mine entrances or the trees were cleared to make space for equipment, leaving these patches of bare earth.'

Jarvis examined the image again and turned to the technician.

'Can you put locations to any of these mines on this image?'

The technician hurried back to his workstation, as Joe looked at Jarvis.

'What are you thinking? That Randy MacCarthy found something up there?'

'Maybe,' Jarvis said, not willing to commit himself until he had further evidence.

The image blinked and three tags appeared, each over a patch of earth but all within about a kilometre of the central gorge.

'Three mines,' the technician said, 'all abandoned, the last in 1915, and get this: the National Forest Service banned access to the area two decades ago due to rock falls and unstable ground in the area of the mines. Public access to these peaks is denied, which is why only the National Guard is allowed to conduct searches in the area.'

Jarvis stood up from examining the image. Fact was, the National Guard wouldn't get out of bed on such a regular basis looking for wandering tourists out in the Idaho hills. They would, however, be mobilised if something had to be protected, even if the guard itself was not informed of what that something was. Being a force derived from militia, the guard was subordinate to the fully deployable military and would obey orders from higher authority without question. Given the unlikely story of tiny mines causing unstable ground on mountains that weighed billions of tons, Jarvis felt almost certain that whatever was up there was the reason for the disappearances.

And it made Randy MacCarthy's encrypted files all the more interesting.

'Keep on this,' he said to the technician, 'but stay quiet about it. Let me know if there are any further movements in the area, either by local law enforcement or the National Guard.'

The technician nodded, and Jarvis left them to their work as he walked out of the laboratory and caught an elevator down to the ground floor. His mind was working overtime as he strode out of the security buffer and into the pale sunshine of the parking lot. He got into his pool car and drove out of the DIA complex, heading for the Capitol.

Fact was, he had no business in the district and should have been at his desk. But what Natalie Warner had said about the surveillance on her family had bothered him immensely, and now the sudden loss of communication with Ethan was another blow to his operation. Images of the grilling by the Joint Chiefs of Staff and William Steel flashed through his mind, and he checked his mirror.

It only took about three minutes of driving and careful observation before he knew what he was looking at. His instincts spoke to him despite his disbelief screaming that it simply could not be true.

A silver GMC followed him, cruising three cars back. Jarvis had been in the business long enough to know how to get a tail to show his colors. He hit his turn signal and changed lanes. The GMC didn't signal or turn but it drifted subtly out to the edge of its lane, as the driver subconsciously reacted to the movement of Jarvis's vehicle on the road.

No doubt then. He was under surveillance too.

39

GOVERNMENT ACCOUNTABILITY OFFICE, WASHINGTON DC

'Project MK-ULTRA,' Ben Consiglio said finally as they climbed out of the car.

They had agreed not to talk about what they'd discovered during the journey back, just in case the car had been bugged. Although Natalie felt stupid about it, as though she were being excessively paranoid and was acting the part of a suspect in a hammy police show, there was still the remote possibility that she was a target both because of the Congressional investigation and because of her digging into Joanna Defoe's past.

'What was it?' Natalie asked as they walked toward the main rotunda.

'It was a nightmare,' Ben replied. 'It's the codename for a covert program run by the Central Intelligence Agency's Office of Scientific Intelligence back in the 1950s and 1960s. They used American and Canadian citizens as subjects for batteries of illegal tests, often without the knowledge or consent of the subjects involved.'

Natalie stared across at him.

'Are you kidding?' she uttered. 'The CIA was experimenting on people without consent?'

'For as long as twenty years,' Ben nodded. 'They spiked drinks with drugs and other chemicals to induce altered states in subjects, used hypnosis and isolation, sensory deprivation, all kinds of abuses and even torture. The idea was to test the limits of how people could be manipulated in order to carry out tasks for government agents, and they killed several people in the process. The most famous was Harold Blauer, the American tennis player who died as a result of injections of Methylene-dioxyamphetamine. Blauer knew nothing of the experiment being performed on him, and after his death the involvement of Project MK-ULTRA was covered up by New York State, the government and the CIA for more than two decades.'

'Jesus Christ,' Natalie said, 'and the CIA wonders why people are suspicious of it.'

'Well, if the agency wasn't paranoid before, they will be now,' Ben said as they walked inside the building. 'MK-ULTRA was exposed by Congress through investigations by the Church Committee and the presidential Rockefeller Commission.'

'This gets better by the minute,' Natalie said. 'So you think that maybe they're doing the surveillance now because they fear we're onto something?'

'I doubt that,' Ben said. 'MK-ULTRA was shut down somewhere in the late 1970s by the director of the agency himself.'

'Where's the evidence from the program?' Natalie asked. 'I didn't see any other references to it in the archives.'

'That's because the same director had all of the files burned in 1973 to prevent the Congressional and presidential committees from learning too much about what went on. There were a few Freedom of Information Act requests that uncovered caches of documents, but despite a Senate investigation nothing much came to light.'

Natalie led the way to their office. Guy Rikard was nowhere to be seen but Larry Levinson spotted them immediately and hurried over.

'Guy's in a meeting,' he informed them, 'but he won't be gone for long. Did you manage to find out anything useful?'

Larry joined them as they huddled down at her desk and sifted through what they'd discovered.

'So Joanna Defoe's father is a former subject of this MK-ULTRA program?' Larry asked after they had filled him in.

'He testified before the Senate in 1973,' Ben confirmed. 'After the incriminating evidence was ordered burned by the DCIA, all the investigating parties had left to go on was the sworn testimony of the victims of the MK-ULTRA program. It was enough to build a picture of the scope of the operation but not enough to bring charges against anyone involved, which was almost certainly the motivation behind the destruction of the files.'

Ben slid one of the papers that they had printed out at the archive to Natalie.

'Harrison Defoe testified in 1973 and gave a detailed account of how, in 1967, he had been a serving officer in the United States Army, working as a translator in Singapore.'

'He wasn't a military man,' Natalie noted, reading the file. 'He was a languages expert.'

'And spoke fluent Cantonese as well as Vietnamese,' Ben said. 'He was part of an electronic intelligence outfit tasked with monitoring Viet Cong communications with sympa-thetic communist parties in the Malay Peninsula. They worked on tracking funding and weapons smuggling that came up into Vietnam from the south, instead of the more normal route down from the communist north and Russia.'

'What was Singapore's role in all of this?' Natalie asked.

Larry Levinson replied immediately. Natalie knew him to have an encyclopaedic understanding of world affairs, but even she was surprised at the depth of his knowledge.

'Singapore's Prime Minister, Lee Kuan Yew, was a staunch anti-communist,' he explained. 'In an economic sense the Vietnam War benefited Singapore. It had just gained its inde-pendence from Britain and was able to build immense infrastructure to act as a staging post for the war effort in Vietnam. When the US military moved into South Vietnam, Thailand, Malaysia and the Philippines were facing armed com-munist insurgents and a communist underground was still festering in Singapore. Indonesia was in the throes of a failed communist coup and was waging *konfrontasi* against Singapore, an underground conflict. America's presence gave Prime Minister Yew the reason and opportunity to rebuild his coun-try's economy on a war footing and create the nation that it has since become. Harrison Defoe's presence there would have been a tiny but pivotal role in the unfolding drama of the conflict.'

'Why would they hit somebody in such a vital role?' Natalie wondered out loud.

'Probably because of his language expertise and his service location,' Larry answered. 'Harrison could talk to local people and so get information from the ground, which is the best way to find things out. But the people he was tasked with watching were largely well-known civilian figures who were discreetly supporting the communists. Popular with people in the region, if the American military had arrested them or the CIA had arranged for accidents to occur, then somebody, somewhere, would probably know about it and expose them, losing the United States respect and support in the region.'

Natalie realized what Larry was saying.

'So they start using Harrison Defoe as some sort of programmable assassin or something?'

Ben laughed.

'Probably not quite like that,' he said. 'Harrison testified that he was asked by the CIA if he would like to use newly developed hypnosis techniques to expand his knowledge of Malaysian dialects. He agreed, of course, as language was his passion. Over the next three months he underwent numerous, extensive hypnotherapy sessions. His testimony says that he did indeed learn a great deal about various dialects but that also he began to develop an inexplicably strong sense of outrage toward communist businessmen in Singapore, especially those whom he knew had links to the Viet Cong.'

Natalie smiled bitterly.

'The Viet Cong were effectively winning the war by the late sixties,' she said. 'We were relying on carpet bombing and Agent Orange, and our boys in the jungles were in a living hell of combat. Harrison was a patriot and a pacifist, which could explain some of his mounting anger.'

'He must have hated the sight of so many body-bags coming back from Da Nang and Saigon,' Ben agreed. 'Couple that with some deeply induced hypnotic suggestions about how evil his friends in Singapore were and you've got a time-bomb waiting to explode.'

'Nineteen sixty-eight,' Natalie read from the sheet, 'and Harrison Defoe is arrested after the murder of four Malaysian businessmen outside a downtown restaurant. Tried and convicted, he served the next three years in a Singapore jail. Christ, they burned him.'

'Left him to rot,' Larry noted. 'His own country abandoned him despite his loyalty and patriotism. Essentially, the CIA programmed him to murder enemies of the state and then melted away when he was arrested and tried.'

Natalie shook her head, a shiver running down her spine as she realized with sudden clarity that in the world of international politics and espionage the value of the individual was always outweighed by the importance of winning a war. No matter how patriotic the subject, no matter how hard-working, they would be sacrificed in an instant for political or military gain. The sugar-coated ideal of American cinema, of no man left behind or of presidents risking their careers and lives to protect individual citizens, was a fallacy as fanciful as it was ridiculous.

'He survived his incarceration,' she said, gesturing to further pages of files.

'Was released in 1971 and repatriated to America,' Ben nodded. 'Looks like the government had an attack of guilt over his suffering, or more likely it feared that he would expose what had happened. Harrison receives a government pension and a Purple Heart, and is offered a position at Harvard teaching languages to students.'

Natalie picked up the trail.

'He takes the offer, settles in, marries. His wife dies in childbirth, delivering Joanna.'

'Leaving Harrison to raise his daughter on his own,' Ben said. 'Looks like the trials of life got him down. It says here that Harrison became somewhat embittered by the hardship and tragedy that he'd endured, and spent much of his time wailing to anybody who would listen about how corrupt the government was.'

'Something that his daughter would not have failed to notice,' Natalie guessed.

'Harrison became involved in all manner of anti-capitalist ventures,' Ben said, 'and made quite a name for himself talking about MK-ULTRA and other alleged government-sponsored programs by the CIA that affected ordinary US citizens. He was preparing a court case against the government when he died unexpectedly at his home.'

'The heart attack,' Natalie said.

'There were no suspicious circumstances, although the coroner noted that his heart was perfectly healthy and strong and that cardiac arrest was a highly unfortunate way for someone in his physical condition to have died.'

'Young, too,' Natalie noted, 'forty-eight years old.'

'People do die of cardiac arrest sometimes,' Larry pointed out, 'often for no apparent reason. If the coroner didn't find anything it's likely a dead end, a coincidence.'

'I don't like coincidences,' Natalie replied, 'especially when politics and the military are involved.'

She looked at the pages for a moment and then had an idea.

'Is there anybody still alive who was involved in MK-ULTRA?' she asked.

Ben chuckled bitterly.

'About a hundred thousand people, if you count all the conspiracy theorists and lunatics claiming to have been involved in government tests, alien abductions and God knows what else. It would take years to sift through them and locate the genuine players, if they even know who they actually are. The available files are so vague that they don't reveal if many of the subjects of the experiments actually knew they were being experimented upon.'

'There must be some,' Natalie said. 'If the program was shut down then they can't have simply killed off everybody who was involved. The people who testified in 1973, what about them?'

'The ones who knew about MK-ULTRA at the time would almost certainly be genuine subjects because they were invited to testify. That wouldn't have happened if there was any doubt about their involvement among the investigating committees.' Ben looked at her. 'Why would you want to talk to anybody from back then?'

'Because I'm beginning to suspect that this may have something to do with Joanna Defoe,' she said.

Ben frowned.

'Joanna was raised in an orphanage after her father died,' he said. 'It's all on paper here. When she turned eighteen she was given the money her father left her, which she used to pay for college. Looks like she inherited some of her father's distrust of government and authority because she spent pretty much her entire career as a journalist exposing government corruption around the world.'

'And here,' Natalie said, 'when she hunted down connections between MACE and our government.'

'So?' Larry asked her. 'There are plenty of journalists doing the same thing on any given day. No reason for the CIA to single her out for special attention.'

'Do we know which orphanage she was sent to?' Natalie asked.

'Yeah,' Ben said, and shuffled through some papers until he found what he was looking for. 'Benedictine School for Girls,' he said. 'Virginia. Spent ten years there in the care of the state system before getting her father's payout and heading for college.'

Natalie scanned the details of the orphanage and made a decision.

'I'm going to check this place out,' she said. 'It's another long shot but they may have records that reveal new information that the CIA might not have thought to erase.'

'Long shot doesn't begin to describe that,' Ben said. 'Want me to come with you?'

'No, you've done enough for one day,' she replied. 'How about you just see if you can uncover any names for me connected to Harrison Defoe who are still alive, who might know about what really happened to him. There may be somebody he confided in who can tell us more about what happened.'

Ben threw her a mock salute as he span in his chair and began typing at his keyboard.

'Going somewhere without me?'

Guy Rikard's rotund face appeared before Natalie's, a limp smile hanging from his face.

'Going anywhere that you're not,' Natalie replied as she slipped past him.

Rikard wrapped his thick fingers around one of her arms firmly enough to stop her in her tracks.

'You're not holding out on me over here, are you?' he asked. 'Looks like you're onto something juicy about the Church Committee.'

Natalie wriggled loose from his grip.

'Guy, if I thought for a single moment that I could share anything with you, trust me, I would. But I don't.'

Guy's features hardened. 'That's not team-play, Nat,' he snapped.

'It's *Natalie* to you,' she shot back.

'Well, *Natalie*, this is a team and right now you're not playing along. Our job is to collate information from the Congressional investigation and present it to the committee, not run around Washington DC like you're in a friggin' Dan Brown novel!'

'I need to follow this lead,' Natalie said. 'It could be important to the committee's investigation.'

'It's a good lead,' Larry Levinson intervened as he moved to stand alongside Natalie. 'It could get us somewhere, and if the Investigator General accepts what Natalie's found as tangible evidence of malpractice within the CIA, this office will be at the forefront of it. You sure you want to miss out on what could be the next Watergate, Guy?'

Natalie looked at Larry in wonderment, unable to conceal the smile on her features.

Rikard looked down at her for a long beat, as though

deciding whether she would even have a job at the end of the day, and then he glanced at Ben Consiglio.

'Ben, you do it.' Rikard looked at Natalie and Larry. 'You two, on the other hand, will stay in this office until I say otherwise, is that understood?'

Hot acid flushed through Natalie's veins as she glared at Rikard but there was little she could do. Ben stepped up alongside her and Larry as Rikard stalked away.

'Good work, Larry,' he said. 'I'll come back as soon as I can. Maybe we can pick up the threads of this outside of office hours without Rikard poking his nose in.'

'Larry!' Rikard snapped. 'Get over here! I need help with these translations!'

'I need to pop out of the office for a moment, boss,' Larry replied meekly.

'You can pop out when I damned well tell you!' Rikard thundered back at him.

'But it's important,' Larry pleaded.

'So is national security! Get over here.'

Larry sighed. Natalie mastered her fury as she turned to them.

'Thanks, guys. I owe you both, really.'

Ben smiled as he grabbed his jacket and slung it over his shoulder.

'You owe me nothing,' he said, 'except maybe a drink later.'

He swept from the office with a flash of a smile before she could respond. Larry raised an eyebrow at her and grinned as he walked toward Rikard's desk, leaving her with a warm tingling sensation in the pit of her belly. She didn't even realize that her anger had melted completely.

40

NEZ PERCE NATIONAL
FOREST, IDAHO

'He's gone.'

Ethan stood alongside Lopez and watched as Kurt Agry pulled the stretcher's plastic cover over Simmons's face, his skin now pale and his eyes ringed by blotchy purple sclera. The rain pattered down on the plastic sheet and ran in rivulets into the mud as they stood in a forlorn circle around the body.

They had walked only for an hour before Corporal Jenkins had noticed that Simmons had stopped breathing, his lips turning a dull blue.

Kurt stood up and stared vacantly at the stretcher for a few moments. Ethan watched the soldier for a moment before speaking.

'We'd have never got him back in time, even if the valley weren't blocked,' he said. 'He wasn't going to survive this mission once we lost our radios.'

Kurt nodded, ignoring the streams of chill rainwater streaming from his shaven head to run down his face. He finally ran a hand over his head, the motion sounding like sandpaper rubbing against drywall, and turned to the group.

'We push on,' he said. 'The way home is blocked, but without the stretcher we can take the high ground and push over the valley, then head north.'

Ethan glanced up at the sky, heavily laden with clouds, the forests forever entombed in their foggy grip.

'Why not just head north right now?' he asked. 'Pick up Highway 14 and get back to Grangeville?'

The climb back up into the valley, weighed down by the stretcher, had taken all of the morning and most of the early afternoon. Everybody was exhausted, especially Dana and Proctor.

'Because we're not done yet,' Kurt growled back. 'I'll be damned if I'll let Simmons, Willis or Lieutenant Watson's lives be lost in vain. We finish what we came here to do, then we head home. We can send a recovery team for the stretcher when we're done.'

Duran Wilkes, his beard glistening with beads of water, gestured back down the valley.

'What makes you think that thing is going to let us head back down anywhere? It blocked our route, Kurt. It did that for a reason.'

'It's an animal!' Kurt yelled as he whirled on his heel and marched up to the old man, getting right in his face. 'It's a creature, a big, hairy son of a bitch but nothing more. It's not thinking, it's not planning and it's sure as hell not chasing a vendetta against us!'

Duran Wilkes stood for several long seconds, not averting his eyes from the soldier's raging gaze.

'Then why are we running away from it, back up the valley?'

Kurt stood immobile in front of the old man, and Ethan sensed his chance.

'It's time to come clean, Kurt,' he said. 'You've lost three of your men and we're stuck up here being chased by God knows what. If you've got some other reason for being here then now would be a great time to share it because we might not survive this if we don't work together.'

Kurt turned away from Duran and looked at Ethan.

'Our task is to protect your team from harm and—'

'Bullshit!' Lopez snapped. 'Do you really think we're all just goddamned idiots, following you and your team up and down this mountain like sheep? Right now I don't trust you as far as I could throw you.'

Kurt watched her for a long moment and then glanced across at Dana and Proctor.

'That a universal opinion?'

Dana nodded once beneath her tightly tied hood, and Proctor shrugged. 'Guess so,' he replied nervously. 'Y'all seem like you've got something on your minds other than the man-eating creature from hell that's on our case, which surprises me a little.'

'That part wasn't in our briefing,' Kurt said. 'Guess they must have omitted it.'

'And what are *you* omitting, Kurt?' Duran pressed him. 'What aren't you telling us?'

'I don't have to tell you a goddamned thing,' Kurt snapped.

'About your mission, no,' Duran replied. 'But I'm eight thousand feet up in the mountains with low supplies and my granddaughter to think about, and that wasn't in *my* briefing either. You're the commander of a heavily armed team of soldiers, so I'm going to ask you again: why are we running away from that thing, back up the mountain?'

Kurt swallowed, seeming to quiver on the spot with impotent rage before he turned away and looked at his men.

'Good question,' he snapped. 'I'm about done with this shit. Any of you guys fancy making a stand and sending that goddamned thing back to hell?'

Ethan heard a chorus of 'Hell, yeah' ripple through the soldiers as they gripped their rifles tighter. Kurt turned to Ethan.

'You, marine. My suggestion is that we find somewhere to hunker down and use Duran's advice. Let it come to us.'

Ethan stared at Kurt for a moment. 'You asking me, or telling me?'

'Both,' Kurt said. 'We're not leaving until the job's done and right now we're three men down.' He reached to the ground by the stretcher, lifted Simmons's M-16 and tossed it toward Ethan, who caught it instinctively. 'You'll take his place, and your partner there can cover the science team and our guides. Oh, and one more thing.' Kurt gestured to Simmons's bergen. 'That's yours now.'

Ethan walked across to the bergen and hefted it onto his shoulders. Despite the overall weight of the backpack, maybe sixty pounds or so, he could still feel the twenty pounds extra from the stashed explosives.

Sergeant Agry turned to Duran Wilkes.

'Okay, old man, this is how it's going to play out. One way or another we need to get out of this valley and we're going to do it in the direction that I tell you because that's where I need to go. We may find some kind of shelter in that direction and a place where we can rest and reorganize ourselves defensively. What I need from you is everything you know about this damned *thing* that's following us.'

Duran hesitated for a few moments and then nodded.

'That, I can help you with.'

Kurt turned to his men. 'Wrap the body real tight in the stretcher bag. We'll rig a line up into one of the trees and hoist it off the ground. Last thing I want is for his family to be handed his corpse after it's been chewed into little pieces by wolves.'

Ethan and Lopez helped the soldiers with the body-bag, double-wrapping the body and then rigging a jury line. One of the soldiers weighted the end of a para-cord and used it to loop a rope over a large tree branch in the forest some twenty feet above the ground.

Moments later and the body was dangling out of reach of anything that lived in the woods.

'A bear might plausibly climb up for it,' Duran said as he got his breath back, rubbing his hands from the rope. 'But hopefully it won't detect any scent of food for a few days with all that plastic around it.'

Kurt hefted his bergen onto his back.

'Let's move out. Duran, with me. Ethan, you too. Lopez, you join Klein and Jenkins as rearguard.'

Lopez scowled irritably but obeyed, heading to the rear of the group with her pistol drawn.

Ethan fell in alongside Kurt and Duran as they led the way up an animal trail that climbed a slope through the forest.

The rain was still falling heavily but within the dense trees it was reduced to fat, heavy drops that splashed down around them in a constant patter.

'Talk to me,' Kurt said to Duran. 'Everything you know.'

The old man took a long breath before he began.

'Sasquatch is not a modern myth like most people think,' Duran said. 'Encounters with large, reclusive bipedal creatures are found among the stories of our earliest ancestors. Members of the Lummi tribe of Washington State speak of the *Ts'emekwes*. The *stiyaha, kwi-kwiyai* and *skoocooms* are all ancient tribal names given to species said to live in the forests, and in 1840 a Reverend Elkanah Walker spoke of stories of nocturnal, hairy giants among the native American Indians living in what is now Spokane, Washington. The natives said that the giants lived near the peaks of mountains and sometimes stole salmon from the fishermen's nets. Even the name, sasquatch, is derived from an ancient tribal name for the creatures the Halkomelem called *sásq'ets.*'

'Fascinating,' Kurt uttered without interest. 'Now tell me what I actually need to know. What does it eat? How does it live? Does it hibernate, or make camps, or sleep?'

Duran sighed as they walked.

'There are so few confirmed, recorded sightings that fine details are hard to figure,' he replied. 'It's omnivorous as far as we know. Large scat samples have been found that do not correspond to any known creature that contain everything from wildflowers, nuts and grasses to the remains of carpenter ants, rodents and fish. That matches other wild primate species like gorillas and chimpanzees, which are generally herbivores but will eat meat when it becomes available.'

'Do they hibernate?' Ethan asked.

'Nobody knows,' Duran replied. 'They're very large creatures, living in a region with harsh winters where food of any kind would be extremely hard to find. I'd say it's likely that their activity is greatly reduced during the winter months, but sightings persist so true hibernation is unlikely.'

'Camps,' Kurt pressed. 'Do they have homes or are they wanderers? Do they have territories?'

'Every now and again in the woods I'll find cedar trees bent over at the trunk with incredible force,' Duran said, 'the branches wedged beneath another tree's branches alongside. That can't happen naturally. Nature also doesn't plug the gaps in the branches with smaller bushes and twigs, so yes, they make camps out of trees and they've been photographed and documented regularly. As for territories, it's possible. Most reports show that they will remain in one area for a number of months. Other wildlife tends to vacate the area when they're around, and there are literally hundreds of recordings of sasquatch howls and communications during these periods.'

Kurt nodded, taking it all in.

'Any evidence of causing harm to humans?'

'Almost none,' Duran said. 'Some people claim to have been pursued but those claims are unsubstantiated. Almost all sightings end with the sasquatch moving off as quickly as it can. They seem almost intimidated by humans despite their physical size, or shy of contact.'

'You said they were inherently curious,' Kurt said.

'They are,' Duran shrugged, 'just like us.'

Ethan peered across at Kurt. 'What are you thinking?'

A grim smile flickered across the soldier's face as they walked. 'Curiosity has a habit of killing things,' he murmured. 'We need to even the playing field here. This thing has wrecked our equipment, killed three of my men and we haven't even had a good look at it yet. If we can see it, we can kill it.'

'Why would you want to kill it?' Duran asked. 'You said it yourself, it's just an animal. If it's just an animal then it will only have killed your men out of instinct or perhaps defense. You can't have it both ways, Kurt. Either it's intelligent or it's not.'

'I want to complete this mission and return to base,' Kurt replied, 'and whether it's a monster or a genius I need it dead because it's in our way.'

Ethan chuckled as he clambered over a damp, dark tree stump.

'Good luck with that. So far it's outwitted us completely.'

Kurt nodded. 'That's what I'm counting on.'

'What do you mean?' Ethan asked.

'You dangle a carrot for long enough, something'll come looking.'

Ethan frowned in confusion and then glanced over his shoulder. Dana and Proctor were just behind them with Mary Wilkes, with Lopez and the other two soldiers were further back. Ethan did a rapid head count and realized with sudden certainty what Kurt had done. Two of the soldiers were missing.

'You baited it.'

Duran understood immediately. 'The body. You weren't protecting it from vermin, you were using it as a lure.'

Kurt nodded and abruptly stopped walking. He turned back the way they had come.

'Time for payback,' he uttered, then raised his fist with one finger pointed at the sky and twirled it around.

All of his remaining soldiers immediately began back-tracking along the animal trail.

'We've gone two hundred yards,' he said as he started back along the trail. 'In five minutes we'll all be on the ridge above the hillside with our weapons trained on whatever goes near that body-bag. Archer and Milner are already there.'

Ethan felt a sudden unease trickle like nausea through his guts.

'We're all going back?'

'We'll be fine,' Kurt said. 'We know what we're up against now.'

'You said we should stick together,' Duran snapped. 'You'll be sitting ducks back there.'

'We're trained men,' Kurt replied. 'We know what to do.'

Ethan stopped in the forest and pointed back the way they had come.

'Damn it, Kurt. It'll probably see us long before we see it.'

'I doubt that,' Kurt replied, not stopping. 'That thing will be dead before the sun goes down. You want to come watch?'

41

The body hung motionless from the trunk a hundred yards from where Ethan lay prone behind the rotting bulk of a Douglas fir tree that had fallen long ago. The rain splattered off ferns that quivered beneath the blows, and dripped off the front of his baseball cap as he lay with his cheek against his M–16 and his right eye sighted down the scope.

'We could be here for hours,' he whispered. 'Days, even.'

'Whatever it takes,' Kurt Agry whispered back from his position ten yards away, completely concealed by the foliage.

The cold had seeped into Ethan's bones again, his lack of movement over the past two hours locking his joints and aching through his muscles. Ten years ago such an exercise would have been an almost daily occurrence in the corps, but he'd also been ten years younger then. And at least he'd known that whatever appeared in the sights of his rifle would be human.

Dana, Proctor and Mary Wilkes were hunkered down beneath a plastic sheet a hundred yards behind them, sitting on a pile of folded tents to keep them off the cold earth. Duran had remained with them, his rifle in his grasp. The old man had refused to take part in what he had called cold-blooded murder, but had no problem with firing in defense.

Lopez lay in the damp undergrowth ten yards to Ethan's right, watching and waiting. Her pistol did not have the range to be effective against anything that may or may not appear before them, but it was still in her grasp, her knuckles showing white around the handle.

'It might not be hungry,' she pointed out.

Kurt's reply came back, touched with an undercurrent of weariness.

'This isn't about food.'

Ethan spotted a tiny motion some fifty yards ahead through the forest, a quiver of bushes and ferns that seemed out of place. Moments later he identified the position of one of Kurt's men, further forward. The others were arranged in flanking positions to the left and right, in the hope of catching the creature in a lethal crossfire. The chances of that happening, he suspected, were minimal. Whatever was hunting them possessed intelligence far greater than Kurt Agry and his men were willing to admit. More even than Ethan was. The thought churned fear within him, a long forgotten neural tract coming alive that perhaps once harboured a more developed sixth sense, the instinct for recognition of intelligence in another, albeit not quite human, species.

Ethan shifted his weight on his elbows and was about to say something when a faint whiff of putrefaction drifted from out of the pristine forest into his nostrils. His throat tightened instinctively and his eyes flicked up to watch the tendrils of drizzle drifting down from the sullen gray sky above.

From the west.

'Enemy,' he whispered. 'To our right.'

Kurt frowned uncertainly at Ethan as he slowly turned his head, unsure of how a marine five years out of the service could have beaten him to it. Then he caught the same smell on the air.

'Fucker's coming in from upwind,' he hissed, slowly repositioning himself and touching his microphone earpiece. 'Enemy to the west.'

Ethan watched as the team discreetly changed their positions, aiming their weapons out to the west through the dank forest. The light was already starting to fade as they waited, and Ethan knew that if darkness fell before they could strike then they would be forced to regroup.

'I don't see anything,' Lopez whispered.

'It's out there all right,' Kurt replied. 'I can feel it.'

'I can sure as hell smell it,' Lopez agreed. 'Can't be far away.'

Ethan shook his head.

'Olivia MacCarthy said that she could smell one of them hiding in a treeline over a hundred yards away. It might not even know we're here.'

Kurt Agry considered this for a moment and made a decision. He keyed his microphone.

'Convex, wedge, go. Advance.'

Ethan knew what he was doing. Forming his men into a sort of 'net', they would advance and slowly encircle the creature. The tactic was as old as warfare itself and used often by the Zulus, who called it the 'Horns of the bull'.

'Let's get this done,' Kurt said, and crept forward through the dense foliage.

Lopez looked at Ethan, who nodded, and they began moving forward together, forming the right flank of the formation as it advanced toward the stale, musty odor of decaying flesh and unwashed skin. As they moved the intensity of the stench began to increase, yard by yard through the forest, staining the air around them.

Ethan watched as Kurt Agry slowed and lowered himself down onto one knee, his rifle raised up in front of him. He touched his microphone again.

'Convex, encircle, go.'

There was no anxiety in his tone, no hurry or fear, just cold professionalism.

The soldiers to the north broke cover and jogged swiftly into position, almost directly opposite Ethan and Lopez, their rifles pointing off center toward them to avoid friendly fire as they began advancing in.

'Convex, break now!' Kurt whispered harshly, and broke cover.

Ethan leapt up behind him and ran with the M–16 pulled tightly into his shoulder as the forest suddenly came alive with running boots and crashing ferns as they all rushed in and converged around a patch of forest where the air was thick with the stench of decay.

'Enemy seen!'

The soldier's cry rang out just as Ethan saw the mass of fur crouched down in the foliage ahead, a bulky mound of russet-brown fur half-concealed by the undergrowth.

'Open fire!'

Kurt shouted his command out loud, and in an instant dozens of high-velocity rounds slammed into the body.

Ethan saw the flesh and hair quiver under the impacts as bullets bored deep into flesh. The soldiers skidded to a halt over the remains as Ethan, his nose clogged by the unearthly stench, stumbled to a halt with his rifle unfired and looked down at the remains.

'Shit.'

The body of the elk lay curled up in a foetal position, its legs tucked underneath it to expose its broad back. Ethan scanned the remains and saw the blood and intestines spilling from its belly, which had probably been torn open by hungry wolves or a bear.

'Goddammit!' Kurt snapped, running his gloved hand over his stubbled head.

Ethan looked down at the corpse, a vein of confusion pulsing in his head.

'How come this kill was abandoned?'

Lopez's voice seemed to reach him from afar. 'And where's its antlers?'

Ethan's gaze flicked to the elk's head. Two bloodied stumps protruded from its skull where the magnificent antlers had been torn out.

'Poachers?' one of the soldiers hazarded.

'They'd have taken the whole head,' Ethan said. 'This elk is a bull male, probably had an enormous set of antlers.'

Kurt Agry looked down at the elk, and then at Ethan.

'Which we'd have seen long before the body,' Kurt said.

Ethan shook his head. 'Damn, we should have realized. It would never have approached us from upwind and betrayed its presence.'

Ethan looked down at the remains for a moment longer,

smelled the stale odor of decay still on the air, and felt something rush upon him like a wave of panic as his own warning cry struggled to make it out of his throat.

'Duran!'

A scream that pierced the forest and rang like a bell through every tree shrieked into the lonely wilderness, and the sound of a rifle firing followed it as though hunting it down.

'It's a deception!' Lopez yelled as she turned and sprinted back into the forest the way they had come.

Ethan followed her, running hard through the dense network of leaves and branches, the rain pouring down in sheets and blurring his vision. The soldiers followed them, keeping pace as they plunged frantically toward the wild gunshots ahead. Ethan heard a man screaming as though his heart was being torn from his body, a sound almost as terrifying as the inhuman howls of the previous night.

They burst out into the narrow clearing where Duran, Mary, Proctor and Dana had waited for them. Proctor and Dana were huddled on the pile of tents, their arms wrapped around each other and their faces blanched white with undiluted terror.

In the center of the clearing, on his knees and shaking with what Ethan could only guess was a volatile mixture of rage and fear, was Duran.

'Where's Mary?' Lopez asked.

Duran, his rifle lying uselessly on the forest floor beside him, quivered as tears spilled from his eyes onto his beard.

'It got her,' he croaked. 'It took Mary.'

42

Ethan stared out into the forest, unable to process the fact that this animal had so comprehensively outwitted them. He was attempting to formulate some kind of response when Klein jogged back into the camp.

'Simmons's body's gone,' he said, and jabbed a thumb over his shoulder. 'Ripped right out of the trees.'

Kurt Agry turned to the soldier. 'It's gone?'

'That thing was twenty feet up in the air,' Lopez uttered.

Kurt Agry turned and looked down at Duran Wilkes, who was still on his knees and staring into the forest where the creature had presumably run off with Mary.

'Duran,' Kurt said, and crouched down on one knee alongside the old man. 'Can you track it?'

Duran stared blankly into the wilderness, muttering to himself behind eyes glazed with emotions that Ethan didn't like to see. He imagined that he might have borne that same, wild-eyed disbelief for months after Joanna had vanished without trace from Gaza City.

'Duran,' Kurt repeated more urgently, grabbing the old man's shoulder. 'Do you want to find Mary alive?'

Duran looked at the sergeant and nodded, the wild look in his eye vanishing in a blink to anger.

'Can you track it?' Kurt asked.

Duran looked into the forest and his paralysis vanished. 'Damn right,' he hissed, and reached down to grab his rifle.

Agry stood up and looked at them all. 'We're not running anymore,' he said. 'We're going after this thing. Anybody have a problem with that?'

Ethan watched as everybody shook their heads. He looked back to where the dead elk lay somewhere in the distance, then at Duran Wilkes, and then out to where Mary had been dragged away into the forest.

'Yeah,' he said finally, 'I do.'

'What?' Kurt snapped, grimacing at him. 'You want to go home instead? I thought you were a goddamned marine?'

'What's on your mind?' Lopez asked.

Ethan gestured back to where they had hung the soldier's body as bait.

'We set a trap for this thing,' he said. 'It then deceives us to distract us away from Duran and his group, steals Simmons's body, and then takes Mary away. Doesn't anybody else think that's a deliberate plan of action on its part?'

'I don't care if this thing reads *War and Peace* every night and plays fucking chess,' Kurt snapped back. 'Only way we're getting out of here is if it goes down, and it's going down.'

'That's what you said yesterday,' Lopez pointed out.

Kurt gestured at Duran. 'He'll take us to it, and we'll kill it.'

'And that's my problem,' Ethan said. 'I don't think it's doing any of this randomly. I think it wants us to follow it.'

Kurt stared at him for a long moment. Ethan noticed that Duran now turned his head and looked straight at him.

'You think?' the old man snapped.

'I can't figure out any other reason for why this is all happening,' Ethan replied. 'It stopped us from getting back out of the valley, but let us travel north. It took Willis, then hurt him so that we'd hear it, to keep us following. Now, it's outwitted us and taken one of our number again, giving us a reason to keep following it. It killed that elk as bait and tore off the antlers so that we wouldn't identify what we were looking at until it was too late.'

Duran clenched his rifle tightly as he shook his head. 'That's not what happened to my wife. It just took her and disappeared.'

'Different circumstances,' Ethan said. 'If we start following it instead of trying to kill it, we might be able to figure out why it's doing what it's doing.'

Kurt Agry turned away from them in disgust. 'This is bullshit. You really think the ape's gone all Einstein on us?'

Duran Wilkes got up from his knees and hefted his rifle onto his shoulder.

'We've done things your way twice now, Kurt,' he said, 'and both times it has cost lives. Now my Mary is gone. You're not my priority right now: she is. I'm going to follow this thing and find out where it leads me.'

Duran looked at Ethan and nodded once before he turned on his heel and walked away between the broken and trampled ferns. Ethan looked at Lopez, who shrugged.

'I'm in, if you want to go for it?'

Ethan nodded and picked up his bergen. 'What we're here for.'

'What you were here for,' Kurt Agry corrected him, 'was to find Cletus MacCarthy's body, and he was killed miles from here in Fox Creek.'

'That's right,' Ethan agreed, 'and we haven't found him yet. This creature just strolled out of here with at least two bodies in its grasp and didn't seem to find it that hard, so my guess is that wherever it takes them is where we'll find Cletus and the answers we need. You got any better ideas, how about sharing them?'

Kurt's features creased with indignation.

'You need to get yourselves out of this,' he uttered.

'Out of *what*, exactly?' Lopez snapped.

Kurt looked at her for a moment. 'Out of this forest.'

'We will,' Ethan replied, and turned to follow Duran. 'Right when we've done what we came here to do.'

43

BENEDICTINE ORPHANAGE FOR GIRLS, VIRGINIA

Ben Consiglio stepped into the office of the principal, an elderly lady named Martha Knight who had overseen the residents of the orphanage for almost forty years. Conservatively dressed and with a sharp eye like a bird of prey, Ben guessed that she was one of the old-school types, a firm but fair hand. Certainly the orphanage itself was immaculate in its appearance.

'Thank you for seeing me,' he said as they sat down opposite each other at her desk.

'We get a lot of visitors,' Martha replied by way of an explanation. 'Often from biological parents seeking to contact their lost children. Lives change, people change, and sometimes parents who could not afford to raise a child in their youth find themselves in different circumstances in later life.' She smiled. 'Was that why you came here?'

'I'm afraid not,' Ben said. 'I was one of the lucky ones, my folks are still together. This is regarding an investigation by a

Congressional committee. I'm on the analytical team and we're trying to gather information.'

'On whom?' Martha asked. 'We have detailed records of all residents here.'

'Joanna Defoe,' Ben replied, 'she would have been resident here somewhere between—'

'1986 and 1996?' Martha suggested with another smile.

'You have a remarkable memory,' Ben said. 'I can barely remember what I did last week sometimes.'

'I have a thing for names,' Martha explained, 'which then leads me to recall everything else. Joanna was indeed a resident here after her father died tragically young, a heart attack I think?'

'Cardiac arrest,' Ben confirmed.

'Joanna was sent here shortly afterward,' Martha went on. 'I remember her well because she was so active, a real handful but in a good way. She was a wonderful sportswoman, keen on tennis and field sports. I thought that she might have pursued a professional sporting career but she seemed more interested in politics and world affairs. She went to college after she left here and then became a journalist, I believe, but I haven't heard from her for some time.'

'When did you last speak to Joanna?' Ben asked.

'She used to come by here if she was in DC,' Martha said. 'I suppose the last time was probably about four or five years ago.'

'And did she seem as if anything was troubling her at all?'

Martha shrugged.

'Joanna was a closed book,' she said. 'She was always upbeat, optimistic, cheerful, but it meant that you could never really tell whether she was actually happy or not. She very rarely opened up.'

'But she did?' Ben pressed. 'Sometimes?'

'Occasionally,' Martha replied sadly, 'when she spoke of her parents. She never knew her mother, you see, which must be an extremely difficult thing to deal with. Then her father passed away. You must understand, Mr. Consiglio, that these things all happened before she was eight years old. Joanna Defoe was scarred even before she reached adulthood. Who knows how she really felt inside?'

Ben frowned as he thought for a moment. 'Who actually sent her here?' he asked.

Martha stood up and strode across to a bank of filing cabinets that stretched along one wall of her office. She pulled one open that was marked with a D, and rifled through for a moment before lifting out a thick file. She sat down again opposite Ben, who saw the name printed in neat ink on the top corner of the file: 'DEFOE, J'.

'Here we are,' Martha said, pressing a finger precisely down on one of the first pages in the file. 'Joanna Defoe was sent here by an agency based in Washington DC. I don't believe that we had any links to them at the time, so it must have been by referral or similar.'

'What was the name of the agency?'

'The John J. Carter Memorial Trust,' Martha read from the page.

Ben glanced up at her in surprise. 'The military agency?'

Ben knew of the trust – in fact most people with a military background had heard of it. It was named after John Carter, the son of a shipping magnate who had forgone the chance

to join his father's empire and instead joined the draft for
Vietnam. A stellar officer, he had been killed in action with
the 101st Airborne Division during the battle for Hamburger
Hill in Thua Thien Province. His grief-stricken father had
founded the Trust in his memory, to help former US soldiers
through periods of financial or professional distress.

Ben's familiarity with the trust was personal. He himself
had been gravely wounded in Iraq: the trust had paid for his
treatment and rehabilitation.

'The agency serves former soldiers,' Ben said, 'but why
would they extend that service to Harrison Defoe's daughter?'

'I don't know that they did,' Martha said. 'I assumed that
it was her father's financial legacy that paid for her education
and time here at the orphanage.'

Ben shook his head.

'Her father didn't have enough money to pay for her time
here,' he said. 'Besides, Joanna received her inheritance from
her father when she was eighteen years old and used it to pay
for her college studies. So who paid for her time here, when
she was younger?'

Martha looked down at the file.

'It just says here that the agency provided the funds for her
upbringing via her father's estate, but it doesn't provide
details.'

Ben thought for a moment. It was possible that Harrison
Defoe's passing had indeed been a tragic natural death and
that the government had perhaps decided that it would provide for his orphaned daughter in recompense. But there
were also many thousands of soldiers who had fought in conflicts around the world who had received no such support

from the government – indeed many of them had been reduced to vagrancy.

A thought occurred to him. If Harrison Defoe had been such a successful member of MK-ULTRA, then perhaps the CIA may have suspected that his daughter would share some of the same characteristics. If they could shape one person to do their bidding, then maybe they could shape another in much the same way. Except that her father had been a patriot willing to do anything for his country, whereas Joanna had inherited her father's later bitterness toward his country and government. Such a mindset would be a difficult thing to overcome, even with the deepest hypnosis or whatever those crackpots had been using to turn ordinary people into ticking psychological time-bombs. Hell, to break a spirit as strong as Joanna Defoc's would need some kind of massively traumatic event, the kind that wipes the brain clean like a computer format and . . .

'Christ,' Ben muttered out loud.

'I beg your pardon?' Martha responded, offended. 'We don't take kindly to idle use of that name, young man.'

'Sorry,' Ben said, his mind racing. 'Something just hit me that I hadn't considered before. Did Joanna ever mention something called MK-ULTRA?'

Martha's eyes narrowed.

'Yes,' she replied. 'Only once or twice, when she was very upset just before she left for college.'

A tingle of excitement whizzed up Ben's spine. 'What did she say, exactly?'

Martha sighed.

'To be honest I didn't listen very well because it sounded

like something she'd picked up from watching the *X-Files* or similar. Joanna was very impressionable, easily whipped up into a frenzy about injustice or the uncaring hand of fate. Considering her past, that's not unusual.'

Very impressionable. The words rolled around in Ben's head as he spoke.

'Anything you can recall may help us,' he said.

Martha nodded.

'Well, the long and short of it all was that Joanna believed that her father was murdered, and that something called MK-ULTRA was behind it all. I never did get to the bottom of why she would think that, but she insisted to me on the rare occasions that she spoke of it that MK-ULTRA was still active. She swore to me that she had evidence that the government was experimenting on its own citizens illegally.'

Ben sat still and silent for a long moment. In the warm office, with the low sun streaming in through the windows, it seemed impossible to consider what he was thinking. And yet all possible avenues pointed in the same direction. Joanna Defoe was still alive, MK-ULTRA was still active and somehow Joanna had got the drop on them. For some reason Joanna knew far more than anybody had realized, and that was something that would make the CIA extremely interested in apprehending her. A journalist with a history of exposing governmental corruption in possession of such explosive knowledge, and perhaps solid evidence too, would be an immense threat to national security.

'Thank you, Mrs. Knight,' Ben said, and stood. 'You've been very helpful.'

Ben walked out of the orphanage to his car, unlocked it

but did not climb inside. Instead, he pulled out his cellphone and dialed Natalie's number.

Almost immediately the line connected with a whining, undulating buzz that sounded like a distant hairdrier. Ben looked down at his phone and then around him at the rolling hills. He had no idea where the nearest mast would be but guessed that he was out of range of a decent signal. He pocketed his cell and got into the car before driving out of the lot. He headed back onto Route 646 toward the main highway into Fairfax and across the Potomac into Washington DC.

The 646 was a narrow road lined with high hedges and trees. Ben cruised north toward the highway and took the sweeping right-hand bend past Nokesville at a steady fifty as a blue sedan appeared heading back toward Aden.

Ben leaned on the driver's door sill and glanced out across the open fields, nothing much but a couple of distant farmhouses and small copses of woods, the trees thinning as the last leaves of the fall were—

The sedan flashed into view as it crossed lanes and screamed toward him. Ben felt a split second of fear lance his spine as the sedan loomed large in his windshield. He yanked the wheel to the left, the car's tires locking up and screeching on the asphalt as the sedan plowed into him.

Ben's head flicked sideways and he felt the muscles in his neck crunch under the impact. The sedan's engine roared as it smashed into the passenger door, shattering the glass and smashing Ben's car sideways as it bludgeoned its way past.

Ben kept his foot on the brakes as the car slewed in the opposite direction. His head flicked uncontrollably back the other way and smashed into the side window with a dull thud that sent a bolt of nausea bowling through his stomach. The car shuddered to a halt in the center of the road, the engine stalled. His vision was blurred and his neck throbbed painfully as he squinted out to his right and saw the sedan slumped by the shoulder, smoke pouring from under the hood.

Ben reached down and popped his seatbelt as he pushed his door open. His arms felt weak and his balance was shot away as he staggered out of the car and promptly jack-knifed forward and vomited. He shoved one hand out for balance against the hood as he coughed up an acidic stream of bile, then wiped one sleeve across his mouth and tried to focus.

The sedan was still smoldering by the shoulder but the driver's door hung open. Ben stood upright and turned as a man approached him from behind. He got a brief glimpse of a long, sepulchral face and cold, gray eyes.

'You okay, man?' the stranger asked in a monotone voice.

Ben was about to answer when he saw the pistol in the man's right hand, held close to his side behind the lapel of his jacket. Ben lunged for the weapon on an impulse, but the man leapt aside with incredible speed and cracked his knuckles across Ben's temple. Ben staggered off balance and stumbled onto his hands and knees on the asphalt.

A heavy boot slammed into his guts with enough force to drive him into the side of his car, the air blasting from his lungs as he gagged and slumped forward, sprawled across the cold surface of the road.

A pair of immensely strong hands hauled him up onto his knees and then dragged him into the driver's seat. Ben struggled against his assailant's grip, but his vision was star-ring and swimming with nausea and his limbs felt weak and feeble.

The tall man with the long face strapped him into the seat and squatted down next to him. Ben peered sideways at him into those emotionless eyes. The man's voice was monotone, strangely devoid of presence as though he were a phantom without a soul.

'One question, only one correct answer,' the man said. 'What have you and Natalie Warner uncovered about the whereabouts of Joanna Defoe?'

Ben, slumped in the seat of the car and with the pistol pressed to his stomach, managed a weak smile.

'Natalie who?'

The tall man regarded Ben only for a brief instant. Then he stood and with a vicious swipe of the pistol struck Ben across the head. Ben's already battered skull flicked sideways and he slumped into unconsciousness.

The tall man slammed the car door shut, turned away and reached into the pocket of his jacket as he walked to the filler cap at the rear of the car. He produced from his pocket a plastic sack filled with a clear fluid, opened the filler cap, tore off the tip of the plastic sack and poured the contents down into the fuel tank.

Almost immediately he heard a hissing sound as the volatile chemical mixed with the fuel deep within the car. He placed the filler cap back on its mount but did not tighten it, balancing it so that a gap remained where oxygen could enter the tank, then turned and walked briskly away from the vehicle.

Moments later another car pulled in alongside the shoulder, this one a nondescript Plymouth with Maryland plates.

Mr. Wilson reached out and opened the door, climbing lithely in as the vehicle drove without haste away from the scene of the wreck.

In the comfortable air-conditioned interior, Mr. Wilson briefly glanced into the wing mirror to see Ben Consiglio's vehicle consumed within a funeral pyre of seething flames.

44

GOVERNMENT ACCOUNTABILITY OFFICE, WASHINGTON DC

Natalie sat behind her monitor and fumed in silence, paying little attention to the rest of the team and studiously avoiding Guy Rikard. Being pulled off her investigation at such a crucial moment had brought her to the edge of a paroxysm of fury like nothing she had ever experienced before. Rikard, the fat arrogant pig, was using his authority to belittle her in front of her colleagues.

She managed to master both her revulsion and her anger and looked down again at the notes that she and Ben had compiled so far. Most of it was showing a general pattern: that Harrison Defoe was involved in a government-sponsored CIA program to create assassins, or at the very least informers, out of unwitting citizens. The program had ruined his life and he had passed on his bitterness to his daughter, who had become a journalist with a mission to stamp out government corruption. That meant one of two possibilities: either she had simply inherited her father's bitterness before he died, or Harrison Defoe had told his daughter everything that had happened.

The fact that her father had testified before the US Senate meant that Joanna would have been hard pressed not to have heard about MK–ULTRA. But then why had she not told Ethan anything? Or if she had, then why hadn't Ethan told her about it when he'd had the chance in Chicago?

The only sensible reason for that would be that Joanna had told Ethan nothing about MK–ULTRA, her father, or anything else. For that to be true, she must have had a good reason.

'She was still investigating it,' Natalie murmured to herself. Then another thought hit her even harder. 'It might still be active.'

She looked down at the files before her as a realization began to dawn. Joanna had vanished from Gaza City years before, while probably pursuing leads against a corrupt arms supplier working in Israel called MACE. There was no evidence that she or anybody else connected to her was under surveillance at the time. Joanna was abducted, Ethan went searching for her but ultimately ended up broke and living in South Chicago. Everything was done, finished, over. And yet then all the surveillance started after Ethan's return from Israel.

What the hell was it that she wasn't seeing?

Natalie leaned back in her chair and looked out of a nearby window at Washington DC's busy streets, home of the Capitol, the White House, the beating heart of America's government. There was nothing connecting Joanna to that government except her investigation into MACE, who had been supplying arms to Israel and . . .

Natalie's train of thought slammed to a halt. What if it wasn't just Joanna herself that was the focus? MACE had maintained close relations with the Pentagon, who in turn had close relations with the CIA. MACE had been shut down due to corruption, but if Joanna had been investigating them at the time and had uncovered information that could have brought down the government of the day then the Pentagon would have cheerfully seen her silenced or somehow removed from play.

Two words flickered through her mind: *extreme rendition*. The CIA's policy of grabbing suspected terrorists or enemy combatants and transporting them to countries outside of the Geneva Convention for interrogation.

Joanna herself might be the key. Joanna may have known about MK-ULTRA. *MK-ULTRA may still be active*. By abducting her, the CIA would have been killing two birds with one stone.

'She's involved in it all, somehow.'

Natalie sifted through the pages at her desk and focused on the files detailing the Senate testimonies of former MK-ULTRA members. She worked her way back through the pages until she found what she was looking for. The original copies of the typed testimonies, signed by the hands of the victims who had made them.

The names were blacked-out, as was standard practice during sensitive hearings concerning the security agencies.

Natalie glanced up at her colleagues behind their desks, and took a chance. She picked up the testimonies and hurried to a side office, closing the door behind her. She turned on a desk lamp and sat down. Fact was that documents that had been redacted properly were available only as copies, the information beneath the blacked-out areas forever lost. But when the original copies were available, a little ingenuity was all that was needed to reveal the information.

One by one, she held the documents up to the light then tilted them so that the light was shining down the surface of the page toward her, and looked closely. Through the black bars of thick marker pen, she could clearly see both the indentations made by the original strokes of the pen and the strikes of letters from the typewriters used to write up the testimonies.

Sometimes using the back of the pages where the indentations of the pens was easier to see allowed the observer to identify the words concealed there. It took Natalie no more than ten minutes to record a list of eight names of former members of MK-ULTRA who had testified before the Senate regarding their exposure to the illegal CIA program.

Natalie turned off the lamp. She hurried out of the office and back to her desk.

Rikard was out of his chair and loping his way toward her even before she'd managed to pick up her phone.

'Got something for me, Natalie?' he asked.

'Not yet.'

'You're taking your time,' he muttered, and glanced at the paperwork on her desk. 'And you're not working on the files I left for you.'

'It's called multi-tasking,' Natalie shot back with an icy smile. 'You should try it someday.'

Rikard ignored her and picked up one of the files from her desk, then leafed through it.

'MK-ULTRA,' he uttered. 'Are you kidding me?'

Natalie set her phone down again. Rikard was an asshole, and right now she felt certain that he was taking a far greater interest in her work than he otherwise might. Usually he spent most of his time ogling her breasts instead. But, she figured, telling as much of the truth as possible was usually the best way to lie.

'Joanna Defoe may have a connection to it,' she replied. 'It's a thin lead but it's got enough potential to chase it down.'

'Again,' Rikard reminded her. 'You've done this before, Natalie, and nothing came of it.'

'I didn't have the information then that I do now,' she replied.

Rikard dropped the file on her desk.

'You don't have shit,' he snapped, his podgy face turning an ugly shade of red as he squinted at her. 'I've given you more leeway than most people here but it stops right now. You're chasing fantasies when other people here are spending their days doing real work, work that matters, work that gets results. You either clear this whole thing up, refile it, and get back to work right now, or I'll fire you and have somebody else hired who can do the job!'

'What's your problem, Guy?' Natalie shot back, standing up from her seat as the entire rest of the office looked on. 'Why the opposition to this work when it might expose the biggest misuse of taxpayer's money and the most disgusting abuse of human rights by a government agency since the Nazis?'

The office fell dead silent around her but Guy shook his head, his features beaming with malicious delight.

'That'll sound great at your dismissal hearing,' he replied, and shook his head. 'I was hired to do a job but I got fired chasing down a huge conspiracy. You really think that anybody *believes* a word that you're saying?'

'Ben believes it, and he's out there right now doing his job too!'

'He's wasting his time,' Rikard snapped, 'and you're wasting *my* time.'

'How the hell can Ben be wasting his time out there? This is relevant to CIA activity, we know that!'

'It's relevant to you personally!' Rikard yelled. 'This office serves Congress not your paranoid little fantasies, now shut up and get back to work! And I want Ben Consiglio back here right now, no arguments!'

Natalie was about to answer back when Larry Levinson walked nervously up to Rikard.

'Boss?'

'What?!' Rikard yelled, turning to loom over the smaller man.

'There's been an accident,' Larry said, and looked at Natalie. 'Ben's been in a car wreck over in Virginia.'

Natalie felt a cold veil of horror sink over her, her limbs feeling heavy as she balanced herself on her desk.

'Is he okay?' she asked.

Larry shrugged apologetically. 'I don't know, Nat. I just know that his car was identified as one of our vehicles and the police on scene called it in.'

Natalie's hand flew to her mouth as she realized what that probably meant. She wasn't a family member, so any details of death would be withheld from their office until Ben's family had been informed. 'Oh, Jesus.'

Rikard rubbed his temple with one hand.

'That's all I need, one man down at a time like this.'

Natalie stared at Rikard for a moment as her mind emptied of conscious thought, and then she stepped forward and swung her fist at him.

Her knuckles smacked into Guy's sweaty temple with a sharp crack. The blow was so unexpected that Guy span aside and sprawled across a desk, scattering a phone and pens onto the office floor. His blotchy face collapsed into rage and he leapt up off the desk toward Natalie, who stepped back out of range as to her surprise Larry put himself between them. The diminutive analyst raised a hand toward Rikard.

'Easy, Guy,' he said in a trembling voice. 'You earned that one.'

'She assaulted me,' Guy growled, his beady eyes cold as they glared at Natalie.

'And there are plenty of people who will attest to that,' Larry replied. 'You hit her back and I'll attest to that too whether you like it or not.'

Guy glared down at Larry, but Natalie sensed that he realized retaliation would only serve to scupper his own career as well as Natalie's. His arm quivered as though alive with unspent energy as he pointed at Natalie's desk.

'Clear your desk and get the hell out of here,' he hissed.

Natalie, still numb with shock, merely turned and picked up her bag and the handwritten names of the MK-ULTRA victims. She turned and strode away from the desk as she called back over her shoulder.

'Clear it yourself, asshole.'

Natalie strode out of the office and down the corridor outside, her mind swimming. She had walked fifteen paces before she realized she was heading in the wrong direction. She turned and saw Larry hurrying after her.

'You okay?' he asked.

'Never better,' she replied vacantly.

Larry fell in step alongside her.

'That's crap. Ben's hurt or worse and you just lost your job after assaulting your boss.'

'It's only Ben I'm worried about.'

'Me too,' Larry replied. 'And about you. As for Guy, I think that every single person in that office has dreamed of doing that for many, many years. It'll go down in Congressional history.'

Natalie reached the elevators and stopped. Larry was watching her with an earnest expression, and she managed a faint smile. Larry gave her a nod as the elevator doors opened. 'Now go and find out what happened to Ben. They said he was out on Route 646, got hit head-on in a hit-and-run. I'll see what I can do here to talk Guy out of filing assault charges.'

Natalie turned and hurried into the elevator, both flooded with gratitude for Larry's help and filled with dread for Ben's safety.

'Thanks, Larry,' was all that she could think of to say.

'Thank me later when this has all settled,' he replied, 'and call me when you find out what's happened to Ben.'

45

NEZ PERCE NATIONAL
FOREST, IDAHO

The light was fading fast.

Ethan's bergen felt heavier than ever as he clambered up the steep hillside, the dense forest around them cloaked in swirling mist and clogged with cold moisture that beaded on his face and eyelashes.

Duran Wilkes was just ahead and moving at a furious pace, as he had been for almost two hours now. How the wiry old man was able to cover ground so fast at his age was a wonder to Ethan, who was struggling with fatigue. Behind him labored Lopez, equally exhausted, followed by Dana and Proctor.

To their flanks, Kurt Agry's soldiers kept pace with Duran, moving through dense patches of foliage with practiced efficiency and near complete silence. Down to five men, they were now taking their predicament very seriously.

'It's getting dark,' Lopez said behind him.

'We'll have to make camp soon if we don't catch up with

this thing,' Ethan replied. 'Duran's not going to like that but we'll not be able to track it at night.'

That was despite the obvious trail left through the forest. Ethan had never been an expert tracker despite his training in the corps. Some people had an eye for that sort of thing, and while he knew enough to follow simple game and the foot patrols of enemy soldiers he had always left point duties to those more gifted. But even he could see this trail. Snapped branches, trodden foliage and deep, obvious footprints wound their way ever higher into the mountains.

'I bet Duran could follow this trail at night,' Lopez pointed out, probably thinking the same as Ethan. 'Hell, even I could.'

'It's carrying two bodies,' Ethan replied, 'one of them hopefully still alive. Even something as big as that must have limitations and . . .'

Ethan broke off as Duran Wilkes slowed and raised a hand. He crouched down in the trees and touched the earth at his feet. Ethan moved slowly to join him with Lopez, and from their right Sergeant Agry crept alongside them and looked at the old man.

'What is it?'

Duran scanned the forest ahead as though the trees themselves would tell him what he needed to know.

'It's slowing down,' he replied.

Ethan didn't miss the old man's use of the present tense. 'How far ahead is it?'

'No more than a couple of hundred yards. We're right behind it.'

Kurt Agry's eyebrows raised sharply. 'And you didn't tell us?'

Duran looked at the soldier.

'It's leading us somewhere. Ethan is right. This trail is too obvious, so it wants us to follow it. And it's got Mary. One false move from you trigger-happy assholes and it could snap her neck like a twig.'

'Maybe it already has,' Kurt pointed out callously. 'No need to keep her alive if we can't see her.'

'That's not your call to make,' Ethan cut in. 'It's Duran's.'

The old man set off again, this time in a low crouch, shifting direction from cover to cover as they advanced slowly up the hillside in the weakening light.

Lopez followed closely alongside Ethan as they climbed, the air frigid and cold and the first hints of sleet drifting down amid the drizzle. Ethan saw it collecting on his jacket in little patches of translucent ice.

He saw the forest ahead start to thin out a little, and the foliage around them began to give way to a loose shale of stones and rocks, as though somewhere up ahead the mountain had crumbled and fallen down into the woods. Ethan spotted sheets of sand shaped by running water from heavy rains, bearing the occasional heavy footprint that dwarfed Duran's as he followed the trail.

Ethan sensed that whatever was waiting for them was now very close, perhaps just ahead in the clearing. Duran reached the edge of the treeline and squatted down to look out across a clearing of gray shale and sand that stretched for a couple of hundred yards to the north up the mountain slope, dotted with occasional trees.

The trail of huge prints disappeared into the opposite treeline.

'Where are we, exactly?' Lopez asked as they squatted down. 'We need to take stock before we go any further.'

Kurt Agry pulled a map from a pouch on his webbing and folded it to their location.

'About three miles north-northwest of Moore's Lake,' he said, and jabbed a finger on the map. 'There's nothing out here. The nearest forest trails are probably eight miles to our east and four miles to our west.'

'Where's the nearest road and town?' Ethan asked.

'The nearest road's about ten miles to our north,' Kurt replied, 'or there's a ranger trail a couple of miles south of Moore's Lake. Nearest town's probably fifteen miles to the northeast. Hell, we're right out on our own here.'

'It's no wonder nobody sees much of these things,' Lopez said.

Duran, who had remained silent, stood up and strode out across the shale clearing to follow the trail. Ethan, Lopez and Kurt exchanged glances before getting up and following him.

It took only a few minutes to cross the shale bed before they were plunged into the darkness of the forest again, but this time there was a clear path slicing through the woods. Partially overgrown, Ethan could still see what looked like tire tracks ground deep into the ancient hillside, as though a vehicle of some kind had passed through.

'Wagons,' Kurt said as they moved. 'There were people here.'

Before Ethan could reply, the smell of decay and putre-faction slithered into his nostrils and the hairs on the back of his neck stood on end. He slowed along with Lopez and Kurt as they approached another clearing ahead.

Duran had stopped again, this time crouching down on one knee near a rock face that loomed up some twenty yards ahead of them. The trail ended there, where a dark rectangular crevice was sliced into the bare rock of the mountain, hewn by the hands and tools of men long dead.

'It's a mine,' Lopez said. 'Probably abandoned years ago.'

Duran Wilkes shook his head. 'People have been here recently.'

The old man pointed out across the patch of clear ground in front of the mine, and as Ethan looked so his guts convulsed inside him.

The bare earth was littered with perhaps a dozen rotting corpses, many of them reduced almost to bare bones from which hung tattered ribbons of flesh. A skull seemed to look right at Ethan, the jaw crushed and the back of the skull collapsed as through struck by something with immense force.

'How long ago?' Ethan asked, glancing across at Kurt.

'Maybe three or four weeks,' Kurt guessed, looking at the state of decay of the bodies. 'It's been cold here for a while now and the bodies don't look like they've been chewed up by predators.'

'No,' Lopez agreed, 'but they look like they've been smashed up by something.'

'Miners, maybe?' Kurt hazarded.

'No,' Duran said. 'They're scientists, or lab workers at the least.'

Ethan squinted at the bodies in surprise, and then realized what Duran meant. Several of them were surrounded by the tattered remains of lab coats, the once white material stained heavily by mud and perhaps dried blood. One thing was clear: every one of the bodies was horribly mutilated, the ribs stoved in or skulls shattered or legs broken. Worse, the earth around the bodies was littered with large footprints, sufficient that they could not tell where the trail they had been following actually went.

'They were running from something,' Lopez said. 'They're all facing out from that mine.'

Kurt nodded and waved his men forward briskly. 'Cover the entrance,' he instructed them, 'while the rest of us head in.'

'We don't know what's in there,' Lopez said. 'It could be a trap.'

'It *is* a trap,' Duran said. 'But I've got no choice.'

Kurt gestured to Jenkins. 'Unpack the video camera and set it up outside the mine entrance,' he instructed. 'We can link it to a portable screen. It'll give us some warning if anything tries to follow us in there.'

Jenkins pulled the camera from his bergen, along with a tripod and a loop of thin black cable.

Ethan checked his rifle and looked at Duran. 'One step at a time, okay? We'll find her but we've got to stick together. Don't go rushing off.'

The old man nodded, and with a deep breath he stood up and walked across the clearing. Ethan, Kurt, Jenkins and Lopez followed with Dana and Proctor as the rest of the soldiers formed a loose rearguard, their weapons trained out into the forests behind them. Jenkins jogged ahead and swiftly set up the camera on its tripod, plugging the cable jack into the camera and then into a small headset that he pulled on, a screen the size of a matchbox suspended over his left eye.

Then, one by one, they entered the darkness of the mine entrance.

46

GOVERNMENT ACCOUNTABILITY OFFICE, WASHINGTON DC

'The hell do you mean, she's been fired?'

Doug Jarvis stood at the door to the office of a low-ranking analytical official by the name of Guy Rikard, who blocked his access with wide, fat shoulders and sneered down at him.

'Pending assault charges,' he spat back at Jarvis. 'The little bitch is going to get everything she deserves.'

Jarvis glanced at Rikard's sweaty brow and saw the thick purple bruise swelling around his left eye. He smiled.

'Not the only one by the look of things.'

'Who the hell are you?' Rikard snapped.

'Defense Intelligence Agency,' Jarvis growled back, and flashed his identity card. 'Either get out of my way or I'll put you on your ass too.'

Rikard stared in amazement at the ID card and then backed away from the door. Jarvis strolled in and glanced around. Several members of staff were looking at him with interest. Jarvis turned to Rikard.

'What was Natalie working on here?'

'I am not at liberty to discuss that with outside parties from any governme—'

Jarvis took one pace toward Rikard, grabbed his testicles and twisted them hard as he yanked them upward. Rikard yelped as he staggered backward on his toes and collided with a water cooler in the corner of the office.

'She was tasked to disseminate from public office records information pertaining to alleged misconduct by government agencies against American citizens!' Rikard sang in a bizarre high-octave voice.

Jarvis nodded slowly. 'Good. Now, why did she hit you?'

Rikard's patchy red face was glowing like a beacon as he struggled to talk in quick, abrupt sentences.

'Her friend was involved in a car wreck. I got mad because it would leave us one man down. She got mad about that and then whacked me.'

'And you were surprised?' Jarvis uttered. 'Who was her friend?'

'Ben Consiglio. He works here.'

'What was he doing?'

'Chasing up leads on Natalie's work,' Rikard squeaked. 'She was looking for somebody called Joanna Defoe, some orphanage or something.'

'Where?' Jarvis snarled and twisted harder.

'Virginiaaaah,' Rikard squealed as tears began flowing from his eyes.

Jarvis thought for a moment. Virginia was a long way to

go to pursue Joanna Defoe's life story, if that was what Natalie had been doing.

'Why was this Ben doing it for her?' he asked, and released some of the pressure.

'Because I wanted Natalie in this office,' Rikard heaved in response. 'She was going off too much on her own mission and not doing her job.'

'Sounds like she was doing her job just fine,' Jarvis said. 'Anything else?'

Rikard shook his head.

'Not much, just some old junk files from something called MK-ULTRA.'

Jarvis let go of Rikard as though he'd been electrocuted. The office manager let out a gasp of relief as he slumped against the wall and slid to his knees, his hands clutching his groin. Jarvis barely noticed. Suddenly a huge missing piece of the puzzle had fallen into place and he realized what the whole charade had been about.

He knew all about MK-ULTRA. In fact, anybody who knew anything about the CIA would know about the controversial program that had been blown wide open by the Senate's Church Committee back in the 1970s. But if Natalie had been researching the files from the testimonials then Jarvis could think of only one good reason why. Either Joanna Defoe was more involved with her father's history than he might have otherwise assumed, or MK-ULTRA was still an active program.

Only one explanation really provided a reason for the extensive surveillance operations now extending to himself at the DIA and to Natalie Warner. A new and unexpected concern flooded his awareness as he considered the implications of Natalie discovering anything about an active MK-ULTRA program that the CIA would want to remain covert.

'How far had she got with her work?' he demanded of Rikard as the office manager struggled to his feet.

'This is assault!' he gasped, 'I'll have you up in front of a tribunal and—'

'People are dying,' Jarvis snapped. 'Your man Ben Consiglio was possibly the subject of an assassination. Anybody involved in the Congressional investigation of intelligence agency corruption could become a target.'

The office around Jarvis went deathly silent. Rikard stared at him for a long moment before he spoke.

'That's insane,' he said. 'They wouldn't dare do such a thing.'

'Believe me,' Jarvis replied, 'they've done far, far worse in the past and nothing's changed, except for the fact that things are covered up much better than they used to be.'

Rikard's slitty little eyes glazed over for a few moments.

'I've got two kids,' he said.

'So have I,' said somebody from across the office.

Jarvis scanned the members of the analytical team and made a decision.

'Go home,' he said. 'Each and every one of you. Take two days off and don't come anywhere near this office. You're all sick with a bug. You don't come here, you don't do any work and you won't be a target for anything more than a disciplinary hearing from your boss, which we'll ensure won't happen, right, Guy?'

Rikard looked at his team and nodded. 'Get out of here.'

The office emptied quicker than a high school at the end of semester. Only one person remained, a thin-looking man with big brown eyes who seemed cautious of approaching either Jarvis or Rikard.

'I'll stay,' he said. 'Nat's had a rough day.'

'This is Larry,' Rikard said. 'He follows Natalie around like a pet puppy.'

'Better than treating her like a dog,' Larry muttered back.

Jarvis looked at Larry. 'Where did she go?'

'To the scene of the accident, out near Aden on the 646.'

Jarvis's mind went into overtime as he considered what had happened to Natalie's colleague Ben. If Rikard had sent Ben out to the orphanage to chase a lead on Joanna Defoe, then whoever made the hit had to know something about it. And for them to have known about it, somebody had to have told them, because the CIA was tasked with tailing Natalie, not random colleagues from her office. Even with the intense security around anything like MK-ULTRA, if it was still running, the CIA just didn't have enough manpower to keep tabs on an entire Congressional investigation. An informer would be a much wiser resource, planted within Congress and most likely within the analytical team itself.

'Who knew where Ben Consiglio was going?' he asked Rikard.

'Me, and anybody who overheard the conversation, I guess,' he replied.

Jarvis nodded. The office had emptied almost immediately. Jarvis had flashed a DIA identity badge in front of all of them, which meant that any CIA mole would most likely have hot-

footed it out of the office with the rest of the team for fear
of being spotted.

All that was left was Rikard and Larry.

'Listen to me very carefully,' Jarvis said to them. 'Nothing
that I tell you can ever be heard by anybody else, understood?'

The two men nodded in understanding.

'Good,' Jarvis said. 'Then this is what we're going to do.
Natalie is in great danger and may need protection. I'll call the
police and have her taken into custody in the nearest station to
the car wreck. I want you both to stay here and search through
Natalie's work – try to figure out exactly what she was doing
and how far she got. Rikard, you gather together everything
the pair of you find out and take it to the Congressional committee, Congress, the Investigator General of the CIA –
anybody, and tell them what's happened, understood?'

Rikard nodded as his bad attitude suddenly evaporated in
the face of a true crisis. Larry whirled and headed toward
Natalie's desk and the piles of paperwork still sitting there.

'Give me Natalie's cell number,' Jarvis ordered Rikard,
who quickly dictated the number from memory.

Jarvis turned and strode out of the office, taking the elevator back down to the ground floor and walking out of the
Capitol. He made no effort to conceal his presence as he
walked across the street to the lot and scanned for the silver
GMC that had followed him into the district. He spotted it
within just a few moments of entering the lot, parked discreetly some fifty yards down from his own vehicle.

Jarvis strode brazenly down the lot toward the GMC and
fixed his gaze on the shadowy form of the driver inside. He

got no closer than thirty yards before he saw the driver's head turn in apparent panic as he started the engine, and then faced a dilemma.

Traffic was flowing through the parking lot toward Jarvis, who had picked his point of entry deliberately as far to the right of his own vehicle as possible, giving any watching spooks little opportunity to get away without being identified. The GMC pulled out. The driver clearly wanted to turn left away from Jarvis but was forced by the cars moving through the lot to join the flow toward the nearest exit.

Jarvis waited until the GMC was almost level with him before he leapt out into the center of the road, his cellphone in his hand with the video function running. The driver ducked his head aside and tried to hide his features, but it did him little good as the GMC lurched to a halt in front of Jarvis.

The old man scanned down to record the vehicle's plates, although he knew that by the evening the GMC would have been dismantled into spare parts and sold to merchants across the breadth of the country. The CIA was nothing these days if not thorough.

Jarvis leaned against the hood of the vehicle and smiled in at the driver.

'You've been made, son, because you're an amateur,' he said to the man, who refused to make eye contact. 'I'm guessing that your boss back at the CIA will be seriously pissed about it, so I'll make this easy on you. You drive around the lot here and park somewhere else, sit there for three hours, and I'll make sure that this film never makes it back to the CIA, okay?'

The driver peeked at him sideways, suspicious.

'I'm not the main mark of this observation cell,' Jarvis said, and waved his cellphone at him. 'All you tell them on the radio is that I'm still in the Capitol. If you tell them that I've left I'll broadcast this across the entire intelligence community. You'll be assigned to an administration desk in an Alabama backwater by tomorrow morning. Catch my drift?'

The driver looked at Jarvis for a moment longer and then nodded once.

Jarvis pushed off the GMC's hood and walked to his car.

As he drove out of the lot, he saw the GMC parked way back in the distance behind him, and that was where it stayed.

47

ADEN, VIRGINIA

Natalie saw the pillar of oily black smoke smeared across the afternoon sky five miles before she reached the scene of the wreck.

Two fire trucks and an ambulance were parked by the side of the road, which was shut off to traffic by two patrol vehicles on either side. Natalie had managed with a quick telephone call to her Capitol office to gain access to the accident itself, the state troopers reluctantly waving her through. Rikard had obviously not yet managed to have her name wiped from the system, although she felt certain that before sundown any authority she had would be erased from existence.

Ben Consiglio's pool car was a smoldering black wreck of tortured metal that sat on the rims of its wheels amid a sea of white foam sprayed by the emergency crews when they'd arrived on the scene.

Natalie felt a plug of nausea lodge in her throat as she detected the acrid stench of burning chemicals, molten plastic and rubber. A dull gray haze hung in the air around the vehicle like a chemical halo.

Natalie approached a group of paramedics clustered nearby, sipping coffee from a thermos flask. They saw her approaching and quietened down as the senior man among them stepped forward.

'Natalie Warner,' she said, 'I'm a friend of the driver of the vehicle. Is he . . .?'

The paramedic's features were strained.

'We found the remains of some clothing in and around the vehicle, ma'am,' he said softly. 'They've been bagged for forensics, but if you could identify them for us?'

Natalie nodded, not able to find the strength to say anything as she followed the paramedic to the rear of the ambulance, where a number of scorched items of clothing were laying in clear plastic bags. In an instant she recognized part of Ben's jacket, and what was clearly a scorched and tattered white shirt.

Natalie sucked in a deep breath of air and turned away as the nausea swilling in her stomach intensified. Hot tears scalded the corners of her eyes as she put her hand to her mouth and struggled to keep her breathing under control.

'That's his shirt and jacket,' she confirmed in a whisper.

The paramedic nodded and gestured to one of his men.

'We've got an identification, Ben Consiglio, works in DC,' he said. 'Soon as the vehicle cools down we'll find him and get him out.'

Natalie blinked her tears away and turned to the paramedics.

'He's still in there?'

'I believe so, ma'am,' he replied. 'The vehicle burned with extreme ferocity, much more than I've ever encountered before in a vehicle wreck. Our hoses weren't having much of an effect, so standard procedure is to drench the surrounding area to prevent the fire spreading and then let it burn itself out.'

Despite herself, Natalie's eyes flicked across to the burning wreck.

'Jesus,' she muttered to herself. 'It was supposed to be me coming out here.'

'Ma'am?' the paramedic said. 'It's normal for people to find a way to blame themselves for the loss of life, but believe me this happens every day somewhere in every county. It's a hit-and-run wreck, and there's absolutely nothing that you or anybody else could have done about it.'

Natalie blinked away some of her tears, knowing that he was right.

'Did anybody get an ID on the other vehicle?'

'Sure did, ma'am,' he replied, and gestured across the road. 'It's against the shoulder, right over there. Weird, though – we can't get identification for the driver. The vehicle's not in our database or on the police files.'

Natalie turned away and walked around the wide patch of churning foam surrounding the burning pool car. She was halfway around when she caught sight of the abandoned sedan on the shoulder opposite. Her heart skipped a beat as she laid eyes on it.

A blue Cadillac Catera.

Natalie began walking quickly toward it as she fished her cellphone out of her pocket. She flipped through a series of images, selected one of them and zoomed in. She read the license plate of the blue sedan that had followed her earlier the day before over the Potomac, and then looked at the abandoned sedan before her.

Same plate. Same vehicle.

Natalie slowly turned around and looked again at the burning pool vehicle and the tire marks on the road that betrayed where the accident had taken place. She walked across to them and then turned toward the scene of the accident.

She saw the marks left by Ben Consiglio's car as it had suddenly locked up and skidded hard left. Ahead of her, the asphalt glittered where thousands of tiny pieces of glass had scattered when the windows in Ben's car had imploded under the impact. A few scattered chunks of fender plastic and chrome trim littered the side of the road.

'Ben travels along here,' she murmured to herself as she walked the course of his car, 'then suddenly brakes and swerves left toward the opposite lane.'

She looked up. Ben's burning car was facing her on the opposite side of the road, and although the foam blocked some of her view she could see enough of the tire marks to tell that it had spun through a hundred-eighty degrees and come to rest where it was.

The sedan, on the other hand, was sitting nose-first into the shoulder, its passenger-side front fender mangled and warped but otherwise undamaged.

And there were no tire marks on the road. No attempt to avoid a collision.

'It swerved deliberately toward Ben,' she went on to herself, voicing her thoughts aloud. 'Hit him, then stopped here.' She walked to the driver's side of the vehicle. 'The driver gets out, and does what?'

The soft earth of the verge bore a couple of footprints heading back onto the road. Which meant that the driver had gotten out and walked back to Ben's vehicle, then presumably vanished.

Natalie didn't need to think about it anymore. Ben had been the victim of a deliberate attack, one probably meant for her. But for anybody to have known he would be coming out here and would in fact pass this spot meant that the killer must have been told about it. Natalie felt a chill run down her spine as she realized that only one person could have known about this, the same person that had been blocking her investigation from the very start.

Guy Rikard.

Natalie rushed across to the Virginia state troopers standing guard near the wreck. Out here, she felt confident enough that they were far enough removed from the Capitol to not be in the thrall of the CIA or anybody else. She showed them her phone and the pictures of the blue sedan from earlier in the day.

'This guy followed me for almost an hour this morning, and it was me who was supposed to come out here this afternoon,' she explained. 'I work for Congress on a team investigating illegal activity by the intelligence community, and we've learned that we're being followed day and night by government agencies that presumably want to prevent us from uncovering too much about their activities.'

The trooper looked at the photograph of the car.

'I appreciate what you're saying, ma'am, but that car could have been driving quite innocently across the Potomac earlier in the day. It could have been stolen since. There's nothing to link it to this accident.'

'No there isn't,' Natalie agreed, and then flicked to the next picture on her cellphone. 'But you guys can't trace the car to a driver.'

Natalie held the picture up to the two troopers, that of the sedan's driver from the previous day. The long, gaunt face was half in shadow but the features were clearly recognizable.

'Good enough for you?' she asked them.

'Damn straight,' the trooper said, and pulled out his own cell. 'Send me the images you have to my cell and we'll get them distributed.'

Natalie did as she was asked and then looked at Ben's burning car. Her cellphone started ringing in her pocket. She looked at it, and frowned. It wasn't a number she recognized. She looked at the cops: if there was ever a place that she was safe, this was it. She shut off the call.

'This was a deliberate attack,' she said to the officers, 'and I think I know who orchestrated it.'

The troopers looked at her expectantly.

'Two men,' she said. 'Guy Rikard, my boss and the only person who knew that Ben would be here this afternoon, and Douglas Jarvis, a senior security specialist at the Defense Intelligence Agency. It's my belief that they're working together to silence anybody who gets too close to whatever they're up to.'

48

NEZ PERCE NATIONAL
FOREST, IDAHO

The interior of the mine was an inky black void that smelled heavily of mold and dust. Ethan glanced behind him to the last pale light from outside that was visible through the entrance some fifty yards away.

In front of him, Kurt Agry and the soldiers advanced with their rifle-mounted flashlights cutting through the dank darkness like strobes in a damp, cold nightclub.

'What would this thing be doing coming in here?' Lopez wondered out loud.

Her voice sounded hollow and rolled back and forth in the tunnel. Ethan looked up at the roughly hewn walls around them.

'Shelter, maybe,' he replied. 'A nest, some kind of lair?'

Ahead, Kurt Agry's voice cut through the darkness.

'We've got a door up ahead,' he said.

Ethan looked up in surprise as the flashlight beams bounced and reflected off a steel panel that blocked the mine ahead. A thick blast door hung on its hinges, the handles smeared with blood that had dried long ago.

'It went in there?' Lopez asked.

Duran Wilkes peered into the gloom within, the flashlight beams reflecting off metallic objects but nothing that appeared to have fur or eyes.

'I ain't sure,' he replied. 'Lot of tracks comin' in and out, but nothin' I can be certain is fresh. No weather underground.'

'No,' Ethan agreed, 'but that doesn't hide the smell.'

The odor was faint but unmistakeable, the taint of unwashed skin and fur drifting in the darkness.

'Jesus, now what?' Proctor asked. 'You want us to actually go in there?'

'You can do what you goddamned want,' Duran said, and got up to move forward into the gloom.

He was stopped by Kurt Agry's firm hand on his shoulder. The soldier looked at him.

'You can go in, but how about we make things a little safer first?'

Kurt hefted a flash-bang grenade in front of Duran's face, and the old man nodded and covered his eyes.

'Fire in the hole,' Kurt whispered urgently, then pulled the grenade's pin and tossed it into the darkness. The device clattered on what sounded like a tiled floor as Ethan and the entire group covered their eyes.

A bright flare of light and a deafening bang shuddered through the mine as the grenade detonated, and in a rush Kurt and his soldiers charged into the darkness ahead, followed by Duran and Ethan.

Flashlight beams sliced through the gloom and the smell

of decay became stronger as they moved into the room. Ethan glimpsed what looked like multiple glass doors, all of them shattered, the soldier's boots crunching on broken glass that littered the floor.

'Some kind of hazardous materials facility,' Kurt Agry said as he swept the room with his flashlight. 'Those glass doors were a pressure barrier, to keep air in and prevent toxins from escaping.'

Ethan watched as Lopez glanced back at the steel wall and hatch, and then approached it. The hinges were bent outward as though warped by an incredible amount of pressure. She touched her hand to them as Ethan looked at the twisted metal bolts and the warped edges of the doors, and then Lopez realized what had happened.

'This wasn't a break-in,' she said. 'Something broke out.'

Duran squatted down and looked at the glass on the floor.

'She's right. It came through here,' he said. 'Picked up bits of glass on its feet as it went. But all of the rest of the glass is on the outside of the pressure hatch, not the inside. Something crashed through here and killed everybody that got in its way.'

Ethan looked back out of the doors to the open mineshaft entrance fifty yards away.

'We should seal these doors shut, keep our tail clear.'

Kurt Agry nodded, and together the soldiers heaved the warped doors closed, then picked up the bent and battered steel bars that had secured the doors and wedged them back into their holders. A thin gap in the battered doors allowed the cable from Jenkin's camera outside into the room.

The soldiers glanced nervously at each other. Kurt Agry pointed ahead. 'We push on.'

Ethan followed as they stepped through the shattered glass doors and entered a narrow corridor of modern-looking paneled walls. The combined flashlight beams illuminated the corridor with shards of white light that reflected off the polished panels.

Ethan spotted smears of blood along the floor, some of them handprints that trailed finger lines along the tiles, the old blood black in the harsh beams of the flashlights. Ahead the corridor opened out into a large room, the flashlights glinting off darkened monitor screens and what looked like a large yellow sack.

Kurt and his men rushed the room at once and fanned out as Ethan and Lopez followed.

They entered what looked like a command center. The room was round, maybe fifty feet across. Computer terminals were mounted into the walls, overturned office chairs littering the floor. Ethan glimpsed a couple of shattered plasma screens, what looked like freezers filled with vials of obscure, colorful liquids, and two large reclining seats with headphones and large helmets dangling from cables beside them. Three further corridors led away from the room, one on either side and a third that led deeper into the facility. In the center of the room was an oval table covered with discarded bits of paper, files and randomly scattered pens and clipboards.

Upon the table lay Simmons's remains, the yellow body-bag tossed aside nearby. In the cold, harsh light of the beams his body looked strangely glossy, reflecting the light as though wet. It was only a moment later that Ethan realized why.

'Oh, Jesus.'

Proctor turned away and gagged a thin stream of bile that splattered onto the tiles at his feet. Ethan just managed to hang onto the contents of his stomach as he looked at the corpse.

Simmons's body was a mass of flesh and bone that remained intact despite having been methodically stripped of its skin. Like some macabre museum waxwork, the soldier's entire innards were displayed. In the wavering flashlight beams he could see the glistening shape of the muscles, tendons and even arteries that sagged from the bones. The soldier's eyes stared like bright white orbs at the ceiling above, lifeless and yet wide open as though alive, and his teeth were white and bared where the lips had receded postmortem.

The dead man's skin lay in tattered strips and ribbons on the floor or dangled like gruesome banners from the table on which he lay.

Dana Ford stepped up to the corpse.

'Ritualistic skinning,' she murmured. 'I've read of this before. Humans have performed precisely the same procedure on victims both dead and alive throughout history.'

'Why would it do that to him?' Lopez uttered, her normally dark features ashen. 'He's gone. There's nothing to gain.'

'Revenge,' Proctor muttered, gulping down water from a bottle. 'To deny the victim his skin, to leave him naked and defenseless. It's another form of stress relief.'

'Christ,' one of the soldiers muttered, 'what the hell is this place?

Ethan scanned the walls of the control center and spotted a fuse box on one wall, the yellow and black warning graphics easily visible. He made his way over and yanked the box open.

A series of columned fuses labeled with locations filled the box, many of them tripped. Ethan tried a handful of them but nothing reacted in the building, the lights remaining dark.

'Look for an emergency power source,' Lopez said. 'Place as remote as this must have run off generators and would have had some kind of back-up system.'

'Fuel oil,' Kurt Agry agreed.

Ethan scanned the fuses and spotted two named E1 and E2 at the bottom of the columns. He reached out and flipped them both.

A distant rattle echoed through into the control center from the adjoining corridors, spluttered for a few moments and then leveled out into a steady hum. Above their heads a series of emergency lights flickered into life on the walls, half of them white and half of them red, casting feeble patches of light across the room.

'Like being in a friggin' submarine,' Lopez uttered and glanced at the huge dissection tables. 'This place gives me the creeps.'

'You and me both,' Ethan agreed as he looked around. 'I'm guessing that this thing wanted us to come here. Question is, why?'

Duran's old features were grotesquely half-lit by the glow from one of the red emergency lights as he turned to look at Ethan.

'I don't care. Either it gives up Mary or it dies.'

'You've changed your tune,' Kurt Agry said as he looked

around the room. 'Thought we were all for treating it like an innocent animal?'

Duran glared at the soldier. 'That was before it started acting like a human being.'

Kurt grinned tightly but said nothing in reply. Ethan looked around at the control room.

'This place must have cost a fortune to set up, and the locals sure didn't know about it.'

'Or the sheriff,' Lopez agreed. 'Place like this would need some serious finance, good security, a way of keeping people out.' She looked at Ethan. 'You thinking what I'm thinking?'

'Military,' Ethan agreed as he paced around the room and came to a stop, 'maybe government sponsored. Either way, I know this wasn't a corporate gig.'

'How do you know?' Klein asked.

Ethan lifted his boot and kicked a large metallic object across the floor. It slid across the polished tiles and clattered against a wall. Klein looked down at the M-16 rifle, the barrel of which was bent over as though twisted in a vice.

'Could have been bought on the black market,' Kurt Agry said.

Ethan nodded. 'And this guy?'

He pointed down to the corner of the room where a body lay slumped against the steel wall units. Kurt's men hurried around to stare at the remains. The dead soldier was dressed in full disruptive-pattern material combat fatigues, and on his shoulder was a distinctive Stars and Stripes patch. His face was an unrecognizable, bloodied pulp of smashed bone and ripped flesh.

'Mercenary,' Kurt replied, turning away. 'Probably an amateur, that's why he went down.'

'Like your lieutenant was?' Lopez challenged. The soldiers
all turned to glare at her, but Lopez stood her ground. 'Stop
bullshitting us, Kurt, you know what this is all about.'

'I don't know anything about this place!' Kurt shouted at
her.

The control room echoed with the sound of his voice,
stark against the lonely silence haunting the abandoned facility. The echo of his voice rolled away and then seemed to
bounce back toward them. Ethan stared at Kurt for a long
moment, and then he heard it. A distant voice, something or
someone calling out.

'You hear that?' he asked.

The group stood in silence for a few moments, and then
the distant cry sounded again. A woman's voice. Duran was
moving before he'd gotten her name fully out of his mouth
as he charged toward one of the laboratory exits, the one that
led deeper into the mountain.

'Mary.'

49

Kurt Agry leapt over one of the table tops and dropped down in front of Duran Wilkes, bringing the old man up short with the barrel of his rifle.

'Get out of my way!' Duran yelled at him.

'Stand down, old man,' Kurt growled. 'We don't know what's down there.'

'*Mary's* down there!' Duran bellowed, and raised his own weapon toward Kurt.

'Don't do it!' Kurt shouted, as the other soldiers turned their rifles on Duran.

'That's enough!' Lopez snapped, and pushed herself between them both. 'Put your weapons down, now, both of you!'

Kurt kept his rifle up. 'Get out of my way.'

'Like hell,' Lopez shot back at him.

Kurt's men switched their aim to Lopez. Ethan stepped forward and aimed his own M-16 at Kurt Agry. The soldier glared at him from the corner of his eye.

'Seriously, Warner? You better be ready to pull the trigger.'

'This is getting us nowhere!' Lopez yelled. She reached out

and bashed Ethan's rifle down with one hand, but kept her gaze on Kurt. 'We've got to find Mary.'

'You both said it-yourself,' Kurt replied, 'this thing led us down here. It's a trap.'

'She's just a child,' Duran pleaded.

'Then more fool you for bringing a kid on an expedition like this!' Kurt yelled. 'You're not my responsibility.'

'That's exactly what we are,' Ethan growled. 'Or are we, Kurt? Why are you really here?'

Jenkins's shout cut Kurt's reply off.

'We've got company!'

Ethan looked at Jenkins, the soldier not focusing on the room around them but peering into the tiny screen in front of his left eye.

'You see it?' Kurt demanded.

'I saw something come by,' Jenkins replied. Ethan detected a tremor in his voice. 'Christ, it was fast, just a huge blur.'

Kurt was about to reply when something smashed into the doors behind them with a crash that echoed away through the facility down endless empty corridors. Ethan whirled around in shock as the steel doors shuddered and then warped to the sound of screeching, rending metal being tortured under immense pressure.

'It's coming in!' Lopez shouted. 'It got behind us!'

'Secure the door!' Kurt yelled.

The soldiers rushed forward as one and slammed into the door, heaving it shut as their boots slipped and slid on the tiles. Ethan dashed in behind them and leaned his weight into the steel. The huge doors rumbled and buckled under the competing forces as Proctor and Dana joined in.

The door was open by a three-inch crack, the steel bars bending under the stress. Ethan heaved against them, his face inches from the darkness beyond. In the dull light he saw something glinting there, and focused on a mass of wiry russet-brown hair bulging into the gap. The breeze blowing in from the mine entrance stank of sweat and he coughed as his eyes automatically flicked upward into the darkness.

A single point of reflected light glowed as it looked right back down at him, touched with a soft hint of red. Ethan felt his guts convulse as the eye glared for a moment longer and then suddenly the doors slammed shut, the pressure released.

Ethan and the soldiers slumped against the doors, breathing heavily as they struggled to regain their composure. Kurt Agry gestured to the doors with a jab of his thumb.

'That's our only route out of here. Damned thing must've slipped out before we got in.'

Ethan nodded as he wiped sweat from his brow. 'We can worry about that later. Right now, we need to find . . .' He looked up. 'Where's Duran?'

Kurt took one look across the room and cursed. The old man had disappeared and Lopez was standing over the dead soldier's corpse.

'Damn it, where the hell did he go?' he yelled.

'Down the south corridor,' Lopez said. 'Let's split up, it'll be quicker.'

'The hell you will,' Kurt snapped. 'You'll stay here. We'll do the searching.'

'Don't be such an ass,' Lopez uttered. 'Ten minutes ago you didn't want anybody to go looking for Mary. Now you want to find Duran in a real hurry. What the hell's going on here?'

Kurt Agry didn't reply to her as he checked the magazine on his rifle. Ethan decided to make the decision for him.

'We go together,' he said. 'That way, you get to see what we're doing and we get to help. Good enough?'

The soldiers all looked to Kurt. Their officer slammed the magazine back into his rifle, cocked the weapon, and gestured to his men to follow him with a flick of his head.

'Fine, let's cover this door and then move out.'

Ethan helped the soldiers as they hauled the large, heavy table with Simmons's mutilated remains on it across the room and into position in front of the main exit. Ethan seriously doubted that the weight of the table would stop the creature outside from coming in, but it would slow it down enough to give them some kind of warning.

If, he wondered, it intended to let them out at all.

'This way,' Kurt waved them forward in a whisper.

Kurt led the way out of the control room and down the main corridor where Duran must have gone, in the direction of the cries of his granddaughter. Ethan watched as Kurt and his men picked their way down the corridor with military precision, moving from cover to cover in natural alcoves in the walls where bare rock had been hewn away by the blows from ancient pickaxes.

The corridor was entirely black, devoid of the emergency lights that illuminated the main chambers. Ahead, perhaps fifty yards away, Ethan could see a dim rectangular light that was another door into what he presumed was another chamber. The soldiers moved forward until they held position just outside the chamber.

As Ethan followed, he felt a gentle tug on his arm. Lopez

looked at him and opened her left hand. In her palm lay a
small access card. Ethan realized that she must have palmed
it from the dead soldier in the control center. He nodded but
said nothing as they moved on.

Kurt made hand signals to his men, and on a silent count
of three they rushed into the chamber with their weapons
pointed ahead.

The room was a large laboratory, roughly the same size
and shape as the command center, abandoned like the rest
of the facility. In the center of the laboratory were three dissection tables, each at least twelve feet long and festooned
with a mess of thick steel-reinforced belts that dangled from
the edges, the buckles glinting in the flashlight beams. In
one corner stood a battery of computer servers, their once
blinking lights dark now. Beyond the laboratory three
doors led off in different directions even deeper into the
mountain.

Then he saw Mary, sprawled across one of the tables and
staring up at the ceiling. Duran dashed to her side and lifted
her up. Mary appeared to emerge from her catatonic state
and flung her arms around him, sobbing uncontrollably as
Kurt's men's flashlights converged on them.

'She okay?' Kurt asked, peering at the girl.

Duran forced himself to release her, tears streaming freely
down his face as he looked Mary over and nodded.

'She's not harmed,' he said in a hoarse, choked voice, and
wiped his eyes as he looked at her. 'You okay, honey?'

Mary nodded but her eyes were wide with terror. Lopez
moved forward without hesitation and took one of the girl's
hands in hers.

'What happened, Mary?' she asked her. 'What brought you here?'

Mary's jaw began working though she could not speak, her throat constricted from the adrenaline rushing through her system, supercharged with fear and anxiety. When a word finally came out it was broken and ragged.

'Sasquatch.'

Ethan watched as Lopez gently prodded.

'The creature that's been hunting us, you saw it, right?'

Mary nodded, fresh tears trickling down her cheeks. Duran opened a water bottle and offered it to her. Mary took the bottle and gratefully gulped down mouthfuls as Proctor, Dana and the soldiers gathered around her.

'What did it look like?' Dana whispered, a mixture of fascination and fear etched across her features.

Mary stopped drinking and sucked in a huge lungful of air as she began to regain control.

'Big,' she said finally. 'Huge. Nine feet tall. It couldn't walk upright in here.'

Ethan's eyes flicked up to the ceiling, a good eight or nine feet high, probably originally that size to allow for mining machinery to pass into the mountain to the rock face.

'Where did it come from?' Lopez asked. 'When it took you?'

'It was behind me,' she replied. 'I never heard it there. Never saw it. Must have been there all the time.'

'Downwind of us,' Kurt said, looking across at Ethan. 'It was probably watching us set that trap for it.'

'Killed an elk and set it up as bait,' Lopez agreed, looking over her shoulder as though the creature were waiting for them in the shadows. 'It's one step ahead of us all the time.'

'Did you see its face?' Proctor asked, excited again now.

Mary nodded, and for a long moment she did not speak, but when she did her words were distant.

'It's not like us,' she whispered. 'It has a face like ours and its skin is like ours but it's dark brown, like leather, like it's been sunburned. And its eyes are black and red, like they're bloodshot, and they're strange, empty.' Mary focused back on the room around her and looked at her grandfather. 'Like it's got no soul.'

Ethan looked at Duran. 'Some animals have red eyes, don't they?'

'Foxes, bats, some raccoons,' the old man nodded.

'It's caused by the *tapetum lucidum*,' Dana explained, 'a layer of tissue in or behind the retina of nocturnal animals. It's the same thing that sometimes causes eye-shine in animals when people take photographs of them, because it reflects light back through the retina and increases the light available to the photoreceptors, giving superior night vision.'

'Some people with severe albinism have red eyes,' Proctor said, 'due to low levels of melanin. Light passes through the iris's blood-rich choroid and is then reflected back out. But this thing clearly wasn't albino.'

'It might have evolved a blood-rich retina and iris though,' Dana suggested, 'as an alternative means to gather light at night.'

'This isn't the time for a science lesson,' Agry cut across them, and looked at Mary. 'What I want to know is why didn't it kill you?'

Mary shook her head and shrugged.

'It barely even looked at me,' she said. 'Just carried me up here and dumped me on this table.'

Ethan thought about Jesse MacCarthy, who had fled from this very same creature, been caught but then allowed to continue his near-suicidal flight through the mountains back to Riggins.

'It spared you on purpose,' he said finally.

'You figure that how?' Lopez asked.

Ethan looked around them at the control room.

'This thing tore a park ranger and Cletus MacCarthy to pieces, but then let Jesse MacCarthy go. Jesse runs to the police and we get sent out here to search for Cletus's remains.' Ethan looked at them all. 'It then herds us all to this spot, either by violence or by indirect coercion. It abducted Mary because it knew we would follow her. She's the youngest and the most vulnerable.'

Kurt Agry frowned at him.

'What possible reason could it have for bringing us all up here on purpose?' he muttered. 'Damn thing wants to be left alone; it wouldn't be risking its neck to get us here.'

Ethan nodded, his mind racing. 'That's what bothers me.'

Kurt Agry checked his watch.

'It'll be dark outside by now,' he said. 'Best thing we can do is hunker down here for the night. Archer, you're on point. That corridor outside the control room is a natural choke point: keep it covered and blow the shit out of anything that tries to get through those doors.'

The soldier hurried out of the control room, and Kurt looked at the rest of his men.

'Search the facility,' he ordered. 'I want to know what's in every room, understood? Report back here when you're done.'

His men responded instantly and jogged out of the laboratory. As soon as they were gone, Kurt turned and walked across to the computer servers in the corner of the laboratory. He reached up and touched them, then began searching around the edges.

'What are you doing?' Lopez asked.

Kurt replied over his shoulder. 'My job.'

Ethan watched for a moment as the soldier moved methodically around the server, his hands following panel lines in the matt black surfaces. He located a panel in the side of one of the servers and pulled it out, exposing a series of power sockets. Kurt stood up and surveyed the laboratory.

'You knew this place was here, Kurt,' Ethan said finally. 'You were briefed on how to locate the power sockets on those servers, so you could jury-rig them and then download whatever data they hold.'

Kurt didn't respond. Instead, he reached into a pouch on his webbing and produced a long cable. He plugged one end into the server's power socket and then lay the coiled cable down on the floor.

Lopez's voice sounded loud in the relative silence.

'What are you going to do?' she asked.

Kurt was about to respond when Milner burst into the laboratory.

'Sir, you need to see this,' he said breathlessly. 'We found Cletus MacCarthy.'

50

Kurt strode out of the laboratory and followed the eastern corridor. Ethan fell into line behind him, walking through alternating pools of red and white light as their boots echoed down the corridor. Ahead, he saw Milner and Klein come to a halt and look down at the floor.

Kurt Agry stopped beside them with Ethan.

A human arm lay twisted and mangled on the tiles amid a congealed pool of blood that looked black under the weak lighting. Ethan could see that it had been torn from its shoulder socket, frayed tendons and ripped muscle spilling onto the tiles.

'There's more,' Klein said. 'Leading down the corridor.'

Ethan followed them with Kurt, Lopez just behind him. Proctor's voice echoed down the corridor from the laboratory where he stared vacantly at the severed limb.

'I'll keep watch. Out here.'

The soldiers stepped over another grotesquely mutilated arm lying in the corridor, this one lanced by snapped bones that had punched through the skin. Ethan gave the remains a wide berth, along with the leg that they found further down.

'Jesus,' Kurt muttered. 'He's been ripped apart.'

Ethan called out to the soldiers just ahead. 'How do you know this was Cletus MacCarthy?'

The two men stopped at a door at the end of the corridor, their flashlights pointing down to an object on the floor at their feet. Ethan slowed as he reached the door and stared down at the remains.

'That's how,' Lopez said softly.

Cletus MacCarthy's bruised, slouching torso lay propped against the steel door, above it his face a gruesome mask of blood and splintered bone. His eyes had rolled up into their sockets and his jaw hung slack, filled with a thick and swollen tongue that poked from between his lips. Completely naked, the skin had been ripped from his chest and abdomen and lay scattered around his remains.

Ethan tore his gaze from the corpse and looked up at the door. It was heavy like the main entrance to the facility, and had a three-bar locking mechanism that appeared to be electronically controlled. With the power having been down the mechanism was stuck in position, the door locked shut. There were no manual locks, only a swipe-card activation device.

'What's in there?' Lopez wondered out loud.

'Must be important,' Ethan replied. 'It's the only door I've seen in here that's locked and needs an access card.'

'We need to figure out what else is down here before we start trying to break into anything,' Kurt said.

The sound of running boots interrupted him as Jenkins and Milner joined them. Milner looked down at the corpse and grimaced.

'Christ, is that the guy we've been looking for?'

'That's him,' Ethan confirmed. 'And it means that Jesse MacCarthy is innocent. He couldn't have killed the park ranger and his own brother, dragged him all the way up here and then got back into Riggins by morning.'

Corporal Jenkins looked at Kurt.

'We've completed the sweep. It's not a big place, seven rooms in all including this one, whatever's inside it.'

'Tell me,' Kurt snapped.

Ethan listened as Jenkins described the layout of the rooms.

The central core of the facility consisted of three large, round rooms hewn from the interior of the mountain in a line facing north–south. The main control room was first, connected to a corridor facing north that led to the laboratory with the huge seats in the center, and then a further corridor connected to a final room in the depths of the mountain that held a series of large containment cages.

'The cages are huge,' Jenkins reported. 'The kind of thing they put tigers in, but heavily reinforced.'

'What about the side rooms, like this one?' Kurt asked, and gestured to the locked door behind him.

'The control room and the laboratory each have two rooms flanking them, one each to the east and west. Those doors aren't locked. The control room leads onto a medical facility on the west side and a living space to the east, probably where the scientists who worked here bedded down. The laboratory leads onto this door, and on the other side is a store room. Nothing much there but racks of dehydrated food, water bottles, shit like that.'

'Self-contained facility,' Ethan said. 'Whoever was work-ing here was probably shipped in by night, stayed over for days or weeks before being pulled out again.'

Kurt didn't reply to Ethan, instead looking at his men.

'You didn't find any power generators?'

'Just the two that are running now,' came the reply from Milner. 'Diesel pumps, they're sealed into a wall cavity some-where above the laboratory. Looks like they're plumbed into what must have been the mine's ventilation shaft. The main generator is right out back. It's a battery system, completely out of juice now. My guess is this place has been out of com-mission for about two weeks.'

Ethan looked at Lopez.

'Whatever was in here broke out, killed everybody on its way and vanished. Somebody sends a team to clean up, they get wasted too. If this is government funded, there must be something up here that's important enough that they can't just level the place with an air strike to hide it.'

'So they send in an elite team instead,' Lopez replied as she put the pieces together and looked at Kurt. 'To grab the data, and then blow the place with the high explosives they're car-rying with them.'

Kurt, his face demonically half-lit by the emergency lights, lifted a service pistol and aimed it at them.

'That's about the size of it,' he said.

51

Ethan and Lopez walked out of the corridor and back into the laboratory with their hands in the air. Duran, Mary, Proctor and Dana stared in surprise as Kurt and his men followed them out, their weapons at the ready.

'I knew it,' Duran spat.

'Everybody, out back,' Kurt snapped.

His men fanned out across the laboratory in a loose phalanx with their weapons drawn, blocking escape. They advanced, forcing Proctor, Dana, Duran and Mary down the north corridor toward the rear of the facility. Ethan and Lopez followed, pacing down the narrow passage until they entered the third and final chamber.

Another pair of reclining seats dominated the first half of the chamber, each of them festooned with wires and strange devices that looked like helmets. Behind the seats was a large mesh fence and beyond that a series of huge cages that lined the rear wall of the chamber. There were no further exits or corridors. Ethan guessed it made sense that whatever was being held captive here would be at the very back of the facility. It only backfired when the creatures somehow escaped and were forced to fight their way out.

Kurt turned to Dana Ford but kept his weapon trained on Ethan and Lopez as he spoke.

'I want to know what was going on here,' he demanded. 'Tell me everything.'

Dana glanced nervously at Ethan as she spoke.

'Judging by the tables, the medical freezers and the seats I'd say it was clinical trials, maybe some sort of drugs testing. The subjects were strapped down and subjected to experiments, probably against their will.'

Ethan looked at the size of the seats. Far too large for a human and the helmets were slightly conical in shape and had large eye-shields attached.

'I'm beginning to figure out why these things hate humans so much.'

Duran glanced at the seats. 'I told you,' he said. 'There would be a reason why creatures like this would start tearing up hikers in the hills.'

Proctor lifted one of the helmets up and looked inside.

'Looks like a spatial-awareness shield,' he said.

'The hell's one of those?' Kurt asked.

'It's designed to deny the wearer any sense of where they actually are,' Proctor explained. 'The eye-shield prevents sight, obviously, while the earphones block all sound. Then images are played to the wearer through the eye shield.'

Ethan looked down at the seats. 'Looks like that's not all they were given.'

The ends of the cables were tipped with electrodes, sharp crocodile-clips that most likely had been attached to bare flesh.

Dana Ford looked at the clasps and Ethan saw her make a connection, one hand flying to her lips.

'Cerebral reprogramming,' she blurted.

Proctor nodded in agreement, speaking before Ethan or Lopez could ask Dana what she was talking about.

'Military-devised assimilation program,' he said. 'The subject is shown endless images of people, locations or whatever, and learns to associate them with either a threat or a welcome. So they'd show these things images of enemy soldiers or whatever, while subjecting them to electric shocks, therefore engendering in them a deep-rooted psychological hatred of enemy combatants.'

Dana lifted an intravenous line that was dangling down from one of the seats.

'Or show them images of their captors while putting drugs into their system to calm them, make them feel better, maybe just straight morphine or similar.'

Ethan quickly got it.

'Programming them to obey. But to what end?'

It was Duran Wilkes who replied.

'War,' he said simply. 'Men have done things like this for thousands of years.'

During his training as a US Marine at Quantico, Ethan and his fellow recruits had been taught about the history of warfare. Even modern combat sometimes made use of tactics developed by military legends such as Alexander the Great and Saladin. Alexander himself had made extensive use of elephants as a sort of ancient version of tanks, using their might and bulk to crush enemy warriors during battles.

'The American military has made use of all kinds of

animals to support troops in war zones,' Duran said bitterly. 'Dogs to sniff out explosives and take down enemy soldiers in the trenches of the First World War and pigeons trained to carry messages over long distances. They even placed pigeons inside cruise missiles after training them to peck at a screen if it was drifting off-course.'

'That's crazy,' Lopez muttered.

'You think that's nuts?' Duran said. 'The military once spent twenty million dollars on a project to implant cats with microphones, antennae and batteries in their chest and tails, then set them loose near the Russian Embassy in the hopes they'd be taken in, allowing the US to eavesdrop.'

Proctor nodded, examining a discarded syringe as long as a pen as he spoke.

'The US Navy regularly train dolphins to detect under-water mines on ships,' he said. 'It's been alleged that they've even trained the animals to *plant* mines on enemy ships, but the military denies it of course.'

'Some armies trained dogs to carry explosives on suicide missions into enemy troop formations,' Dana said. 'When it comes to winning wars there's not much that mankind won't stoop to.'

Ethan looked at the size of the tables in the laboratory.

'If one of these things were trained to obey US soldiers in a combat environment it could tear the crap out of enemy infantry, move freely at night, be hard to spot and almost impossible to shoot.' He shook his head. 'It would be a major tactical asset in the field.'

'So this stuff is being done out here because it's illegal,' Lopez said.

'Tests on animals are legal in this country,' Dana said, 'but the ways and means to do that testing is heavily regulated. The animals in question have to be under the care of a licensed and accredited veterinarian. Protocols have to be reviewed by an Internal Animal Care and Use Committee who have to agree that the tests are both humane and worthwhile, in that they would result in useful information being gained.' She looked at the room around them. 'I think it's obvious that whatever went on in here was neither humane nor worthwhile to science.'

'Especially,' Proctor said, 'if the work involved attempting to create para-humans.'

'What?' Kurt asked.

'A human-animal hybrid,' Proctor said, 'a chimera. Some work has already been done on mixing the genes and cells of different species. Mass production of spider-silk proteins for armour and insulin have been achieved by adding human genes to bacteria. The military have a long-standing interest in producing *bio-genetically* enhanced soldiers with greater endurance, strength and resilience to injury. Splicing sasquatch genes with those of a human could plausibly create such a chimera.'

'They'd never create a viable fetus,' Dana argued. 'Humans are genetically too distant from whichever ancestor sasquatch evolved from. But they could create tissues, muscles, bones and suchlike, which could then be grafted onto soldiers' bodies.'

'True,' Proctor said, 'but scientists have already found ways to enhance muscle mass by injecting gene-manipulated viruses. Researchers at the University of Pennsylvania have caused rat muscles to increase by up to thirty per cent in size using a gene called IGF1, and the enhancement lasted for the life of the animals. If the same procedure was used by borrowing genes from a sasquatch, they could bypass any evolutionary mating obstacle and simply insert the genes directly into troops, creating super-soldiers.'

'Who would most likely be involved in something like this?' Lopez asked, horrified.

Ethan already knew the answer but it was Duran Wilkes who replied.

'The CIA,' he said. 'They're the ones who have done all the strangest experiments in military history, on animals and on their own citizens. If this is the work of a government agency then that's where my money would be.'

'And if somebody exposed the operation,' Ethan said, and turned to Lopez, 'they'd be facing a huge backlash.'

'Randy MacCarthy,' Lopez replied. 'If he managed to get photographs of what was going on up here then the CIA would do just about anything to silence him, or anybody else who came wandering up too close to this site.'

'And the National Guard would take over the search for any missing persons,' Ethan went on, looking at Agry, 'which would then ensure that no civilian or park ranger accidentally stumbled on the site. The Guard wouldn't question an order from the Pentagon to stay away from this area.'

'And the rangers would be none the wiser,' Lopez agreed. 'The only people who would find themselves in trouble would be unfortunate hikers and tourists who strayed off the beaten track and somehow got too close—'

'They'd be silenced and disposed of,' Ethan finished her

sentence for her. 'Nobody would ever know anything and they'd be assumed to have died of exposure, injury or animal attacks.'

Lopez looked around at the ruined facility.

'And if something went wrong up here,' she said, 'then the Pentagon would have to send people to clean it all up and remove the evidence.'

'Top work,' Kurt Agry said. 'If I ever need a private investigator, I'll call you.'

'Who are you, really?' Ethan asked.

'Twenty-fourth Special Tactics Squadron, United States Air Force Operations Command,' Kurt Agry replied.

Ethan had heard of the 24th STS, a unit specializing in paramilitary operations and often tasked with high-value missions by the CIA.

'You're here to clear out and destroy any remaining evidence.'

'And we need to be getting along,' Kurt confirmed, casting a glance of distaste at the room around them. 'We've had enough delays already.'

'That's why you were in such a rush,' Ethan said to him. 'Why you didn't want to backtrack down the mountain with the lieutenant's body. You're on a deadline.'

Kurt nodded.

'Whole place is about to go boom, I'm afraid,' he replied. 'We're going to bring the whole damned mountain down on this place and seal it underground for about the next quarter of a million years. Our extraction is due to pull us out at first light.'

Ethan let a grim smile crack his jaw. 'And I guess we have to stick around for it.'

Kurt did not reply as his men joined him in the laboratory. He gestured with quick flicks of his gloved hand as he spoke.

'Separate them,' he ordered.

The soldiers barged between them, forcing them into two groups.

'This is a mistake, Kurt,' Lopez snapped at him. 'You're taking down the wrong people. You really believe that you're in control here? That you're alone in betrayal?'

'I'm not betraying anybody,' Kurt replied. 'I'm doing my job.'

'And so is the CIA,' Ethan shot back. 'My boss made a request for soldiers to escort us from the National Guard. That request was intercepted and your platoon sent in place of the reservists. Somebody up the line burned us. What makes you think that the same thing won't happen to you?'

The soldiers all stopped moving, Klein, Jenkins, Milner and Archer all looking at Kurt. The sergeant slapped a grin on his face but Ethan could sense the uncertainty in his voice.

'We're the ones doing the burning here, Warner, not you or anybody else.'

'This is a covert program,' Lopez intervened, 'probably classified at the highest level. You really think that the CIA is going to go out of its way to ensure a little team of soldiers survives this any more than some investigators and scientists? Wake up, Kurt!'

The sergeant shook his head.

'Our extraction is planned, and you're forgetting that we're carrying the explosives.'

'Get real,' Ethan shot back. 'My guess is this place will be hit with an air strike the moment you send the data from those servers back to the CIA. You get out, the extraction will most likely be an ambush to finish off any one of you left standing.'

'We'd hardly go to the extraction if we were bombed,' Jenkins pointed out.

'You got anywhere else to go?' Lopez challenged. 'You've been burned, just like us. We're in the same boat here.'

'That's an issue of perspective,' Kurt replied without interest.

'There's nothing to be gained from this, Kurt,' Ethan said, keeping his voice reasonable. 'We need to finish our job and get out of here, alive. Sooner we do that, the better I'll feel.'

'Your work is done,' Kurt snapped.

'This isn't you, Kurt,' Ethan said, searching the soldier's face. 'You were willing to go after Mary. Murder isn't your thing.'

'Obeying orders is my thing!' Kurt snapped. 'We're done here, Warner. All of you, turn around and keep your hands in the air.'

Ethan stared at the soldier for a long beat and then obeyed. Lopez stared at him in dismay.

'Seriously, you're going to just fold for this asshole?'

'I'd rather die in the blast than let that scum have the pleasure of shooting me,' Ethan replied. 'He's not worthy of pulling the trigger.'

'Shut up,' Kurt snapped, and jammed the muzzle of his rifle into Lopez's chest, forcing her backward until she staggered into a desk unit. 'Kneel down or I'll finish you right here and now,' he growled.

Lopez's eyes flashed with unconcealed fury, but she obeyed.

'Keep Warner and Lopez separate,' Kurt advised his men. 'Don't let them communicate.'

'At least let the girl go,' Duran pleaded. 'Mary's been through enough.'

Kurt did not look at the old man as he shouldered his rifle and replied.

'Her problems will soon be over, as will yours.'

'No doubt you'll be putting us in the cages,' Lopez uttered in disgust.

'No, although not by choice,' Kurt replied. 'Fortunately for you the cages are remotely locked and we haven't worked out how to open them, so you'll be held elsewhere.' He turned to his men. 'Duran, Mary and Warner go into the store room. Put Proctor, Lopez and Dana in the living quarters, and make damned sure all of the doors are secured.'

Ethan shook his head as he was gripped by the arm and led out of the room.

'You'll regret this, Kurt. Your men can't get out of here alone. Have you forgotten that creature is out there, waiting for you?'

Kurt did not look at Ethan as he replied.

'It'll be no match for our weapons. If we can't walk out, we'll shoot our way out.'

Kurt looked up as Duran Wilkes was led past him.

'Like I said,' Duran murmured softly, *you're* the real animals.'

52

While Kurt's men escorted everybody from the laboratory into the adjoining chambers and secured them there, he connected the computer server's power cable to a battery pack specially designed for the purpose of the mission. When his men returned, he gathered them together in front of the server.

'Okay, this is how we're going to do it.'

On the main table they had unloaded the entire contents of their weapons arsenal, a metallic mountain of assault rifles, pistols, ammunition magazines and explosive charges.

'We can't clear that creature out of the tunnel using explosives otherwise we might collapse it ourselves and block our escape, so we're reduced to small-arms fire until we're clear: then we blow the charges. Archer, you get the easy job. Stay here and cover the mine exit in case that *thing* tries to break in.'

Kurt turned to his other two men as Archer moved off.

'Klein, Milner, you're with me. We'll place the charges throughout the facility and set the timers.'

They nodded and gripped their rifles tighter.

'Once we're done,' Kurt went on, 'we're out of here. Check watches.'

Kurt called out the time and they synchronized together. He then flicked a switch on the battery pack and was rewarded with a loud beep from the servers and an array of lights flickering into life.

'Get the flash drives ready,' he ordered Jenkins. 'Let's get this over with and then get the hell out of here.'

Jenkins obeyed without question, unpacking from his bergen a glossy black portable hard drive the size of a large diary. He handed the drive to Kurt, who plugged it into the computer server's main panel.

Klein and Milner stared at Kurt. 'We can't send any data you pull from there. All of our communications gear was destroyed.'

'We're not sending anything,' Kurt replied.

It only took a moment for them to realize what he was doing.

'You think that Warner's right,' Milner said.

Jenkins and Klein stopped what they were doing and looked at Kurt. He checked the downloading data was being picked up by the portable hard drive, then turned and looked at them.

'You want to take the chance that he's wrong?'

'So what are we going to do then?' Jenkins asked.

Kurt gestured to the corridor that led to the control center and the mine entrance.

'We get this stuff downloaded and then we set the charges to blow the facility. We get the hell out of here and use copies of this data as insurance.'

Klein shook his head.

'Jesus, Kurt, we head back to our unit we'll be dead men.'

'They can't touch us as long as we've got this,' Kurt replied, tapping the hard drive.

'That's probably what Randy MacCarthy thought,' Milner pointed out. 'We all knew it was wrong to string up a civilian. Now look where it's got us.'

'Those were our orders!' Kurt growled. 'That's what you all signed up for. You got a problem with that now, that's too bad.'

Jenkins stood for a moment as though uncertain of whether to challenge his sergeant. The rest of the men watched him, waiting to see what he would do. When he spoke there was an edge of defiance in his tone.

'And what about the civvies, and Warner and Lopez?'

Kurt glanced down at the hard drive, checking its progress.

'They're a liability we can't afford. They walk out of here we compromise ourselves even further. They know enough about this place to expose it even if it's buried under rubble.'

'They're civilians,' Jenkins protested. 'We were assigned to protect them.'

'We were assigned to protect this facility!' Kurt shouted. 'We were compromised the moment Lieutenant Watson went soft on them! You'd listened to me, they'd have never made it up here and wouldn't be an issue now!'

'I didn't listen to you because you weren't in command,' Jenkins shot back. 'Since the lieutenant died we've gone from being an escort team to becoming an execution squad!'

'Randy MacCarthy died when Lieutenant Watson was still in command,' Kurt pointed out, dropping his voice to a reasonable volume. 'The mission is the priority, and our mission is to extract data from this facility and then blow it back into the Stone Age. It's also our best means of proving to the top brass that we're worth keeping alive. We got burned but we stuck to the mission regardless. If we run, if we break, then we'll be targets for the rest of our lives.' He stared Jenkins down. 'Question is, are you in or are you out? Because if you're out you won't last a day alone.'

Jenkins fumed on the spot, and glanced at Milner and Klein. Neither of them moved. The corporal rubbed his hand across his face.

'We can't shoot our way out of here,' he said finally. 'Duran Wilkes said our rounds won't stop that thing out there.'

Kurt winced and waved dismissively.

'We've got four M-16s. It's an animal, not a fucking tank. It'll go down just like anything else.'

'I agree,' Jenkins said. 'But it won't go down quick enough to stop it from breaching that door the moment we open it. Some wild animals survive for minutes, despite taking shots to the heart. They just keep on going, driven by the pain or whatever, like crazy folk. We can't just start shooting and hope we drop it. We want to get out of here, we need a clean shot, straight through the brain. We don't stall it, Kurt. We *kill* it.'

Kurt regarded the corporal for a moment. *Give him some slack and he'll start toeing the line.*

'You got any ideas?'

Jenkins took a breath and looked out toward the control center.

'The corridors from the medical center and the living

quarters open out on the control center. So does the southern corridor. We could shut down the majority of the lights,
set up in each of the three corridors and catch the thing in
a crossfire. The breeze from the tunnel entrance will put us
downwind of it so it won't smell us. It won't know we're
there.'

Kurt nodded and looked at the other men.

'There's only one thing missing,' he said.

'What's that?' Milner asked.

Kurt turned and strode toward the store chamber.

'Bait.'

53

'This isn't good,' Mary Wilkes said.

Ethan's mind raced as he searched the room for some way to escape.

The chamber was devoid of anything other than aluminum racking, the metal too soft and thin to be useful against solid walls and the steel door. A few dusty boxes of equipment adorned the racking. The floor was concrete and covered in dust, the ceiling just lightweight panels bolted into the bare rock above. A ventilation shaft high up on the rear wall of the chamber was only a few inches deep and two feet wide, not nearly large enough to clamber into and escape.

Duran Wilkes shook his head as he examined one of the boxes.

'It's not worth it, Ethan,' he said. 'Even if there was a way out, that sasquatch out there isn't going to let us leave.'

'It's not going to blow us up in here, though, is it?!' Ethan shot back. 'I'll take my chances.'

'Ethan's right,' Mary said. 'The sasquatch might attack, but those soldiers are definitely going to kill us.'

Ethan felt certain that Kurt's team were attached to the

CIA. Paramilitary teams spent a great deal of their time supporting the intelligence community when the need for subtle
observation and digital intervention was replaced by the need
for muscle and firepower. Kurt's team would not let them
leave the mine alive, for to do so would compromise them
if their parent agency had indeed burned them.

'If Kurt's on a deadline,' Duran asked, 'then what the hell
for? Why not just vaporize this place and be done with it?
Why send a special-ops team up here?'

'To keep an eye on us,' Ethan surmised. 'They probably
didn't expect us to find much, or hoped that we'd find Cletus
MacCarthy's remains before getting this far and then pull out.
That's what they wanted. They'd then be free to come in
here and do their job before the place was leveled.'

'They didn't bargain on us being hunted down by that
thing out there,' Mary Wilkes muttered. 'Which means they
probably weren't told much about it.'

Ethan nodded.

'Kurt was telling the truth,' he said in the darkness. 'He
doesn't know much about what's been happening in here.
He was probably told to expect resistance, but not from
whom or what.'

Duran opened one of the boxes and pulled out a large
flashlight. Ethan guessed it was maybe one of those million-
candle-power lights, probably used by sentries patrolling the
site. Duran humphed as though satisfied and set the flashlight
down on the racking.

'What are you going to do with that?' Ethan asked.

Duran shrugged and said nothing. Ethan studied the old
man for a moment before he decided to push his luck a little.

'What happened to your wife, Duran?' he asked.

The old man's eyes flicked up to look at Ethan, and Mary froze as she looked at her grandfather. Duran turned away from the flashlight as he spoke.

'She vanished,' he said, 'abducted by something just like I told you.'

'And you're an expert tracker,' Ethan pointed out. 'You telling me you didn't bother following the trail?'

Duran seemed to be having trouble breathing as though he were suddenly afraid. 'I didn't find a trail,' he said. 'There was nothing to follow.'

'And yet,' Ethan said, 'you claimed that your wife shot something, that you found blood on the rocks by the river. If something had bled, it would have left a clear trail for you.'

Mary was watching her grandfather silently. Duran sighed, some of the tension draining from his body as he replied.

'The trail only went as far as Fox Creek,' he replied. 'After that, there was nothing for me to follow.'

'So whatever captured your wife just stopped bleeding?' Ethan asked.

Duran shook his head. 'Somebody stopped it bleeding,' he said. 'My wife was not taken by an animal, Ethan. She was almost certainly taken by men, one of whom she wounded and who was patched up or otherwise carried out of there by his companions. The fact that they were professional enough not to leave a trail means they were trained.'

Ethan rubbed his temples and nodded as he put the rest of the story together.

'Troops, protecting this facility,' he said. 'They didn't know you were nearby, so they just took Harriet.'

Duran nodded, and then turned away from Ethan. Mary looked around at the facility.

'They must have done a lot of research here,' she said, changing the subject. 'It's probably why the sasquatch learned to hate humans so much all of a sudden.'

'Whatever happened here, it wasn't pretty,' Ethan agreed. 'Looks like the creature escaped and tore the hell out of everybody on its way out. After being cooped up in here and subjected to God knows what tests, I'm not surprised.'

Duran nodded.

'But that begs the question: how did it escape? This seems like a very secure facility.'

Ethan could not think of a way in which a powerful but supposedly dim-witted creature could have formulated an escape plan from such a secure base manned by armed guards. The escape must have been a surprise, catching the guards out.

'You think that Kurt and his men have been betrayed,' Mary said. 'But what about you? If your boss requested the soldiers, isn't he implicated too?'

'Maybe,' Ethan replied. 'But not directly. This is the work of somebody further up the chain of command.'

There could be little doubt that Jarvis's request for troops to support them out here would have gone through the Director of the DIA. At some point, perhaps with his knowledge, the escort team would have been replaced by the CIA-controlled STS, and the process of eliminating all witnesses to the secret program high in the Idaho mountains complete.

'Maybe Kurt and his men took down Randy MacCarthy too,' Duran suggested.

'I don't know,' Ethan said. 'Seems a little heavy-handed.'

'That's Kurt's goddamned signature,' Duran muttered bitterly.

'He wasn't in command of his unit when Randy died,' Ethan said. 'Lieutenant Watson was.'

'A far better man,' Duran replied, and then added, 'albeit a killer himself. It wouldn't have been hard to fake a suicide.'

'No,' Ethan agreed thoughtfully. 'Especially if they did it subtly enough that it seemed like an amateur job, maybe one of the locals and not a squad of elite troops. That would send the cops in the wrong direction.'

'Kurt Agry would do that,' Mary said. 'Kill an innocent civilian if he had to in order to complete his damned mission.'

'The man's a fool who's going to get us all killed in here, himself and his men included,' Ethan agreed, and gestured to the facility. 'That damned creature led us here on purpose, right? Whatever we're supposed to do, it ain't going to let us out until we've done it. I don't care how many weapons Kurt and his men possess, they're not in control here. It's got us right where it wants us.'

Duran shook his head slowly. 'Trust me, there's more than one of them out there.'

Ethan was about to respond when the chamber door unlocked and Kurt, Milner and Klein strode back inside, their features hard as iron.

'We've got a problem,' he said to Ethan.

Kurt yanked him to his feet and dragged him toward the exit corridor.

'Where are you taking him?' Mary demanded.

Kurt grinned over his shoulder at her. 'He's going to meet the natives.'

Ethan said nothing as Kurt pushed him ahead, the muzzle of his pistol never far from his side as they walked out through the laboratory and then on into the control center. Kurt prodded Ethan toward the table that had held Simmon's body. Ethan noted that the corpse had been moved and the table dragged back from the main door.

'Get on the table,' Kurt ordered him.

Ethan turned and faced the sergeant, but did not obey. 'The hell for?'

Kurt moved forward until his face was barely an inch from Ethan's.

'Because I fucking said so,' he hissed. 'You either get on here of your own accord or I'll break your arms and your legs and haul your sorry ass onto it. Understood?'

Ethan stared down into Kurt's raging expression and decided that he didn't have much choice in the matter. He was pretty sure that he could disarm Kurt, the soldier's fury clouding his judgement and putting the Beretta pistol easily within Ethan's reach. But there was no way he could take Kurt down and then shoot Klein and Milner before they retaliated. He knew without a doubt that they would shoot straight through Kurt in order to stop him, to avoid failing in their mission.

Ethan pushed Kurt away hard enough to make him stagger and then turned and climbed onto the table.

Kurt gestured to his men with a flick of his head and they instantly moved forward and began strapping Ethan to the seat using cables ripped from useless computer terminals.

'I don't know what you think this will achieve,' Ethan said, managing to keep his voice level despite the cold dread flooding his stomach. 'There's nothing that I can tell you that you don't already know.'

Kurt looked down at him for a moment and then smiled.

'Oh, don't worry, I don't have any questions for you.'

'Then what the hell are you doing?'

Kurt watched as the two soldiers stood back and checked the restraints, tugging on them before picking up their weapons again. He nodded at them, and they retreated back down the corridor into the facility. Kurt waited until they were gone before he moved forward to stand over Ethan.

'That thing out there,' he said, 'is in our way. I don't know why, but as long as those doors stay shut we can't do our job.'

Ethan thought for a moment.

'You can't blow the facility,' he said. 'No way out.'

'Top marks, Mr. Warner,' Kurt replied. 'We could go out there with all guns blazing and take it down, maybe, but I figure why waste the ammunition? Let's offer it some dinner and see if it sits down at the table, right in our sights.'

Ethan stared at Kurt for a long moment before he managed to get his breathing under control enough to respond.

'You're going to lure it in here into a crossfire,' he replied. 'And I'm the bait.'

'Yes, Ethan, you are.'

Kurt walked across to the steel doors and hauled the bars out from their mounts, then pulled the doors open, his rifle aimed out into the inky blackness beyond. Then he turned and stalked away into the darkness of the south corridor, leaving Ethan strapped to the table in full view of the mine entrance.

54

CORAL HILLS, MARYLAND

Natalie drove down between rows of battered clapperboard single stories that lined the steeply inclined street, searching for the address she'd gotten for the name deciphered from the files at the National Archives.

Coral Hills was a rundown residential area just to the southeast of the district border, where the Maryland side led down toward Joint Base Andrews Naval Air Facility and the capital beltway. There wasn't much here, but for the increase in drug-related homicide that kept the police departments on their toes.

Natalie spotted the home she was looking for and pulled into the sidewalk. The single story was painted an off-white that had faded over the years, the paint flaking away to reveal patches of undercoat. The two properties either side of it were well maintained with brickwork walls and broad lawns, but only a warped chain-link fence and weeds adorned the tiny house between them as Natalie pushed open a metal gate that squealed in protest as she passed through.

The porch was bare but for an old chair stacked with

frayed cushions. Natalie walked up to the shutter door and
rapped lightly on it. She waited and watched as someone
inside shuffled about and made their way to the porch. To
her surprise, she found herself looking down into a wizened
old face that peered up at her suspiciously through a crack in
the door, restrained by a thick metal chain.

'Hank Anderson?' she asked.

'Who are you?'

Anderson's voice was throaty. Crooked fingers grasped the
edge of the door and threatened to slam it shut at the slightest provocation.

'My name's Natalie Warner,' she replied. 'I work for
Congress.'

Anderson's face folded in upon itself in disgust and he
shoved the door shut. Natalie called through as she watched
the old man's silhouette turn and shuffle away.

'We're working on an investigation into corruption within
the intelligence community,' she called after him.

He kept walking.

'One of my colleagues has already been killed as a result of
the investigation. They're trying to silence us.'

He kept walking and turned out of sight. Natalie raised
her voice even further.

'MK-ULTRA is still active.'

Nothing but silence issued from the house. Natalie clenched
her fists in frustration and glanced around for some other
means of accessing the property. She considered smashing a
window when the front door suddenly snapped open in front
of her.

Anderson peered at her for a long moment before speaking.

'What would you know about it?'

Natalie took a breath and picked her words with care.

'A friend of mine vanished several years ago, and the investigation has uncovered links between her and her father, who
was a member of MK-ULTRA.'

'Who?' he demanded.

'Harrison Defoe.'

Anderson's eyes widened, and he hesitated for a moment
before he dropped the latch on the door and opened it.
Natalie walked in and saw Anderson peer suspiciously out of
the door again before closing and immediately locking it
behind her.

The house was as tiny inside as it looked from the outside,
more so because of the incredible amount of junk piled from
floor to ceiling in all of the rooms. Making it into the lounge
was an obstacle course in itself; Natalie was forced to step over
piles of boxes, newspapers and glossies to get through the door.

'Excuse the mess, obsessive-compulsive disorder,' Anderson
croaked in explanation. 'And I don't want to forget another
day like they made me forget all the others.'

Natalie looked at him curiously but said nothing as she
picked her way toward an armchair in one corner of the
lounge and perched on the edge. Anderson slumped with a
sigh onto a couch littered with copies of *National Geographic*.

'I get you anything?' he asked. 'Coffee? Juice?'

'I'm good,' Natalie decided, wondering if the juice in
Anderson's cooler would be as old as the 1982 copy of the
Washington Post on a coffee table next to her. 'I just need to
know about MK-ULTRA.'

Anderson humphed as though sick of the subject.

'Read the conspiracy websites or the books,' he replied. 'You'll find everything you need right there.'

'No I won't,' she responded. 'I'll find out about the MK-ULTRA from the 1970s, and that's not the one I'm interested in.'

'How did you know Harrison Defoe?'

'I didn't,' Natalie admitted. 'I knew his daughter, Joanna. She disappeared from Gaza City several years ago and hasn't been seen since.'

Anderson's wrinkled face creased into a faint smile.

'Ah, Joanna. I only met her the once when she was barely five years old. Harry was so proud of her.'

For a brief moment Natalie glimpsed the man that Anderson had once been, the bitter old eyes melting with warmth and the hard line of his narrow lips softening. Anderson noticed her gaze and the moment passed as though the warmth had been physically drained from his body.

'Harry died a few years back,' he said. 'Heart attack.'

'So it was said,' Natalie replied.

Anderson chuckled without mirth and waved one thin hand at her in dismissal.

'Harry wasn't assassinated,' he said. 'He was still a patriot despite what those bastards did to him. He would never have done anything to compromise security and they knew it. All he did was draw attention to the illegal aspect of CIA programs, not the fact that they were ultimately designed with the best intentions in mind: the protection of our country.'

'He testified against the CIA in front of the Senate,' Natalie pointed out, 'and spent most of his life railing against governmental corruption.'

'Yes, he did,' Anderson agreed, 'and quite rightly so. But he didn't slate government itself, or the CIA, or the fact that many covert operations have to stay out of the public eye for all kinds of reasons. Harry just wanted those reasons to be good ones, not the kind of betrayal that sent him into a god-damned Singapore prison.'

Natalie gathered her thoughts.

'Mr. Anderson, Joanna may have something to do with MK-ULTRA.'

Anderson's gray eyes narrowed. 'How so?'

'My entire family is under surveillance by the CIA,' she replied. 'We couldn't figure out why until we realized that they were not watching us, but were instead looking for Joanna, as though hoping she'd make contact with one of us.'

'You two were close?'

'Not as close as she was to my brother, Ethan,' Natalie replied. 'They were together for four years and worked as investigative journalists, exposing corruption in countries all over the world.'

Anderson slapped his thigh in apparent delight.

'Good old Jo,' he said. 'And good old Harry. He brought her up to continue his work, and, hell, she went and did just that.'

'And got herself abducted,' Natalie continued. 'Now my brother has vanished along with his work partner. My own colleague was killed this afternoon in a hit-and-run auto-mobile wreck, and the car that hit him spent much of this morning tailing me around DC. To cap it all, I've been con-veniently fired from my position by my boss just as I've collated enough evidence to expose the CIA's interference in our investigation and a possible homicide.'

Anderson thought for a moment.

'You think your boss is working for the CIA?'

Natalie inclined her head but said nothing.

Anderson raised an eyebrow. 'What do you want me for?'

'I want you to tell a Congressional committee and the CIA's Inspector General what happened to you when you were a part of MK-ULTRA, and to give them your best estimate of what such a program would be doing today if it were still active.'

Anderson chuckled, then the chuckle turned into a deep, rattling cough. He managed to bring himself back under control and looked at her with his rheumy old eyes.

'I'm dying, Miss Warner,' he said finally. 'Government's got nothing on me so I've nothing to fear from them. I'll testify if that's what you need, but I wouldn't have a clue what they might be up to right now if MK-ULTRA is still active.'

'You must have some idea,' Natalie pressed. 'You were there. You saw what happened.'

'Yes, I was,' Anderson agreed, 'but these are different times. The technology is so much more advanced. It makes what they were doing in the 1970s look remedial. They can track brainwaves and use magnetic fields to influence what a person is thinking. They can do things with a single microchip now that an entire division of scientists could not have achieved forty years ago.'

Natalie thought for a moment.

'That may be true, but the technology is only the means to an end. What was the purpose of MK-ULTRA? What was the ultimate goal?'

Anderson sighed and stared at his hands as he spoke.

'The mission objective was to create assassins who would undertake their work without the slightest hint of emotion. The purpose was to develop a means to temporarily, via hypnosis or drugs or whatever, entirely erase an individual's personality so that nothing remained but their pre-programmed mission: they would become like a robot, utterly devoted to their cause. A terminator, if you like.'

Natalie sat in silence for a long moment before she spoke again.

'They wouldn't know anything of this?'

'Not a thing,' Anderson said. 'MK–ULTRA was specifically working toward a method of ensuring that not only would people be purged of any memory of their involvement with the program, but that they would also undertake their assas-sinations before then taking their own lives. They were the perfect way to commit murder, Miss Warner: a human, pro-grammable suicide bomber who would take all evidence of their crime and their motivation to the grave with them. No person, no country, could ever be held accountable for their actions.'

Natalie felt a cold chill embrace her as she realized the implications of what MK–ULTRA had set out to achieve. If it had indeed been operating beneath the veil of the Pentagon's Black Budget, for some forty or more years, then the scope of its operations could be vast.

'And these experiments were conducted on American cit-izens?'

Anderson chuckled bitterly.

'On any citizen, of any nation on earth,' he replied. 'You have to remember that this was a paramilitary program, designed to ensure that the United States of America had on hand a number of programmed killers living, working, marrying and reproducing in countries all across the globe. At any time, if the need arose, they could be sent into action to do the bidding of the CIA, including murder.'

Natalie sat in stunned silenced for a long time. 'They could take down unfavorable world leaders, dissidents or dictators.'

'Or otherwise innocent people whose world view didn't fit with that of the United States,' Anderson pointed out.

'How many victims were there of the program?' Natalie asked.

Anderson shrugged. 'Nobody knows.'

'Do you know how many people might have been programmed by MK–ULTRA over forty years?'

Anderson stared at the grimy carpet beneath his feet for a long time before he replied, his voice softer as though he himself had not considered the question before. Natalie heard his words cross the room to her as though from another world.

'Hundreds,' the old man whispered. 'Thousands.'

55

DEFENSE INTELLIGENCE AGENCY ANALYSIS CENTER, WASHINGTON DC

Doug Jarvis drove back into the parking lot at the DIAC just over an hour after he'd left the district. He'd used every trick in the book to ensure that his tail was clear, and had taken the final, paranoid step of parking his pool car in a side street in Anacostia before renting a Ford Taurus to drive back across the border.

If his vehicle had been tagged with a GPS tracker, it would be useless to the CIA now.

Jarvis hurried into the building and took an elevator up to the fourth floor, hoping against hope that his team had managed to crack the decryption on Randy MacCarthy's flash drive. He walked into the laboratory and was greeted by his lead technician, who leapt to his feet with a bright toothy smile bent across his beard.

'We did it,' Hellerman said. 'And, man, are you gonna want to see this.'

Jarvis felt a wave of relief flush through his body.

'Tell me everything.'

Hellerman waved him across to a plasma screen that showed a blown-up image of the technician's monitor. Jarvis instantly saw a file folder that he had not seen before.

'Photographs,' Hellerman identified them for Jarvis, 'and get this – they were all taken around mountains in the heart of the Nez Perce National Forest in Idaho, right where we found those hard-rock mines and right where most of the missing persons have been reported.'

Jarvis watched as Hellerman opened the folder. Two more folders were within: one named 'EVIDENCE' and the other named 'ACTIVITY'. The technician opened the evidence folder, revealing a huge mass of photographs. He double-clicked on one and then began scrolling through them.

Jarvis saw endless images of enormous five-toed footprints, with a ruler set alongside to give scale to them.

'I've never seen so many images like these,' Hellerman said. 'Absolutely incredible, unassailable evidence of Bigfoot.'

'Absolutely incredible, unassailable evidence of big *feet*,' Jarvis corrected him. 'This isn't what we're looking for.'

'Isn't it?' the technician asked. He looked at Jarvis, and then tapped to the next image.

Jarvis glanced up at the screen and froze. There, captured in broad daylight, was the image of a pair of footprint casts that had been taken *in situ* alongside the actual prints, part of a track running along the floor of a dry creek bed. Judging by the sunlight and foliage in the image, it had been shot in summer.

What was striking was that one foot was deformed, the toes splayed and twisted.

'It's caused by gout,' the technician said, 'or perhaps a bad case of club-foot. Point is, this is a record of a sasquatch suffering from a disease that affects humans. You think that a faker would bother to think to do something like this?'

Jarvis shook his head. Even the most determined of fakers would probably not be able to create a convincing example of such a track, especially not one that carried on for tens of metres along the creek bed.

'The strides are almost two metres apart, much too large for any human to fake and convince even amateur trackers. And look at the roll pattern in the dried mud,' Hellerman said, 'caused by the ball of the foot digging in as the creature walked. This thing was real. Even using stilts, no human could produce enough weight and momentum to produce a set of tracks like these.'

Jarvis gestured to the other file.

'What's in there?'

The technician closed the evidence file, and opened the activity file.

'This one you're really going to have to see to believe.'

Jarvis watched as the file opened and he saw images of what looked like an old abandoned mine set into the steep hillside of a mountain high in the forest. Hellerman flipped across a couple of images and then paused on one.

'I'll be damned,' Jarvis said.

From the mine a group of men were walking out, dressed in civilian clothes. The technician moved on to images of a jet-black, unmarked helicopter landing near the mine and picking up the men before flying away into the distance.

'You got an ID on that helicopter?' Jarvis asked.

'Not a thing,' Hellerman said. 'No identifying marks what-soever. All I can tell you is that we matched the date and time of the image to air traffic records from Boise, Idaho. That helicopter flew from there to Mountain Home Air Force Base.'

Jarvis's mind began racing.

'Where the National Guard are based.'

'And that's not all,' Hellerman said, flicking across to another set of images.

The new pictures were not taken near the mine, and were shot a couple of days prior to those of the helicopter. Jarvis squinted for a moment before he realized what he was look-ing at.

Dense forest cloaked with thick foliage, a mass of greenery that seemed devoid of anything interesting until his mind had spent a few seconds processing the image and doing what it did best: looking for patterns. Moments later, as though appearing by magic, a pair of eyes stared out past Jarvis, focused on some distant target over the barrel of a rifle.

'M–16,' Jarvis uttered to himself, 'under-slung 203 launcher, and that guy's not wearing standard-issue disruptive-pattern material. Looks like foreign stuff, maybe German.'

'Special Forces soldier,' Hellerman confirmed. 'We can't confirm the location from this image but it's likely that it was taken in the same region, maybe even the same mountain. Point is, whatever's going on up there is important and it's off the record because that area is not military owned.'

'That everything?'

'No,' the technician said, and flicked to the next image.

Jarvis looked at the screen and saw that the soldier with the rifle had fired, the muzzle of the M-16 aflame as a high-velocity round was released. The technician's voice was heavy as he spoke.

'Next image is not a good one.'

Jarvis watched as the image flipped. This time, it was of a man in hiking gear lying flat on his back, his face turned toward the camera. A bloodied red hole was punched through the side of his face just below the right eye, and his hair on the opposite side of his head was a matted mess of blood and bone.

Jarvis took a pace toward the screen as Hellerman flicked across the images.

The man's ruined face, close up.

Then more men standing around the body, heavily armed and camouflaged.

The body being hoisted into a large black bag and being carried away by the soldiers into the forest. The fourth image showed them vanishing into the woods somewhere just below the mountain peak that was obviously the same one that contained the supposedly abandoned mine.

'Oh Christ,' Jarvis said.

Hellerman's voice was somber as he replied.

'We used a basic facial recognition program on the close-up shot of the photograph that Randy, or his brother Cletus, must have taken. The victim's name was Aaron Hall, forty-two, out of Michigan. A keen hiker, he was reported missing in the Nez Perce National Forest two months ago.'

Jarvis turned slowly to face the technician as he went on.

'National Guard conducted the search and it was reported that they found Hall's jacket and a few belongings high in the

mountains. They concluded that he was attacked and killed
by a bear. His body was never found.'

Jarvis turned back to the screen.

'They're killing anybody who gets too close to the mountain,' he said in disbelief, then shook himself from his stupor.
'Get me Earl Carpenter at the Riggins Sheriff's Office on the
line, right now.'

The technician called up the office details, and moments
later he put the phone down as he looked up at Jarvis. 'Sheriff
Earl Carpenter was retired this afternoon on a full pension,' he
said. 'He's no longer available for duty.'

Jarvis felt the blood in his veins run cold. Everything had
been planned. Everything had been done at once.

The whole thing was a trap.

'Make copies of the files and send them to each other,' he
snapped to Hellerman. 'Do it now before anybody can stop
you.'

'Who would want to stop us from—'

'Do it, now!'

The technician flinched as Jarvis shouted, then hurried
away. Jarvis called after him.

'Then make hard copies and send them via the postal service to yourselves. You'll need them, keep them safe and tell
nobody about any of this, okay?'

The technicians in the office all nodded, their features
creased with concern as Jarvis stormed out of the laboratory
and across to the elevators. He was on the seventh floor a few
minutes later as he charged down the corridor and burst into
the director's office before his secretary could even get up out
of her seat to stop him.

'You've burned them!' Jarvis shouted.

Abraham Mitchell looked up, as did four other men all holding files and wearing surprised expressions. For all Jarvis knew they were high-ranking Pentagon officials but he didn't care as he growled at them.

'Get out. Now.'

Whatever they saw in his eyes was enough to kill any notions of pulling rank. The four men stood up and filed silently out of the office. Jarvis kicked the door shut behind them and glared down at Mitchell.

'You've burned Ethan and Nicola.'

'I haven't done any such thing,' Mitchell snapped back at him. 'What the hell do you think you're doing?'

Jarvis walked forward and slammed his hands down on the director's desk.

'The security unit you dispatched is a CIA paramilitary cleaning-team,' he shouted. 'I've got hard evidence of them killing civilian hikers in Idaho to protect some kind of facility the CIA is running up there.'

Mitchell's anger flickered out like a candle in the wind as he stared at Jarvis in disbelief.

'I didn't dispatch the team,' he said. 'I handed control of the military request to . . .'

Jarvis stared at his boss and realized what had happened.

'The Pentagon,' he finished the sentence for Mitchell. 'The CIA must have intercepted the request and channelled it through to the 24th STS or similar.'

'William Steel knew that Warner and Lopez were operating in Idaho,' Mitchell said. 'But he knew nothing about what they were doing.'

Jarvis stood up and touched a hand to his head.

'That may not be true, sir,' he said. 'The CIA has been mounting surveillance on Ethan and Nicola. They've even had me tailed, perhaps even bugged. It's likely that if they've got something to do with what happened to the MacCarthys in Idaho, they know why Ethan and Lopez were sent up there.'

Abraham Mitchell folded his hands beneath his chin thoughtfully for a moment.

'What do you want from me?'

'Get them out of there,' Jarvis replied. 'Whatever's going on just pull them out before they're captured or killed. Do we have any information on missions being flown by the National Guard out of Gowen Field?'

Mitchell turned to his desktop computer and accessed a series of files detailing in real-time the sortie profiles of literally thousands of United States military operations worldwide. Within a few moments, he looked up at Jarvis.

'A pair of A-10 Thunderbolt IIs of the 124th Air National Guard are detailed to perform a low-level night-strike training flight out of Gowen. It says here it's a weapons-cold sortie, no active ordnance.'

'I bet it does,' Jarvis said bitterly. 'When are they due for wheels-up?'

Mitchell looked at the screen. 'An hour from now.'

'Christ, Abe, this is a murder plot!'

'We don't know that, Doug,' Mitchell shot back. 'You got any idea what you're insinuating here? That the CIA is murdering civilians?'

'They're doing a hell of a lot more than that,' Jarvis said. 'In fact, they've been doing more than just that for the last forty years. You remember MK–ULTRA?'

'Sure I do,' Mitchell replied impassively. 'Shut down in the 1970s.'

'So they said,' Jarvis replied. 'What we've stumbled upon here is not one but two illegal CIA programs. MK–ULTRA is still active, Abe, and the agency is conducting some kind of experiments on either people or hominid species in Idaho. An agent named Mr. Wilson, whom we've encountered in the past, is likely to be behind much of it,' he explained quickly. 'A guy called Ben Consiglio was killed this afternoon. He was part of a GAO Congressional investigation into misappropriation of resources by the CIA, who must have had a mole in the GAO to know where Consiglio and his team would be at all times. You see a picture developing yet?'

Mitchell's brow furrowed as he struggled to digest the new information.

'Director Steel will be behind all of this,' he said. 'This Wilson must be the muscle, an enforcer.'

'Sure he is,' Jarvis agreed. 'And if he's taken his job too far it'll cost lives. The man's a friggin' psychopath, Abe. You need to call the DCIA and have Wilson pulled before anybody else dies.'

Mitchell reached for his phone just as the door to the office opened, and Jarvis turned to see two armed security personnel burst in, their weapons pointed at Jarvis.

'Sir,' one of them said to Mitchell. 'I'm afraid we have to take Mr. Jarvis into custody.'

'You have to do what?' Mitchell demanded, rising from his seat to tower over them like a Greek Titan.

'Mr. Jarvis has had a warrant for his arrest issued,' the security guard explained, 'from detectives investigating a homicide in Virginia.'

Jarvis blinked in amazement. 'What homicide?'

'The detectives are outside, sir,' the guard said. 'They're here to arrest you for complicity in the suspected murder of a Ben Consiglio.'

'On what evidence?' Jarvis uttered.

'The accusation has been made by an associate of the deceased, a woman named Natalie Warner, Congressional aide.'

Jarvis gaped at them for a moment and then looked at Mitchell. 'Wilson.'

Abraham Mitchell rubbed his temples.

'This is a civil case, Doug,' he said. 'I can't protect you from arrest.'

'Then at least get Ethan and Nicola out,' Jarvis said. 'Find a way before that air strike hits. And find out who the hell the mole is in the GAO! We need them arrested as evidence or they'll be in the wind by tomorrow!'

56

NEZ PÉRCE NATIONAL
FOREST, IDAHO

Ethan lay on his back on the cold metal of the table and tried to peer down the corridor to his right that led to the mine entrance. He could feel the cold mountain air whispering through the mine tunnel and raising bumps on his skin beneath his jacket, could smell the damp but fresh scent of the forests beyond.

He looked away from the darkness and searched the control room, desperately seeking some means of escape. Kurt's men had yanked the cables fixing him to the table savagely tight. Ethan's chest felt constricted and he was struggling to get enough air in as it was, but if he could maybe free one arm then he'd be able to undo the cables and get away.

He pulled on his arms, but they were also held fast by smaller wires that secured his wrists. He twisted his hands sideways, trying to create a gap large enough that he could begin wriggling free, but it was no use. He finally gave up

after fifteen minutes of scraping the skin from the back of his
hands against the unyielding bonds.

His only real hope lay with Lopez, but she was sealed up
with Proctor and Dana in the living quarters, while Duran
and Mary were locked in the store room. Only way out of
that room was down the corridor into the laboratory, where
Kurt's men would most likely have set up.

Ethan turned his head and looked at the other two exits,
those to the east and west. Both were dead ends but both
corridors provided a field of fire into the control room where
Ethan lay. If it were up to him he'd have posted two snipers
in each, with the heavy firepower to the south in the laboratory, aiming down the corridor. Anything that came in
through the entrance from the mine tunnel would instantly
be caught up in three fields of fire.

Size didn't count for so much in the face of that kind of
lethal barrage.

The breeze drifted over him again and this time his skin
crawled with fear as a faint but unpleasant odor stained the
air. Ethan felt his heart quicken in his chest as he slowly
turned his head and stared out of the laboratory entrance,
down into the utter blackness of the mine tunnel.

Nothing moved, the blackness was absolute. He realized
belatedly that to be able to move freely in the dead of night,
out here when darkness was so complete, the beast must have
evolved excellent night vision. The explanation for the red
eyes, increased vascularity to the optic nerves. Ethan blinked.
His mind was racing as a distraction and he knew it, trying
to focus on anything but what he knew was approaching
from somewhere out there in the dark.

Wild. Dangerous. Curious.

Something shifted, a tiny sound as though a single grain of sand had trickled down from the wall of the mine to land gently on a metal tile. Ethan's gaze was fixed upon the dark maw of the tunnel, unable to tear himself away from it. He could hear his lungs sucking in air in short, sharp breaths. And then he realized that wasn't the only breathing he could hear.

Ethan held his breath.

The sound came in long, slow rasps from out of the darkness. Ethan was briefly reminded of the sound a diver's oxygen tank makes, though this was far deeper in tone.

Ethan stared at the darkness, and then in the faint glow he saw two discs of light near the top of the door briefly reflect the emergency lights in the laboratory, like translucent red orbs floating nine feet high in the darkness.

It's here. It can see me.

Ethan saw a slow movement against the tunnel, like a shadow upon a shadow as a tuft of brown hair glinted in the soft light. All at once Ethan's brain digested the information and identified the tuft of hair as being from an immense, muscular arm, and in an instant Ethan could see it standing there on the edge of the light.

His gaze flicked instinctively up and once again he looked straight into a pair of dull red eyes, the retina occasionally flashing as they reflected the emergency lights. Ethan swallowed as his stomach twisted upon itself and shuddered involuntarily. It was fear, but not like he had ever felt before. This was something ancient, buried deep in the cerebral cortex, a flashback from prehistory when men huddled together naked and afraid

in the night, listening to the sounds of huge, dangerous creatures prowling nearby.

Whatever is watching me is far from human.

It moved again, a tiny step forward until the soft glow
bathed its thick fur in a pale red light. Ethan stared at a huge
form, bipedal just like a human but with thick, stocky legs of
immense musculature. Even with the thick, knotted fur that
covered them it was still obvious that this creature was possessed of incredible strength.

Ethan could see ranks of abdominal muscles beneath the
finer fur covering its belly, each as big as his fist, bulging
prominently outward and flexing slowly as the creature drew
its breath. The chest was broad and muscular, thickly forested
with more hair, and the shoulders were like cannonballs.

The arms hung long by its side and almost reached its
knees, as though it were stooping slightly. Ethan saw that its
legs were not straight but slightly bent at the knee, as though
acting like shock absorbers.

Ethan looked into its eyes again and felt the same ancient
fear course through his veins.

The features were unmistakeably human, far more so than
a gorilla or chimpanzee. The nose was more pronounced,
not flat, and the line of the mouth was wider than a human's.
Even in the low-light conditions Ethan could just make out
that the creature's head was conical in shape, but that the skull
was round like that of a human. Only the thick fur coating
the top of the head gave it a conical appearance, perhaps an
adaption to prevent heat loss from the scalp during the cold
mountain winters.

No gunshot broke the silence. Ethan realized that although

he could see the creature's skull from his position on the table, the creature was too tall for Kurt to spot its head or even its eyes from his position down the south corridor. Without a clean shot at the head he couldn't be sure of a kill. All that was saving this immense creature's life was the fact that it was too tall to walk into the control room. It would have to stoop to get in.

Ethan shivered as he became aware that the creature was looking directly at him. The eyes seemed black now, bottomless pits beneath a slight ridge running along the skull above them. He could see that the creature's facial hair was like a man's, thick around the jaw and the sides of the face, but the nose and cheeks were hairless, the skin there darkened by exposure to a thousand Idaho suns.

The eyes remained transfixed upon his as they stared at each other. Ethan searched desperately for some kind of recognition, an emotion to appear on that face, but he saw nothing. The eyes stared back at him blankly for what felt like an eternity.

Then, they began looking around the control room.

Ethan felt a new kind of fear tingle uncomfortably through him as he saw the creature slowly scan the room, sweeping methodically from one side to the other. Watching. Observing. Waiting. He realized without a shadow of doubt that it was thinking.

Ethan flinched in shock as it suddenly sniffed loudly, sucking in air like a hoover. It looked at him for a long moment and then softly let the breath out, its huge chest sinking as it did so. Now it focused on Ethan again and seemed to look at the cables securing him to the table. Thinking. Assessing.

Ethan took a chance and whispered.

'Hey.'

The dark eyes flicked back onto his and bore into him like laser beams. The face remained impassive but Ethan was in no doubt that he had its attention. He swallowed, and then looked up at the east corridor before looking down at the west corridor. Ethan looked back at the creature, saw it still focused directly upon him, and then repeated his gesture, checking out the two corridors and looking back at the creature.

It stared at him blankly.

Ethan tried the whole routine again. The animal just looked at him, unreadable. Ethan tried again, looking at the corridors intently and then back at the creature.

It wasn't looking at him. With a chill that ran down through his bones he saw it looking from one corridor to the next, the big dark eyes rolling from left to right before looking down at Ethan. Ethan could not tell if the creature was simply mimicking him or actually understanding what he was trying to do.

Ethan repeated his gesture one more time, and then looked at the creature and shook his head slowly.

The vast majority of human civilizations used identical means of indicating 'yes' and 'no'. Ethan had once read that the origin of this universally accepted gesture was conceived shortly after birth, when hungry babies would search for milk from their mother's breast by moving their heads up and down, and would generally decline milk by turning their heads aside.

And if this creature could understand that, then it might

also have recognized that Ethan was trapped, perhaps just as it had once been.

The creature looked at him again, that blank and inhuman expression still cast across its face. Ethan repeated the entire gesture again and shook his head. This time, he put on a worried expression.

The creature stared at him for several long seconds, then looked at the corridors again.

Slowly, ever so quietly as though it were not walking but floating above the ground, it began to melt back into the darkness.

'Open fire, now!'

Kurt's voice shouted out, shockingly loud in the silence. It was instantly drowned out by a salvo of deafening shots. Ethan heard a shriek of rage and pain and then the creature vanished as though it had never even existed. He heard footfalls receding swiftly into the night beyond the mine tunnel.

Ethan stared at the darkness for a few moments, and then he breathed out.

The entire encounter had taken less than a minute, but it felt as though he had been watching the creature for a lifetime.

'Damn it!'

Kurt burst into the control room, his rifle pulled into his shoulder as he worked his way around the table and kicked the steel doors shut. Two of his soldiers emerged from the other corridors and helped him seal the doors with the bars before Kurt turned to look at Ethan.

'You see it?' he asked. 'Did we hit it?'

Ethan nodded and then let a grim smile curl from the corner of his mouth.

'I saw it,' he said, 'and, believe me, we're not getting out of here alive.'

Kurt Agry used a combat knife to slice the cables off Ethan's body and hauled him onto his feet.

'*You're* not getting out of here alive,' he corrected, and shoved Ethan toward the south corridor.

Ethan did not resist, his mind filled with the image of the sasquatch's face, those blank yet intelligent eyes, that other-worldly essence.

Agry waited as one of his men unlocked the door to the store room and opened it. Ethan was shoved inside, and Kurt was about to slam the door behind him when all three of them stopped and stared at the room.

It was empty.

Duran and Mary Wilkes had vanished.

57

DEFENSE INTELLIGENCE AGENCY, WASHINGTON DC

Jarvis was led by the two detectives to an unmarked police car, probably a pool vehicle like his own. He saw that it had no grilles on the windows, no means of preventing escape should he decide to make a run for it, although his wrists were cuffed in front of him.

The sun had long gone down, the car park lit by the harsh fluorescent glow of street lights as the detectives drove him out of the lot and onto the main highway south for the district.

'I have an alibi for the time of the murder,' Jarvis said to the two detectives in the front of the car.

'Is that so?' one of them replied. 'That's convenient, especially as we haven't yet told you the time of death.'

'I've already been to the Capitol,' Jarvis explained, 'and visited Ben Consiglio's colleagues. That's where I heard that he'd been killed.'

The older of the two detectives turned in his seat to look at Jarvis.

'And why would you be doing that?'

'Ben was working for a Congressional committee looking into the CIA's activities,' Jarvis explained. 'So was his partner, Natalie Warner, who is the sister of a man who works for me. Natalie visited me earlier today but because I couldn't tell her what she wanted to know due to national security, she thinks I'm part of some conspiracy to derail the committee. Now that Ben's been killed she's implicated me.'

The detective nodded.

'And rightly so. Consiglio was killed in an automobile wreck and the vehicle that hit him was untraceable.'

'As expected,' Jarvis replied, 'it was CIA.'

The two detectives looked at each other and chuckled.

'Sure it is, Mr. Jarvis,' the younger man replied. 'But don't worry, I'm sure Jack Bauer's on the case for you right now.'

Jarvis was about to shout his reply when a set of headlights flared like nuclear detonations through the side of the car. Jarvis threw his cuffed hands over his head and bent forward in his seat as the vehicle slammed into the side of the car with a deafening crash of metal and shattered glass. The detectives in the front seats were hurled violently sideways by the impact as the car screeched along the asphalt and shuddered to a halt in the darkness.

Jarvis, his body doubled over forward to protect him from whiplash and to hide himself from view, reached forward between the front seats and grasped under the older detective's jacket. His hand fell upon the pistol in its shoulder holster, the unconscious man unaware as Jarvis pulled the weapon out. He fumbled for the keys to his cuffs on the detective's belt, then lay down silently on the back seat. He worked the key into the cuffs and felt the restraints loosen as they slid from his wrists.

The lights from the car that impacted them illuminated the steam pouring from the detectives' vehicle, the vapour glowing in white clouds as Jarvis waited silently, listening to the tinkling of the engine as it cooled.

Moments later he saw a shadow appear, cast by the same lights as the driver of the other car approached them. Jarvis saw the pistol in the man's hands first, the weapon held out in front of him as he reached the car. An amateur. He'd announced his arrival by not masking his approach, letting his shadow be seen by Jarvis. Maybe some kind of punk hired by Mr. Wilson to trash the car and kill the occupants, like maybe a jacking gone wrong.

The man, still holding his pistol aimed at the detectives' heads, reached out and opened the passenger door. Jarvis watched silently as the man reached in and rested a finger on the unconscious man's neck. Jarvis masked his surprise and waited for the man to reach in further and check the driver.

Jarvis watched the man's hand move further into the car.

He leapt outward, grabbed the hand and yanked it into the car as he slammed the detective's pistol up against the man's head.

'Move and I'll blow your brains out across the windshield.'

The man squinted sideways at Jarvis, his dark eyes smeared with blood from the crash impact. It took a moment for Jarvis to realize that the man had already bandaged his wounds.

'Douglas Jarvis?' the man croaked.

'Who the hell are you?'

The man raised a hand slowly, palm up at Jarvis, and with the other he set the pistol down on the dashboard of the car.

'My name's Ben Consiglio. We have to leave, now, before these two wake up.'

'They'll be onto us real fast,' Jarvis said. 'You just T-boned a police vehicle and I've stolen a detective's pistol.'

Jarvis scrambled from the back seat as Ben led him to his vehicle.

Ben Consiglio drove, joining the freeway headed south. His face was a mess, caked in dried blood and hastily applied bandages, the skin around his left eye turning purple and yellow with bruises.

'I know,' Ben said. 'What I didn't know was that you were under arrest.'

'Natalie put them onto me. She thinks I'm out to sink the investigation.'

'Are you?' Consiglio asked.

'I'm a victim here too,' Jarvis said. 'This is a CIA-sponsored operation. How the hell did you survive the assassination attempt, by the way?'

Ben shook his head.

'Pure luck. This guy hit my car then gave me a beating. He strapped me into the seat and pistol-whipped my head. Then he used some kind of accelerant and poured it into the filler cap. I watched him do it in the wing mirror.'

'You were still conscious after being pistol-whipped?' Jarvis asked in amazement.

'I feigned unconsciousness,' Ben replied, and tapped his skull. 'Four titanium plates, fitted to hold my head together after I got hit by shrapnel in Iraq. They're not due out for another couple of years once the bones have healed.'

Jarvis shook his head.

'Okay, lucky strike. You want to tell me why the hell you haven't checked into a hospital, or a police station?'

'I'm a target,' Ben said. 'Long as they think I'm dead, I'll be alive. This was a professional hit and I'm not taking any chances until I've figured out what the hell's going on here.'

'I might be able to help with that,' Jarvis said.

'First things first,' Consiglio insisted. 'Where's Natalie?'

'I don't know,' Jarvis said. 'She visited me and then swore she'd get to the bottom of it all. I didn't know at the time what she meant. You got any leads on her?'

'Last I heard she planned to go see one of the survivors of MK-ULTRA, some old guy living out near the Edwards Base. But I don't know the name or exact location. We need to find out.'

Jarvis thought for a moment. 'You think she's a target?'

'I don't know,' Consiglio replied. 'What I do know is that somebody in our office must have been an informer to whoever's doing this. Nobody but the people in our team had any idea of where I was going or what I was doing.'

'Your team have gone home,' Jarvis said. 'Only people left are Guy Rikard and someone called Larry. They know the risks.'

'Yeah,' Consiglio chuckled bitterly, 'I bet they do. Most likely person working for the CIA is Rikard. He's got a photographic memory, something that the intelligence agencies would find very useful, and he's had it in for Natalie ever since the investigation started. If he already knew she was being treated as a person of interest to the CIA that might explain why.'

Jarvis frowned.

'Doesn't fit,' he said. 'Rikard's an ass but he was first to act when he realized what was really going on. He agreed to sending the team home for their own protection and he's already put himself on the line for Natalie.'

'How come?'

'I sent him to tell the committee everything that had happened. Left him collating the evidence with the other guy who stayed back, Larry.'

Consiglio looked at the traffic streaming past them on the freeway as he thought furiously.

'He'll never let that happen. Larry could be in real danger. We need to find them both, now.'

Jarvis nodded and pulled out his cell. 'I'll call ahead. Then I'd better call my boss and explain what's happened.'

'Good luck with that,' Consiglio said as he accelerated.

Jarvis dialed in a number and held his cell to his ear. Almost immediately the dial tone changed to a strange humming noise. Jarvis stared at his cell for a moment and then shut it off. He opened the car window and tossed the phone out into the night.

'The hell you doing?' Consiglio asked.

'Cell's being jammed,' Jarvis replied and closed the window again. 'They're trying to close us down. You got a cell?'

'No,' the younger man replied. 'It burned with the car. I didn't try to buy a new one either. I've got no cash on me and using an ATM would be suicide right now.'

Jarvis clenched his fists in frustration and then made a decision.

'We turn up at the GAO, the entire Metropolitan Police Department will be on us within minutes. Only chance we've got now is to find Natalie and use whatever she may have discovered as evidence. The fact that you're not dead proves me innocent of any crime.'

'We need to find Larry,' Consiglio insisted. 'He's in real danger and Rikard might destroy all of the evidence Natalie had collated.'

'There's nothing that we can do for Larry,' Jarvis snapped. 'We can't go back there. You said that you watched the man who tried to kill you pour accelerant into your fuel tank.'

'Sure.'

'You get a good look at him? Good enough to pick him out?'

Consiglio looked across at Jarvis.

'I'll never forget his face as long as I live. You find him, I'll pick that bastard out from a line-up of a thousand people.'

Jarvis nodded. 'Find a store. We're going to need a disposable cellphone first, and then we need to find Natalie. Fast.'

58

NEZ PERCE NATIONAL
FOREST, IDAHO

'Where the hell have they gone?'

Kurt Agry swept the room with the flashlight beam on his rifle, but there was no sign of the tracker and his daughter. Ethan stared in disbelief as Kurt kicked boxes across the floor and ran a gloved hand over his stubbled skull.

'How would I know?' Ethan uttered. 'You've had me strapped to a table in the control room.'

'Don't fuck with me!' Kurt yelled, ramming the muzzle of his rifle against Ethan's chest. 'You were in here with them. They must have said something.'

Ethan said nothing. Just stared down at Kurt in disgust. One of the soldiers called out and Kurt walked across to him. Ethan watched as Milner pointed down at the locking mechanism on the door.

'The screws are loose,' he said. 'Looks like they got out and then rigged the locks back in place to hide their escape.'

Kurt looked down the corridor from which they had come.

'They must have slipped past us while we were watching for that thing to come in here.'

'Don't see how,' the soldier replied. 'I was in the corridor.'

'You were at the other end of the corridor,' Ethan corrected him, 'with line of sight to the mine entrance. Both Duran and Mary are adept at moving quietly through the forest – in here it would have been child's play. Factor in the low light and your attention on the mine entrance, it's my guess they slipped past you.'

Milner scowled at Ethan but did not respond.

'They're still in here,' Kurt muttered. 'They can't have gone out the main entrance so they must be holed up out back someplace. Bring the men forward into the laboratory. That way we control the front of the facility. We get the data uploaded and then we move out.'

Ethan laughed.

'You're not in control of anything, Kurt,' he said. 'You're trapped and you're doomed. The CIA has burned you. None of you is going anywhere.'

'That's for me to decide,' Kurt snapped back. 'You're done, Warner.'

With that, he stepped out of the store room and slammed the door shut behind him. Ethan heard the locking mechanism slide back into place on the outside, and found himself alone in the room.

59

'This isn't working.'

Archer squatted in the control center, his shotgun trained on the door to the mine entrance.

Klein nodded in silence. Jenkins could hardly blame them. With their officer lost, communications gone and their sergeant apparently losing his authority and their respect, the situation was as bad as anything faced in a true war zone. The one thing that a soldier relied upon was a clear picture of who was calling the shots. Even among such a close-knit and elite team like the 24th STS, a breakdown in the chain of command could be lethal.

Worse, Jenkins knew that every single man in the squad, himself included, was now aware that even if they did manage to escape the mine they had been marked as an expendable asset by their superiors. Their job, to extract and send the data kept in the facility's computer servers, was expected to be their last living act.

'What are we going to do?' Archer asked him.

In the gloomy darkness, two pairs of eyes swiveled to look expectantly into Jenkins's and the weight of responsibility bore down upon him. Officially the third-ranking soldier when they set off on this mission, the men were clearly now looking to him for decisions while Sergeant Agry was out back.

The prospect of outright mutiny would have scared the corporal enough, but the idea of being hunted down by the CIA for the rest of his life scared him even more.

'We need that data. It's the only thing keeping us alive right now.'

'Kurt's not going to just hand that shit over,' Klein pointed out. 'He'll cover his own ass, even kill us before giving it up.'

Jenkins nodded slowly in the darkness. Agry was already at the tipping point, unable to take the stress of command to the point that he was abandoning the basic principles of humanity. Locking up the civilians wasn't any part of the briefing they'd received from Lieutenant Watson before deploying. Even if the CIA *had* decided to burn them, wasn't it worth trying to find a solution that fit all parties? They could still salvage something from this mess. That was what they were trained to do: get results, not kill fellow country-men and flee into the woods.

Yet he was the corporal, and Kurt Agry would be relying on him to maintain the morale and cohesion of their unit in his absence.

'I'm going to take the drives from him,' Archer said finally. 'We can figure this out once we've sprung Warner. He seems to know what he's doing.'

'Are you fucking *kidding*?' Jenkins hissed. 'What the hell will that achieve? We'll still be here and the sergeant will shoot you on sight.'

'That's a chance I'm willing to take,' Archer snapped. He looked at the other men. 'Who's with me?'

Klein nodded. Archer got to his feet.

'Let's do it.'

Archer turned and stared straight into Kurt Agry's eyes staring at him over the barrel of a pistol. Before Jenkins could intervene, Kurt's voice growled in the shadows.

'Let's.'

The gunshot was shockingly loud in the confined space of the corridor. Archer's head flicked backward and his body flailed as the impact of the bullet into his skull hurled him into the control center.

He hit the floor hard, the back of his smashed skull crunching across the tiles.

Kurt Agry lowered his pistol. Jenkins stared at Archer's lifeless corpse and then looked at the sergeant.

'Jesus, Kurt, that didn't help anything. We're a gun down now.'

Kurt glared a challenge into the eyes of the remaining soldiers as Milner joined them and stared in disbelief at Archer's body

'Gentlemen, our survival depends upon our ability to stick together. We split now, we'll be dead before dawn. Anybody else tries to take control of this situation I'll put a bullet in them too, understood?'

Klein stood up and pointed down at Archer's body.

'That what you call sticking together?'

'That's what I call mutiny,' Kurt shot back. 'We've got to get the hell out of here, and the only currency we have is the civilians. Unless any of you would like to set foot out there and tempt that fucking thing inside?'

'We tried baiting it,' Milner snapped. 'It didn't go for it.'

Kurt's thin lips curled into a grim smile.

'We're not going to bait it,' he replied, 'just keep it occupied. Milner, get Proctor and Dana out here, and bring Lopez too.'

Milner hurried down the west corridor toward the living quarters as Kurt glanced at the mine entrance. The warped metal bars could hold the creature back, but not forever. Sooner or later it would come through.

He turned as Proctor, Dana and Lopez were marched into the control center, Milner prodding them along with his rifle.

'This won't work,' Dana said. 'We could hear what you were up to earlier. You tried this with Ethan and failed.'

Dana Ford stood with Proctor at the door to the mine entrance, their hands cuffed as Kurt Agry aimed his rifle at them.

'It's better than nothing,' the sergeant replied. 'It'll have to come through you to get to us, and that's all the extra time we'll need.'

Proctor swallowed thickly, his eyes quivering behind his spectacles.

'It'll kill us,' he said, his voice trembling.

'Better you than me,' Kurt grinned, 'and it'll save on bullets. Move.'

Dana Ford stood her ground.

'Go to hell,' she spat. 'You're going to kill us anyway, so the way I see it, it's better to die quickly from a bullet than get torn to pieces out there. You want to escape so badly? Go do it yourself, asshole.'

Kurt Agry stared at her for a moment in what might have been surprise. He performed a brief calculation.

'Have it your way.'

Kurt Agry fired his rifle.

The shot impacted Dana Ford's chest. Her body jerked as it was thrown backward, the bullet passing through her heart and exiting her back in a fine mist of blood that splattered the paneled wall behind her.

She collapsed to the floor and slumped against the wall, her eyes wide but sightless.

'Jesus Christ!' Proctor blurted as tears flooded from his eyes. 'You've killed her!'

Kurt sneered at him. 'I can see why you're a scientist.' He swung the rifle to point at him. 'You too?'

Proctor stared in terror at the rifle as his hands flew into the air beside his head.

'Don't shoot!' he blubbed, his legs jerking and swaying as he tried to stay upright. 'I'll do it.'

Kurt, his rifle pulled tight into his shoulder, gestured with the weapon for Proctor to move to the main door. The scientist shuffled miserably across as Klein reached out and pulled the steel bolts out of the locks before hauling the door slowly open.

The dark, damp interior of the mine entrance yawned open in front of Proctor as he stood with his hands in the air and stared into the blackness. His legs trembled and he seemed to crouch forward slightly as though he wanted to crawl into the tunnel.

'Get moving,' Kurt snapped, and with one boot shoved Proctor forward.

The scientist cried out as he plummeted into the darkness and crashed down onto the rocks, his sobs echoing down the tunnel. The rocks dug into his palms and his knees as he struggled to his feet and reluctantly started pushing one foot in front of the other.

60

Ethan walked to the door and knelt down beside the lock. In the dim light he could see that the screws in the mechanism had indeed been loosened, a few dull scratches in the steel betraying Duran's efforts to disassemble the lock. Ethan ran a finger over the gouges and frowned. The scratches were deep, as though great force had been applied. Too much force. Duran was a patient man who preferred thought and planning over desperate measures; a man who would have thought his way out of his predicament first and acted second.

The door locked from the outside via the simple electronically controlled system that was now being manually shoved into place by Kurt and his crew. Three solid-steel bars an inch thick and six inches long securing each door. Even without the electronic locking, it was hard to see how Duran could have gotten the door undone from the inside. A single word infiltrated Ethan's mind.

Deception.

Ethan stood up and turned to look around the room. The only logical solution to the mystery was that Duran had only tampered with the lock as a diversion, and that he had escaped from the room some other way.

There were six racks of aluminum shelving, each six feet high and maybe ten feet long, stacked with cardboard boxes containing medical supplies, dehydrated food sachets, coveralls and the flashlights. While Ethan could entertain the idea of Duran fashioning a lock-pick out of syringe needles or similar, it was easy to reject an image of the old man frantically tunnelling his way out of the room. Ethan realized that Duran had known he was going to escape from this room the moment he entered it: that was why he'd been satisfied when he'd found the flashlights. It was dark outside.

Ethan checked his watch. Dead of night. Perfect timing. If there was to be an air strike, or if Kurt and his men were successful in blowing the facility, nobody would hear anything at this range from civilization and anybody camping within ten miles would pay little attention to what could probably be passed off as a rock fall or some other natural event.

'Come on, Ethan,' he murmured to himself. 'If Duran could do it . . .'

Ethan closed his eyes and stood for a moment in the center of the room. He let his mind grow calm and then built a mental picture of the facility in his mind. The mine entrance led into the circular control room, which itself was connected in a straight line to the other two circular main rooms – the laboratory in the middle and the stimulus and containment cages deepest in the mountain. From both the control room and the laboratory extended two corridors to the left and right; the armoury and living quarters from the control room; and further down from the laboratory the mysterious locked room and the store room in which he stood. As far as he knew there were no rooms extending from the containment area at the back of the facility.

Ethan kept his eyes closed, thinking hard. He retraced their steps through the facility, from where he stood and back, from being disarmed by Kurt to finding Mary Wilkes and Simmons's body. All the way back to following the tracks laid down by the creature that had led them here.

In the dim light, Ethan's eyes flicked open. Lopez's words of hours before drifted through the field of his awareness. *Something broke out.*

Ethan stared vacantly into the darkness, not seeing the room now but studying at the mental map he had created of the facility. The place had once been a hard-rock mine, which was dug for the extraction of minerals and ores like gold, silver, zinc and so on. To access the ore before the presence of modern machinery, miners were forced to dig decline ramps that descended from the mine entrance in a sort of spiral that circled the deposit. But in those days, haulage of rock to the surface would not have necessarily been performed by mules working alongside the men in the tunnels. Sometimes, vertical shafts were sunk and the ore hauled out via mules turning a mechanical wheel on the surface.

Ethan saw the facility in his mind's eye again.

The corridors were level, not declining. Those excavations were known as adits, where the ore bodies in the mountain were horizontal rather than vertical and there was no need for ramps or shafts to transport the ore to the surface.

But if this mountain had contained shafts also, they would not necessarily have been used by the construction teams that had built the facility. They would only have used the parts of the mine easiest to access.

Suddenly it all became clear.

The facility sat at the bottom of *vertical* excavations made into the mountain, making use of the cavities but placing false ceilings. That was why the three central rooms were the same size: the same size as the three ore bodies that had been extracted from the rock, one after the other.

Ethan whirled on the spot. The laboratory was behind him, to the northwest. If the original miners had used a tunnel that circled the ore body in a declining spiral, then it must have run somewhere close by where he now stood, essential ventilation for the shafts themselves.

Ethan walked in between the racks and studied the ceiling, lifting the back of his hand and running it along the seams between the metal panels. It took him only a few moments to find what he was looking for – a soft breeze that felt cool on his skin, seeping down between the panels.

Ethan turned and grabbed the side of the racking, seeing as he did so a boot print in the dust that betrayed where Duran Wilkes must have done the exact same thing. Ethan vaulted up until he was standing on the lower of two adjacent shelves, then reached up and pushed against the panel.

It was heavy, solid metal, but it moved as he pushed, and with a squeak of metal against metal it popped out. Ethan hefted it to one side and then reached up and hauled himself out of the room and up into a low tunnel that smelled of dust and mold and was completely, utterly black.

He reached into his jacket and yanked out his cell, turned it on until the screen glowed brightly and illuminated the tunnel.

It was roughly hewn and descended to his right while ascending gently to his left, curving in both directions as it circled the central columns where the ore had once been.

'I'll be damned,' he murmured to himself, and smiled as he saw Duran and Mary's footprints leading up the tunnel and away from him. They would probably be clear of the mine and on their way home by now.

Provided the sasquatch didn't intercept them.

It was then that he smelled something on the air, an over-powering odor like raw sewage and sweat that caked itself thickly across the back of his throat. Ethan covered his mouth and nose with one hand and pressed himself against the wall of the tunnel in the darkness as he looked left and right.

Fear crept like lice on his skin as he searched for glowing eyes in the gloom, but nothing appeared, and he could not hear the deep, heaving breath of the creature despite the confined space in which he was cramped.

A sudden awareness dawned upon him, as he looked at the roughly hewn walls of the tunnel and thought of the immense bulk of the sasquatch. There was no possibility that such a huge creature could have worked its way down through this maze of winding tunnels.

Ethan sat in silence within the tunnel for a long moment, and then suddenly he realized what had happened. The reason why the creature had led them here, had gone to such extraordinary lengths to ensure that they reached this remote mountain. He thought about his mental map of the facility, of where he actually was in relation to the chambers below him.

Another waft of putrid air drifted toward him and he looked left, down the tunnel to where the slim grating of a ventilation shaft glimmered in the faint light from his cellphone. He crept down toward it, trying to make as little noise as possible on the rough floor of the tunnel, until he was able to peer down through the grating and into the room.

It was larger than most of the other subsidiary rooms, and in the faint glow he could see an oven-like structure built from unadorned metal. A wide cylinder extended up from the oven into the ceiling. Ethan looked to his right and saw the open face of the central ore shaft. He guessed that the oven was some kind of incinerator, which made the room he was looking into the one with the locked door.

He peered back down and saw a heavy-looking cage against the rear wall of the room. He tried to hold his breath but the stench was too great to avoid a tight, strained cough.

Instantly, he heard a movement from within the cage. A rustle of wiry, dense fur.

Through the darkness, two silvery discs flashed briefly within the cage, reflecting the pale light from his cellphone.

'Duran was right,' he whispered to himself.

This was why they had been herded into the facility.

A low growl came from somewhere within the cage. Ethan backed away from the grating and eased his way down the tunnel until he reached the ore shaft. The ceiling of the locked room was visible as a narrow strip of steel girders that formed the floor of the tunnel: the rest of the room below him was hacked from the bare rock. Ethan carefully stepped over the girders and passed a vertical cylinder half set into the bare rock wall, an exhaust stack of some kind. He guessed that the locked room must have been some kind of crematorium or similar waste disposal room, most likely connecting to an existing ventilation shaft somewhere above Ethan's position.

He continued on until he reached the far side of the ceiling, above the door. A pair of thickly sealed power cables extended out from a junction box atop the door structure and turned to his right, passing into a hole drilled into the bedrock. From his position, Ethan guessed that they ran to the main and reserve power generators, providing power to the door itself. With the power down, the door would have remained locked.

But why had it not opened again when he had activated the emergency generators?

Ethan backed out of the tunnel and turned left, following the direction of the cables and searching for another point of access to them.

He found it fifty yards later, directly above the store room in which he had originally been held. In the darkness and his haste to examine the tunnels he had passed by a small access passage that took him to his left until he was directly above the corridor between the laboratory and the containment area at the rear of the facility. There, set inside the tunnel, was a power junction. As Ethan approached he could see that it had been sabotaged.

Both the main and the emergency lines had been hastily severed, the cables frayed, bare metal glinting in the light from his cell. But the junction itself was active, powered by the emergency generators in the containment area nearby. Ethan looked at the floor of the tunnel, picked up one of the two cable ends poking from the bare rock below and examined them. They had not been torn but instead severed by a hacksaw or similar.

'Cletus MacCarthy,' Ethan said softly.

He must have watched the mines and found these passages, then worked out what was happening inside. Jesse had told them that he hated tourists visiting the area and preferred to be alone in the wilderness. Some kind of government operation might have remained concealed from casual hikers, but Cletus would have known all about it. Maybe even witnessed the suffering of the creatures detained in the facility.

He must have sabotaged the operation. But even if he managed to escape the area and the Special Forces soldiers guarding it, he would have left evidence, maybe fingerprints. Local enquiries would have been enough to track him down, along with his brothers. Randy's mother had said she felt her home had been searched in her absence.

'They got the wrong brother,' he muttered bitterly to himself.

They had staged Randy's suicide, believing him to be the culprit. Yet in a strange twist of fate, Cletus had also died, victim of the enraged sasquatch attack that had claimed the life of ranger Gavin Coltz. That left Jesse, a man the authorities that owned this place would no doubt be happy to see jailed for life.

He looked down at the power junction box and at a digital display on the front that provided timed power cycles, probably meant for internal heating and hot-water supplies.

The timer had reset itself to zero when the emergency gen-erators had been started. Ethan looked down at the power cable in his hand and the one still lying on the ground as an insidious idea formed in his mind.

He knelt down in front of the power junction, checked his watch, then set the timer to activate in five minutes.

He reached down and shoved both of the power cables back into position, careful not to touch the exposed metal, and then used strips of his shirt to tie them into place. He stood up, satisfied, and then hurried away toward the living quarters where Lopez, Dana and Proctor were being held.

Kurt Agry was about to get what he deserved.

Payback.

61

CORAL HILLS, MARYLAND

Natalie Warner stepped out of the battered house into the night air, her head filled with a thousand revelations that fell like the rain pouring down from the cold dark sky above. As Anderson closed the door behind her, she knew that there was no way the CIA could keep its illegal program covered up if Anderson agreed to testify to the Senate and maybe even the Supreme Court. Burning the papers might have worked in 1973, but now she had hard evidence of CIA intervention in the investigation that would be virtually impossible for any district attorney to ignore.

The CIA would have a hard time stopping the commission now.

The last time the agency had tried to conceal evidence was after video tapes of the CIA 'waterboarding' a suspected jihadist after the victim was rendered from the USA into a prison believed to have been in Thailand. The videos, which had shown the victim screaming and vomiting, had been destroyed by the then head of the CIA's Counterterrorism Center. When the trials of major terrorists began, their

defenses hinged on the fact that waterboarding at the hands
of CIA interrogators was, in any sensible way, considered to
be a form of torture. Along with other known forms of
extreme punishment such as sleep deprivation, often for
weeks at a time, enforced nakedness, stress positions and suchlike, which the CIA and the US Department of Justice had
referred to as 'enhanced interrogation techniques', the defense
would argue that under such torture anybody would confess
to just about anything in order to gain relief from their suffering. Natalie herself had read of men who had experienced
extreme rendition to CIA-run prisons in countries non-sig-
natory to the Geneva Convention, who had confessed
afterward that they had become expert liars in order to avoid
torture. Their lies had cost the intelligence community millions of taxpayers' dollars wasted chasing phantom agents and
nonexistent cells, all from the imaginations of men who had
committed no crime at all.

Now, she finally understood what had happened to Joanna
Defoe. She had not been abducted by militants in the Gaza
Strip. She had been the victim of rendition by the CIA in
order to silence her investigation and prevent a scandal in the
White House, the support of the then president for a corrupt
arms company called MACE and to prevent her exposing
whatever she knew about the still operational MK-ULTRA.

Joanna was still alive. If Natalie could somehow contact
her and tell her what she now knew, the evidence she had
collated, then she could blow the whole damned thing wide
open. The results would no doubt echo through government
for decades to come.

Natalie pulled out her cellphone and started to dial a

number as she hurried to her car, using her jacket to shroud her head from the rain.

Natalie had no problem with the intelligence community extracting information from the kind of insane bastards who sought to burn Western civilization to the ground for nothing more than imaginary religious ideals. What she did resent was the heavy-handed way in which the CIA sought to do so. There were smarter ways to get results, and she intended to make sure that—

The blast did not register in her mind at first.

For a split second Natalie believed that she had tripped on the sidewalk in the dark as her legs crumpled beneath her and she felt herself in midair. Then something plowed into her from behind and she thought that she'd been hit by a truck as she span through the darkness, the street lights around her flashing crazily past.

Then the heat hit her like a blast furnace, stinging her eyes as they dried out instantly as the heat wave washed over her. Natalie hit the asphalt hard, rolling as the force of the explosion rattled her brain in her skull and caused her vision to blur.

The noise hit her last, a roaring crash of thunder and shattered glass as behind her Anderson's home suddenly vanished within a snarling fireball. Chunks of scorched clapperboard and twinkling jewels of glass crashed down around Natalie as she sat dazed on the sidewalk, blinking and staring into the crackling flames.

She shivered slightly and then bent over as she coughed and spat a globule of phlegm onto the sidewalk. She felt sick but managed to control herself, sucking in a lungful of night air as doors to other houses opened, people looking out and pointing at the flaming wreckage of Anderson's home.

Natalie turned and saw her phone on the sidewalk, the screen still glowing and a soft ring tone just audible over the flames and the shouts of alarm. She crawled forward on her hands and knees and picked up the cell. Her voice was croaky and weak as she spoke.

'Hello?'

'*Natalie? Where are you?*'

The voice sounded familiar, but she couldn't place it.

'Who is this?'

'*It's Douglas Jarvis.*'

Natalie's fists clenched on the asphalt beneath her. 'You son of a bitch. You killed him.'

'*Shut up!*' The voice crackled down the line with enough force and venom to both surprise and silence her. '*You've got it all wrong. I've been fired. The CIA are coming after all of us, Natalie. Get away from the case as fast as you can.*'

Natalie blinked in confusion.

'My chief witness just got killed in an explosion,' she said meekly.

'*Natalie,*' Jarvis said. '*Run. Now!*'

Natalie staggered to her feet, one hand reaching out to balance herself on the trunk of her car as she wobbled around to the driver's door. Her hand, the knuckles scuffed and bleeding, reached into her bag for her keys and she climbed into the seat.

People were emerging from their houses, some of them pointing at her as others stared, cellphones to their ears. Natalie switched on the engine and pulled away in a screech of rubber.

She saw the headlights behind her almost immediately as they followed her down the road, heading north as she drove out of Coral Hills and toward the district.

Shit. She didn't care about the potential CIA mole in her office now. The only place that seemed even remotely safe was the Capitol. Then she thought of her parents. Christ, if the CIA's cleaning team didn't get her, maybe they'd head for her parents' home instead. They could blackmail her, do anything. Worst of all, Ethan was gone, unheard of in days.

The net was closing in and suddenly there seemed to be no safe place to turn.

Natalie yanked the wheel of the car to the left and headed directly for the Sousa Bridge. Pennsylvania Avenue would take her in a near-perfect straight line into the heart of the district, where even the CIA would find it hard to make a hit on her without leaving some kind of evidence behind. The avenue was a two-lane that became a three-lane as it crossed the river into the district. Heavy traffic and plenty of witnesses – if she could get there.

The car headlights behind her grew larger as the vehicle behind accelerated, and then suddenly it swerved out to her left wing and smashed across the trunk of her car. The vehicle swerved to the right as she fought for control along Marlboro Pike, but the car smashed up onto the sidewalk and skidded out of control onto an abandoned forecourt just off the main road.

Natalie grabbed the steering wheel and turned the key to restart the engine, only to see the huge form of an SUV bump up onto the sidewalk in a flash of headlights and screech to a halt in front of her car.

From within climbed a tall man, one hand holding a pistol
that was pointing directly at Natalie as she sat behind the
wheel and stared at him. His outline was distorted by the rain
streaming down her windshield.

'Step out of the car!'

Natalie froze, unsure of what to do. A moment later and
the man fired at her vehicle, the gunshot deafeningly loud as
the bullet shattered one of her headlights.

'Get out now!'

Natalie reached down with a trembling hand and opened
her door, then stepped out into the rain. It pummeled her
hair and streamed down her face as she stood beside her car
with her hands in the air and stared at the long, gaunt face
of the man. His voice, when he spoke, was low and murderous.

'My apologies, Miss Warner, but you'll have to come with
me.'

'Where's my brother?' she uttered, trembling from more
than just the cold. 'Where's Ethan?'

The long face cracked with a cold little smile that made
the man seem even more cruel.

'Busy,' he replied.

From somewhere inside of her a spark of the Warner spirit
flared into life, and she dropped her hands. Behind him, a car
slid in alongside the sidewalk, its lights extinguished. Natalie
kept her eyes fixed on her assailant.

'You followed me this morning, and you killed Ben,' she
said with sudden, unshakeable conviction.

The man shook his head.

'I didn't kill anybody,' he replied. 'They got themselves

killed because they didn't understand the importance of national security.'

Natalie's anger flared brighter.

'The only thing the citizens of this country need security from is people like you,' she snapped back, 'because you're the ones killing us.'

The man inclined his head. '*C'est la vie.*'

He raised the pistol and aimed at Natalie's head.

Natalie barely saw the figure that lurched out from behind the parked SUV and rushed at the tall man from behind. The splashing of footfalls on the wet asphalt alerted the agent and he span, but not soon enough. The figure plowed into him and sent them both sprawling to the ground.

In the light from the SUV's headlights, Natalie stared in disbelief as she saw Ben Consiglio crash to the ground on top of the CIA man.

'Get out of here!' Ben yelled at her. 'Run!'

Natalie staggered backward as Ben smothered the CIA man with his weight and struggled to keep the man's gun arm on the ground. She whirled and leapt into her car, started the engine and slammed it into reverse. The remaining headlight beam flashed across the two men as they fought on the ground in the pouring rain, and she heard another gunshot and saw a flash of light as the shot went off into the air. Ben twisted the weapon from the agent's hand and hurled it across the lot.

Ben's head jerked awkwardly as a knife-edged hand sliced across his throat, and then another slammed palm-first up under his jaw and he was hurled off the CIA man's body to sprawl onto the asphalt as he struggled to get away.

The agent rolled sideways and came up onto his knees behind Ben. Two arms folded around Ben's neck, the CIA man interlocking them with one hand cupping the opposite elbow as the forearm crushed the knuckles of the opposite fist against Ben's throat. Natalie saw Ben's eyes bulge and his tongue leap from between his teeth as he fought for his life in the pouring rain, his fingers scraping across the agent's face, searching for his eyes.

She could hear their agonized growls as they strained against one another, saw Ben's features turn a shade closer to pallid, and made her decision. She leapt out of the car and dashed across the lot to where the pistol lay in the rain. She picked the weapon up, surprised at how heavy it felt in her grasp, and turned back just as she heard a terrible gagging sound above the hiss of the rain.

Ben's head was tilted back, his tongue poking from between his lips and the veins in his neck bulging. Natalie raised the pistol. The CIA man violently twisted Ben's body to one side. A shiver of horror snaked down Natalie's spine as the agent glared at her.

'You want him to live, you'll drop the weapon.'

Natalie gritted her teeth.

'You let him go,' she snarled, 'or you'll get nothing.'

The agent watched her for a long moment. In the distance she could hear police sirens wailing, could see far off down the freeway the flashing lights closing in on them. The gunshots must have alerted people close by.

'Time's running out,' she snapped. 'Let him go, now!'

The agent smiled coldly, and was about to twist Ben's neck further when another voice called out.

'Mr. Wilson.' The agent turned as Doug Jarvis appeared, a pistol in his grasp aimed at the agent. 'Game's up.'

The agent released Ben, who slumped forward. His head smacked against the cold, unforgiving asphalt. The agent stood up, watching Jarvis.

'You're out of your league, old man.'

Jarvis didn't reply, simply keeping the pistol trained on Wilson. Wilson looked at Natalie.

'Time for us to leave, Miss Warner.'

Natalie kept the pistol pointed at him, ignoring the rain that had plastered her hair in across her face.

'Go to hell.'

In a flash the agent dropped down onto one knee as his hand flicked to his waist and whipped out another, smaller pistol with frightening speed, the snub-nosed weapon flashing up to point at Jarvis.

Natalie pulled the trigger.

The huge noise and recoil of the pistol shuddered through her arms and threw her backward as the muzzle flash lit up the shards of rain pouring down around her. As she fell she heard another gunshot that echoed across the parking lot as the agent's pistol fired uselessly into the air. She landed flat on her ass in a deep, cold puddle and stared blankly in front of her.

The tall man lay motionless on his back in the rain, the pistol lying by his side.

Natalie looked down at herself. The rain had drenched her jacket, blouse and skirt, and her legs were splashed with muddy water. She ran one shivering, numb hand across her chest but could find nothing to suggest that she had been hit.

The sirens were closer now, flashing red and blue as they tore down Pennsylvania Avenue toward her.

Doug Jarvis ran to her side. 'Natalie, come with me, now!'

Natalie stared at Jarvis for a moment, and then she got up and dashed to Ben Consiglio's side.

Ben's face was slowly regaining color and he was now breathing in short, ragged bursts. Fresh blood was oozing from a savage cut in his forehead, running in rivulets down his face in the rain as his dressings fell away.

'Ben?'

Somehow the former soldier managed a crooked smile as he looked up at her. 'Afraid so.'

Doug Jarvis hurried across to her, looked at the pistol in her hand, and then at the man lying motionless twenty feet away. Jarvis glanced her over once, then hurriedly searched the surface of the parking lot around her until he found what he was looking for. He bent down and picked up a brass casing, then turned and pointed at her vehicle.

'That yours?'

Natalie nodded and was surprised to see Jarvis hurry across to her car and jump in. The old man shouted at Ben as Natalie helped him to his feet.

'Get her out of here. I'll meet up with you both in the district in one hour, corner of Fourth and Maine.'

Before Natalie could respond Jarvis drove her car out of the lot and vanished.

She stood in the rain with a smoldering pistol in one hand and stared at Ben Consiglio, who leaned against her for support.

'You coming?' he asked.

She obeyed without thought and staggered with him across to the car and climbed in.

Ben said nothing as she drove out of the lot and accelerated away, leaving the approaching sirens and flashing lights far behind.

62

NEZ PERCE NATIONAL
FOREST, IDAHO

The light from the control room reached only a few yards into the darkness, glinting off damp rocks that smelled of mold. Proctor shuffled a few paces more until he reached the edge of the light, and looked back over his shoulder.

Kurt Agry was on one knee, his rifle aimed directly between Proctor's eyes.

'Nothing back here but pain, Einstein,' Kurt growled. 'Keep movin'.'

Proctor swallowed and edged further into the inky black grip of the tunnel. He could not see the forest or even the entrance to the tunnel itself, so complete was the darkness. He shifted one foot at a time, wary of tripping over the loose rubble scattered across the tunnel floor. He could smell the clean, fresh air of the night drifting toward him, and realized that he must therefore be alone in the tunnel.

A wave of relief crept over him as he advanced, begging a god that he didn't believe in that it would be all right.

Suddenly he saw a tiny pinprick of light ahead, and then another close by. The clouds must have passed by in the night, stars twinkling in their place. He walked forward, more confident now, and let his hands drop to his sides as he called out.

'It's all clear!'

As his voice echoed down the tunnel behind him, the two stars blinked out together and then reappeared. Proctor had just enough time to realize that he wasn't looking at stars when he smelled the thick stain of decay that hung heavy on the air at the tunnel entrance. He froze, standing absolutely still as he stared into dull red eyes glinting back at him in the distant glow from the control-room lights.

'Oh Jesus.'

Proctor's legs gave way beneath him and he dropped to his knees, his eyes adjusting enough to the darkness of the night to detect the huge form looming over him. He heard a rustle as it shifted position, its immense back stooped as it entered the tunnel, the eyes glowing deep into Proctor's.

'You see anything?'

Kurt Agry's voice rolled down the tunnel toward him, but Proctor's voice was already a long-lost faculty. He merely kneeled, paralyzed on the floor of the tunnel as the huge creature stooped over him and one vast hand, thick with fur, clamped over his face and squeezed with an unimaginable force.

Proctor screamed into the damp, rough palm that closed over his face, reached up and tried to prise the huge hand away, but it was utterly useless. He saw sparks of light through his closed eyes and a searing blaze of agony soared through his skull as he felt the bones crunch and crack as they were shattered in the creature's savage grasp.

Proctor felt his body twist as it was hurled aside and smashed into the wall of the tunnel, and then everything disappeared.

'Answer me, Proctor!'

Lopez watched as Kurt shouted down the tunnel but heard nothing in response. The goddamned idiot had probably taken his chances and fled into the night, not that she could blame him. There was no sense in worrying about him. If the coast was clear then they were good to go, but she could not hope to get out of the facility past all of the soldiers' weapons.

'All right, let's move out!'

Kurt stood up and headed for the tunnel as Klein, Jenkins and Milner moved in behind him.

Lopez saw it from the corner of her eye, a white flash that seemed to fly out of the tunnel's gloom ahead of them. All at once she saw Proctor's body arcing toward them, six feet off the ground.

'Cover!'

A soaring, keening scream of rage pierced her eardrums, as deep as a gorilla and yet gabbling like some kind of ancient dialect. Kurt hurled himself to one side as Proctor's body flew past him and smashed into the control room doors, the scientist's skull crushed like an eggshell.

'Open fire!'

Kurt aimed his weapon down the corridor and let off a three-second automatic burst of fire as Klein, Jenkins and

Milner did the same. The lethal hail of gunfire roared down the confines of the tunnel as the muzzle flash illuminated its depths.

And what Lopez saw there sent a lance of icy fear thrusting down into her belly.

There wasn't just one of them.

The tunnel was filled with sasquatch charging toward them, a raging mass of fur and fury.

Lopez turned in terror and looked straight down the corridor opposite. There, in the shadows, she saw the power light to the locking mechanism flashing bright red. The power was back on.

'Fall back!'

Kurt hurled himself backward over Proctor's body and rolled over the restraining chair as one of the creatures burst into the control room. Lopez heard Milner's scream of terror as one of the animals plowed into him like a freight train and smashed the M-16 out of his grasp before grabbing his chest with one hand and folding the other over his jaw. A moment later and Milner's head was ripped from his neck with a sound like tearing denim as a fountain of dark blood splashed across nearby computer monitors.

The creature hurled the severed, bloodied head across the control room to smash with a dull thud into the opposite wall as Kurt backed down the corridor, firing as he went. The bullets hammered into the creature's chest and it wailed as it backed up into the tunnel again to shelter from the hail of gunfire.

Lopez staggered backward, trying to seek her chance to cross the control center and flee down the corridor.

'Fall back!'

Klein and Jenkins managed to hold the sasquatch back as they fired, wracked with fear as they stumbled toward Kurt.

'Control your fire!' Kurt yelled at them, and then took up position on one knee and aimed carefully at of the nearest of the massive creatures as it charged toward the control room.

He took a breath, held it, and fired.

The shot hit the creature just above the eyes, smack in the center of its forehead. The huge head snapped back and the animal toppled onto its haunches as thick blood spilled across its face.

Klein saw the animal go down and lowered his rifle as Jenkins covered his retreat.

Lopez took her chance and hurled herself at him.

63

Lopez ran across the control center even as Klein whirled at the sound of her approach. His rifle snapped across to aim at her. Too slow.

Lopez smashed into the soldier with all of her weight as she drove her shoulder into his chest and battered his rifle aside. The weapon fired at the ceiling as they crashed onto the floor, Lopez's grip on the barrel failing as it was seared by the passage of the bullets. Klein threw her off of him, twisting the weapon as she grasped it. Lopez felt herself flip over him and onto her back on the hard tiles, the M-16 pinned between them.

'Let it go,' Klein hissed. 'We're not the enemy!'

Lopez didn't respond as she yanked her knee up into Klein's groin and simultaneously jerked her head up toward his. Her forehead smacked into his nose with a dull crunch, the soldier's face folding upon itself in pain as her knee thumped into his testicles and crushed them.

Klein gagged, his eyes streaming as blood spilled in globules from his nose and down across Lopez's face. She let go of the M-16's barrel and smashed her upper forearm across

Klein's throat, driving her elbow deep into his thorax. Klein tumbled off of her and she rolled and leapt to her feet.

Klein whipped the M-16 around toward her, but Lopez blocked the barrel with one hand as she lifted her boot and smashed it down across Klein's head. The soldier shuddered as she reached down and yanked the weapon from his grasp.

'Lopez is free!'

Jenkins's shout was audible even above the din of the rifle fire, but Lopez ignored it as she turned, lifted the M-16 and fired a salvo of rounds across the control room. Kurt and Jenkins hurled themselves clear of the hastily sealed doors as her wild shots clattered against the metal walls and rattled down the tunnel.

In an instant the M-16's clip emptied, and Lopez turned and sprinted down the corridor toward the laboratory. She burst into the chamber and ducked to her right just as a hail of bullets zipped through the corridor and smashed into the dissection tables in a shower of sparks. She rushed across to the computer server and grabbed Kurt's hard drive before sprinting down the adjoining corridor toward the crematorium.

The sound of running boots was amplified by the narrow passage as Kurt Agry raced after her, the thundering footfalls rushing ever closer.

Lopez ran across the chamber and plunged into the eastern corridor. She leapt over the gruesome remains of Cletus MacCarthy's body and reached the locked door, the mechanism glowing with a tiny, bright red light.

Lopez reached into her jacket and yanked out the access card she'd palmed hours before from the fallen soldier. She slammed into the steel door and slid it through the magnetic strip. The bright little light changed to green and the three-pin locking mechanism snapped out of place. Lopez heaved the door open and hurled herself inside.

'Lopez!'

Kurt appeared behind her in the corridor, his rifle raised and pointing at her. She turned and slammed the door shut, then punched the access card through the slot on the inside. The mechanism clicked shut just as she heard Kurt slam against the door outside.

'Lopez! Open the goddamned door, right now!'

She stood back from the door, breathing hard as she swiped one sleeve across her face and wiped some of Klein's blood off. Kurt pounded on the metal from the other side, but there was no way he could break through such a heavy door.

'And you can't break out,' she murmured to herself.

Not, at least, until Kurt and his men were dead, torn apart by the creatures now invading the facility. She was about to formulate some kind of plan when something caused the hairs on the back of her neck to stand on end, as though a bitter wind had blown across her skin. She smelled the dank, stale odor of sweat and rotting meat.

Her stomach twisted upon itself as she felt a presence nearby, something watching her from the impenetrable blackness.

64

Ethan eased his way to the ventilation gratings of the living quarters and peered through the gaps. The dim light in the room and the awkward angle made it hard to see much, but he was almost certain that the room was empty.

He checked his watch. *Three minutes.* And then he heard the gunshots start.

Even in the confined spaces of the facility he still recognized the sound of M-16s and the shouts of men at war. Suddenly he realized why Proctor, Dana and Lopez had been taken out of the room.

Ethan crawled over the false ceiling, careful to stay on the girders until he reached a panel roughly over the center of the room. He reached down and prised the panel upward enough to get his fingers underneath it before hauling it to one side and dropping down into the room.

For a brief moment he considered the possibility that Lopez had figured a way out of the room much as he had, but then he saw the door sitting slightly ajar, a thin strip of light from the corridor beyond slicing into the darkness.

Ethan sprinted toward the control center and almost

immediately ran into Jenkins. The soldier was down on one knee, firing wildly at the mine entrance. Ethan rushed up behind him just as Jenkins heard his approach and whirled in shock.

'Warner, no!'

Ethan grabbed the barrel of the M-16 with one hand as he drove his left boot with tremendous force into Jenkins's face. The soldier's head snapped backward with a savage motion as his hands went into spasm and released his rifle. Jenkins sprawled onto his back on the floor as Ethan yanked the M-16 from his weakened grasp and aimed down at him.

'Where's Lopez and the others?' he demanded.

'Proctor's dead and so is Dana!' Jenkins spat from his bloodied mouth. 'Lopez stole the hard drive from Klein and then locked herself in the crematorium!'

Ethan felt a sudden chill flush through him and looked instinctively again at his watch.

Thirty seconds.

'Oh no.'

Jenkins looked up at him and then his face went pale. 'What have you done?'

Ethan turned away to run back toward the living quarters, but Jenkins leapt to his feet and grabbed Ethan by the throat and hauled him sideways into the wall.

'How did you get out of the store room?' Jenkins screamed, wrapping his arms around Ethan's throat and squeezing hard.

Ethan felt his throat collapse and his eyes bulge as Jenkins locked his arms into place and strained with the effort of trying to kill him. He reached up and grabbed the soldier's arms but he had too good a hold of Ethan's neck, locked rigidly into place and driven by what Ethan could only guess was an insanity of panic: Ethan could hardly tell him how to escape when he was being throttled to death.

Ethan leaned forward, forcing Jenkins's feet off the ground. His vision began to star as his brain was starved of oxygen but Ethan kept his panic under control. Instead, balancing with Jenkins locked around his throat, Ethan moved his right leg and hooked it behind Jenkins's own flailing leg, pinning it in place.

In that instant, as the shift in weight proved too much for Ethan to hold and he felt himself topple to the right beneath Jenkins's weight, Ethan twisted to his right and hurled himself off the ground as though leaping backward out of an aircraft, just as he had done many times before in the corps.

Ethan rolled in midair with Jenkins on his back as they fell, and then they hit the ground hard. Ethan's full body-weight smashed down on top of Jenkins, the back of his head cracking across the younger man's jaw and smashing it sideways. The massive impact crunched down on the soldier's chest and ribs, crushing his lungs and forcing the air from them in a blast that puffed past Ethan's ears.

Jenkins's arms fell aside from Ethan's throat as the winded, injured man sagged beneath him. Ethan rolled off to one side and scrambled to his feet. He had made a single pace when he heard the voice behind him.

'Stay where you are.'

Ethan turned, and saw that Klein had managed to force the mine entrance door closed once more. Kurt Agry stood with a pistol pointed at Ethan's chest.

65

Lopez turned and stood in total silence, her back pressed to the wall as she stared straight ahead and tried to breathe as silently as possible. The paneled wall was cold on her back through her jacket, hard and unforgiving. The gunshots from the control room had fallen silent, either because the attack had been repulsed or because Kurt and his men were dead.

The smell of decay drifted again on the stale air in the room, rising over the clinical odor of unknown chemicals. Lopez guessed the room was maybe thirty feet by twenty feet and filled with impenetrable pools of blackness that seemed to reach out for her, swelling with every passing moment.

It was impossible to tell where the creature was, so deep were the shadows. But she knew that the size of the room meant that it could not be much more than ten feet away. Maybe fifteen, if she was lucky. The emergency generator that powered the rest of the facility's emergency lights was obviously not connected to this room, which must be supplied by a system of batteries or similar. The stench of the chemicals suggested to her that it was some kind of chemical crematorium, probably to keep the facility self-contained,

so there must have been a secure power supply to handle
ventilation and containment in the event of a chemical fire.

She tried to close her eyes and let them adjust to the inky
darkness, but it was no use. So complete was it that she
would not have been able to see her hand in front of her face,
had she the courage to move it far enough to check.

Her heels ached from standing utterly motionless and she
shifted her weight slightly. The movement caused her jacket
to rasp against the wall, and in the silence it sounded as loud
as somebody sanding down a wall.

She shut her eyes tight, clenched her jaw and fists as she
listened for even the tiniest sound.

From the darkness came a soft rustling, like the sound of
millions of tiny ants scuttling across sawdust. Lopez knew that
it was the sound of fur bristling and she felt her guts turn to
slime within her. The sound came from her left again, maybe
ten feet away.

Slowly she turned her head to the left, the sound of her
own long black hair scraping across her jacket. Somehow,
something told her that whatever the hell was in here with
her, it could detect her much easier than she it. Better ears,
better sense of smell, although in this darkness nothing could
see. Only bats would be able to get a handle in here.

She let her head tilt upward. She could not see the ceiling above but she knew that it had to have vents of some
kind. They may not be very large, given that this was a mine
and not a twenty-story in downtown Chicago, but there
might just be the chance that she could climb out of here and
escape.

There was only one thing that she would need.

Light.

And in order to get light, she would have to expose herself to whatever was in here with her. Maybe get herself torn to pieces like Cletus MacCarthy, whose head she knew was just a few feet away from her, the grisly memento lying on the other side of the locked door.

Her common sense told her that the creature knew she was here. Her fear told her it was better to be helpless and alive than courageous and dead. She knew that Kurt and his team might come back at some point, and she would be forced to tell them what was in here, the reason why they had been led to this point. It hadn't been a trap.

The sasquatch imprisoned here had somehow been freed, but the electronic locks in the crematorium had entrapped one of them. The sasquatch were unable to free it, hence their elaborate baiting of Warner, Kurt Agry and the team.

Only *we* know how to control the locks to the doors.

Lopez's throat constricted tightly as she struggled with her dilemma. *Get a grip, Nicola.* Fact was, she couldn't do anything as long as she couldn't see. If she lit the room, the thing in here with her would either kill her or prevent her from moving. If she stayed in the dark, it might kill her anyway, and there would be nothing she could do about it.

Rock. Hard place.

Lopez cursed in the darkness and yanked out her cellphone. Before she could let herself regret it she stabbed a button with her thumb, turned to her left and held the cell up in the darkness.

The screen flashed into life and cast a soft blue glow across the entire room.

A deafening crash sent a bolt of terror through her as something thundered away from the light with a gabbled growl. Nicola shrieked in horror and staggered backward as she saw a huge, muscular form huddle away from the light some twenty feet away.

And the glow from the cell reflected off the bars of a containment cage dominating the opposite side of the room.

Lopez stared at the cage, the huge solid-steel bars some two inches thick. An equally sturdy roof of four-inch steel matched the floor, and the door to the cage was sealed with a large blocky contraption that had a wire protruding discreetly from one side that vanished into a hole in one of the steel bars. Her eyes traced the bar, and the cable that reappeared from beneath the cage and ran to the opposite wall where a control box was fixed.

Remote door lock.

Lopez pushed stiffly off the wall against which she had been leaning and crept forward, holding her cell in front of her and watching the blessed cone of blue light as it advanced ahead of her. The light swept further down the cage, and touched upon a mass of thick fur. Lopez hesitated and then edged a pace further forward.

A thickly forested thigh, curled up, came into view.

She moved a little further and saw a huge torso, a thick arm with bulging muscles the size of her head beneath heavy matted hair wrapped around it while another was swept up over the animal's head. In the light from the cell, she saw two small discs of reflective material flash from behind the thick forearm as the creature peered at her.

The cone of light filled the cage as Lopez stopped some

four feet from it and stared down at the immense form hud-
dling away from her.

It was hard to tell by the way it was crouching, but she
guessed it must be around six hundred pounds and probably
eight feet tall. The stench coming off the thing was almost
unbearable, not helped by the mounds of scat lining the
edges of the cage. She couldn't tell how long it had been
trapped in here, but judging by its reaction to even the cell's
feeble light and the bodies they'd found outside the facility,
not less than two weeks.

A creature as large as it was must have been literally dying
of thirst and starvation.

Lopez turned and looked over her shoulder. Along the
back wall of the room were large steel sinks and five-gallon
containers of water, probably used for washing away the
remains of other, less fortunate occupants of the room. She
backed away from the cage and turned, walked across to the
nearest water canister and heaved it off the sink. She dragged
the heavy canister across to the cage, then squatted down
alongside it and unscrewed the cap. She sniffed the contents
and satisfied herself that it was water inside and not some
awful chemical before she pushed the canister toward the
edge of the cage.

The sasquatch peered at her from behind its arm but did
not move.

'C'mon,' Lopez said. 'I know you can smell this.'

The animal did not move. Lopez set her cell down on the
floor next to her, and with a heave of effort tilted the canister over and put her lips to the cap. Cold water spilled out of
it across her lips and trickled down her jacket, but she

downed a few mouthfuls before righting the canister and shoving it back up against the cage.

Then she picked up her cell and backed away.

As the cone of light retreated from the sasquatch it suddenly unfolded itself from the corner of the cage and reached out. One huge hand passed between the bars and lifted the canister off the ground. Another reached out through another gap in the bars and tilted the base of the canister up as the head appeared just on the periphery of the light and touched its lips to the cap.

Lopez watched as water splashed and drizzled onto the floor and down the immense creature's chest as it sucked and guzzled the five gallons down in little more than two minutes.

She turned and looked up at the vents in the wall.

Both of them were little more than twelve inches high and maybe three feet wide, faced with metal grills and likely led out to an equally impassable ventilation shaft.

There was no other way out of the room.

Lopez turned and saw the sasquatch squatting on the floor of the cage watching her, its eyes flashing as they caught the blue light of the cell. The animal growled, a low, throaty and menacing sound that vibrated through her chest like thunder. She saw the thick hairs on its back bristle upward as a muscle twitched in its shoulder.

And then the cage door clicked and the heavy latch slipped out of place .

With a high-pitched whine, the door drifted open.

CENTRAL INTELLIGENCE
AGENCY, LANGLEY, VIRGINIA

Abraham Mitchell stood in front of William Steel's desk, his fists clenched by his sides and his gaze boring directly into the DCIA's like laser beams.

'You've burned my people.'

Steel remained in his seat, as he had done so when Mitchell had barreled past his personal assistant outside and thundered into the office.

'Nobody has been burned,' Steel replied.

The man was hiding behind his desk and a thin veneer of professional immunity. Mitchell knew that Steel could have half a dozen security guards inside the office within seconds, and he was also aware of why the director had not done so immediately. He knew that what they were about to discuss was not just classified but highly illegal: any exposure could see Steel not just hounded out of his office but up for a grilling in front of Congress and the Senate. Or worse.

'Whatever you're hiding up there in Idaho, it stays

between us,' Mitchell growled. 'Right up until a single one of my people gets killed. Then, it's all over Congress.'

'Is that a threat?' Steel asked, looking idly up at Mitchell.

'A promise.'

'Based on what evidence?' Steel challenged. 'Fanciful claims made by dope-smoking hippies from the Idaho hills? You've got nothing.'

'We've got more than you think,' Mitchell pointed out. 'My guys have been on the ground for a while, William. They've already pieced enough together to know that whatever's in that mountain, it's got CIA written all over it.' He leaned forward, resting his balled fists on the desk top. 'And you've been tailing not just my people but Congressional aides for weeks now, perhaps longer. You think that'll look good when it crops up in the investigation reports?'

Steel's eyes narrowed.

'You haven't got any evidence of surveillance operations on-going in the district and—'

'We have photographic evidence,' Mitchell cut across him. 'Enough to identify CIA agents at work and their possible involvement in the assassination of a Congressional aide right here in Virginia.'

William Steel leaned forward on his desk, the casually dismissive expression draining from his features.

'Who? When?'

Mitchell raised an eyebrow.

'You weren't aware?' he mocked. 'That's not good, considering you almost certainly personally sanctioned the operation itself. And we have names, too. I take it that Mr. Wilson is leading the charge?'

Steel's features paled a little further. 'Where did you hear that name?'

'My people are doing their job,' Mitchell snapped back. 'Which is to figure things out and report back to me. Let me guess: your man in the field has gone too far and now you're starting to realize that if you don't rein him in he'll blow the whole damned thing up in your face?'

Steel swallowed and his eyes quivered as Mitchell watched him thinking furiously.

'This is too big to break publicly,' he said. 'You do that, we'll both go down.'

'No, we won't, and you know it,' Mitchell growled. 'You said it yourself in front of the Joint Chiefs – you've got an operation on-going up there and the DIA investigation was in danger of exposing it. But you're not concerned with the lives of agents on the ground; you're only interested in covering your own ass regardless of the collateral damage it might cause.'

'That's not true,' Steel uttered.

'What, then?'

Steel stared into Mitchell's eyes for a long moment before he replied.

'What do you want?'

Mitchell kept his features impassive. 'My people out, safely. Doug Jarvis to be cleared of all involvement in the suspected murder of a Congressional aide, Ben Consiglio. I'm sure your man Wilson will be able to fill you in on what really happened there.'

Steel ground his teeth in his jaw. 'I can get Jarvis out of trouble but your people in Idaho are on their own. It's too late.'

'The air strike,' Mitchell rumbled, and was rewarded with a nod from Steel.

'Once we get the data out the whole place will be nothing but a memory. Terrible underground gas leak and explosion, lack of ventilation.' Steel sighed. 'No survivors.'

Mitchell's thick hand whipped across the desk and grabbed Steel's collar. He hauled the DCIA across his desk, the smaller man gagging as his shirt crushed his throat. Mitchell glared deep into Steel's eyes.

'If my people are killed I'll blow the whistle on this.'

'They're not your people,' Steel coughed. 'They're just two-bit losers out of Chicago, they're nothing.'

Mitchell dropped Steel face down onto his desk, pinning the back of his head with a forearm as he leaned down close.

'They're also patriots,' he rumbled, 'a word that you're clearly no longer familiar with. They die, so does your career, your reputation and your future.'

Steel's voice squeaked back at Mitchell.

'I'd be careful if I were you. I'm not the only one with something to lose.'

'Like hell,' Mitchell snapped. 'This stops at your door.'

'Not if Mr. Wilson is going off the range. He could target anybody.'

Mitchell considered this for a moment and then tightened his grip.

'Not before you're sunk,' he replied. 'Jarvis told me that there must be a plant in the Government Accountability Office in the district, a CIA mole. Give me the name.'

'Or what?' Steel coughed.

'Or I'll drag you down to Congress myself, right now, and

tell them in advance about the air strike that hasn't happened yet. Our own National Guard using live weapons on American citizens on American soil under CIA control? That alone will be enough to finish you, and start a much more interesting investigation into CIA programs.'

Steel strained against Mitchell's iron grip.

'How do I know you won't squeal anyway?'

'You don't,' Mitchell said as he twisted Steel's neck further. 'The mole, who is it?'

Over his pain, Steel coughed a name loudly enough for Mitchell to hear.

GOVERNMENT ACCOUNTABILITY OFFICE, WASHINGTON DC

'This is it.'

Guy Rikard held aloft a piece of paper from Natalie Warner's collection of files. The piece of paper was filled with scribbled notes that she had made during the day, and one of the notes caught his eye.

'MK–ULTRA,' Larry Levinson read from the notes. 'She's been talking about that all day.'

'CIA program from the seventies,' Rikard confirmed. 'Was cancelled after a congressional investigation. Natalie claimed that some or all of the program is probably still active, perhaps under a different name, and that she had the evidence to prove it.'

'Can't be that easy,' Larry pointed out reasonably. 'Something like that would be buried deep.'

'She's been to the archives office,' Rikard noted, flicking through pages of recently printed documents tagged with the

NARA logo. 'What if she managed to find some piece of evidence, something forgotten in the original cover-up? It might have generated new leads, uncovered new information. Natalie was willing to punch me in the face and lose her job rather than lose this investigation. Whatever she found it must have been colossal.'

'Huge enough to get Ben Consiglio killed,' Larry replied softly.

Rikard nodded, and looked up at Larry. 'Enough to get *us* killed. You can go home if you want, Larry. I can find Natalie from here.'

Larry shook his head. 'I'm in, all the way. Let's finish this. How will you figure out where Natalie's gone?'

Rikard grinned and stood up. He grabbed a pad from Natalie's desk and a pen.

'She wrote down a series of names on this pad,' he said, 'then took it with her. Child's play to reveal what she wrote.'

Rikard rubbed the pen over the blank page on top of the pad, and instantly revealed the impressions from Natalie's scribbles on the now missing page. He was about to read it out when his cell rang in his pocket. He pulled it out and answered. Doug Jarvis's voice sounded muted and distant on the line.

'*It's Jarvis, you got anything yet?*'

'She's gone to an address in Coral Hills. That's a housing project just north of Edwards Air Force Base. There's a name: Anderson.'

'*Excellent work. Get out of there now, both of you. We'll go after Natalie.*'

The line went dead, and Larry stood up from the desk.

'You think we should do that?' Larry asked. 'Surely we're not in any danger?'

'That a chance you're willing to take?' Rikard challenged. 'No, this goes to the Capitol. I'd better call the Investigator General, let them know we're bringing this data in.'

Rikard fished out his cellphone and hit a quick-dial number.

He frowned as his phone buzzed in his ear, and looked down at it in confusion.

'Line's out,' he said, and pocketed the phone.

Rikard got up and picked up the hefty stacks of paperwork from Natalie's desk, then dumped them into his briefcase.

'Maybe we should finish collating everything else she's worked on first,' Larry suggested. 'We need a solid case before we take this further.'

'There's too much paperwork here,' Rikard said. 'By the time we get through it all and figure out what's really been going on, it could all be over. I'll take this to the Investigator General right now, get his people on it.'

Larry stood up. 'You sure that's the right thing to do?'

'It's the *only* thing to do,' Rikard said. 'That's what this department is for. Too much has happened to risk keeping this under the carpet now and we're out of our depth. Jarvis virtually said it himself: we need to blow it open before Natalie or anybody else gets hurt.'

'You mean like Ben did?' Larry said.

'Exactly like that,' Rikard replied and closed the briefcase. 'Somebody in this office was watching what was going on. We need to get this data out of the office and into safe hands.'

Larry stood up, his features taut.

'And what if you're the mole?' he suggested. 'You could take all of that and disappear. Whoever killed Ben must have been informed of his location from this office and it was you who sent him out to Virginia.'

Rikard stared down at Larry and grimaced.

'Seriously?' he uttered. 'I've worked for the GAO for twenty years. If I was in the business of selling out I'd have done it long before now, believe me.'

Rikard turned for the office door. Larry shifted position and blocked his way.

'I can't let you do that, Guy,' he said.

Rikard glared at the little man in his way. 'Natalie could be in danger, Larry. The longer we leave this the greater the chance she'll get iced just like Ben.'

'And if you're the mole,' Larry countered, 'then you'll ensure that everything Natalie and Ben have done and sac-rificed will be for nothing.'

'Jesus, Larry, that's crap and you know it!' Rikard snapped. 'Whatever Natalie's onto here has been running for decades. This could be bigger than Watergate. God knows how many people in this office might have been under observation since the investigation started. Even you might have been watched.'

Larry grinned. 'Yeah, just in case I go all Julian Assange on them.'

Rikard laughed out loud and clapped a hand on Larry's shoulder. 'Yeah, something like that. Come on, let's go together: that way, nobody's in danger of losing anything.'

Larry grabbed his jacket and an expensive pair of Ray-Bans as he turned to follow Rikard for the office door. They were halfway there when Rikard slowed down, his brow furrowed.

'What?' Larry asked.

'Something I just said,' Rikard replied. 'Anybody could have been watched in this office. Ben drove out to Virginia, so his killer must have been informed. But how could the killer have known when Ben would leave the orphanage in Aden, to hit him like he did on the road?'

'Maybe he didn't,' Larry suggested. 'Maybe the killer was lying in wait somewhere along the road?'

'But then why not hit Ben's car before he got to the orphanage and remove any chance of his making any discoveries?' Rikard persisted. 'Unless the killer wasn't informed of Ben's visit until later and had to hurry to make the—'

Rikard stopped walking. Larry took another pace before stopping between Rikard and the office door. Rikard stared down at Larry.

'You were working with me in the office for almost an hour after Ben left,' he said. 'You couldn't make the call. You wanted to leave to make a call but I kept you here.'

Larry shook his head. 'That's ridiculous, Guy. You're getting paranoid now.'

Rikard's features hardened.

'Get out of my way or I swear I'll put you on your ass.'

Larry, his features twitching nervously, stood his ground.

Rikard snarled and swung the briefcase in his hand around at Larry's head.

To Rikard's surprise, Larry didn't flinch. The little man hopped inside the swing of the briefcase, then jammed his right arm under Rikard's and whirled. Rikard felt his body flip over Larry's as he was hurled over the smaller man's shoulder and slammed down onto the carpeted office floor.

The hard surface knocked the wind out of Rikard's lungs. He saw Larry grab his wrist with terrific speed and yank it around on itself. White pain bolted through Rikard's arm and shoulder as the tendons were strained within. His hand flexed open as he cried out in agony and the briefcase toppled from his grasp.

Larry's right shoe slammed sideways into Rikard's face, the cartilage in his nose crunching beneath the impact as blood spilled into his mouth. The back of Rikard's head smacked into the floor and stars sparkled before his eyes as he felt the pressure on his arm vanish.

Rikard squinted up and saw Larry standing over him with the briefcase in his hand, blocking the way to the office door. The nervous, twitchy expression was gone. The small man looked down at Rikard with a face devoid of emotion as though examining a small insect, his eyes hidden behind the Ray-Bans. In his other hand, he held a cellphone to his ear. He began speaking as Rikard hauled himself away toward the opposite wall.

'It's me,' Larry intoned into the cell. 'I'm still at GAO, one hostage. I've got the files.'

Rikard stared in disbelief for a moment as Larry listened to the reply on his cell and nodded.

'It will be done. What about this asshole?'

Larry listened to the response, nodded once, then shut off the cell. He slipped it into his pocket and put the briefcase down.

'You?' Rikard uttered.

Larry did not reply. He simply walked toward Rikard without fear, without compromise, without hesitation. No weapon, and yet Rikard somehow knew without a doubt that Larry, if that was even his real name, would be able to kill him without using one.

Rikard scrambled to his feet as his back hit the water cooler in the corner of the office. His hand rested on a desk beside him, nudged a thick ballpoint pen. He grabbed at it as Larry came within arm's reach and swung it wildly toward the small man's face.

Larry swatted the blow aside with one iron-hard forearm and then smashed his own forehead into Rikard's mouth. Pain seared his jaw as his teeth crumpled backward in his mouth under the force of the blow. He felt his elbow being pinched hard and his legs and arms jangled and twitched in response as he collapsed onto his back on the desk.

Larry's elbow slammed into Rikard's solar plexus, driving the air from his lungs and smearing his vision into a blur of hazy light as he gagged and folded up.

Larry turned, one hand still pinching the nerves in Rikard's elbow. He reached out and grabbed a Styrofoam cup from the stack alongside the water cooler, filled it with water and promptly poured half of it across Rikard's chest and half of it across his shoes.

Rikard, blinded and almost entirely helpless, spat a spray of blood as he cried out.

'What the fuck are you doing?'

Larry did not reply. He grabbed a nearby desk fan, dumped it on the desk and pinned it with one foot before he grasped the power cord and yanked hard. The cord snapped from the fan's base, two copper wires glinting in the overhead lights.

Rikard's vision sharpened as his body twitched beneath Larry's grip. He saw the exposed wires plunge toward his chest.

'No!'

The last thought that went through Rikard's mind was that the office used 110-volt electricity. He'd once read that it was not strong enough to kill from a touch, unless it went straight through the chest. Electricity always traveled along the route of least resistance to the ground.

Larry hauled him off the desk and onto his feet as the wires touched Rikard high on his chest, just to the left of center. Rikard felt a tremendous surge of pain sear through his ribcage as the current plunged through him, his limbs trembling as he collapsed to the floor in a quivering mass.

Larry followed him down with the exposed wire, pressing the live copper against his chest until Rikard's eyes rolled up in their sockets and foamy white saliva spilled from his mouth. Rikard twitched and quivered for several long seconds, and then slumped. Larry pulled the wires away and stared down at Rikard's motionless corpse for a brief moment.

Then he turned and unplugged the desk fan cord from the socket, rolled it up and put it in his pocket. He grabbed Rikard's briefcase and then strode from the office without looking back.

68

NEZ PERCE NATIONAL FOREST, IDAHO

Ethan dropped the M1le and raised his hands, watching as Kurt advanced a pace alongside Jenkins, who still lay sprawled on the floor, gasping for breath.

'Start talking,' Kurt snapped at Ethan. 'How did you get out of the store room and into the living quarters?'

'It doesn't matter,' Ethan replied. 'There's no way out of here other than the mine entrance.'

'You expect me to believe that?' Kurt sneered. 'Where the hell are Duran and Mary?'

Ethan shrugged.

'Hiding out in the tunnels, maybe,' he said. 'Waiting for you and your little bunch of assholes to blow yourself sky-high.'

'We're not assholes,' Jenkins spluttered. 'We didn't want this to happen!'

Kurt ignored Jenkins and raised the pistol to point at Ethan's head.

'Spill it, Warner, all of it, or I'll blow your head clean off.'

Ethan glanced down at Jenkins and saw his opportunity. If you can't defeat the enemy by pure force or guile, then turn your enemy against himself. He let a grim smile curl from his lips.

'Do that, and you definitely won't be getting out of here. Probably just a few minutes until that air strike arrives, Kurt, and it looks to me like you and your team are going nowhere.'

'Don't waste my time!' Kurt yelled. 'Answer me or I'll shoot you just for the goddamned hell of it!'

'And doom your own men to death down here?' Ethan challenged. 'Seems to me you've lost your way, Kurt. You're supposed to lead your men not bargain their lives away. I'm guessing that you've got the data from those computer servers stashed away somewhere safe, out of your men's reach?'

Jenkins looked up at Kurt, who shook his head.

'I wish I had,' he said, 'but your partner decided to cover her own ass and stole the hard drive from me.'

Ethan glanced down at Jenkins.

'I'm guessing that this asshole killed Dana Ford?'

Jenkins nodded.

'He sent Proctor into the tunnel. Those things killed him too.'

'Divide and conquer,' Kurt said with a wry, cold grin as he stepped closer to Ethan. 'You don't think that you can turn my own men against me, do you?'

Ethan shrugged.

'Don't really need to. You've been doing a fine job of that yourself.'

Ethan saw Jenkins look over his shoulder. The mine

entrance doors behind them started shuddering as the enraged creatures outside began trying to smash their way in with brute force, the blows echoing through the lonely facility.

'That door's not going to hold much longer, Kurt,' Ethan said. 'You kill me, you've achieved nothing and you still can't get out of here.'

Kurt Agry stared at Ethan for several long moments, his jaw grinding as he suppressed the latent fury seething through his veins. Then, he straightened and made his decision.

'You're right, Warner,' he said. 'I can't kill you. But if there's one thing I learned in Afghanistan, it's that if you apply the right kind of pressure you can make people tell you anything.'

Kurt lowered his aim and pointed his pistol at Ethan's right knee.

'You shoot, Kurt,' Ethan warned him, 'and you can be damned sure I'll let myself die rather than tell any of you how to get out of here.'

Kurt grinned. 'Thought you said there was *no* other way out of here?'

'Not without me there isn't.'

Kurt sneered at Ethan. 'Let's find out.'

He squeezed the pistol's trigger.

The shot crashed out, but it flew wide as Jenkins reached up and smashed Kurt's pistol to one side. Behind the sergeant, Klein rushed up and grabbed his shoulders and arms and together they dragged the kicking, screaming man to the ground.

Jenkins hurled his weight onto Kurt's body, then looked at Ethan in desperation.

'How do we get out of here?!'

Ethan made a decision of his own without conscious thought.

'The crematorium,' he said.

Before any of them could reply he turned and sprinted back down the corridor. He dashed into the living quarters and slammed the door behind him, then dragged two of the beds across the room and pinned the door shut from the inside.

Then he jumped up onto the bed and clambered back up into the ceiling cavity, praying that he wasn't too late.

69

Lopez stared in disbelief as the sasquatch looked at the open door.

'Oh shit.'

She backed away slowly from the cage as the huge creature leaned forward, one thick, heavy arm as thick as her thigh reaching out to the door. The door swung open as though hit by a car and clashed against the bars.

She realised that with the power back on to the room, the locks on the creature's cage must also have activated, maybe even shorted out.

Lopez reached into her pocket for her access card and backed up another pace.

'Easy,' she said, keeping her gaze on the sasquatch as she slowly turned and reached out to slide the card through the mechanism. The door light turned green as the locks clicked open.

The sasquatch lunged forward, its massive chest slamming against the bars in its haste as a huge and hairy arm shot out toward her, the stale-smelling hair on the hand sweeping across her face as she crashed down onto the tiles. The huge hand flashed down and before she could kick away it folded around her ankle like a vice.

Lopez felt her scream snatched from her throat as an intense pain bolted up through her leg, as though her ankle were being driven over by a train. She felt the bone inside trembling under the immense stress as she was yanked back toward the cage, and the sasquatch let out a terrible gurgling cry as it tried to reach her with its other hand.

Lopez screamed and kicked out, but her boot folded sideways against the immense strength of the arm as it crashed down across her hip and gripped her jacket. With a growl the sasquatch hauled her toward it, those terrible eyes flashing in the light from the cellphone.

Lopez's cell slipped from her grasp and skittered across the tiles, the light spinning and flashing across the floor as she struggled against the might of the beast hauling her in. The animal's eyes flicked across to the glowing screen of the cell, and in an instant it released her as it reached out curiously for the light.

Lopez scrambled backward and turned for the door.

'Lopez, up here!'

She stopped and looked up in surprise to see one of the ceiling panels removed and Ethan's face staring down at her. His arms appeared and reached down toward her.

'Move, now!'

The cage door crashed open as the sasquatch lumbered out, holding Lopez's cell in one hand and staring into the screen's blue light. Then it turned as Ethan's voice attracted its attention. The cell dropped from its hand as it turned and lumbered toward Lopez.

She let out a cry of terror as she leapt up into the air and flung her arms up toward Ethan. Ethan caught her and with a heave of effort hauled her up until her hands gripped the edge of the support beam.

'Pull me up!' she yelled.

Ethan jerked himself up into a squatting position and then grabbed Lopez's wrists and heaved her up through the open panel. Her feet cleared the gap as she scrambled out of reach of the sasquatch and struggled to get her breathing under control, but her chest heaved wildly and her vision starred in her eyes. She staggered sideways and collapsed onto one of the girders as the sasquatch pounded at the panels beneath them. Ethan staggered out of its range with Lopez just behind him, and then she dropped to her knees in the darkness.

'You're hyperventilating,' Ethan said. 'Nicola, get control.'

Lopez tried, but her breath rasped in her lungs and all of a sudden she slumped and felt herself crying as Ethan pulled her to him. She buried her face into his chest and clung to his jacket for what felt like hours but in reality was probably just a few moments, until her body stopped heaving and her breathing calmed.

'Easy,' Ethan said, one of his hands cupping the back of her head. 'I think you were on the menu for a midnight snack.'

'Jesus,' she uttered. 'I thought that was it, Ethan. I thought I was done.' She looked up at him. 'Where the hell did you come from?'

Ethan stood up and offered her his hand.

'The mine wasn't dug horizontally,' he said. 'The ore bodies were vertical, with a surrounding warren of tunnels and ventilation shafts. I got out and came looking for you when I realized what must be in this room.'

Lopez looked back down through the open panel, where the sasquatch was watching them both with hungry eyes.

'The other ones led us here to free this one,' she said. 'What are we going to do? Where's Kurt and his men? What about Duran and Mary?'

'They've got away,' Ethan said. 'Proctor and Dana are both dead.'

'I know,' Lopez said. 'That was down to Kurt.'

Ethan nodded. 'We need to move, fast. It's time to get out of here.'

'What about the rest of them?' Lopez said. 'If they get out, they'll come after us.'

A grim smile formed on Ethan's features.

'They won't. I've made sure of that.'

70

'You're dead men! I swear I'll kill you all myself!'

Jenkins and Klein struggled to keep Kurt on the ground as Klein looked over his shoulder.

'They're coming in!'

The mine doors were buckling as they were smashed and battered from the opposite side, and although the steel bars were holding, the mounts they were attached to were being smashed clean out of the walls. Several thousand pounds of enraged muscle and bone were literally tearing the door clean out of the bedrock behind the paneled walls.

Jenkins, his weight pinning Kurt to the ground, saw the first of the metal bars burst from the wall and clatter noisily onto the tiled floor. He leapt up off Kurt's body and grabbed his rifle.

'Cover the doors!'

Klein whirled and ran back into the control center as Kurt Agry scrambled to his feet and grabbed his pistol, shouting as he went.

'Give them everything! Take them down!'

The huge doors screeched and groaned, and then the

remaining two restraining bars smashed clear from the walls and skittered across the floor as six huge sasquatch thundered into the command center, their banshee wails deafening even above the sudden crash of gunfire.

Kurt fired a burst of rounds into the mine entrance, saw a shadowy form of russet-brown fur shudder as the bullets plowed through thick flesh and bone, but nothing could stop the creatures from plunging into the dull red and white light of the command center.

For the first time he got a good look at it as it stood upright.

Perhaps nine feet tall, with shoulders almost five feet across, its chest a vast forest of thick fur splattered with blood from where bullets had hit it. Huge, muscular arms and thick, short legs, a slight stoop to its stance. A face that was fascinatingly and horrifically both human and primate, the skin dark like leather and covered with fine hair. Then its eyes swiveled to look into Kurt's, as an unmistakeable expression of anger spread across its face.

'There's no way out!' Klein shouted, his face smeared with his own blood.

'Hold them back from the southern corridor!' Kurt yelled. 'If we can't get out we'll blow the charges!'

Kurt leapt backward and ran down the corridor into the laboratory as Klein and Jenkins began firing again with wild abandon into the control room as they retreated toward him. Kurt headed for the door to the store room. Somehow, Duran and Mary Wilkes had gotten out of the facility from that room, and he intended to do the same damned thing.

He pulled the locks out of their shafts and yanked on the door handle.

Nothing happened.

Kurt pulled on it again, harder. Nothing happened. In an instant, he knew that Warner had barricaded the door before leaving the room, and he would have done the same thing to the living quarters.

He turned and dashed back into the laboratory just as Klein and Jenkins backed into the chamber, firing down the corridor in deafening three-round bursts.

'Blow the charges!' Klein screamed. 'Take them down with us!'

Kurt dashed to the center of the doorway and opened fire on the creatures now charging toward them down the corridor. He saw splatters of blood splash against their massive chests and arms but they kept coming, their faces masks of fury.

He turned and dashed to the detonator, picked it up and flashed a grim smile at the huge creatures storming toward him.

'Too late, assholes!'

He pressed the button.

Nothing happened. He pressed it again. Still nothing. Kurt yanked the top of the detonator box off and spilled the contents out. His guts turned to ice water inside him as he stared down at a pile of smooth, polished stones. An image of the riverbed, way back in the valley where Willis had been killed, flashed through his mind. Warner.

'No!'

In a moment of dreadful, terrible realization, Kurt remembered Ethan Warner being made to carry Simmons's bergen. Simmons had been the team's demolitions expert. It would have taken Ethan only a few moments to gut the detonator and make the switch. Kurt felt suddenly empty inside, as though all emotion had been drained from him.

Kurt turned to Klein.

'All out,' he said.

'What?!' Klein yelled.

The animals thundered into the laboratory as Kurt opened fire. Klein screamed something unintelligible as the creatures smashed into him and hurled him into the air as though he were something to play with. Klein smashed against the ceiling and tumbled down among the writhing mass of enraged sasquatch, his agonized screams competing with the roars of the animals as they shredded his body in a frenzy of destruction.

Kurt began to back away as he saw Klein's arm torn from its socket and hurled across the room.

'We need covering fire!' Jenkins screamed.

Kurt glanced over his shoulder and looked at his watch.

Two minutes remaining.

The containment cages in the rear of the facility were a dead end, and with the door to the stores blocked there was only one direction left for him to go. The crematorium; the only remaining room where the electronic locking mechanisms still worked. If he could figure out a way to get out of that room in the same way Duran had escaped from the stores, then maybe he could still get away.

He looked up and saw Jenkins pinned against the opposite wall, firing his last remaining rounds.

'Kurt!' Jenkins yelled.

Kurt took one last glance at his corporal and then he turned and dashed down the corridor to the crematorium.

He heard the gunfire cut short and then the growls and screeches of the sasquatch competing with the harrowing screams of Jenkins as he was torn limb from limb, the horrific cries pursuing him down the corridor as he ran. He leapt over the remains of Cletus MacCarthy and slid to a halt at the crematorium door. To his relief, a bright green light glowed in the darkness.

The sound of heavy footfalls thundered toward him from behind, the sasquatch charging down the corridor.

Kurt said a prayer to himself as he reached out and turned the handle.

The door opened, and Kurt almost cried out as he burst into the room and slammed the door shut behind him.

He stood for a long moment, breathing heavily in the darkness. The creatures beyond the door thundered into it, their huge fists beating against the solid steel door, but even their immense strength could not break through.

Kurt breathed a sigh of relief, and turned to see the light from a cellphone illuminating the room in a soft blue glow. As his eyes adjusted, he saw a shadowy form squatting beside the phone.

'Lopez, we need to make a plan to get out of here,' he said. 'Warner's abandoned you.'

The figure looked at him and then stood upright. Kurt felt a shudder of fear lance through him as he realized that the figure was far too huge to be Lopez. He smelled a sickening waft of putrid air wash over him as the immense sasquatch loomed over him.

He raised his rifle up.

A huge, muscular arm swept down like a falling tree and

smashed into his arm with such force that he both felt and heard the bones in his forearm splinter beneath the impact. Kurt howled in pain as he was driven to his knees in shock, and he turned and looked up at the huge beast towering over him.

He grabbed the rifle with his good arm and squeezed the trigger. The beast smashed the rifle aside, the weapon torn from Kurt's grasp. It clattered to the floor beyond his reach, and as he looked at it he saw the cage in the back corner of the room and the open door. With absolute certainty he knew who had opened the cage.

Warner.

The creature bent down, its broad, tanned face glaring and its wide mouth sneering as it examined him curiously. Kurt stared up at it, and then in a flourish of false bravado he hawked up a globule of phlegm and spat into the creature's face.

'Do your worst, you ugly son of a bitch.'

Moments later, with the last vestiges of his awareness Kurt Agry felt his own head being twisted off of his body, before oblivion closed around him.

71

'Keep moving.'

Ethan hurried along at a crouch as he followed the winding path of the access tunnel, Lopez following close behind him.

He knew that they were close now, could smell the fresh air flowing down the tunnel as though the earth itself was breathing. Moments later he saw the faint outline of the entrance, a ragged hole hewn into the living rock that looked up at the night sky, clouds drifting across star fields.

A metal grating was fixed in place across the entrance, thick mesh wire with a steel border and 'X' crossbeam. Ethan crouched down alongside the grating and illuminated the fixing bolts with the light from his cell.

The aged bolts were freshly scraped, bright metal glinting in the light. Ethan smiled as he gripped one of the bolts tightly between his forefinger and thumb and turned them. The bolt squeaked as it rotated. Duran and Mary had come through here, and the ever cautious Duran would have sealed the grating loosely back in place.

'This is how Mary and Duran got out,' Lopez said.

'And how Cletus MacCarthy got in,' Ethan confirmed. 'He must have found the sasquatch being held inside. Maybe he was a staunch conservationist or something, either way he didn't like what he saw. I found a sabotaged junction box that controlled power to the cages in the rear of the facility.'

'So Cletus gets in here and frees the imprisoned sasquatch,' Lopez said. 'But he leaves a trail enough afterward that he's followed.'

'Probably by a CIA team,' Ethan nodded as he twisted the bolts from their sockets, 'who then took down Randy instead of Cletus, thinking that he was the infiltrator when they found the files on his computer, the images that Cletus took.'

'Jesus,' Lopez said. 'Cletus then gets killed by the same damned creatures he probably liberated.'

'Ironic,' Ethan said.

He removed the rest of the bolts and lifted the grating out. He pushed himself forward and burst out into the fresh air, pocketing his cell as Lopez hurried out behind him.

They were on the same flank of the mountain, no more than fifty yards from the main entrance to the mine. As Ethan stood and got his breath back he saw that the access tunnel was completely hidden from view of the mine's main entrance by the thick foliage and trees that stood between the two excavations, the access tunnel slightly higher on the hillside than the main entrance.

'They could be out here,' Lopez whispered as Ethan carefully set the grating back in place, just as Duran had done.

Ethan nodded and looked up into the night sky. The clouds were breaking up, their edges glowing blue-white in the light of a full moon blazing low over the mountainous horizon. The glow illuminated the forests brightly enough for the trees to cast ghostly shadows that could conceal any number of murderous sasquatch, but right now some visibility was far better than none.

'We'll have to take the chance,' Ethan whispered back as he stood. 'Come on, let's move.'

He led the way down the hillside and ran out across the open ground near the mine entrance, trying to move as lightly as he could to avoid attracting attention to himself. As he ran, the sound of muted screams drifted ghoulishly from the mine entrance and out into the night air, competing with low growls and whining screeches that sent a shiver down his spine.

'Ethan,' Lopez said, slowing.

'There's nothing we can do for them now,' he replied, knowing damn well that Kurt Agry and his men would not have hesitated to abandon either himself or Lopez to their deaths in the air strike now only moments away.

All of a sudden the screeches and growls became louder, echoing and bellowing from the mine entrance in a tumult of what sounded frighteningly like dialect, a babbling, rumbling noise that echoed out across the lonely forest.

'Shit, they're coming out,' Lopez said, and turned to sprint for the treeline.

Ethan turned away from the mine entrance, and then froze as his eye caught upon a metallic object standing unobtrusively near the trees beside the mine. A narrow tripod stood with a camera affixed to the top, pointed out toward the narrow animal trail that they had followed up to the mine hours previously.

Lopez was already past him as she ran in front of the camera toward the treeline. Ethan raised a hand in sudden panic.

'Nicola, wait!'

Lopez turned as she ran, looking over her shoulder in surprise. Almost instantly she tripped and tumbled onto the rocky ground. Her head cracked against rocks and she slumped face down on the cold earth. As Ethan stepped forward to help he saw the shadows at the treeline change shape, and felt his guts plunge as from the darkness emerged an immense sasquatch. The creature lumbered toward Lopez and loomed over her, its eyes glowing with that horrific red haze as it looked down at her crumpled body and then up at the camera mount in front of it.

In the strange blue glow of the moon Ethan saw its features change to anger as it recognized a piece of technology belonging to man, and it lumbered two paces toward the tripod and reached out to swipe one gigantic arm across it.

The camera smashed off the tripod and flew through the air toward Ethan, who ducked to avoid the missile as it clattered down onto the ground behind him. The sasquatch turned and grabbed the tripod, then hurled it away into the darkness of the trees before it turned and looked directly at Ethan.

Ethan carefully took a pace backward from it and glanced at Lopez. She was still lying motionless on the ground, her long black hair snaking away from her head and a trickle of dark blood staining her forehead.

The sasquatch stood up from its crouch and towered into the night sky, nine feet tall and as broad as a barn door. With measured, controlled strides that thumped down heavily onto the earth at its feet it moved toward Ethan.

Ethan backed up as behind him he heard a terrible screech, like the cry of an eagle the size of a car. He turned as three sasquatch burst from the mine entrance. One of them carried something in its giant hand and it tossed the object out into the air with what sounded like a cry of jubilation.

The round object span in a graceful arc and landed ten feet from where Ethan stood with a weighty thud. He looked down at Kurt Agry's head, the features twisted with agony and one side of the skull crushed inward.

Two more sasquatch followed the first three out of the mine and came to a halt, watching Ethan in silence.

Ethan stepped back another pace and his boot hit the edge of the video camera. He looked down, and saw that it was no longer recording. But a tiny orange power light still glowed in the darkness.

The sasquatch advanced further toward Ethan, towering over him like a pine tree. He stared up at it just as a voice whispered urgently in the darkness.

'Don't move.'

Ethan swiveled his gaze to his right, and saw Duran Wilkes hurry across to him and pick up the camera. The viewing screen flopped open in front of him, glowing in his face and showing files with the videos they had recorded during the expedition. Ethan stared at the screen in desperation, as though wanting to look at anything other than the huge beast bearing down upon him.

Duran selected one of the files and pressed play.

In the silence of the forest, an audio track began playing.

The camera's internal speaker was not loud, even as Ethan saw Duran nudge the volume up to maximum, but in the relative silence it carried far enough. A long, low, mournful howl echoed out into the night, rising in pitch with each passing second until it wailed like a banshee into the sky.

The awful cry rang in Ethan's ears as Duran held the camera toward the sasquatch, as if willing the sound to cut them all down.

The big sasquatch stopped in mid-stride and stared at them in silence. The long howl faded away into the silence as the camera's video ended.

Duran punched the screen again and the same horrible cry rose up out of the camera and soared into the heavens once more.

Above the sound of the recorded howl, Ethan heard a distant sound, a bizarre humming, buzzing noise that echoed faintly as it chased through the mountains somewhere to the south. The sasquatch heard it too, their heads turning to listen to the distant noise, their noses quivering as they sniffed the air.

'This isn't working,' Ethan whispered anxiously.

'No, but this will,' Duran replied, and called out. 'Mary, now!'

From the pitch blackness, Mary ran out into the open. Ethan glanced at her just as she held up something in her hands and pointed it at the enormous sasquatch as it turned to look at her.

A blaze of blinding light flashed into existence, a bright blue-white beam that cut through the night and hit the sasquatch square in the face. The huge beast cried out and turned aside from the searing light, flinging one giant arm up across its face as it stumbled away. Mary turned the powerful flashlight on the faces of the other sasquatch, and they ducked away from its glare. A soft gabbling exchange shot between them, and then in utter silence they turned as one and strode off the hillside, the alpha-male passing with its arm up to protect its vision from the glaring light no more than ten feet away from where Ethan and Duran stood.

He watched the animals stride into the forest to the east and vanish from sight, and then Ethan turned and dashed to Lopez's side.

'Get up!'

Lopez groaned and struggled to her feet, blinking wearily at Ethan. She saw Duran Wilkes already running away toward the treeline.

'What happened?'

'Run!'

The whining, buzzing noise grew louder as Ethan pushed Lopez in front of him and began running for the cover of the trees. He knew exactly what the sound was, having heard it many times with the marines in Iraq. The buzz of turbofan engines were some of the most distinctive of any aircraft, and powered the A-10 Thunderbolt II ground-attack fighter.

Above the whine of the engines Ethan heard a sudden series of whooshing noises as though somebody had let off a box of massive fireworks.

'Hit the deck!'

Ethan's last word was drowned out by the rocket propelled roar of eight Maverick air-to-ground missiles that roared overhead and plowed not just into the mountainside but directly down the open mine entrance with precision, laser-guided accuracy.

Before Ethan and Lopez had even hit the ground the side of the mountain exploded in a supersonic cloud of fragmented rock and superheated gas as the powerful missiles sliced into the facility and then detonated deep within the hillside.

Ethan hit the ground and felt his back being hammered by chunks of shrapnel and debris, and then his vision blurred and his consciousness was ripped brutally away from him.

72

FAIRFAX, VIRGINIA

Douglas Jarvis sat behind an oak-paneled table in a conservatory that looked out over a perfectly manicured lawn that he had spent many years carefully cultivating. Most all of his colleagues over the years were highly amused to find that a former marine captain and veteran of several conflicts liked nothing more than to spend his spare time gardening.

Jarvis reminded them, when he could be bothered, that there was little more peaceful in life than a simple garden, especially when his entire career had been spent fighting in war zones or trying to prevent wars from starting in the first place.

A career that was now over.

Winter was coming now, the fall almost over and the lawn littered with the last red and brown leaves. He would have to clear them again soon enough, and at least now he'd have the time to do it properly. The sky above was laden with gray clouds, a fine drizzle spilling down against the glass windows.

'Any word?'

Natalie Warner stood in the doorway to the conservatory.

Dressed in jeans and a loose cardigan with her hair hanging across her shoulders, she looked five years younger than she had in the Capitol. Only her face carried the weight of her worries.

'Nothing yet,' he replied. 'Ben okay?'

Natalie nodded, and walked into the conservatory.

Ben Consiglio had been admitted to hospital in Washington under Jarvis's strictest orders, even though he no longer had the authority to enforce them. The younger man's injuries were not serious, they'd learned, but he had been suffering from exhaustion and dehydration, enough that they had kept him in overnight before releasing him in the morning.

Natalie had insisted on staying by his bedside until he was released.

Jarvis had likewise insisted that she accompany him to his home rather than return alone to her apartment in the district. Fact was, she wasn't safe and there was nobody that she could turn to except Jarvis for protection.

'They haven't found him?' she asked.

'No,' Jarvis replied. 'And I don't believe that they will.'

Wilson had been gone by the time the emergency services converged on the crime scene. Most probably Wilson, a long-service agent with enormous experience, would have worn a protective vest. The bullet would have knocked him out cold but would have caused nothing more serious than bruising on his chest. Had Jarvis been quicker he would have taken the head shot, but Natalie was not experienced with firearms and had done the right thing: aimed for the biggest target, the torso.

Guy Rikard's homicide was being investigated by the

Metropolitan Police Department, who would be unlikely to find themselves making connections to the CIA. The murder would most likely become a cold case, maybe the victim of a random freak accident or a crude suicide bid. Rikard was split from his wife and had financial difficulties, was a known drinker and womaniser and suchlike. His past would be trawled by the detectives on his case but the extinguishing of his life would be forgotten by all but those closest to him by the following morning.

'You think he'll come here for us?' Natalie asked him.

Jarvis looked out of the window for a moment and then shook his head. 'No. Too obvious. He'll lie low for a while, avoid attracting any more attention to what's happened. The death of one Congressional investigator can be put down to bad luck: another one and everybody will start to take notice. It would defeat the object.'

'Which is what?' Natalie asked. 'He was going to kill me.'

'He almost certainly was not,' Jarvis said.

'The CIA had Guy Rikard killed,' Natalie snapped.

'Larry Levinson was a CIA agent, that much is for sure, but there's no way he'll be traced back to them,' Jarvis said. 'The name will be an alias, his entire history forged: it's unlikely he'll even be on the CIA's payroll: the kind of units Mr. Wilson and Larry Levinson work for are funded through the Pentagon's Black Budget, which is protected from Congressional scrutiny.'

Natalie stared down at the floor for a moment.

'So what happens now?'

Jarvis stared at the news channel and then leaned forward and turned up the volume as a newscaster read a report.

Behind her on the screen was a large image of a forested mountain range.

The National Guard was called out last night after an enormous blast at the site of an old abandoned mine in northern Idaho where several people are believed to have been killed. The explosion, believed to have been caused by a build-up of heat and gas inside the mine, was heard more than twenty miles away in Grangeville. The National Guard has placed a ten-mile exclusion zone around the blast site to prevent any further fatalities due to rock falls or subsidence of unmapped mine tunnels beneath the mountain.

Natalie's hand flew to her mouth as the newsreader went on.

The bodies of a man and a woman were pulled from the rubble but the force and heat of the blast means that it's unlikely the two victims will ever be identified. The remains of a third person were found outside the mine but also defied identification. Local officials say the area will be closed to the public until a full clean-up of the area has been completed under the control of the National Guard.

'Oh Jesus,' Natalie gasped, and whirled away out of the conservatory.

Jarvis muted the television and sighed as he leaned back into his chair.

A cleaning team would be put into the mine now that a suitably convincing cover story had been put in place. They would remove any last pieces of evidence of whatever existed there and then seal the mine shut.

Nobody would ever get in there again.

Jarvis wanted to hope that Ethan and Lopez had gotten out of the mine before the blast, but he had no idea who the remains that had been found belonged to. The admission that any fatalities had occurred meant that the CIA most likely would be forced to hand over the bodies at some point, perhaps due to the inevitable pressure that would be applied to the Sheriff's Office and the National Guard by concerned families of people missing in the Idaho wilderness. But nobody would ever be informed of exactly who had died, or what they were actually doing there.

He stood up from his chair and stared out of the window for a moment longer.

Mr. Wilson had done his work well, and now there was nothing left and nothing that Jarvis could do to change it.

It was over.

He turned and walked out of the conservatory. As he did so his cellphone rang in his pocket. He pulled it out and glanced at the screen before answering the call. An unidentified number waited for him. He punched the answer button and lifted the cell to his ear.

'Doug Jarvis.'

The answer was brief.

'*Doug, it's Ethan. We're on the run and dark until further notice. Whoever did this to us is going to pay.*'

The line clicked off and the dead-line tone buzzed in Jarvis's ear.

He slipped the cell into his pocket and walked through to

the kitchen, where Natalie sat at a table with her head in her hands.

'You'd better write down everything you found out about MK-ULTRA,' he said. 'Your brother's alive, and he's on the warpath.'

ACKNOWLEDGEMENTS

As more and more books in the Ethan Warner series are published I've come to realise that writing novels is no longer a solitary pursuit, and the knowledge that I have so many people supporting my efforts is a huge comfort when staring at a computer monitor and wondering where the story should go next. As ever, I owe an immense debt of gratitude to my literary agent Luigi Bonomi and his team at LBA, to the publishing team at Simon & Schuster who all work so hard to develop and promote my work, and to my family and friends who all champion my work so enthusiastically. There cannot be many people who feel that they have the best job in the world, so I am very fortunate to count myself as one of them.

AUTHOR'S NOTE

The history of mankind is filled with stories of monsters, some real and others imagined. The origin of werewolf legends have been traced to medieval cases of lycanthropy in Eastern Europe, the origin of vampires found within the deity myths of ancient cultures around the world. But while most such stories are legends, others remain tantalisingly within the realms of possibility. Separating the fact from the fiction is often difficult, but today's proliferation of video cameras on mobile phones and explorers willing to traverse the harshest terrain in search of the impossible have vastly increased our knowledge of life upon this planet.

The vast majority of the creatures described within these pages are real. This might surprise some readers, but one only has to consider the dinosaurs to realise that it is possible for species to reach truly terrifying proportions without being considered either supernatural or the product of pure human imagination. From the magnificent silver serpent *Regalecus glesne* to the extinct ape *Gigantopithecus*; from dragonflies with wingspans equal to that of eagles to giant squid large enough to bring down sailing vessels: all were once considered fantastical legends yet all have now been documented either by direct observation or through the study of their fossilised remains.

Sasquatch remains to this day an enigma. No solid evidence of its existence has ever been presented, yet credible and knowledgeable witnesses continue to encounter some kind of ape-like creature in high mountain regions across the entire globe. Our species has endured enormous catastrophes throughout its history, from meteorite strikes to super-volcano eruptions to tsunamis and Ice Ages, and has prevailed. Is it so ridiculous to consider that another bipedal species of ape might have likewise prevailed in deep forests and mountains, far from human contact?

It is said that we know more about the moon than about our own oceans. Over three quarters of our planet is covered by water, little of the ocean's mysterious depths explored by humans. Somewhere out there something lives that is unlike anything we have ever seen, because the sounds recorded by the United States Navy's SOSUS network in the deep sound channel of the Pacific Ocean are also real. A creature with a mass some five times that of a blue whale would be an incredible sight to behold, and one that I hope will be found and documented someday along with so many others that might be waiting out there in the farthest reaches of our planet.

Dean Crawford
London 2013

Dean Crawford

COVENANT

Some things man was never meant to know . . .

Humanity has always believed it is the only intelligent species of life in the universe. But while excavating in Israel, an archaeologist unearths a tomb that has remained hidden for 7,000 years. Inside lies a secret of such magnitude that the story of mankind is instantly rewritten – and its future thrown into terrible danger.

Only one man can piece history back together again. Only one man will risk everything to prevent a catastrophe that could tear the world apart.

That man is Ethan Warner.

Paperback ISBN 978-0-85720-469-1
Ebook ISBN 978-0-85720-470-7

Dean Crawford
IMMORTAL

What price are you willing to pay for eternal life?

While carrying out an autopsy on a body recently brought
into a Santa Fe morgue, county coroner Lillian Cruz makes
a surprising discovery. Lodged in the dead man's thigh
bone is a bullet which, carbon dating reveals, was fired
some 200 years earlier during the American Civil War. But
before she can notify the authorities, Lillian disappears.

The Defense Intelligence Agency calls in Ethan Warner
and his partner, Nicola Lopez, to discreetly find the
missing coroner. But the closer they come to unlocking
the terrifying truth, the nearer they unknowingly bring
a warped and dangerous individual to achieving
a catastrophic goal: immortality.

Paperback ISBN 978-0-85720-472-1
Ebook ISBN 978-0-85720-473-8

Dean Crawford

APOCALYPSE

In the notorious Bermuda Triangle a private jet vanishes without trace, taking with it scientists working for world-famous philanthropist Joaquin Abell. In Miami, Captain Kyle Sears is called to a murder scene. A woman and her daughter have both been shot through the head. But within moments of arriving, Sears receives a phone call from the woman's husband, physicist Charles Purcell.

'I did not kill my wife and daughter. In less than twenty-four hours I too will be murdered and I know the man who will kill me. My murderer does not yet know that he will commit the act.'

With uncanny accuracy, Charles predicts the immediate future just as it unfolds around Sears, and leaves clues for a man he's never met before: Ethan Warner.

The hunt is on to find Purcell, and Warner is summoned by the Defense Intelligence Agency to head up the search. But this is no ordinary case, as Warner and his partner Nicola Lopez are about to discover, and time is literally everything.

Paperback ISBN 978-0-85720-475-2
Ebook ISBN 978-0-85720-476-9